da

G000167226

promise

BOOKS BY SARAH CLUTTON

Good Little Liars

the
daughter's
promise

SARAH CLUTTON

bookouture

Published by Bookouture in 2020

An imprint of Storyfire Ltd.
Carmelite House
50 Victoria Embankment
London EC4Y 0DZ

www.bookouture.com

ISBN: 978-1-83888-032-3
eBook ISBN: 978-1-83888-031-6

For my mother, Helen, and my big sister, Sam.
And for my granny, Jude.

CHAPTER ONE

Willa

Willa stamped the snow from her boots. She placed the bundle of letters on the cluttered mud-room bench and peeled off her coat and gloves.

In the kitchen, the warmth of the huge black Aga began to penetrate her frozen bones. She'd walked around the entire suburb; more than six kilometres – four miles, she mentally translated for Hugo as she filled the kettle. It amused and annoyed her in equal parts that she was still translating distance for her husband after nineteen years here. The British were so outdated. Kilometres made much more sense. There were more of them, for a start, so you felt better about how much exercise you'd achieved. And you could divide them by a thousand, so it was much simpler in all respects. Still, she'd chosen to raise her family here in Oxford, so she supposed she'd just have to keep on translating.

'Mum, there's nothing to eat.' Hamish loped into the kitchen, leaned his six-foot-two frame down towards her and gave her an easy kiss on the cheek. Her little boy had taken up residence inside the body of a gangly stranger, and Willa was unsure why this sometimes made her feel like crying. It shouldn't. She should be happy he could get things down from the top shelf for her. That he was alive, here in their kitchen, towering over her. Giving her a *kiss*, for goodness' sake. How many teenage boys kissed their mother for absolutely no reason?

Hamish pulled open the fridge and stood staring at the shelves, sending waves of cold air towards Willa's chair.

'Close it,' she said, suppressing a smile. 'If you've already looked and can't see anything, it won't have magically restocked itself. I'm going shopping soon.'

He grabbed the box of Cookie Crisp from the pantry shelf and headed back out of the kitchen towards his bedroom. 'Can you get some more strawberry yoghurt, Mum? And some orange juice?'

Willa heard his words from the end of the hallway, a moment before the sound of a banging door. He'd be on his computer, probably playing some shooting game with his friends that involved headphones and yelling at each other and, according to Hamish when he was helping her to see the positives, lots of teamwork to find and exterminate all the baddies. Yes, there were rivers of blood, and disturbingly graphic and gruesome killings, but it also involved plenty of lovely synergistic collaboration, thereby making it excellent for future career skills. So that put her mind at rest. Obviously.

Willa sighed. She was just glad he liked being at home. She made a mental note about the yoghurt and orange juice, then looked down again at the letters and began sorting through them. Most were for Hugo. Investment, superannuation, insurance. She stopped as she noticed her own name on the final letter. Underneath the postmark was an unfamiliar business name: *Enderby Jones Lawyers, 31 Elliot Street, Burnie, Tasmania.*

A letter from Australia. From lawyers. Willa felt a swoop of anticipation in her gut, followed by a vague hum of unease. The whistle of the kettle interrupted her thoughts, and she placed the letter gently on the table before pulling a mug from the cupboard. She had never travelled to Tasmania. She knew no one who lived there. Well, not that she was aware of, although by now she was bound to have an old school friend who'd needed a change from Sydney and had uprooted their family to move to the furthest southern corner of Australia to grow organic mushrooms or start an alpaca farm.

Willa adored those life-change stories in her favourite Australian *Rural Style* magazine, which arrived monthly in the post. So many photogenic families living the dream: children in crisp cotton dresses and pristine wellington boots running through wheat paddocks or climbing gum trees or stirring home-made jam on stovetops in glamorous yet casually styled designer kitchens.

She dipped the tea bag into the mug of boiling water and added milk as she considered the possible reasons for an Australian law firm to be writing to her. Her mind was blank. Her mother's estate had been finalised eighteen months ago. She'd barely kept in touch with her cousins in Perth over the years, so they were unlikely to send her anything through lawyers. She couldn't be being sued for anything – she hadn't been back to Sydney since her mother's funeral three years earlier. And she wasn't a witness in anyone's court case, as far as she knew. And they were *Tasmanian* lawyers, from a town she hadn't heard of, so she really had no idea what they could possibly want.

She sat down at the table, digging her toes deeper into her Ugg boots. She pushed one frozen foot towards the Aga and with the other, rubbed Kettles along his black shaggy coat as he slept on his mat. She paused, trying to make her foggy brain think. No. Nothing. Her imagination had deserted her. She stared at the letter again and turned it over. No clues. She picked it up and in one quick movement ripped open the envelope and unfolded the thick sheaf of papers.

Dear Mrs Fairbanks,

Re: The Estate of Lillian Nora Brooks
Bequest to Wilhelmena May Gilmore Fairbanks

We act as executors for the estate of Ms Lillian Nora Brooks. Ms Brooks died on 15 November 2018, and enclosed is a copy of her last will and testament. As you will see, Ms Brooks has bequeathed to you a property, The Old Chapel, at 3 Lighthouse Lane, Sisters Cove. The property is a small converted church sited on a parcel of land of approximately three acres in the semi-rural beachside hamlet of Sisters Cove in Tasmania.

Ms Brooks knew that you had few ties remaining in Australia, and that you were resident in the United Kingdom, but it was her expressed intention that you visit the property before you make any decisions as to how you would like to proceed with respect to this bequest.

We are bound to advise you that there are two interested parties who would like to discuss purchase of the property from you, should you wish to sell it.

Enclosed are some documents that will need to be completed and witnessed, so that the title of the property can be passed to you in due course.

If you would like to visit the property and are able to travel to Tasmania, we would be happy to advise and assist you in this regard. Please confirm by return email that the following documents contain your full and correct details and provide us with your instructions. Please do not hesitate to contact the writer if you have any questions.

Yours faithfully,
Ian J. Enderby
Solicitor & Barrister

Willa stood up, her chair clattering backwards. Behind her, Kettles grunted and shuffled his shoulders before settling back to sleep. She looked nervously around the kitchen, as if someone might be watching her, waiting for her reaction, but it was empty and silent apart from Kettles' gentle snoring. She picked up the letter and began rereading it. *Lillian Nora Brooks.* She knew no one called Lillian. Or Mrs Brooks. Or Miss Brooks, for that matter. She looked at the letter again. Actually, it was *Ms* Brooks.

Why would this woman – whatever her marital status – leave Willa a house? An old chapel? She scrolled through her mind, trying to drag up the names of religion teachers she'd known at school who might own a little church. People she'd met through her parents, perhaps? Her mother had had a religious aunt who had sent Willa fifty dollars and a white leather-bound Bible for her confirmation when she was fourteen. At the time, fifty dollars had been a small fortune, and Willa remembered spending it on a gorgeous floral skirt and a matching midriff top. Her mother had been horrified. It definitely wasn't something she could wear to church. Although since they only went at Christmas and Easter, Willa didn't think it particularly mattered.

Aunt Enid. That was the woman's name. She'd lived in Darwin, or maybe Cairns. Somewhere up north and hot, and so far away that they'd never visited her. Willa had written a thank you letter and that was the last she'd heard of the woman. But surely Aunt Enid would be long dead by now. Maybe she'd had a child called Lillian Brooks, who'd grown sick of the heat and moved south. Although, now that she turned her mind to it, she remembered that Aunt Enid had been a *maiden* aunt. A spinster. The word conjured an image of a crinkly old witch; someone with a withered womb. It felt like a long shot – giving poor old Enid an illegitimate daughter in Tasmania.

She looked at the letter again and felt a tiny shiver run up her spine. Her shoulders reacted by jumping upwards. She shook her head, annoyed with herself for allowing a frisson of excitement to enter into the equation when the only logical conclusion was that the whole thing must be a mistake. Was bound to be! It simply didn't make sense any other way. In a few weeks' time, Hugo would be regaling their friends with the story at a dinner party, telling them how they'd sorted out a strange case of mistaken identity with lawyers on the other side of the world. The real Wilhelmena Fairbanks actually lived in New York, or Budapest perhaps (much more interesting). Willa imagined her namesake wandering down cobbled streets between medieval buildings, ducking into a trendy café to drink a hand-roasted single-origin coffee, leaning against the ancient brick wall and admiring the quirky light installation suspended from the thousand-year-old ceiling, all the while wondering why she hadn't yet had news of her inheritance from Great-Aunt Lillian.

The discovery of the *real* Wilhelmena had been no mean feat, she could imagine Hugo saying as he topped up the red wine glasses and their friends exclaimed in appreciative awe, speculating about how such a screw-up could actually occur in this day and age of technology and data-checking. But wouldn't it have been fascinating, they would murmur, if *their* Willa had actually been the Wilhelmena in question? Imagine that. A mysterious woman leaving you a house on the other side of the world!

Willa picked up the letter again.

Ms Brooks knew you had few remaining ties in Australia and that you were resident in the United Kingdom.

She shivered. The real Wilhelmena lived in the United Kingdom. And how on earth would a stranger know that she had few ties in Australia? And, now that she reread the subject of the letter and noticed her full name at the top, how likely was it that there was more than one Wilhelmena May Gilmore Fairbanks living in the UK? Gilmore was an odd middle name, passed down through the women on her mother's side. Passed down, without fail, for many generations, to every daughter. Willa felt a heavy, dislocating sense of panic beginning to press in at the base of her lungs. Her arms started to tingle. She leaned forward and caught the table for support. *Stop it. Stop it. Stop it.* It had been months since she'd had a panic attack. She dragged up the mantra she was supposed to use: *Deep breaths, let your stomach expand. Remind yourself that everyone is safe and well. Remember that you can handle this. You've done it before. You can do it again.*

She heard the back door open, then shut. She forced her eyes open and made herself stand up straight. There was the sound of stomping feet, then a brief pause before Hugo appeared around the corner and dropped his briefcase on the floor.

'Hello, darling.'

'Hi.' Willa tried putting a normal sort of smile on her face while holding tightly to the table with one hand. She glanced down at the letter on the table, then back at Hugo.

'What's wrong? You're white as a ghost.' Hugo strode across the kitchen and put his hands on her forearms, trying to hold her gaze.

She looked down. 'Fine. I'm fine.'

She took another deep breath, then picked up the letter and handed it to him. 'I got this in the mail. Cup of tea?'

He began reading the letter, ignoring her offer of tea, and Willa slumped back against the kitchen bench, waiting for him to finish.

After a minute, he looked up at her, his head cocked to one side, his eyebrows drawn together. 'Goodness. Who's Lillian Brooks?'

'I don't know.'

'A friend of your parents?'

'Really, I don't know.'

'A distant relative, perhaps?'

'Maybe.'

'You said you didn't have anyone left in Australia apart from your cousins in Perth, though.'

'I don't.'

'Well who can she be, then?'

'I don't have a damn *clue* who she is, Hugo! Honestly!'

'All right, darling, all right.' Hugo put the letter on the table and came towards her, drawing her into a hug.

Willa stiffened as she tried to force back the burning tingle of tears, but Hugo pulled her tighter, refusing to let her go as she sniffed and pushed ineffectually against his chest. Eventually she slumped against him and breathed out.

'Well it's a mystery, but not one we can't solve.'

'What's a mystery?' Hamish stood at the entrance to the kitchen with an empty glass in his hand.

'Your mother has inherited a house in Australia from someone she's never heard of,' said Hugo, as he finally let go of Willa.

'No way!'

'Yes way.' Hugo picked up the letter again, taking a second look before handing it to Hamish.

Hamish scanned it. 'Holy shit!'

'Language,' said Willa irritably. Her head was beginning to throb with the telltale aftermath of her almost-panic-attack. She supposed she should be dancing on the table. What sane person wouldn't be after finding out they'd just inherited a house? Except they didn't really need the money it might bring. And she'd quite like to know why a strange woman – who had obviously done a fair amount of research on her – had singled her out from across the globe to inherit a house in a town so tiny she'd never heard of it.

A *church*, for pity's sake. She wasn't even religious. And in *Tasmania*. All she knew of the smallest and least populated state of Australia was that it was generally cold and was full of forests and people who loved to bushwalk. They were probably all lovely people, but if she was being honest, Willa didn't really enjoy bushwalking all that much. She knew it was the sort of thing people like her were *meant* to enjoy – fit, environmentally focused people. She considered herself a prime candidate for enjoying a bushwalk; she was a strict devotee of recycling, she had a worm farm, last year she'd bought an electric car, and she did like to walk. It was just that she preferred to do it on the streets, and within mobile reception range where at all possible, so she could download podcasts to listen to as she paced out her kilometres, later to be translated into miles, all within shouting distance of lots of other humans in case she should fall and twist her ankle, or require directions or a quick stop for a cappuccino.

'You must have heard of her somehow, Mum,' Hamish was saying.

Willa looked across at her beautiful boy and noticed a large pink pimple that was forcing its way out from underneath the stubble at the corner of his lip.

'Mum?'

'No. I haven't,' she said sullenly.

'Let's look at it on Google Maps,' said Hamish, striding past her and across the living room to the family computer on the antique writing desk in the corner. He plonked himself onto the leather chair and began tapping furiously at the keyboard. Hugo followed him.

Willa felt an odd reluctance to make the letter into any kind of reality, but after a few moments, she joined them anyway.

After Hamish had clicked a few times, a patchwork quilt of green and brown paddocks came into view. They butted right up against the vast blue-green ocean. Small clusters of houses dotted the edges of the narrow laneways and roads that divided the paddocks. Every so often a blackish oval delineated a dam or a lake of some kind.

Willa realised she was holding her breath.

'Go on Street View,' said Hugo.

Hamish clicked a couple more times and a photo of an uneven hedge and a postbox appeared. To the right of the picture, the edge of a small white weatherboard building with a dilapidated paling fence could be glimpsed. It was partially surrounded by a garden full of colourful plants. In the background, a paddock swathed in white appeared to hold some sort of crop.

'Let me see,' said Willa. She pushed Hamish's hand off the mouse and manoeuvred the photograph around, but all she could see were trees lining a narrow dirt road, and an ocean backdrop stretching into infinity. She spun the photograph around and landed in the branches of a tree. 'This is silly.'

'Do you want me to show you the rest of the neighbourhood, Mum?' asked Hamish, easing the mouse out of Willa's hand.

'Sure,' said Willa, annoyed that she was so inept.

Hamish flew over the tops of the trees and within a few seconds had stopped at a lavish-looking garden and large house. 'Mansion' might have been a more appropriate word given the scale of it, except that it looked to be made from weatherboard and brick and there was a certain casualness of style. It had the feel of a grand farmhouse. Around it were several other buildings.

'Check out the neighbour's place. Very fancy,' said Hamish, sweeping the mouse across the length of the property. Willa counted four of five outbuildings and cottages. At one end were symmetrical rows of trees in what looked like an orchard, and formal gardens surrounded the house.

Before she had a chance to comment, Hamish moved the mouse again and they were flying across a stretch of white sandy beach below a smattering of beach houses. Directly in front of the sand, the colour of the ocean changed from a deep blue-green to a pale sparkling aqua. He moved the mouse onto a larger building that edged the shore and was set away from the other houses. A label popped onto the screen: *Sisters Cove Farmgate Café and Lifesaving Club*.

'Lifesavers. Cool!' said Hamish.

'It does look rather idyllic,' said Hugo, rubbing his hand up and down Willa's arm.

'Mmm,' said Willa, feeling oddly discomforted. It felt impolite to be staring into people's back yards, and really, the whole thing was too much to take in. She stepped away, leaving Hugo and Hamish zooming across the screen, exclaiming at the remote, picturesque village and surrounding farmland.

She needed to get something for dinner or they'd be forced to eat Hugo's famous bacon omelette again, and she wasn't sure she could stomach that. She looked at her watch and closed her eyes, realising she'd missed Antonio's closing time and wouldn't be able to serve their gorgeous artichoke and quinoa lasagne for dinner as she'd planned. She'd have to make do with a Tesco ready meal instead. She had no energy to cook. *Lillian Brooks and her silly church house.* A wave of foreboding made her shiver and her head throbbed. Still, headache or not, she needed to go shopping. Tesco it was.

'I'm going to the supermarket,' she said. She picked up her keys and handbag and headed towards the mud-room.

'What about this house, Mum?' asked Hamish. 'Aren't you going to ring the solicitor to see what you can find out?'

'It's night-time in Tasmania, Hame. I'm pretty sure he's not waiting by the phone.'

'Be careful, darling, the roads are icy,' said Hugo. 'Would you like me to go? You look a bit peaky.'

'I'm perfectly fine,' said Willa. *I, Wilhelmena May Gilmore Fairbanks, am perfectly fine.* She closed the mud-room door as her breath began to come in short, shallow gasps, the air receding just out of reach of her lungs. She held onto the bench top. *Everyone is safe and well. Everything is all right. Deep breaths. Remember you have experienced this before and you will survive. Everything is perfectly fine, perfectly fine, perfectly fine.*

Except Willa knew that it wasn't.

CHAPTER TWO

Annabelle

'I've finished Elm Cottage.' Indigo dropped the mop bucket on the hallway floor and stepped towards Annabelle's desk, flicking her dark-blonde hair away from her face.

'Great. Now I need you to take those flowers to the annexe, then help me set up the chairs in front of the arch, please,' said Annabelle.

Indigo wiped her hands on her elephant-print harem pants, then dipped her hand into her pocket. 'Found this under the cushions on the day bed. I reckon it'll fit me. The woman who checked out looked about my size.' She grinned at Annabelle, holding up a black lacy G-string like a prize.

'Eww,' said Annabelle, grimacing. 'Surely you're not going to wear it?'

'Why not? It's designer.' Indigo grinned and stretched the panties across her groin.

'Right,' said Annabelle, swallowing hard. 'Waste not, want not, I guess. I don't suppose she'll ask for them back will she?'

'Nah. Reckon she'd be too embarrassed. No one wants to admit they had sex on your couch, do they?'

Annabelle felt a bit queasy. 'Did you check the scatter cushions were clean?'

'Yeah, all done.'

Indigo grinned and strolled towards the door, and Annabelle felt a pang of jealousy at her unhurried, relentless positivity. So much Zen on what could only be a stress-addled day. One that could be the start of Annabelle's new and incredible career, or could sink her before she'd even begun. She could feel her heart zinging in her chest already and it was only ten a.m. She needed to pace herself. The wedding wasn't until four.

'Annabelle, have you turned the water off?' Pete, her farmhand, stood in his socks at the door of her office.

'What? No! Is it off outside?'

'Seems to be. I just tried the kitchen tap too. Nothing.'

'Blast,' said Annabelle.

'Want me to check the pump?' asked Pete.

'Would you mind? I can't think what would have tripped it this time, but you'll need to prime it. Or something like that.'

'Righto. Robbie used to do it, so I'm not the expert, but I'll look up the instructions on the internet.'

'Lord save us,' muttered Annabelle under her breath as she followed him towards the door. She thought about all the reasons they would be needing water between now and the end of the wedding. Flowers, cleaning, showers, hand basins, washing-up, drinking water. *Bugger bugger blast.* The bride and her party were already in Bay Cottage getting ready. The hairdresser, the make-up girl – they'd all probably need water. And definitely flushing toilets. And the ceremony was taking place in front of the water feature. *Double blast!*

'Let me know when you get it going,' she called after him.

She felt a little panicky flutter in her stomach and picked up her running sheet, nervous energy buzzing through her. The phone rang and she fished it out of the oversized front pocket of her gorgeous new denim apron.

'Annabelle Broadhurst speaking.'

'Hi, Annabelle. It's Kevin here from Barry's Bus Line. I'm in your side lane near the entry gate. Just wondering if you're around. I've got a bit of a problem with a tree.'

'I'll be there in a minute, Kevin.' She ended the call and looked across at Indigo.

'Bus problems now. Brilliant. Luckily I love a challenge!' She rolled her eyes comically and Indigo laughed. 'Actually, Indi, you'd better take some water bottles down to Bay Cottage. Be super-apologetic and tell them the water will be back on in a minute. Maybe leave the flowers until after that.'

Annabelle hurried towards the front door, conscious of her loud, heaving breaths as she balanced herself against the balustrade to pull on her boots. Her pants bit into the rolls of her belly and she sighed loudly again, a combination of frustration at the unwanted problems of the morning and annoyance at herself for having eaten most of the packet of mint-chocolate biscuits last night. Not a brilliant start to her new diet.

Outside, the perfect blue sky and sparkling ocean views across the paddocks made her stop and take a calming breath. A perfect mild summer's day. That was one good thing, at least.

She glanced across at the dirty white weatherboards of The Old Chapel. Its wild garden framed the endless blue backdrop beyond. The grass on the verge of the lane needed mowing. She would have to send Pete over in case the bride wanted photos near the barn with the ocean in the background. Farm chic was apparently the latest and best in photo opportunities. She supposed Lillian's now neglected garden would fit the theme if it made it into the shots.

Lillian had been gone for a couple of months now, but it had been a shock for all of them when the contents of her will had come to light this week. Annabelle wondered yet again about The Old Chapel's new owner. Wilhelmena Fairbanks. She didn't even live in Australia. How was she supposed to contact the woman? Today wasn't the day to worry about it though, she supposed.

At the gateway flower beds, masses of dark pink dahlia heads were swaying in the breeze. Beyond that, down the pebbled driveway, the back end of a tour bus was poking out from behind the boundary hedge. As she reached the laneway, Annabelle gasped. A huge branch from the old maple tree was slung in a monstrous leafy mess alongside the bus. A man – Kevin, she presumed – was rubbing his hand along the bus door. The shattered wing mirror dangled pathetically from exposed wires.

Stay calm. Be in control. You are now a professional wedding ceremony host.

'Good grief. What happened?' she asked.

'Oh. G'day,' said Kevin. He looked at Annabelle momentarily, then down at the branch. 'I just dropped a tour group in Stanley,' he began, scratching his chin. 'Thought I'd work out the best place to park for this wedding lot you've got coming this arvo. Looks like the lane's a bit narrow.' He pointed to the corner, where the bend in the main road met the laneway entrance. 'Branch was hanging too far across.'

Annabelle stiffened. *No. No it wasn't, Kevin! The branch was hanging in perfect balance with the rest of the tree, which has been extending its lovely branches across this lane for as many decades as I can remember!*

She looked up at the huge gash in the side of her beautiful deciduous maple, the showstopper of the front entrance to Merrivale. It looked traumatised. Unbalanced. She felt a little unbalanced herself. The tree was currently covered in tiny rust-red flowers before its main autumn display of deep-red leaves, many of which were now on the ground, about to wither. She *loved* that tree.

'I see,' she said, as her breathing returned to normal. 'Well, you'll need to get rid of that branch.' She gave a tight smile of encouragement in direct counterbalance to her thoughts. Actually what she wanted to do was cry. After she'd strangled Kevin. 'You can put the wood on the bonfire pile in the far paddock. Borrow our chainsaw if you need to – Pete will know where it is.' She pointed in the direction of the pump house. 'Sorry, but I have to get going.'

She walked back up the laneway and stood for a moment at the first tree in the orchard, still covered in walnuts that were fast going to the birds. They'd harvested plenty to pickle in the week after Christmas, but the trees were still heavy with pretty green spherical nuts that might or might not yet be picked, depending on Annabelle's energy levels after this wedding.

She closed her eyes and reordered her thoughts. Priority one: water. She deviated past the studio and headed down towards the pump house at the base of the hill, where Pete was standing with his hands on his hips. His shirt was stuck to his chest. He was drenched.

'Any luck?' she asked.

'Can't seem to get the pressure valve going. Reckon it's something to do with the flow rate from the council side.'

'Right. What do we do?'

'I've rung the usual pump guy in Burnie. He reckons his technicians are all booked today.' Pete squatted down and twisted his screwdriver to open a valve. Water spurted out, hitting him on the forearms.

'Really?' said Annabelle. She had a sudden image of an angry bride in Bay Cottage who was probably wanting to shower at this very moment.

They both turned their heads to look at the pump as it hummed into life. Annabelle held her breath, but after a few moments the motor sputtered and died.

'That's what it keeps doing,' said Pete. He stood up to face her. 'The other pump mob in Yolla said they were too busy too. Tried them straight after.'

'Bugger,' said Annabelle, staring dumbly at the silent pump. 'Right. Let me talk to them.' She pulled out her phone and dialled as Pete read out the number, then drummed the fingers of her other hand against her apron as the phone rang.

'Burnie Pumps. Gary speaking.'

'Hello, Gary. My name is Annabelle Broadhurst and I believe you just spoke with my farmhand, Peter Bledham, about a broken pump at our place in Sisters Cove. I understand your technicians are very busy today.' She listened to the murmur of agreement on the other end. 'The thing is, Gary, I have a wedding at our property at four p.m. today and a hundred guests who will require flushing toilets and drinking water, and caterers who will need to wash their hands and...' she paused, mentally flailing around for some sort of culinary practice that required water, 'steam their canapés!' she blurted.

'Right.'

'In the meantime, I can't hose down the exterior tables, I have a bride who is unable to shower or wash her hair and a mother-of-the-bride in complete hysterics in one of our cottages.' Annabelle was amazed at how the slightly fabricated dramatics flowed off her tongue. She felt no concern about the lies – every bit of that scenario would come true if she didn't get the water back on in the next hour, she was certain. 'Now, I know this isn't your problem, Gary, it's mine. But I am begging you, if you have any romance in your heart, if you've ever been married, you'll understand that I am utterly desperate and I cannot do without your urgent assistance straight away. I'll pay whatever you want.'

She listened to the slight delay on the other end, and wondered if she'd taken the right approach.

Eventually Gary spoke. 'My wife left me last year. Ran off with my best man on Valentine's Day. Known him my whole life.'

'Oh,' said Annabelle, momentarily blank at this absurd bit of bad luck. Why had she felt the need to mention romance? *Stupid, stupid, stupid.* 'I'm so sorry, Gary.'

'Just kiddin' you, Annabelle.' Gary laughed.

Annabelle wanted to scream with frustration. She looked at the broken pump and wondered if she might be about to lose her mind.

'Look, if you give me half an hour, I'll lock up the office and come out myself. See what I can do. Send me a photo of the pump so I can bring a replacement with me in case I can't get yours fixed.'

'Gary, God bless you. I'll make sure my firstborn grandchild is named after you,' said Annabelle, letting the tight belt of panic around her stomach unwind slightly. That promise was an easy one to make. She and Dan had no children, so they were unlikely ever to have any grandchildren. And if the fairies somehow magically delivered her one in the future, she was sure Gary would never find out. Some promises were obviously meant to be broken. She ended the call.

The pump sputtered into life, then died again.

'I'd better go and see how the bridal party are coping with the drought,' said Annabelle.

She marched up the hill towards Bay Cottage, leaving Pete squatting by the pump. As she passed the machinery shed, her eye was caught by the sun glinting off the breakers along the coastline as far as she could see. Such a shame The Old Chapel got in the way of the view. 'Well, Lillian,' she muttered. 'Apparently you and your silly bequest haven't been the worst thorn in my side this week. It turns out that water pumps and idiot bus drivers have beaten you to the prize.'

The sound of crickets clicking and skittering in the grass and the gentle swish of the breeze through the gum trees was her only reply.

She sighed. She couldn't quite shake the feeling that Lillian was having the last laugh. The identity of this mystery woman who was inheriting The Old Chapel kept rubbing at the edge of her thoughts, like a freshly formed blister.

Ahead of her, the door to Bay Cottage was ajar and she peered through the fly screen. 'Hellooo.'

A blonde girl in her late twenties in a floral silk kimono-style bathrobe came to the door, her hair in hot rollers. 'Oh, hello!' She smiled, and Annabelle found herself entranced by the girl's incredibly prominent front teeth with a large gap in the middle. She lost her train of thought for the slightest moment.

'I... er, I just wanted to pop my head in and see how it's all going.'

'Oh, great. I'm Leanne. One of the bridesmaids. We're pretty good. Although Petra's a bit stressed.' The girl smiled again, then leaned towards Annabelle and whispered, 'Hates her hairdo. Wants to start again. I'm trying to convince her it's fine. Although she does look a bit like Cleopatra,' she added, widening her eyes.

'I'm sure she looks lovely. You wouldn't want to get the timing of the day out of whack by starting again,' replied Annabelle conspiratorially. *Plus, there's no water to wash it.*

'Exactly.'

The two women shared a moment of silent agreement and Annabelle realised she was waiting for the girl to smile again. There was something about her strange teeth that turned her from ordinary-looking into alluring.

Another girl in an identical floral robe came out of the living room towards them, a man with a large camera around his neck behind her.

'Petra's just thrown up,' said the girl nervously. 'Hopefully it's just wedding-day jitters.'

Annabelle felt her own stomach begin to churn with all the possible implications.

'Really?' said Leanne. 'I felt a bit off after that seafood we had last night. Hope it's not food poisoning.'

'I'm sure it's not,' said Annabelle. 'That comes on within a couple of hours. As you said, it's probably just nerves.'

'She can't get the toilet to flush,' said the girl miserably.

'Oh gosh,' said Annabelle. 'Look, I'll bring a bucket of water over to flush it manually. The pump has just gone down briefly. I've called an emergency technician. Sorry, girls. It's the council's fault. The flow to the area has been reduced due to some technicality, and the pumps don't like it.' She wondered if that sounded feasible. In any case, it was better than blaming it on their own temperamental infrastructure.

She waved goodbye to the girls and headed towards the shed to get a bucket to fill from the pond. Her stomach clenched as she dialled Dan's number. It went to voicemail. She hung up. The phone jangled in her hand as she neared the shed.

'Annabelle Broadhurst speaking.'

'Annabelle, it's Gary. From Burnie Pumps.'

'Yes, Gary. Are you nearly here?'

'That's the thing. I was about to come out, but we've had an emergency call-out to a school camp facility, so I need to give them priority. But one of us will be at your place soon. Not sure when. Could be after lunch.'

'Oh Gary, I really need you *now*. If I don't get the water on, this wedding is going to be a nightmare.'

'Sure. Well, hopefully someone will be there by two. Three at the latest.'

Annabelle hung up and recalled the last time the pump failed. She calculated. Two o'clock arrival. Then it might take an hour or so to fix the damn thing. Then it would have to be primed, the tank refilled. Another couple of hours after that for the tank levels to rise. Then all the taps in the house would need to be run at the same time to get the air out of the system. This was officially a complete nightmare.

She dialled Dan's number. It went to voicemail. She dialled it again and the same thing happened. Her head felt like it might explode. Why wouldn't her husband ever answer the dratted phone when she needed him urgently? She dialled it again and after a few moments he answered, his voice humming with irritation.

'Annabelle, I've had to leave a settlement conference to take this. Is it an emergency?'

'Yes, darling! It is! The pump's on the blink and Pete can't fix it and the pump guys are too busy and the bride's vomit can't be flushed down the toilet and the silly bus has torn apart my beautiful maple at the front gates! It's an emergency!' She felt tears welling in her eyes. 'You need to come home and fix the pump, Dan. You managed it last time.'

'I can't come now.'

'Dan, I need you here. You're the one who told me I needed to earn some money to keep this place going. Well, this whole venture is going to fail if I don't get the water back on! You need to come home. *Please.*'

'I can't. There's at least another hour till this is finished, then I'm due in court at two.'

'Well I'm sorry, but you'll need to miss court. Get one of the others to step into the settlement conference for you. Say you have a stomach bug. Nobody will want to be near you then. I need you here!'

There was a silence on the other end of the phone. Then Dan whispered, 'For Christ's sake, all right. Tell Pete to look at the second pressure gauge under the white pipe at the back. If it's showing red, he needs to let some more air out of the lower tank. Ring me if you sort it.'

'Okay. I'll see you soon, though. Yes?'

'Yes, *all right*, Belle.'

Annabelle listened to the silence. He'd hung up. She leaned down with the bucket and scooped some murky greenish water out of the pond. A huge, shiny orange carp opened its mouth and blew air at her, then ducked away under the surface as she pulled the bucket out. She thought enviously of all the people in the main township and down on the beachfront who had direct access to the town water supply and didn't have to rely on pumps. The town supply stopped just before the main entrance to Merrivale. The Old Chapel was the final house in the area to have it. Maybe they could use The Old Chapel's water if they were desperate.

She looked across the lane and wondered how tidy Lillian had left her bathroom last November, the day she'd died. Lillian had been a hoarder. It didn't bear thinking about. Although Sylvia said she'd cleaned a lot of it up. Still, Annabelle definitely couldn't send her guests over there. Any way she looked at it, the place was a bit of a hovel.

She picked up the bucket of water and began the slow, sloshing walk back to Bay Cottage, running through her list again. Flowers, glasses, bathrooms, finger food, chairs, water feature. *Water feature.* Hmm. She might need to go into Lillian's garden and run some hoses across the laneway, over the lawn and into the catch tank below the water feature. The guests might not have flushing toilets, but the bride would have her water feature tinkling musically away as she said her vows. Sometimes emergencies just meant you needed to be creative, and Annabelle was sure that Lillian would be smiling down at her from heaven and clapping her hands at this inventive line of thought. Lillian had never been one to run away from a challenge. Lillian had never run away from anything.

CHAPTER THREE

Sylvia

From behind her eyelids, Sylvia visualised the warmth of the room rising up and engulfing the man like a swarm of bees. She smiled inwardly.

'I promise you, we are certified as having the highest compliance for our resorts by the International Sustainable Tourism Network.' The man stopped and tried to catch the eyes of people in the front rows. 'Sisters Cove's ecosystems will be carefully considered and managed at all times. Our organisation has had years of experience in building resorts that work in synergistic harmony with pristine environments.'

Sylvia opened her eyes. The man's suit had some sort of bright-blue plaid pattern running through the navy. The jacket looked like it had been expertly moulded and sewed over his elegantly muscled frame. Tight-fitting must be the latest thing.

'What the hell does that mean?' Jeremy Anderson stood up next to her, his usually ruddy face now an alarming shade of purple. Sweat was beading at his temples. 'Don't give us all that corporate crap. If you build a resort down the end of the cove, you're going to disrupt the waterways!' He was jabbing his finger angrily towards the man giving the presentation. His sleeves were rolled up and his hairy forearm was weathered and speckled with sun damage.

'Sir, I know—' The man tried to continue, but Jeremy's voice boomed through the clubhouse, unperturbed by social niceties.

'The freshwater crayfish have been dying out for the last two decades, mate. It's one of the last areas where we see healthy activity from them. They're not going to survive if this development goes through. That's all there is to it.'

He sat down as the mutterings from the room full of Sisters Cove residents began to rise in a humming crescendo, some ripe with agreement, others scoffing and annoyed.

Len Pickington from the local council stood up at the front of the room and cleared his throat.

'We're here to listen to information from Greenways Resorts about the proposal. Why don't we let Alistair continue so we can hear how they plan to manage these issues?'

Sylvia uncrossed her legs and wriggled her shoulders. She glanced to her left and watched the waves roll in and recede on the beach outside the wall of glass. The sun was beginning to hang low in the sky and shadows obscured the rock pools.

'We're going to work closely with Parks and Wildlife Tasmania to reduce human impact in the area,' said the man from the resort group. 'If we damage the environment, we won't have an eco-resort worth visiting. Nature is the hero of this venture.'

'Good to know it's not the dollars then,' jeered someone in front of Sylvia.

She listened to some chortling from the people around her and sighed. If this resort went ahead, the whole fabric of the community would be changed. The village of Sisters Cove was set down a narrow, winding road that came to a dead end at a pristine white sand beach of unparalleled beauty. The small habitable stretch of beachfront had long ago been filled to capacity with old fibro shacks that jostled for prime position. More recently some had been knocked down to be replaced with substantial family homes, some so box-like and ugly they were enough to make her weep.

But still, the place was relatively undeveloped and she wanted it to stay that way.

Most locals had assumed they were safe from this kind of proposed development because of the geography of the area. For about a hundred metres behind the beach, narrow roads had been built to allow for another thirty or forty houses, but the nature of the bushland further up the hill, and the encroaching national park, meant that beyond that, development had stopped. About ninety houses sat inside the Sisters Cove beach precinct in all, and most people had assumed it was at maximum capacity. But now there was a proposal to build into the second cove that sat behind the headland, which had previously been dismissed as inaccessible and too expensive to develop.

Roger, the owner of the Farmgate Café, which operated out of the other end of the surf lifesaving clubhouse, was standing, twitching his fingers nervously. 'If you say this will take two years to build, that's a major impact on the community. There is one narrow, already degraded road in and out. The tourists tell us that the views they get along the way in, from the little parking bays, are part of the charm. You're going to be blocking that road and causing all sorts of problems. You can't tell us this won't impact our businesses. All the trucks, the cranes or whatever. It'll be a nightmare.'

The resort builder nodded encouragingly. 'That's why we've been in talks with the roads department to build another road in. Coming in from Delaware, behind the headland.'

'That's sacrilege! It's pristine bushland through there!' Eleanor Belingen remained sitting, three seats down from Sylvia, her arms folded tightly across her chest. Sylvia noticed her awkward, bristling posture. Eleanor wasn't very supple. She often had difficulty with the yoga moves that Sylvia tried to teach in their Monday classes. Downward Dog gave her a head spin. Bridge Pose made her feel weird and off balance. Eleanor seemed passionately devoted to complaining about most things, although this time Sylvia agreed with her sentiment.

'My bees?' Tippy Heokstrom stood up, a great shambling hulk of a man. His jeans were dirty and sagged low on his hips and his old coat was frayed at the cuffs. He stared blankly at the resort builder, his mouth hanging open.

The resort builder nodded and waited, but nothing more came. Tippy was intellectually disabled. As a child, he had spent so much time following the local builders around and asking them to make their trucks tip up and down, that he'd been given the nickname Tippy. Nobody even remembered his real name any more.

'My bees,' he said again. For nearly fifty years, Tippy had supplied honey to the locals. Everyone knew he kept illegal hives up in the national park behind Sisters Cove where the leatherwood trees grew.

'Tippy's wondering about the impact to the forest in the national park where his bees gather pollen,' said Dan, standing up next to Tippy.

Dan had always looked out for Tippy, even when they were young.

'Yeah,' said Tippy.

'We'll manage it sustainably and any protected species will be saved,' said the man.

'You've been involved in resorts before, Dan, what do you reckon about all this generally?' asked Roger, turning to Dan, who was still standing.

Dan motioned to Tippy to sit down.

Sylvia wondered where Annabelle was. Usually her sister loved community meetings and the chance to chat to all her many friends. It was strange that she wasn't here, hanging off Dan's arm, nodding at his sage words.

'Look, I don't know,' said Dan, stroking his short grey beard. 'I'm no expert but I reckon resorts are always a gamble in a place as remote as this. It'll bring jobs and tourist dollars, but with no direct flights to most of the mainland capital cities, it's hard to know whether it's sustainable.' He shrugged. 'Plus the site's pretty tricky and hasn't got the best views. I'm not sure I'd put my money in it, but good luck to you if you do.'

The meeting droned on, Alistair from Greenways Resorts answering questions when he could, the local council members interjecting, residents bickering. When the meeting finally ended, Sylvia was the first to get up and leave quietly from the back.

A cool breeze was coming off the ocean, and outside the clubhouse she stopped to pull off her shoes. She felt strangely calm, and the cold sand on her feet cleared her head. The moon sat high in the sky and the sun had begun to slip away as nine o'clock approached. Summer in Tasmania meant more than enough daylight for fitting everything in.

'Reckon I'll have a couple of beers before I go to the next meeting. Might make it more bearable.'

Sylvia lifted her head towards the sound of Dan's voice, but remained facing the ocean. 'It could wreck this place if it goes ahead,' she said.

'I wouldn't be so sure,' said Dan.

Sylvia shrugged, not wanting to extend the conversation with her brother-in-law. 'Where's Annabelle? I thought she'd be keen to hear from the developers.'

'She had the first wedding ceremony in the garden today. When the guests finally left to go to the reception, she fell in a heap. A pretty stressful day all round.'

'Why?'

'The pump broke. No water till the last minute. A bridezilla. You name it. She had a migraine coming on when I left.'

'Oh.' Sylvia had a sudden pang of guilt for not going up to help her sister get ready for the wedding. She'd forgotten it was Annabelle's first big event today.

'Have you finished sorting out The Old Chapel yet?' Dan asked.

A group of people came out of the clubhouse, talking loudly about the proposed new road. Sylvia and Dan looked towards them and waited for the chatter to disappear into the car park.

Sylvia hesitated. She wondered whether to tell him about Indigo's plan for The Old Chapel, but he continued before she could.

'Ian Enderby rang me – Lillian's solicitor. Said he couldn't get hold of you, but he's contacted the beneficiary. The woman in England. He's waiting to hear whether she's coming out to see it.'

'I know. I rang him a couple of hours ago. I've cleaned out quite a lot of Lillian's junk and delivered the stuff she'd marked to go to charity, but she left most of the artworks to stay with the house.'

'Who do you think this beneficiary is? A distant relative?' asked Dan.

'Maybe. Lillian didn't ever mention her, though.'

'I want to buy the place,' said Dan. 'I've left an offer with Ian. Makes sense that The Old Chapel comes back into Merrivale.' He put both hands in his pockets and looked over her shoulder into the distance. The wind had picked up and was now cold and insistent.

Sylvia shivered. 'Really?' She buried her toes in the sand, wondering why Annabelle hadn't mentioned this. 'Well, Indigo wants to buy it too.'

'What? How can she afford it?' asked Dan.

'Lillian left her a few thousand in the will. And somehow Indigo's managed to build up quite a nest egg. She's a hard worker.'

One corner of Dan's mouth turned up just a fraction, and Sylvia thought: why does this situation upset you so much? The tiny inflection of annoyance disguised as a smile might have fooled most people, but she had known him her whole life.

'Indigo wants her own space. And the solitude,' she said.

'Her mother's daughter, then,' said Dan, and Sylvia wondered if there was criticism in the words, or if she'd imagined it. Perhaps she was getting thin-skinned in her old age.

'Goodnight, Dan. If my sister has a migraine, you should probably go home and check she's all right.'

Sylvia turned and walked up the beach in the direction of her house. She focused on the low, rumbling sounds of the waves running up onto the sand then receding; breaking and rolling, back and forward. Crash, swish, swoosh. Her feet dug into the wet sand, and as she walked closer to the ocean edge, rivulets of cold water ran across them. The sun had almost disappeared now and the beach was in dark shadow.

'Sylvia.'

Sylvia turned. 'What?'

'Annabelle asked me to deliver a leftover roll of chicken wire to you. For your new coop. It's in the ute. I'll drop it in on the way past.'

'I can get it tomorrow.'

'I'll need the ute empty for Pete in the morning. I'll just leave it by your back door.' He turned and walked back to the car park, and Sylvia watched him go, resenting his help. His insistence.

As she continued walking towards the end of the beach, she noticed the outside light of her veranda flickering through the branches of the gum trees that lined the front of the hill. By car, Dan would beat her. Her house sat off the road, down a long, rutted, unsealed driveway through the bush. But on foot, there was direct beach access, although the hill path through the scrub along the ocean front was steep.

Her breathing was heavy as she climbed, and she stopped as a loud crackling sound came from the bush to her left. She flipped her head towards the shadowy treeline. A huge wombat emerged into the grass clearing, its brown fur sleek and beautiful. It stopped and looked up at her, then, without a second glance, proceeded nonchalantly across her path, straight into the bushes on the other side. She smiled to herself and continued up the hill.

She crossed her front garden and slipped down the side of the house to see if Dan had left the chicken wire. He was leaning against the door frame.

'Thought I'd wait to check you got home okay,' he said.

'There was no need. I'm a big girl.'

He pushed himself off the wall and took a step towards the ute. 'I put the chicken wire around the other side.'

'Thanks.'

He hesitated, then turned back to look at her. 'There were a few things that worried me in that meeting. Feel like making me a cuppa and we can chat them through?'

'Not really.'

'You're a tough woman, Sylvia Glendenning.'

Sylvia raised her eyebrows and pushed open the door. Nobody locked their doors around here, so she should be grateful Dan hadn't just let himself in. She turned and noticed that he hadn't made any move to leave. She flicked on the lights and let out a heavy sigh, holding open the screen door for him but refusing to meet his eye. *Bugger him.* He was forcing her into this chat. She didn't want a cup of tea. She wanted a gin and tonic. Preferably a double.

Imagine what her yoga students would say if they knew that their lentil-eating, herbal-tea-drinking, meditating yoga teacher was craving a very large gin. Actually, they'd probably just give a knowing chuckle. She was a local girl after all. Forty years away from the place didn't change you. Not really. She'd been to the Wynpark primary school with them, smoked cigarettes behind Jim's market on Saturdays while their parents drank in the pub, had her first kiss with the pot-smoking Bogie Thomas – although she'd heard that Bogie, aka Aiden, was now a leading Melbourne QC who did pro bono work for Amnesty International. His success probably meant that her brief fling with him didn't count any more if they were tallying up all the ways she was just an ordinary local girl.

Dan walked past her and stood next to the fridge. 'On second thoughts, got any beer?'

'No. I have about thirty types of Pukka tea, though. I'm having the turmeric. But the spearmint is nice.'

'Right,' said Dan, 'excellent.' He gave Sylvia a sarcastic half-smile that made her itch with irritation.

She opened the cupboard and looked longingly at the gin on the top shelf. She took out two mugs and closed the door with a firm click.

'So the wedding was hard work then, was it?' she asked as she flicked on the kettle.

'Let's not talk about it.'

'Why not?'

Dan cocked his head and widened his eyes. 'Because I don't want to.'

'What would you like to talk about then?' Sylvia poured the hot water into the cups and opened the brightly coloured tea bags.

'What about why you barely give me the time of day? Why every time I come home to find you visiting Annabelle, you practically run away the minute you see me?'

'That sounds like a stupid topic of conversation.'

'It's not. It pisses me off. Why won't you answer my calls? It's not right, Syl.'

Sylvia felt the anger like an electric shock. Like a blowtorch through her chest. '*Fuck you,* Dan.'

'What?'

'*Not right*? Are you insane? What *we* were doing was not right. Coming into my house at night, asking me for a drink and for God knows what else, when Annabelle's at home in bed, sick – that's *not right*!'

'Syl, don't.'

'I know you think there's still something between us, Dan, but there can't be. There just *can't* be. I told you it was over and I meant it.' For a moment Sylvia forgot to breathe. She dropped her eyes to the floor and forced her breath to come out evenly, but she felt herself crumbling inside.

'I didn't mean to upset you.'

'Just go.' Sylvia walked to the door and opened it. She looked out into the darkness, holding herself rigid, forcing back the tumble of emotions. The last thing she wanted to do was cry in front of him.

She felt him stop just behind her, then registered the warm, strong weight of his hand on her shoulder.

'I'm sorry, Syl. I know it's wrong, but every time I see you, I want to put my arms around you, kiss you. It makes me sick that I feel like this. But I can't be sorry for it. The last few months have been hell without you.'

Sylvia felt every muscle in her body tensing. She'd been through this torture twice since she'd returned to Sisters Cove – falling back into his arms for a few weeks, dragging herself back out – wanting to peel off her skin as she boiled in her guilt each time. She couldn't do it to herself again. But more than that, she couldn't do it to her sister. 'Dan, I just can't.'

She felt him move closer behind her, both hands now on her upper arms. He pulled her against him and she wanted to turn and slap him. But instead she let herself lean back. Tears began running down her face, and a sudden, unexpected sob echoed through the silence. She turned around and buried her face in his chest, letting the tears fall with great heaving gasps into his T-shirt.

'I hate you, Dan.'

'I love you, Syl. Always have. Always will.' He put his finger under her chin, tilted her face upwards and looked into her eyes. She knew he wasn't really seeing her lined and tear-streaked sixty-two-year-old-face. He was seeing her as she used to be. The person he'd first loved when he was twenty-one and she was seventeen, before she'd abandoned her life here. He was seeing the person she was under all the hard layers of life.

'Can I close the door?' he asked.

She reached out and pushed it shut and then reached across and turned out the light. She let her face rest against the warmth of his chest and listened as his heart beat a firm, fast rhythm in the darkness. It was so comforting. The smell of his aftershave, the heat of his body. From the day she'd come back to Sisters Cove, she'd been fighting the torrent of teenage memories unleashed by his familiar scent, the force of his personality, the tiny, appreciative movements of his eyes as they rested on her, always for a moment too long.

She looked out of the kitchen window. Darkness had fallen now and the moon was throwing a warm, silvery splash across the ocean. She wondered what the universe had meant by sending her back to Sisters Cove to care for Lillian when she was dying. Sending her back to the only man she'd ever loved properly; the only man she could never have. Perhaps it was playing a cruel joke.

'Can you stay for an hour?' she asked.

'Yes.'

She took his hand, and in the dim light she pulled him towards the bedroom. They lay down on the bed, fully clothed, and she put her head on his chest and let the scent of him close down her thoughts.

'I love you too, Dan. But I'm just so sorry I ever came back.'

CHAPTER FOUR

Willa

'I've been researching Tasmania, Mum,' said Hamish. He had wandered into the kitchen in his tracksuit pants and a crumpled pullover, holding his laptop. His hair stood up in a thick wedge where he'd slept on it, and a crease ran down one side of his face. 'Apparently Sisters Cove was voted one of the top ten beaches in Australia.' He plonked himself at the table and grinned.

Willa scraped marmalade onto her toast. 'Was it?'

'Yeah. Nearly as good as Whitehaven. We should go visit.'

'You've got exams coming up. We can't.'

'In the Easter holidays, then?'

'Dad's busy. He's got projects going on for the next few months.'

'Don't you want to go and see your new house, Mum?'

'It's not that simple, Hame. Eat your breakfast or you'll be late for school.'

Willa pulled the Weetabix box from the shelf and milk and yoghurt from the fridge. She handed him a bowl and spoon. She knew she shouldn't mother him so much, but she couldn't help it.

'Why was the regatta cancelled?' she asked.

'Weather. Anyway, Louis did something to his shoulder. He reckons he'll be right by next Friday, though.' Hamish poured milk onto the six Weetabix he'd piled into the bowl. He picked up the family-size tub of yoghurt and tipped it up. Willa held her breath as half the tub landed on top of the mountain of cereal in a huge dollop.

'Use a spoon with that,' snapped Willa. She hadn't slept well. She felt shivery; as if she was coming down with a strange virus. She'd stared at the ceiling for half the night, wondering about the little house in Tasmania, tossing and turning, thrumming with anxiety. It must have done something to her immune system.

'Good morning.' Hugo kissed the top of her head on his way to put the kettle on the hob. He was wearing jeans and a button-up shirt and the beautiful brown loafers she'd bought him for Christmas. Casual Friday.

'What do you have on today?' asked Willa, admiring his bottom. Hugo had a very nice body for a man in his mid forties. He often went jogging, and if the weather prevented it, he lifted weights in the spare room.

'Not much. I thought we could meet for lunch. Maybe try out that new café, the Rectory, I think it's called. Near Christ Church. Amy told me it was very good.'

'I'm not sure. I'll see. I didn't sleep well,' said Willa, ignoring Hugo's worried look and gazing out of the window at the dreary sky, the bare trees, the hard, icy ground.

She used to think January was the worst part of winter. Nothing to look forward to except weeks more cold and ice. December, with Christmas and the markets and the lights and carollers, had been her favourite winter month, and February had been tolerable, with its cool promise of spring in the air. Now, though, the entire winter was unbearable, but February was the worst. Willa could feel February coming, feel it spreading into her bones like cancer in concrete, something insidious creeping through the part of her that should be unshakeably solid. But in the last two years, she had come to realise that a person's foundations could be precariously balanced. Bones, muscles, emotions. With the approach of February, she felt as if she might collapse and shatter with the slightest touch.

She focused her eyes on the screen saver of Hamish's laptop. A photo taken in Ireland, three summers ago. The four of them looking so together. So *ordinary*. Hugo leaning against her, laughing. Hamish, not so tall then, his arm slung around Esme, an expression of comical, exaggerated impatience on his face – penance for making him pose for the photograph. Esme smiling radiantly, putting up with Hamish's constant tomfoolery. *Esme.* Willa felt the breath halve inside her chest. As if the bottom part of a lung had collapsed and there was only a little bit of capacity left to take in air. She clutched at the worktop, making her breath become slow and full.

'… at home, then?'

Hugo was saying something. She hadn't heard. She was thinking about her session with Dr Lee yesterday morning. *What if you could find happiness in just a few everyday interactions this week? If it's a thing you decide to be, just for that moment? Choose to acknowledge a spark of happiness, just as you acknowledge the other emotions that may also be present.*

'Sorry?' Willa picked up the kettle. She steadied her hand and poured water into cups that Hugo had readied with tea bags.

'I said I could come home instead, and we could go for a walk, see where we end up. A little adventure for our lunch.'

'Mmm,' said Willa. She jiggled the tea bags.

Hamish was scooping mushy, yoghurt-covered slop into his already full mouth, without pausing between spoonfuls. She was transfixed. It was repulsive, but also comforting. The nourishment, the energy needed to keep him growing. He was becoming a man, and she would have to watch carefully in case something went wrong and he needed her there to fix it.

'Darling?' said Hugo.

'Yes, okay. Sure.' She needed to focus. Concentrate.

'What time is it in Australia, Mum?' mumbled Hamish through his mouthful.

'I guess about six p.m. on their Friday night.'

'You should have called them last night then. To find out about the house. Now they won't be in the office.'

Willa was counting on it.

'She can email them any questions,' said Hugo, picking up his tea.

'Will you, Mum?'

'I don't know, Hamish. I can't leave here at the moment and the letter says I need to go and see the house in person. You and Dad have commitments.'

'Go on your own then,' said Hamish, as if the answer was obvious. As if it was well within her power to catch a train to Heathrow, board a plane to the Australian mainland, then another to the island of Tasmania, then after thirty hours in transit, hire a car and drive a couple more hours to an unknown place called Sisters Cove and turn up to a seaside cottage to… to do what? Take ownership from a mysterious dead woman? The idea was ludicrous. She wasn't capable of that sort of momentum.

Once it would have been easy, but now, well, she felt panicky at the idea of being away from Hamish. What if he contracted some sort of random illness that meant he had to be put on life support? Or if he needed to be picked up from a party in the middle of the night? Although he didn't really go to parties – he was too dedicated to his sport and also a bit of an introvert. But still, that might change at any moment. Hugo had the same sort of personality, yet he'd liked parties at seventeen, so you could never be sure. A hot flush of worry swept through Willa again, and she wondered if perhaps this was just a symptom of perimenopause. That would make her normal. Hot, normal sort of flushes. Not crazy panic-woman flushes. The thought comforted her.

'You could, you know, darling,' said Hugo. 'It might be fun.'

Willa narrowed her eyes at him. 'I don't think so.'

She could sense his disappointment. Almost see the cogs of his mind turning over. *When will it end? This isn't the woman I married.* But the fear that he might give up on her didn't feel quite as real as the terror of setting out on such a huge journey all by herself.

Hamish looked from his father to Willa, then gave a shake of his head. 'I'll have that house if you don't want it, Mum. I could learn to surf if I lived in Australia for a while.'

'The water would be freezing,' said Willa. But despite the sick feeling in her stomach, she smiled at the thought of her lily-white English son next to the bronzed Aussie surfer boys with their overgrown, sun-bleached hair.

'Not for me,' said Hamish.

He was right. Here, the water was always cold. And the idea of her boy surfing in the freezing waters of Bass Strait made her feel strangely warm. As Hamish dumped his plate in the dishwasher and grinned, she thought: this is happiness. This moment is happiness.

She tidied up the kitchen and then sat and drank her tea, as her husband and son hurried themselves to get out the door.

'I'll see you around one, then?' asked Hugo as he kissed her goodbye.

'All right. Bye.' She smiled, then looked down, pretending to be engrossed in the newspaper. The moment of happiness had made her feel untethered, as if she might blow away at any second, as if she might not always feel so weighed down. It frightened her that she might feel happy again one day.

As soon as they were both gone, Willa walked into the laundry and began to fold, wash, iron, clean out the cupboards. Dr Lee said she needed to keep busy. Needed to give herself other things to think about. After she'd finished ironing, she went into the bedroom and pulled out the drawer full of summer clothes. She tossed them onto the bed. Time for giving to charity. She held up each item, assessed whether she could ever imagine wearing it again, whether it gave her joy. Wasn't that the latest trend in decluttering from that Japanese woman? 'Joy' as a measurement of working out her summer wardrobe was a little bit over-the-top, in Willa's opinion. She held up a beige pair of chinos. She quite liked them. They were very functional and fitted her perfectly. A feeling of joyousness at the sight of them eluded her though. She put them in the 'to keep' pile and decided she couldn't possibly be influenced by a woman who got her joy from her choice of trousers. It was a highly suspicious sort of personality trait.

She stopped as she came to a pale-green sundress with silver embroidery down the front. She held it up to her face and smelled it. A gift from Esme, years ago. The splash of a tear made a dark green spot on the material.

'Baby girl, I miss you so much,' she whispered. She felt the tide of grief begin to overtake her. Sometimes it happened without warning. Less these days, though. She let herself collapse backwards onto the bed and curl up in a ball, clutching the dress. She shook with tears. After they stopped, she lay there wondering how long it would go on; if it would ever be easier; if the tiny moment of happiness this morning had really happened.

An hour must have passed and Willa eventually got up, went back into the kitchen, and made herself another cup of tea. She sat at the desktop computer. The letter from the solicitor taunted her from the desk. She lifted her hands and typed in *Lillian Brooks Sisters Cove Tasmania*.

Several articles popped up, and she clicked on the first one. It was from a newspaper called *The Coastal Herald*. From the look of the article, it was a local paper. A woman of perhaps sixty was pictured in a bright-yellow long-sleeved shirt, red shorts and a red sun hat, leaning on a yellow lifesaving board outside a building at the beach. She was short, with hunched shoulders and a leathery, lined face. Her eyes twinkled straight into the camera. The caption read: *Sisters Cove's second-longest-serving lifesaver, Lillian Brooks, gets ready for the Tulip Time Ocean Race.*

Willa began to read the article, but she could feel Lillian's eyes staring out from the screen at her. She looked back up at the photograph and was suddenly overcome with a cold sense of dread. This funny little woman knew her. She had singled Willa out for her final act of giving.

She pressed the back arrow on the screen and flicked down the menu of articles about Lillian. The next one showed her with a group of women inside the surf club. Some sort of craft group fund-raiser for charity. Lillian was holding up a painting. The woman next to her was holding a knitted jumper. They had raised more than six thousand dollars for a children's charity. Willa scanned the text, which mentioned details of each woman's particular talent and how they had gone about raising the funds over twelve months.

The next article showed Lillian sitting in a chair next to another woman, who was standing. The other woman was tall, slim and fit-looking. She might have been fifty or so, and was quite beautiful, with long grey-blonde hair pulled back in a ponytail. She was wearing yoga pants and a fitted tank top. The article talked about yoga during illness and about the women's long-standing friendship and how yoga and meditation were helping Lillian through her battle with breast cancer.

Lillian must have lost her battle, thought Willa. She looked at the date of the article: 28 February 2018. A cold, churning nausea flooded her gut. She pushed back her chair, walked into the mud-room, and grabbed her coat.

'Kettles!' The dog looked up from his mat. 'Here, boy. Walk.'

She attached his lead and pulled him outside to the gate. She tried to force herself to step into the lane. But she was trapped. She was stuck on the date of the article: 28 February. She couldn't think what to do next. She was still standing there a few minutes later, Kettles waiting patiently on his lead, when Hugo arrived back for lunch.

'Willa? Are you all right?'

'Yes. Yes. I…' She had to pull herself together. 'I knew you'd be coming so I thought I'd wait.'

'All right. Shall we take Kettles for lunch?' Hugo was looking at her oddly.

'I… No. I'll put him in.'

Willa took the old dog back into the kitchen. In the hallway, she looked at her face in the mirror. It was blotchy, her eyes puffy and pink. She brushed her hair with her fingers and put on a blue woollen hat that Hugo liked. It hid the mess of her hair.

Outside, Hugo took her gloved hand and they walked towards the city centre. She wondered where they were going, but she didn't have the energy to ask. She wanted Hugo to decide. She might like a cup of coffee. Yes, a cup of coffee would be very warming. Very nice.

At the entrance to a new café on Little Clarendon Street, Hugo said, 'Wait here a minute, darling.' He went in and spoke to a man and came back out with a pretty hessian bag.

'I ordered a picnic earlier,' he said. He smiled at her kindly. So kind, her husband. It occurred to her that it was too cold for a picnic, that there was nowhere to go where they wouldn't freeze, but she smiled back, because she knew she was letting him down. She needed to try. She loved him, and she needed to make things normal.

They walked past the stunning brick edifice of Keble College Chapel, then crossed the road into the University Parks. Hugo led her down the familiar paths towards the Cherwell, where the wind bit into their faces and the bare beech and chestnut branches swayed. They kept walking along the banks of the river and eventually reached a grove of yew trees, and Willa felt her knot of anxiety lifting at the familiar, lovely sight of her favourite spot. They passed a lamp post, and ahead of them, between some large oaks, bare of leaves, a dark green fir tree sparkled with remnants of ice.

Hugo led her to a park bench – a high-backed wooden seat with wrought-iron arms, but instead of turning around to sit, he said, 'Here it is.'

Then Willa understood. It was finally here. She bent over. In the centre of the seat was a small metal plaque:

In memory of our beautiful girl
Esme Katelyn Gilmore Fairbanks
11 November 2001–28 February 2017

She took a breath and let the emotions jostle in her mind. *This is where we will come to remember you, darling.* Her eyes tingled with heat and she squeezed Hugo's hand.

She sat on the bench and ran her glove along the black iron of the arm. Hugo sat down next to her and gave her shoulder a squeeze. He picked up the bag and placed it on his lap, and pulled out a thermos and two cups. After he'd poured the coffee, they sat and watched a young woman with a toddler. The little boy was running and falling in his huge, thick duffel coat. The girl must be his nanny, thought Willa. *So young.* Hugo was watching them too, and after a while, just as Willa was beginning to think they might see what food was in the bag, he said, 'I was thinking about the house in Tasmania.'

'Me too,' she said.

'I was thinking about who the woman might be.'

Willa could hear the hint of forced cheer in his voice.

'Yes, me too.'

'I… I know you won't want to hear this, but I think there's only one person who it can be,' said Hugo. He turned and looked at her, and Willa looked back. She could see his love, his open, trusting heart, but beneath all that she could see a hint of fear, and she almost couldn't bear it.

He squeezed her gloved hand.

Willa was holding the coffee cup with her other, bare hand and focused on the warmth of it in her palm, the cold air against her knuckles. She reached down and placed it at her feet.

'Yes,' she said. 'I suppose you're right.'

She closed her fingers around the iron rail of Esme's seat. Her beautiful daughter. Her little girl, who she would never see again. And now she had to think about that house. That *woman*. It was too much. How dare anyone interrupt this moment? This special day? Today was for Esme.

Hugo reached into the bag and pulled out a large polystyrene cup and a plastic spoon.

'Chicken soup,' he said.

'Thanks,' said Willa. The anger had gone as quickly as it had arrived. She took off her other glove and wrapped her hand around the cup and stared at her fingers, long and elegant. Her mother had called them pianist's fingers. Her mother was within her, part of her. The part of her that needed to keep living. Her mother would have liked to sit here on this bench, remembering Esme.

The cold pushed into her, but Willa felt strangely warm, as if a small piece of her might nearly have been restored. The sharp fragment of a broken teacup, glued back together by a delicate line of glue. She needed the pieces to stay together now. She owed it to her husband and her son.

'Perhaps we can stop by the travel agent on the way home,' she said.

Hugo gave her an uncertain smile.

'I imagine you and Hamish can do without me for a week or two if I go.'

Hugo didn't answer immediately. But she could feel his relief that the burden he'd been carrying for both of them might have an end in sight. That there might be light at the end of this awful dark path she'd been treading.

'We'll have a lads' week in,' he said gently. 'Steak every night.'

Willa looked back at the little boy. His nanny was holding both of his hands and swinging him around. She gathered pace and lifted him off his feet. Hugo was looking too. The girl began turning faster and faster, and they listened to the child's gurgling squeals of laughter as he spun through the air, and Willa thought: yes! Yes, little one! You can fly.

CHAPTER FIVE

Annabelle

'It just doesn't make any sense,' said Dan. He finished the last of his red wine and refilled his glass. He put the bottle back on the table, picked up his knife and fork and attacked the lamb.

Annabelle glanced at her own empty glass. 'Well, I suppose Lillian had her reasons, darling.'

'What reasons? It's selfish. This woman in England has probably never even been here. Certainly not that we know about. She inherits a broken-down house on the other side of the world and Lillian tells her she has to visit it before she sells it.' Dan sighed and gulped down another mouthful of wine. 'She'll end up selling it anyway, but it will just cost more. Selfish.'

'Why will it cost more?' asked Annabelle.

'Two transactions. Legal fees and so on. The cost of the woman's travel. It's just a big fat expensive hassle. Lillian knew I would have bought it off her and let her stay in it until she died.'

'Maybe she didn't know that.'

'I told her last year. When she was looking half at death's door. She knew all right.'

'What?' Annabelle cringed. She pushed the rare lamb to one side and finished chewing on a bean. She tried to swallow, but Dan's revelation was weighing on her oesophagus and she couldn't get it down.

Dan was looking at his phone.

She picked up her beautiful navy and white tasselled serviette, part of a set she'd found on a shopping trip to Melbourne last year. Dan had told her she needed to use the trip as a tax deduction, so she'd visited a wedding expo on the same weekend.

She coughed into the serviette. 'What do you mean, you told her? Surely you didn't mention the fact that she was dying?'

He looked up. 'She *was* bloody dying. Everyone knew it.'

'Yes, but… still.'

'Anyway, Ian Enderby says this Englishwoman has arranged a time to see the place on Thursday. He'll bring her out. I might try to have a chat with her. You should too. Be nice to her. It'll be easier to get her to sell to us if you're friendly.'

'I'll be busy on Thursday. I've got a meeting for the garden fete committee. Then I'm setting up for Lola Peterson's wedding.'

'You can do that on Friday. Anyway, Indigo cleans the cottages and Pete sorts the mowing for you. And you told me they have their own florists coming to set up the arches and that other crap.'

'There are lots of other things I need to do,' said Annabelle, sniffing.

Dan began playing with his phone again and Annabelle had a sudden urge to slap his hand. The idea was so foreign that it gave her a little buzz. She felt invigorated. She'd never in a million years do such a thing. If she were to make a point about his rudeness, she might do something like place her hand gently over his and laughingly say, 'Darling, I'm still here! Silly thing.'

Dan kept scrolling, probably looking at football scores or his email.

'It takes hours to get everything perfect for the weddings. And the garden doesn't do itself, you know.' Her voice sounded whiny, and she thought: I am making the best garden and wedding ceremony venue on the north-west coast. Maybe the whole of Tasmania. You should be proud of me!

'Sure. Still, just a quick cuppa with her.' Dan looked up. 'Talk gardens or something. Don't you want to get your hands on The Old Chapel so you can offer it in your wedding options?'

Annabelle prodded the lamb. 'Maybe. I don't suppose it would be popular with brides, though – thirty guests would be a squeeze in there. Forty at most. And we'd have to renovate it. But I suppose an ocean view would be nice.'

'Exactly. Brides would love getting married there and having that view right behind them.'

'No, I mean the view from here. Or from a marquee if we put one up where The Old Chapel is and start offering receptions as well as ceremonies. We could knock The Old Chapel down. We'd have a wonderful view from our bedroom then.'

Dan looked at her oddly. Then he pushed back his chair and took his wine glass to his armchair in front of the television. Annabelle put down her cutlery and decided she was finished too. She looked forlornly at the pile of untouched Brussels sprouts on Dan's plate and felt a stab of annoyance. She took the plates to the kitchen and then went into her office and sat down at her computer.

Half a dozen emails about the garden fete had arrived since four p.m. She felt jittery just looking at them. It had felt like such a coup to be selected as the show garden for the Sisters Cove Autumn Festival and Fete, but now the whole thing was making her feel a bit wobbly. She had four weeks to get the garden up to scratch, or Mary Trelawney would never let her forget it. It wasn't Annabelle's fault that her garden had gotten more votes than Mary's. Lots more votes! Still, it had to be absolutely perfect or Mary and her crew of complainers would make snide remarks for the rest of time.

She sighed. They'd probably make the remarks anyway. She really needed Pete to work more hours to help her make the garden sparkle. The edges around the old elms needed redoing, but Dan would get cranky if she asked him to increase Pete's weekly pay from their account. Maybe she could work out a way to set it up from the new wedding account so he wouldn't notice. Alan from the bank would tell her how to do it. He was lovely about helping her with all that online business.

The sight of the seaweed tea flowing through the mulch soothed Annabelle's headache. She hadn't slept well. Too much screen time and answering silly emails before bedtime. She aimed the watering can away from the Japanese windflowers and towards the marigolds, emptying the can across the first golden row. The windflowers wobbled their white heads in the breeze and she caught the faint scent of the native frangipani tree.

'Morning.'

She looked up. Sylvia was wearing her yoga pants and a fitted singlet top. It defied logic that a sixty-two-year-old woman could look forty. Well, forty-nine perhaps. Much younger than she should look, in any event. They were not at all like sisters, although people often commented that they both looked younger than their years. The only thing that saved Annabelle from withering away to old womanhood was the fact that the chubbiness around her face smoothed out the lines. Sylvia's face relied on lentils and meditation to do the same job. Annabelle thought her own method, involving a scandalous amount of chocolate, was far more sensible.

'What are you up to?' asked Sylvia.

Annabelle smiled. 'Hello, Syl. Just getting organised for wedding number three and the garden fete.'

'Mmm. About that,' said Sylvia.

'Yes? Are you keen to do some pruning to help out? I won't say no!'

Sylvia laughed. 'No. Not really.'

'Seriously though, Syl. If you want to put your skills to use for these weddings, I'd say there's lots of scope for extra income for you. I hear yoga for brides is all the rage.'

'Is it?'

'You could come and run a private class for them on the morning of the wedding. Calm their nerves.'

'Maybe,' said Sylvia.

'Or use your calligraphy skills. I had one of them asking me about people who could help with place cards and little sign boards. You'd be brilliant.'

'God, no,' said Sylvia. 'I haven't done calligraphy for decades. Anyway, I'm here about the fete, not the weddings. A couple of the women in my sunrise class this morning wondered if you're going to include Lillian's gardens around The Old Chapel in the fete tours. I don't imagine the new owner would mind. Lillian did have an amazing eye for planting.'

'In her own haphazard way, I suppose,' said Annabelle, turning back to the marigolds. She knew she shouldn't feel miffed. Lillian was dead for a start, and being jealous of a dead person felt just a little bit, well, childish. Still, she looked over at the tall blue artichoke heads swaying amongst the parched dahlias in the overgrown beds on Lillian's side of the lane, and supposed the wild extravagance of the garden might draw in a few extra people. Everyone seemed so entranced by The Old Chapel for some unfathomable reason. Paint was curling off the weatherboards and the whole thing would probably blow over in a decent storm.

Sylvia followed her gaze. 'I think I can rustle up a couple of volunteers who might help get it in order. Leandra Pickle seemed keen. And her husband too, apparently.'

'Well *I* won't have time. You should probably talk to Lillian's solicitor about it, though, before they go in and start digging around.'

'I already have,' said Sylvia.

Again Annabelle felt a surge of something like jealousy.

'I asked him when the new owner is coming out. And I passed on an offer from Indigo to buy the place.'

'Really? Indigo wants it?'

'Yep. Why not? Great views. I was surprised Lillian didn't leave it to her in her will, actually. It would have been a nice godmotherly thing to do.'

Annabelle turned back to her watering can and splashed in another black dollop of concentrated seaweed mixture, then leaned down to get the hose. 'I should probably tell you that Dan and I want to buy it too. It makes sense for it to be returned to the estate, don't you think? For the heritage. Obviously.'

'Really?' said Sylvia.

Annabelle considered the raised eyebrow and the inscrutable smile. Actually a sort of smirk. And Sylvia's tone. It sounded superior. Big-sister sort of superior. As if she knew better.

'Absolutely!' she said.

'I've only ever heard you whinge about the place,' said Sylvia.

'No,' said Annabelle slowly. She felt certain that wasn't right. Yes, she'd been perplexed that Lillian had ignored all the maintenance the house had needed and had let it become an eyesore for her neighbours. Well, she and Dan were the only neighbours, but plenty of tourists visiting the lighthouse stopped to look at the little weatherboard church building that, from a distance, seemed to sit right on the cliff edge, with the ocean as its only backdrop.

It was so dilapidated that she had no idea how Lillian had managed to paint her canvases in the building – or live in it for that matter. It was so dark and dingy inside; you could tell just from standing on the doorstep how bad it was. But she'd never *whinged* about it. Had she?

Annabelle turned up the pressure on the tap and the hose flew out of the watering can and began whipping around like a lunatic snake.

Water sprayed across Sylvia's knees, then the hose lurched through the freshly turned flower bed towards Annabelle and sprayed jets of water through the dirt, leaving her soaking and covered in muddy flecks. She stamped on the hose and turned off the tap.

'Sorry.' She dropped her eyes.

'It's fine,' said Sylvia. She held up a key. 'I'm going to go through a few more things of Lillian's. Try to clean the place up a bit more. I can't think who this Englishwoman is, but it looks like we'll find out on Thursday.'

'Yes. Dan thought I should invite her for a cup of tea,' said Annabelle, squeezing out her shirt.

Sylvia made a strange guffawing sound.

'Well, if we're going to be neighbours, it makes sense.' Annabelle tried not to pout. 'I'm going in to have a shower.'

Sylvia gave her a wave and headed off towards the boundary fence.

From the verandah, Annabelle spied her sister pushing on the boundary gate and crossing the lane. Sylvia hesitated at the door of The Old Chapel, seeming to take in the view of the ocean. Then she fitted the key into the door and disappeared into the little front entry.

Annabelle pulled off her boots and went through to the shower. Dan had been so concerned about money lately. So keen for her to start this wedding business when he found out how much people would pay. She wondered how they could afford to buy The Old Chapel if they were meant to be watching the pennies. Apparently they'd had some investments go bad, but she hadn't asked the details. She didn't really want to know. Dan had always looked after the money side of things.

She picked up her new bottle of shower gel and smelled the fragrance of white lilies. It made her think of the last of the flowering lilies in the top beds by the shed. What a shame they'd be gone by the time the fete came around.

She turned up the heat on the shower, rubbed the delicious fragrance into a lather and soaped off the stress of the morning, letting the hot water pour over her head. Since Sylvia had returned to Tasmania, things hadn't been as Annabelle had hoped. There seemed to be a gulf between them that she couldn't bridge. They didn't share any interests. And Sylvia was so self-sufficient. She wouldn't let Dan or Annabelle come and help her clean up that messy, bush-covered house block she'd bought. Annabelle wanted to reach out to her sister. She wanted things to be right between them. But they were just a little bit skew-whiff, and she didn't know what to do about it.

She let her soapy fingers slide down by her armpit. She stopped, lifted her hand, then placed her fingers back down on the spot where her breast started. It felt like there was a hard little pea under her skin. No, larger; a marble. She pressed it. It was unmoving under her skin.

She dropped her hand to her side and washed off all the soap, then ran her finger firmly over the side of her breast. It slid up and over the round bump and then off again, like a perfectly formed little ski jump on a mound of soft snow. She got out of the shower, ignoring the urge to check the lump again. She felt a flame of fear as she looked in the fogged-up mirror.

'Stop it. Just stop it.'

The harsh sound of her words bounced around the bathroom tiles. She had found a cyst. Plenty of women had cysts. Abigail Beddingham had two breasts full of them! Fibrocystic breasts, or something like that. Abigail adored telling stories after garden club about her cysty breasts and how every new doctor she visited always wanted to send her off to have them squashed flat as a pancake in the toasted-sandwich-maker thingy at the breast clinic. Apparently a mammogram was performed using a cold version of a sandwich press. Very, very painful. Although Annabelle had never seen the need to have one, so she didn't usually comment during these conversations. The idea of medical people fondling her breasts made her feel icky. She shuddered.

The cysts went away after a while. So Abigail had told them, at least. Besides, she couldn't think about it now. She had too much else going on.

She pulled out the bathroom scales and stepped on them. The digital counter flicked over to 90.2 kilograms. She smiled. See. She had lost nearly a whole kilogram. And if she was counting in pounds, she was now under the two-hundred mark, which was a very satisfying thought. She was healthier now than she had been last week. And the cyst probably accounted for some of that weight anyway. It was just a little bit of extra water retention. That was all it was.

She pulled on her best tummy-controlling underpants and some black trousers. Then she chose a fuchsia silk top to wear to the meeting later. It was her best colour. And she would wear lots of lipstick. As soon as she lost a few more kilograms – twenty would be ideal – she would be fit and gorgeous and everything would be fabulous.

She would email the lawyer, Ian Enderby, right now and get him to bring this Wilhelmena Fairbanks in for a cup of tea on Thursday. And she'd bake her orange poppy-seed cake. That was sure to put the woman in a good mood. A negotiating mood. If Dan wanted to buy The Old Chapel, it was her job to help make that happen.

She got her nicest black bra out of the top drawer and deliberately avoided touching the area near the cyst as she put it on. Then she threw on her top, added a contrasting floral cardigan, slid on her dark pink leather loafers and without looking in the mirror went down to her computer to send the email to Ian. Nice fellow, Ian. A bit boring, but kind eyes. These days he had an interest in succulents, she recalled from her discussion with him at last year's legal practice dinner. So all in all, it might be a very nice little gathering on Thursday. And she would only eat the very smallest sliver of her cake.

CHAPTER SIX

Sylvia

The arched window of the entry porch to The Old Chapel was so grimy it was impossible to see through it. Over the years, several of the stained-glass panels had been replaced with ordinary glass, and now they were thick with dirt and sea salt. A fine covering of spider webs was draped across the top.

Sylvia knew she should have cleaned the window months ago, when Lillian was still alive. But instead they had used their time for other things. Meditation. Yoga. Drinking herbal tea, or Lillian's favourite whisky, depending on their mood. Talking about Indigo, and about the past. Or at least the bits of it they had wanted to remember.

As she turned the key in the front door, she noticed lines of dirty red paint cracking along the wood grain. Inside the tiny foyer it was dingy and cramped, and although she had left the back window open a crack last time, Sylvia was assaulted by the familiar mix of smells. Linseed oil, turpentine, antique furniture. Tempered with old cigarette smoke, it combined into a sickly-sweet fragrance that was distinctly Lillian's.

She turned on the light and stood at the entrance to the living room. It had once been the nave in the days when Merrivale's original family had attended church services here, a hundred years ago or more. It was so small that Lillian's sparse furniture barely fitted. A faded and squashed couch with colourful throws across its back was pushed close to a sideboard, an armchair and a small television cabinet. At the end of the space, on the left-hand wall, a set of narrow stairs led to a loft platform, where Lillian had slept as a girl, and then as a young woman until her father passed away. Now it held dozens of canvases and boxes that were yet to be dealt with. Underneath the platform, the open lower area was divided through the centre. On the right there was a kitchen bench and a table for two with a pot-bellied fire in the back corner. On the left, a proper bedroom had been partitioned off with a bathroom hidden behind it. Nothing had been renovated for decades, and the place made Sylvia feel trapped in time.

'Hello, old girl,' whispered Sylvia.

She picked up the framed photograph on the dresser. It was from the early 1970s – her and Lillian arm in arm, holding their hockey sticks aloft and grinning. She put it down and felt a heavy loneliness descend, as if the last good part of her had died with Lillian. Except, of course, that wasn't true. She still had Indigo. And Annabelle, sort of. A picture of Dan floated through her head and she strode across to the kitchen and yanked open the blind above the sink. The window let in a grimy ray of light.

Wrinkling her nose at the bad smell coming from the sink, she turned on the hot water and scrubbed the basin with an old cloth. After wiping down the dusty kitchen bench, she climbed up to the loft. The cathedral-style timber-lined ceiling sloped down sharply, and she had to duck her head as she wandered around looking at the labels on the boxes.

She'd already taken Lillian's clothes to the charity shop and cleaned out the cupboards as she'd promised she would do. The boxes were filled with more substantial bric-a-brac – the bits that Lillian hadn't already given to her friends. The solicitor would know what to do with them. She picked up a small box of books and lifted it on top of a larger one, shunting and tidying to make the space easier to walk around. A large canvas portrait of a woman emerged from behind one of the boxes. It was painted in muted colours and the woman's upper body was naked. Her face and figure were elongated and distorted as she leaned back on the grass. The thick, bold strokes of paint forming her face made her look anguished somehow. She was staring off to the side. Sylvia regarded the painting for a few moments, then descended the narrow timber stairs.

She picked up the cloth from the kitchen bench and wiped along the railings of the stairs and down the dark lining boards of the walls, where spiders had begun spinning webs. She'd done this once already, before Christmas, a few weeks after Lillian's funeral. But she was happy to do it again. She wanted the new owner to find the place habitable, or at least bearable for an hour or two. Of course she hoped the woman wouldn't fall in love with it, and would instead want to sell it to Indigo, but there was no need to make her first experience of The Old Chapel an unpleasant one. Lillian wouldn't have wanted that.

A church pew with a high back and box seat sat along the bedroom wall on the lower level, facing the entry. Large art books and other volumes on philosophy and gardens had been lined up along the seat, as if it were a bookcase. Their colourful fading spines were arranged with artistic flair. Sylvia supposed she should box them up, although they gave a lovely insight into Lillian's personality and interests. But she didn't want to create more work for the new owner, so she fetched some flat-pack boxes from the top level and assembled them before pushing the filled cartons into the corner, below the staircase. Behind the books, dead insects and dust had collected, and she ran the cloth along the pew.

A sudden intrusion of a voice into the silence of the little church startled her.

'Hello, beautiful.'

Dan stood in the open door at the entrance to the living room. She was so accustomed to noticing sensations in her body that she felt her stomach clench and her shoulders tense. She took a deep breath and loosened them.

'Hello. I'm just cleaning.'

He smiled. 'I can see that.'

'Are you wanting something?'

'Just to see you. I saw you arrive from my office.'

'Dan…' She paused, looked down at the worn sisal rug under her feet, then back up at him. 'Please don't. We can't…'

'Syl, I need you.'

'No, you don't.' She dropped her head and began cleaning again. She could feel him watching her. 'You've survived perfectly well without me for forty years. Don't be daft.'

'I was thinking, maybe we can go away. Move to the mainland.'

'Dan, don't. Not here. If you talk about this any more, I'll…' The words caught in her throat. It would break Annabelle to hear him talking like this. To know what they'd been doing behind her back. Sylvia needed to be away from here; away from Dan and the strange persuasive hold he had over her. 'Just… don't say another word, please. You are married to Annabelle. She loves you. There is nothing else to say.' She turned back to the pew and pretended to be cleaning. She heard him sigh, then he was silent for a minute.

'This place could use a coat of paint,' he said.

She turned back around. 'Yes. Well, whoever ends up here will make it their own.'

He was looking at her strangely when she caught his eye again. He turned, embarrassed perhaps, and fixed his gaze on something through the window. 'I'm sorry that Andrew sold this part of the estate to Lillian. Back in the seventies, we didn't think about views, beach access and so on. You'd never do it these days. Lil paid half a pittance for this place.'

Sylvia said, 'It was the least Andrew could do after Len's accident, don't you think? Anyway, that's ancient history. I don't want to talk about it.'

Dan huffed a little laugh. 'Don't worry, Syl. I'm all for living in the present. I've had to. Constance has kept me in my place, waiting for Merrivale. She's as fit as a fiddle. The bane of my bloody life.'

Sylvia pondered the conversation she'd had with Annabelle the other day about Dan's aunt. It was true. Constance was ridiculously energetic for a woman who must be nearly ninety. 'Well, Annabelle seems to adore her. And anyway, she's let you live in Merrivale for years, so what's the difference if you don't get the deeds until she dies?'

Dan shrugged and avoided her eyes.

'You're lucky, you know, that Annabelle's so good to Constance. You're the one who should be checking in on her. She's your kin,' said Sylvia.

'Coo-ee!'

At the sound of the shrill voice, they both turned towards the door. Dan stepped back as Annabelle came into the cramped, shadowy porch in a ghastly bright-pink top that did nothing to flatter her.

'What are you two up to?' Annabelle smiled from one to the other.

Sylvia lifted her cloth. 'I'm cleaning. I'm not sure what Dan's doing here.' She turned sideways to the staircase and began wiping down each of the railings with swift strokes.

'Oh good. Well it's Dan I'm after, actually. Pete needs the hedge trimmer, darling. He can't find it. Didn't you use it along the orchard boundary at the weekend?'

Dan walked out the door without answering. Annabelle raised her eyebrows in Sylvia's direction, then turned back to watch him go. Sylvia saw him through the window, striding across the grass.

'He's been a real grumpy bear lately. I don't know what's gotten into him,' said Annabelle.

Sylvia made a murmuring sound in her throat, and kept cleaning.

'He's been so angry. I don't know if it's just about Lillian leaving this place to a stranger when he wanted it.' She paused. 'I think there must be something else.'

Annabelle was looking at Sylvia as if she might have some answers.

Sylvia walked across to the sink and rinsed out the cleaning cloth. 'Men,' she mumbled.

'Do you think men go through the menopause too?' asked Annabelle.

Sylvia noticed the uncertain smile, the forced little laugh, and she wanted to curl up and die. She didn't want this burden. This knowledge, that she was responsible for causing such angst in her kind, sweet sister.

'I mean, if that's what it is,' continued Annabelle, 'maybe there's a hormone treatment for men. He might just need some of my excellent little pills!' She laughed again, more loudly this time.

'Are you on hormone replacement therapy?' asked Sylvia, frowning.

'Absolutely!' said Annabelle. 'Best thing I ever did.'

'Really?' said Sylvia. 'There are some good herbal remedies if you're interested. Much better for you.'

'No fear!' said Annabelle. 'I adore my little pills. The doctor keeps trying to make me stop taking them, but I say, no, thank you very much! They changed my life.'

'Menopause can be brutal,' said Sylvia.

'Exactly,' said Annabelle. 'I was just so depressed there for a while. Flat and exhausted. And, you know, all the other symptoms too. Hot flushes, dry eyes, drying up of... you know...' She nodded downwards and Sylvia felt her chest constricting. 'Those pills gave me back my sex life,' continued Annabelle earnestly. 'Well, not that I have a huge sex life or anything, but after menopause I really hated all that moochy stuff. The lack of hormones made it, you know... really awful. Now at least it's bearable.'

'Good,' said Sylvia mildly, trying to convey her disinterest without sounding rude.

'I think three-weekly is a good compromise,' said Annabelle thoughtfully after a moment. 'I mean, Dan probably wants it every third day, and I'm about every third month, absolute tops, so I think every third week is a perfectly good middle ground. He gets the better end of it, obviously. But you have to feel sorry for men, don't you? Such slaves to their testosterone.'

Sylvia could feel her gut churning. It was her own fault. Her penance. She knew she deserved to suffer through this conversation. She tried to tune out, but it didn't work. Images of her lovemaking with Dan the other night kept spinning through her head.

Annabelle was still talking. 'I mean, not that I chat about it much with my friends, but after the garden club meeting one night, Gail Beecroft was telling us she was going home to have a nice bit of sex with her partner. We all nearly fell off our chairs! I mean, we were looking at each other as if to say: you're looking forward to sex! Really? Ugh!' She made an exaggerated grimace, then laughed. 'Mind you, she's a lot younger than most of us. Doesn't know what's coming.'

'Probably not,' said Sylvia. She crossed the room and began dusting the television cabinet.

'Did you have lots of lovers when you were travelling?' asked Annabelle. Her eyes were wide with interest.

'A few.'

'What about Indigo's dad. How long did that last in the end?'

'About two years, I suppose. Lovely guy, very spiritual. Just a bit… aimless. Couldn't seem to hold down a job.'

'Mmm.' Annabelle made a noise of agreement. 'Well, everyone likes a breadwinner.'

'I was okay on my own. I managed.'

'Sorry. Of course! Of course you were.' Annabelle looked chastened, and Sylvia felt an unwelcome rush of guilt.

'I'd better see if Dan found the hedge trimmer. I'll see you later,' said Annabelle. She waved and walked out.

Sylvia collapsed onto the pew seat and looked back towards the entrance door. The walls at that end were painted a deep moss green and the colour felt calming. She closed her eyes and did some meditative breathing, placing her middle fingers on her third eye, in the centre of her forehead, then alternating her thumb and pinkie finger to each side of her nose, closing off one nostril at a time. In, out. In, out. She focused on the flow of the breath, letting the jumble inside her head loosen and float away.

After a moment, she opened her eyes and dropped her hands to the seat, curling her fingers under the front lip. The wood felt cool and the old divots along the edge were smooth under her fingertips. As she stood up, her fingers lifted the seat a little. It made a clunking sound as it dropped. She turned around and squatted, pushing it up again a fraction. It was a storage seat. She lifted the lid and rested it against the back of the pew. Inside were stacks of old leather notebooks. She picked up the top one. On the inside page, in gold cursive font, was the word *Diary*. Underneath, Lillian had written the year: 2018.

Sylvia stared. There must be fifty books in there. Fifty years of diaries. Her chest tightened as a searing flush of grief overcame her. She leaned down and picked up another one, at random, from towards the back: 1999. She flicked through it. Some pages had barely anything written on them. Others were full of Lillian's curly, almost illegible scrawl. She let the pages flutter through her fingers and landed on 2 September 1999.

> Kant says inaction is an action. Both action and inaction
> can be evil or good, it just depends on the circumstance.
> Neither is inherently better. It is the reason behind the
> action or inaction that is important.
>
> The consequences do not matter.

She looked up. Outside the window, across the fence, Dan was talking to Pete and holding a large garden implement in his hands. Annabelle was standing next to him, nodding at whatever was being said.

Sylvia let the diary drop back into the seat. It fanned out, then snapped shut, and the quote was gone. No, Lillian, she thought. Consequences matter. Sometimes they're the only things that matter.

CHAPTER SEVEN

Willa

At the junction on the dirt road, Willa stopped the car. Her GPS announced that she had arrived at her destination. To her right she could see a lighthouse looming out of the paddocks on the clifftop like a white mirage. Behind it, from where she sat in the hire car, she could see the blue of the ocean, but much larger was the endless blue sky intermittently broken up with streaks of white cloud. Gum trees clung to the hills in the distance, but mostly the land had been cleared for crops. On her right, a field of what looked like long bright green grass swayed in the breeze, different from the grass of the surrounding paddocks.

She looked left. Trees blocked her immediate view on the ocean side, but further along the road, on the other side, she could see a sprawling house painted dark grey. This must be the grand neighbouring house Hamish had found on Google Maps.

She wriggled in the seat, her back still stiff from the twenty-four-hour flight from Heathrow to Melbourne, then the second flight across Bass Strait into Launceston airport. She could barely believe she was actually here, when just days ago, the mere thought of this journey had felt like a distant impossibility. Something inside her was changing.

She indicated left, then wondered why she'd bothered. The road was deserted. She slowed the car to a crawl. Adjacent to the beautiful big house there was a pebbled laneway. Willa admired the large iron gates and some beautiful deciduous trees planted at the entrance.

Ahead of her, the dirt road came to a dead end. She drove a little further, and after she had passed a battered old hedge, the most delightful sight emerged. A tiny wooden church was perched just a little way back from the cliff edge, suspended above the ocean, surrounded by a wild, colourful garden.

She drove closer. A white hatchback was parked on the edge of the road. She pulled in next to a pedestrian gate that gave access to the large house and turned off the ignition.

The little church was white, although dull and shabby. The iron on the steeply pitched roof was rusty in patches, and a dormer window jutted out from the roofline. Its pretty square-panelled style contrasted with the traditional lancet windows below, and she wondered if it had been added later.

Willa got out of the car. The thump of the door closing made her cringe. She was comforted by the raucous call of seagulls that started a moment later, breaching the silence. Would she attract attention? That was the last thing she wanted. She wasn't supposed to be here until tomorrow, when the lawyer was bringing her to view the place. But she had wanted to come alone, to see this strange home that she now owned, or soon would when she signed the documents.

The lane remained deserted and she walked across towards the little church, almost holding her breath. Along the front entry, ornately carved bargeboards were attached to the gables. There was one large gable for the main building, and a smaller pitched roof below it for the entry porch, which had identical gables and bargeboards. Around the front and the rear of the building, overgrown garden beds were awash with flowers – pink dahlias, green and purple artichoke flowers, red geraniums, blue and white agapanthus, garlic plants and yellow lilies. Huge lilac allium heads danced and swayed. At the end of the front flower bed, a single, beautiful maple tree arched over the front of the garden and threw shade across the steps. For the first time in as long as she could remember, Willa had the urge to laugh. The place was *beautiful.*

Wind whipped at her hair and she brushed it from her eyes as she wondered if she was brave enough to walk through the gate and peer into the church windows. She looked around. In the distance she heard the sound of a low-powered motor starting: garden machinery. It whirred loudly then died down, the engine revving repeatedly. To Willa it was the comforting sound of neatly clipped civilisation.

She closed her eyes and listened to the wind rustling through the long grass on the road's edge and the melodic notes of a wren or a finch as it whistled and twittered in the large elm trees inside the boundary fence behind her.

She turned in a slow circle, taking in the glorious endless inky blue of Bass Strait in front of her, then the little church and its garden, then over the lane where the lighthouse now loomed in the distance, and across the spectacular formal gardens of the house behind her. The setting was unbelievably glorious.

A noise startled her. She spun around to see a woman locking the front door of the church house. She had a box at her feet, and when she'd finished with the key, she picked up the box and began walking towards the road. Willa fled back to her car. She fumbled with the key and started the ignition. When she looked up, the woman had stopped in the middle of the road near the white hatchback and was staring at her. Her hair was drawn back in a long greyish-blonde ponytail. She was tall and slim in exercise clothes, and Willa felt sure she had seen her before. *The woman from the newspaper article.*

A sudden unsettling sensation grew in Willa's chest. There was something about the way the woman moved, the angles of her face, that chimed at her consciousness. She put her car into gear and indicated to pull out. The woman walked towards the hatchback and opened the back door, putting the box inside. Willa drove past her to the lane's dead end, then turned the car around and drove back, keeping her eyes glued to the road. She glanced towards the woman, who smiled and raised her hand in a friendly wave. Willa tried to smile back, but she wasn't sure if it had shown on her face. She kept driving, turned right at the junction and headed back down the dirt road, dust flying behind her. The woman's smile was warm and familiar. Willa was filled with a worming sense of unease. When she reached the main road, she turned right, drove past a roadside strawberry stall, a few ugly brick houses and some farmland. She just needed to keep driving.

At the next junction was a sign: *Sisters Cove Beach 1 Kilometre.*

She turned and drove down the narrow, winding coastal road, past little beach houses clinging to the side of the hill and a hand-made archway decorated in colourful ceramic tiles that announced: *Welcome to Sisters Cove Beach.* As she rounded the corner, she slowed down and pulled into a parking bay. She felt steadier now, and she took some deep breaths as she closed her eyes. *Everything is all right. You are strong and capable.*

After a minute or so, she opened her eyes. Below her, a gleaming white patch of beachfront meandered across the base of a semicircular cove. Inside the cove, a sparkling half-moon body of azure water stretched out to the headland, where the deep blue of the ocean rejoined it. She spotted a single windsurfer and two swimmers. It was like a postcard.

Willa started the car back up and continued on down the winding road cut into the side of the hill, past the jostle of beach houses that had been built at odd angles, scattered across the hillside. The car park at the bottom was half full. She got out, and was hit by a gust of wind. Sand whipped around her legs, and the sound of the ocean and the smell of the salt air combined to make her shiver. She was alive, and healthy, and here she was at the prettiest beach imaginable.

Thank you, Lillian Brooks, she thought. Thank you. Whatever your intentions were.

'I'm afraid she didn't give me any clues at all.' The solicitor glanced across the car at Willa, then turned his attention back to the road.

'Really?' said Willa. 'Is that even legal? To leave your house to a stranger and not tell them why?'

'Yes, completely legal… of course.'

Ian Enderby seemed on edge, and Willa wondered why. Perhaps she had lost her knack. Her Australian-ness. Her ability to put people at ease. She used to have it. In the last two years, though, people had been different around her. Nervous and cautious; not knowing what to say and not wanting to say the wrong thing to make her grief worse – as if that were even possible. But Ian Enderby didn't know about Esme. Perhaps he was just an uptight lawyer.

'Here we are.' He turned left at the same junction on the dirt road that Willa had stopped at yesterday. He drove down the road confidently and parked in the driveway of the little church.

'It's beautiful,' said Willa, after a moment of silence.

'Yes, it's certainly unique. It used to belong to the neighbouring house – Merrivale.'

'That would make sense, I guess,' said Willa.

'They were both built in the late 1800s, I think. By a wealthy merchant and his wife who were quite religious. Lillian took ownership of The Old Chapel in the 1970s. But she lived in it all her life.'

'Was it rented to her family before then?'

'Yes. Her father was the head farmhand for Merrivale before his accident, so I guess it was part of the package.'

'Oh,' said Willa, wondering what accident he was talking about. But it didn't feel polite to ask. Instead she said, 'When was it deconsecrated?'

'No idea,' said Ian.

They both stared at the little church for a while, and then Willa got out and took in the sight of the incredible garden again. She walked a bit further in through the long grass and noticed an old, greying wood heap and a raised timber compost bed with a rake and shovel leaning up against the side. Behind the compost bed, a mottled grey headstone was poking out of the long grass. She wandered closer and bent down to inspect it. The writing had almost been worn away by age and weather, and it was spotted with black dots that looked like spreading algae.

Maisy Elizabeth
Beloved daughter of Thomas and Edith Dalrymple
4 August 1902–12 September 1904
Sleep on Sweet Angel

Pain swamped her.

'Apparently she came off the back of a cart being pulled by her dog.' Ian had arrived beside her silently. 'Lillian told me about it when I came out to finalise the will.'

Once, Willa would have revelled in the poignancy of this snippet of history; stood soberly beside Ian inside a shared little puff of imagined sorrow. Perhaps even taken a photo to show Hugo. Now she just felt angry. What idiot would put a toddler on the back of a dog sled? Poor, poor Maisy.

'Shall we go in?' Ian asked.

'Yes,' said Willa. She took a deep breath. *You're fine. Keep it together.*

Inside, it was dark and the smell was musty, with a chemical undertone of some sort. The lawyer turned on the lights and Willa walked into the centre of the cramped living area, admiring the dark old antiques mixed with a few mid-century pieces. Along the sides, artworks covered the walls – colourful semi-abstract depictions, thickly painted, mostly of women, mostly close-up. There was a harmony to the works, a boldness, but also an eerie sadness. Willa wondered if they were all by the same artist.

'Would you like some time alone in here?' Ian asked her.

She smiled at him. 'Thank you.'

When he left, she wandered towards the back and poked her head into the bedroom, which was filled almost entirely by a double bed. There was barely room for the old French armoire that must have stored clothes. Behind the bedroom was a tiny bathroom. Willa inspected it by the dingy light of the single narrow window. Yellow-speckled wall tiles and beautiful mosaics in yellow, brown and orange on the floor dated it to the 1950s or so. A pale-yellow bathtub tiled to match the wall, and a matching free-standing porcelain sink completed the picture. A daddy-long-legs hung from the corner of the ceiling. The room smelled damp and old.

In the kitchenette, she ran her hand along the Formica bench top and stared through the grimy window into the garden and across the lane to the imposing grey house.

'You're invited for a cup of tea with the neighbours if you feel up to it.' Ian stood in the doorway, smiling.

'Oh,' said Willa. She wondered if the tall, slim woman in the exercise clothes lived across the road. She felt suddenly unsettled at the idea of meeting her in person.

'The neighbours are one of the two parties I told you about, who have offered to buy this place from you.'

'I see.'

'Of course, if you'd prefer not to linger, that's absolutely fine too,' he said. 'You're probably feeling quite jet-lagged still, so it's completely up to you.'

Willa stared at him, not really thinking about what he was saying. 'Did Lillian Brooks have any children?' she asked.

'Not that I'm aware of,' said Ian.

'Had you known her long?'

'Well, I grew up around here. I knew her a little. We've both lived in or around this area our whole lives. Apart from when I was in Hobart for a few years, at university.'

'Do you think the neighbours knew her well?'

'Yes, very well. She and Annabelle Broadhurst grew up together. Dan, too. They were neighbours for decades.'

'Annabelle and Dan – they're who's invited us for tea?'

'Yes.' He turned and looked out into the garden, then raised his hand in a wave and stepped backwards.

A woman burst through the exterior doorway and stood at the entrance. She was wearing a flowing bright purple blouse that showed off her ample bosom. It was teamed with ankle-length cream pants and fabulous expensive-looking purple leather loafers. 'Hello, Ian! How lovely to see you again!'

Willa watched as the short, round little woman reached upwards to the solicitor and offered her cheek for a kiss. Then she turned to Willa.

'You must be Wilhelmena! How lovely to finally meet you. We've all been absolutely agog to find out who the mystery woman is that's inheriting this old wreck. I'm Annabelle!'

The woman was beaming through her bright-pink lipstick. Her large blue eyes sparkled with welcome. She looked as if she was in her fifties, with a soft, pretty face and greyish-black curls that stopped at her shoulders.

Willa was momentarily mute.

Annabelle made no move to come into the house, and eventually Willa remembered her manners. She crossed the room and held out her hand.

'Yes, hello.'

Annabelle pulled her downwards for a hug, and Willa was overwhelmed by a comforting floral scent.

'Well,' said Annabelle, looking around. 'Do you like it?' She flung her arms out wide.

Willa smiled. 'It's gorgeous.'

'Ha!' said Annabelle, frowning. 'Aren't you funny.' She took Willa by the arm and guided her towards the door. 'Shall we have a cup of tea at my place? It's not so smelly and the garden is much less likely to be full of snakes.'

'Oh. Right,' said Willa. She thought of the long grass she'd just walked through in the garden. The warm log pile, a perfect hideout for snakes. She'd been away from Australia for so long, she hadn't even thought of it.

As they neared the door, Ian cleared his throat.

'Now, Annabelle,' he said, 'why don't you go ahead and put the kettle on while I just finalise a few things with Wilhelmena here. We'll be over shortly.'

Willa smiled at him gratefully and Annabelle laughed.

'Oh, of course! No need to rush. The cake is still cooling,' she said.

Willa watched her walk back across the road. As she moved through the garden, she leaned down and broke off some dead flower heads with quick, efficient motions, barely breaking her stride.

'Wow,' said Willa.

'She's quite something, isn't she?' smiled Ian. 'Heart of gold.'

Willa smiled too, and picked up a book that was sitting on the side table. *Identity and the Artists of Early Tasmania*. She flicked through it, admiring the photographs of ink sketches – men and women in heavy old-fashioned clothing, loggers standing next to ancient felled trees holding long saws, bark huts, dogs and children playing in the bush.

'I wish I knew who Lillian was,' she said after a moment.

'It is unusual. Perhaps the mystery will be solved when you go through her things. She left you the lot, apart from some named items that have already been distributed, and a sum of money for her goddaughter.'

'How old was she?' asked Willa.

Ian looked into the distance for a moment and seemed to be thinking. 'Early sixties, if I recall correctly from the paperwork.'

'Well, that might make sense.'

'How so?'

'She would have been young, and unmarried.'

'Sorry?'

'When I was born. I was adopted, you see. At birth. I was born in Launceston General Hospital. I believe...' Willa took a deep breath and looked back out through the window towards the ocean. 'I believe Lillian Brooks was my birth mother.'

CHAPTER EIGHT

Annabelle

'Are you a gardener, Wilhelmena?' asked Annabelle. She leaned forward and filled the woman's teacup from the pot, then turned the handle of the milk jug towards her.

'Not really,' said Willa. 'But sometimes, when I see gardens like yours, I wish I was. And please, call me Willa.'

'Willa. Okay, I will,' laughed Annabelle. 'I inherited the bones of this garden. Dan's Aunt Constance was a keen gardener.'

They were sitting on the veranda in the wicker lounge chairs, with elegantly patterned scatter cushions propping them up. Ian was sitting across from them, but all the chairs were angled out for the best view over the gardens. The old rhododendron tree reached across in front of Annabelle, the last of the vivid pink blooms providing a pretty frame to the flower beds just beyond their feet.

'How long have you lived here?' asked Willa.

'More than twenty years now. When Constance moved into a retirement village, she let us move in. She and Andrew – he was Dan's uncle – they didn't have children. Dan was Andrew's closest relative, so he inherits eventually.'

'Oh,' said Willa.

'The Broadhurst family have been big property owners in the north of Tasmania since settlement,' said Ian. 'Dan's Uncle Andrew inherited this farm. It was passed down from his parents. He was a lawyer by profession, though. Worked for my father in the early days. Nice chap. It was a tragedy, what happened to him.'

'What happened?' asked Willa.

'He was killed. Fell from the cliffs here,' said Ian.

Annabelle busied herself with the teapot.

'How awful,' said Willa.

'Yes, terrible. Absolutely terrible,' muttered Annabelle.

'It really was,' said Ian. 'He was the sort of bloke where you thought, why him? He was such a good person in the community. Every Christmas he used to run a fund-raiser where people would drive from Burnie to Devonport in their beautiful old classic cars and the money would go to the community children's fund. Do you remember that, Annabelle?'

'Yes,' said Annabelle. She'd been at the starting line for the event a few times as a child. She remembered Andrew Broadhurst standing next to the loudspeaker, then on the running board of his silver Jaguar, handing out huge bags of sweets and Christmas hampers to the children and their parents before the race. Annabelle had once begged her father to be allowed to go and take some of the sweets, but he had admonished her: *Those sweets are for the needy. We're not poor, girly.* They might struggle a little, survive on hand-me-downs, but apparently that was different.

'Dan was very close to him,' added Annabelle as she reached over to refill their teacups, 'Still, it was decades ago. Constance managed the place very well on her own after he died. It's a wonderful legacy she left here. Merrivale is very precious to us.' Talk of the death had put a cloud over the conversation, and Annabelle was irritated at Ian for bringing it up. She needed Wilhelmena to be in a positive mood for this chat. She wondered how to mention The Old Chapel and its significance to the property without sounding rude.

As she was casting around for an idea, Banjo rounded the corner of the house and wandered towards them, his hindquarters swaying in a loping gate.

'You'd better watch your cake,' said Annabelle, pointing to the dog.

Willa seemed to soften as the old yellow Labrador lumbered towards her. 'Hello, beautiful,' she said. Banjo sat at her feet and let his head be scratched.

'Careful,' said Annabelle, 'you'll be covered in hair. He's shedding. It's ridiculously annoying if you happen to be wearing black.'

Willa gave her a look that Annabelle couldn't quite interpret.

'So,' said Annabelle, 'how did you know Lillian?'

'I didn't,' said Willa. She kept one of her hands buried in the folds around Banjo's neck.

'Really?' said Annabelle. 'How bizarre! What's the connection, then?'

There was a pause, and Willa looked across at Ian.

'I think Wilhelmena is still trying to work that out too,' said Ian.

'Oh,' said Annabelle. 'Isn't that intriguing!' She pondered this for a moment as she forked a piece of blueberry cake into her mouth. Looking at a whole blueberry bulging out of the moist vanilla sponge, she suddenly had an image of the lump in her breast. She bit down hard and jumped in with both feet. 'Do you think you'll be keeping The Old Chapel? I imagine it's of no use to you if you're living in England.'

Willa had both hands on the sides of Banjo's neck and was scratching him with all her fingers. She didn't say anything.

'I mean, it's not exactly easy to pop back to Australia for a weekend at the beach, is it? You'll be selling, I should think,' laughed Annabelle tightly.

'I don't know. I'll need to talk about it with my family.'

'Of course. Sorry. You're married, I see,' said Annabelle, motioning to Willa's ring finger.

'Yes,' said Willa, looking up briefly again before returning her gaze to the dog.

Annabelle sighed internally. So, Willa was one of *those* people. They always made her feel like she was at the beginning of a gym workout she hadn't wanted to come to in the first place. Hard work. There were no easy offerings, but you just had to get stuck in.

'Children?' she asked.

'Yes,' said Willa. Her face was inscrutable.

'How wonderful. Boys or girls?'

'One of each.'

'How lucky!' said Annabelle.

'Yes,' said Willa, after a beat.

Annabelle felt as if she'd hit a brick wall. 'Would you like some more cake?' She motioned to Ian's empty plate. Willa's cake had barely been touched.

'No thank you,' said Ian. 'It was lovely, but we'll have to be getting back shortly.'

'Oh, of course!' said Annabelle, cutting another slice of the cake for her own plate. She needed fortifying. This woman was making Dan's plan to acquire The Old Chapel seem like a marathon task.

She broke off a small piece with her fork and popped it into her mouth, closing her eyes momentarily to enjoy the moist sweetness of it. She'd realised this morning that she hadn't got any poppy seeds, so she'd had to abandon her favourite orange cake recipe in favour of this. It was silly. Unlike her to run out of supplies. She was just so scatty lately. When she opened her eyes, she noticed that her guests were looking out towards the lawn. Sylvia and Indigo were walking across together. Annabelle's heart sank.

When they reached the veranda, Sylvia smiled at Willa and Ian. 'Hello. I'm Sylvia, Annabelle's sister. And this is my daughter, Indigo.'

Annabelle was always struck by the differences between her sister and her niece. Sylvia could have been a cover-girl model in her day. She had the lithe figure and the interesting, angular face. Her hair was pulled back in a pigtail and she was wearing tight-fitting jeans and a button-up green shirt, sleeves rolled to her elbows. Indigo was shorter, and dressed in her usual colourful harem pants and a blue long-sleeved T-shirt. Her father must have been exotic – Indian, or perhaps Nepalese, pondered Annabelle for the millionth time. She knew Sylvia had been living in some yogi-type place when she'd gotten pregnant. Indigo had a lovely rich brown skin tone and thick dark-blonde hair. Today the mess of her hair was hidden beneath a mustard-coloured turban.

Ian and Willa both stood and shook hands with the new arrivals. There was an uncomfortable moment as Annabelle wondered what to do. She really didn't want them to sit down and discuss buying The Old Chapel, but she knew for certain that was what they were here for.

'Ian and Willa were just about to leave,' she said.

'Oh, what a shame,' said Sylvia, turning to Willa. 'We were wondering if you'd like us to talk you through some of the artworks that Lillian left in the house. Obviously we don't want to keep you, though. You might be all up to speed.'

Banjo had abandoned Willa and wandered across to Indigo. She squatted down and ran her hand along his back, taking out handfuls of creamy hair in the process. She and Willa were smiling at each other.

'Oh, that would be lovely,' said Willa.

'Great,' said Sylvia. 'Lillian was my oldest friend. We were at school together. I know she would have liked me to show you around.'

Willa smiled and stood up. The wind blew her dress against her body. Annabelle wondered if the woman was eating. She was so unpleasantly thin.

'Ian may have to get back, though.' Willa looked at Ian.

'I'm afraid I do. I have a meeting shortly.' He turned to Sylvia. 'Would you be able to drop Wilhelmena back to her lodgings if I head off?'

'Sure,' said Sylvia, at the same time that Annabelle said, 'Oh, I can do that!'

Willa looked from one to the other. 'You're both so kind. I'll just fit in with your plans.'

'If you're finished your tea, we can head over,' said Sylvia. 'Lillian was an accomplished painter. If you've been in the house, almost all the works you saw were hers.'

'They're amazing,' said Willa.

'I'll come too,' said Annabelle irritably. Why should she miss all the fun? Besides, she didn't want Sylvia getting in Wilhelmena's ear about buying The Old Chapel if she wasn't there to plead Dan's case.

Annoyingly, she was due to meet a bride's mother shortly. The woman wanted to talk about seating and locations for the ceremony on Saturday if the weather turned wet. Annabelle would have to keep watch from The Old Chapel doorway in case she arrived early. She turned to gather the tea things onto the tray, but froze when she saw the dog.

'Banjo! Stop!' she screeched. Banjo had his front paws on the coffee table. His head was bent to the side and he was licking the blueberry cake, which sat on top of a delicate ceramic cake stand. Annabelle stepped around her chair, shrieking, and as she did so, the cake stand toppled onto the tiles of the veranda and shattered. 'Bad dog! Bad, bad dog!' She stamped her foot and shooed him away just as Banjo gulped down a huge chunk of cake. He slunk behind an armchair.

'Oh, I'm so sorry!' said Annabelle her hands covering her mouth as the others looked on. 'You're such a naughty dog, Banjo!'

The dog lowered his head and shuffled further away.

'If only he'd eat the snails from my agapanthus, we'd all be a lot happier.' Annabelle was trying to make light of the situation, but the words came out a little bit shrill.

'Banjo, you crazy dude,' said Indigo, giggling. She shook her head, and Willa laughed too.

Annabelle leaned down and picked up the larger pieces of the broken cake stand, putting them on the table. 'You all go ahead,' she said, not daring to look up. For some unfathomable reason, she felt tears welling in her eyes. 'I'd better tidy up here. I have someone popping in soon about a wedding anyway.'

Ian coughed. 'Ah, Sylvia, I really should get the key to The Old Chapel back from you now, actually.'

'Oh,' said Sylvia.

'You've been a great help to the estate, saving me from having to employ a maintenance person. But, now that Wilhelmena is here I need to formalise things.'

Willa interrupted. 'I don't mind. If she's always had the key, and she's able to keep an eye on the place for a while longer, then…' She shrugged her shoulders.

'Of course I can,' said Sylvia.

'Well, I suppose so,' said Ian. 'If you're sure, Wilhelmena.'

'It's fine.'

'Great,' said Sylvia. 'Let's head over.'

'Do you need some help, Annabelle?' asked Willa.

'No, no. Not at all. You carry on.'

'Thank you for the cake. It was lovely.'

They both looked sideways at her barely touched piece of cake.

'You're more than welcome,' said Annabelle.

Annabelle put the broken fragments of the cake stand on the tray and carried it into the kitchen. There was something unusually defiant about the way Sylvia had turned up today. The way she was pursuing The Old Chapel. Usually she was much more laid-back – left things to fate or karma or some other cosmic force that seemed to float about and sprinkle fairy dust on whatever she touched. Although, of course, Annabelle hardly knew her sister these days. She'd only been back in Tasmania for eighteen months, and even though Sylvia was living so close, sometimes a week or two would pass between them running into each other. They'd seen each other more when Lillian was dying, of course. Sylvia had taken care of her, so she was in and out of The Old

Chapel every day. But since then, hardly at all. Sylvia didn't like coming over in the evenings for dinner, and so Annabelle had to push her to have lunch now and then. They occasionally ran into each other at the surf club if there was a community meeting or they were both there having coffee or dinner with friends. But it didn't feel like enough. It didn't feel sisterly.

After she'd cleaned up the mess, Annabelle checked her diary for the day's jobs. She really must make a doctor's appointment to get a script for her hormone pills. The lump popped into her mind again. *Silly.* That little cyst certainly wasn't worth bothering poor Dr Collins about. A waste of time. And Annabelle had hours of work to do in the garden, then a garden meeting tonight with the ridiculously large subcommittee to discuss the autumn garden festival. What a busy, busy bee I am, she thought as she hurried to the office to deal with her emails. As she sat down, she felt a strange little wave of nausea, and wondered if the tea was reacting with the blueberry cake.

'I think the money raised should go to the church,' said Patrice Richards. She was perched on the edge of her chair, her perfectly combed hair sitting prettily in grey waves around her face. She wore pink lipstick the exact shade of the roses on her blouse. 'After all, they let us meet here for a very reduced rental each month.' She sniffed. Patrice was the church organist, and spent most Fridays tidying up the gardens around the little graveyard at the rear of the church where her husband was buried.

'No way!' said Elaine Yellowstone, her cranky face set in its usual scowl. 'The bloody churches have fleeced the community for too long. And what do they give us back? A prayer and a pat on the back, and if you're really lucky, they'll lend us a priest who will later be moved on to another parish but in the meantime he'll molest your kids for free. A fat lot of good that does for the needy!'

She drummed her fingers on the table and directed a withering look at Patrice, who had slunk down in her chair.

'Let's keep it civil, Elaine,' snapped Lucy Benson.

There were eighteen of them sitting around four large trestle tables that had been pushed together. Lucy was standing at one end, directing the meeting. Every so often she stopped to make notes on the whiteboard.

'Did you say your children were molested by someone?' asked Vera Haysworth. Her voice crackled across the meeting from the other end of the joined tables. Everyone turned to look at her. 'That's terrible, dear.'

'Turn up your hearing aid, Vera,' said Mary Trelawney in a loud stage whisper. Her posse of friends tittered, but several others tutted and scowled at her.

You are a cow, thought Annabelle. A jealous, bitter, dreadful woman.

Lucy tried to get the meeting back into order. 'So far I think the majority are keen on donating the money to one of the environmental groups or a charity for cancer.' She turned and underlined *cancer* and *environment* on the whiteboard.

'My Stan's really struggled after his prostate operation. It's the mental bit they find hard, isn't it?' said Abigail Beddingham. 'You know, erection difficulties, which is tough on a man, isn't it? I vote for the cancer charity.'

Annabelle cringed. This was a public forum. And there was a man present! It was all very well to say these things to close friends or family, but seriously, Abigail had no sense of occasion. She was only about fifty, but was married to a much older man. A retired judge. He was so withered and creaky-looking that Annabelle had sometimes wondered how on earth he'd managed to woo the glamorous Abigail. And anyway, the fact that he was about a hundred was much more likely to explain his problems in the erection department.

The meeting had been dragging on for over an hour, and they were only up to the second item on the agenda, the fund-raising aspects of the garden fete. They were supposed to be donating half of the funds to a local charity, but nobody was agreeing on which one. It was hot in the church hall and Annabelle was sweating. She pressed her arm against her side as she felt a trickle of sweat from her armpit run down into her bra. She knew she was pressing against the lump, and she imagined it dislodging and floating through her body, leaving toxic cells in its wake. Which was silly, because it was a perfectly harmless cyst.

'Let's get this show on the road. Can we agree that it's between the cancer counselling service and Landcare?' asked John Boyle. He was very good at getting things back on track, thought Annabelle. Men were so much better at sticking to agendas.

There was a general murmur of agreement.

'All right. All those in favour of the cancer counselling service, then?' said Lucy.

Everyone except Annabelle, John and Patrice raised their hands.

'Well, that's settled,' said Lucy. 'I think the important thing is that the funds will be going back into the local community. The cancer counselling service in Burnie is really worthwhile, and I know we've all had experience of cancer. It just seems to be getting more and more frequent. They'll be really happy to have our support.' She smiled around at the group, but Annabelle refused to meet her gaze. 'Let's take a break and have a cup of tea, shall we?'

Annabelle looked down at her hands as the buzz of voices around her rose. Chairs scraped and people began moving towards the tea table. She felt sweaty and a bit queasy. The whole thing was irritating. She had very much wanted to support the local Landcare chapter, who were busy pulling weeds out along the river near Sisters Cove. Surely her vote should have counted for more than the others given that she was hosting the damned fete? She stood, but a sudden dizzy spell made her sit back down. A sick, clammy coldness come over her. Her heart was pounding. She could hear it drumming in her ears. *Something's wrong. Something's wrong with me.*

'Are you all right, Annabelle?' Mira put her hand on Annabelle's shoulder.

Annabelle tried to speak, but the nausea became a violent whirlpool and her throat felt like it was closing. She opened her eyes, but her vision was blurred. She could hear herself making a noise – *Help. Help me* – but it wasn't coming out properly. The chicken sandwiches! They must have been off. She'd sneakily taken two chicken and walnut finger sandwiches from Lucy's platter as she came into the little rear kitchen to get the teacups ready. They'd just looked so delicious! Perhaps she had salmonella. Or something worse! She was certainly poisoned. Terror gripped her – sheer, utter terror – ice-cold and heavy. She was dying and Dan wasn't even here. She hadn't helped him with The Old Chapel, and now Sylvia and Indigo would get it, which was fine, but still. How would he manage without her? What about the wedding on Saturday? She wasn't *ready* to die.

Through the awful blackness, Annabelle could sense people gathering around her. Then she heard someone say, 'Call an ambulance! She's sick. She's having a heart attack or something.'

'Annabelle! Can you hear me?'

She couldn't breathe, she could feel herself becoming giddier. She needed *air.*

'Help me get her onto the floor,' she heard a voice say, and Annabelle lurched sideways and toppled into somebody's arms. The last thing she heard before she passed out was Mary Trelawney's bitter voice hissing to someone, 'How's she going to host the fete if she's having a damned heart attack?'

CHAPTER NINE

Sylvia

The box of diaries sat in the corner of Sylvia's living room, next to the old slow-combustion fire. There had been a cold snap over the last two nights, and each time she had twisted newspaper into long sticks and stacked neat piles of kindling into the mouth of the fire, she had glanced guiltily at the box before striking the match. For just a millisecond before coaxing the flame into life – stacking small logs onto the sticks, then larger ones – she would imagine burning the diaries. But of course, that would take courage and a certainty of morals, and Sylvia knew she was lacking in both.

Instead she would move her gaze back across to the fire, ensure that it was burning, let it draw for a few minutes with the door ajar, stoke the flames with the metal poker, and allow defeat to settle into her bones. *Perhaps I'll just read a little. Just enough to know there is nothing there.*

It had been the morning she'd seen Willa that she had finally succumbed. She had picked up the diary on top of the pile and flicked to the date page inside. She had checked the year of each one in turn before putting it back and wondering if she really dared to read a single page. She hadn't packed the diaries into the box in chronological order. That would have been too premeditated. What she had done was the opposite, telling herself she probably wouldn't read them – she had no right – but if she did, then she would just choose one at random, and if fate intended that there be anything in there – anything that might give her answers – then it would place the right diary into her hands. And in her own defence, she had only brought about a dozen of the diaries home with her. Did that lessen her crime, she wondered?

Either way, now, she wished she hadn't begun. The first diary she opened had almost stopped her. It was 1987, and Lillian had talked about a new lover. She had dissected his passionate devotion to her, talked about his daughter, one of Lillian's art students, and about Lillian's desire to be free when he wanted her to be tethered to him. Sylvia knew about the need to be free. Here, in Tasmania, she didn't feel free. She felt suffocated by the past. It was meant to be her home, but she had been away so long that perhaps she didn't belong here any more.

It was true that she had known happiness in Tasmania, and she'd also experienced the thrilling terror of being in love for the first time. But mostly she had known sadness. Lillian wasn't the first person she'd nursed to the grave. Her mother had died of cervical cancer when Sylvia was eighteen, and she had cared for her through the whole of 1975, taking time out of her nursing training course. She'd also looked after Annabelle and their father at the same time. Annabelle had been fourteen and completely caught up in her own world. She was vivacious and tempestuous, but she was also squeamish. Illness, hospitals, their mother's fading health – they had all terrified and repulsed Annabelle. She would stand at the doorway to their mother's room and whisper, 'Mummy, are you all right?' Their mother would raise her arms as much as she could off the bed, and Sylvia could see that her little sister wanted to run in and fold herself into those arms, but instead she would freeze. As the disease raged through their mother, leaving patches around her eyes the colour of bruises, her skin became so translucent and taut that Sylvia feared it would tear at the slightest touch. Annabelle, who loved their mother with ferocious devotion, couldn't bring herself to witness the daily withering away.

But in the end, Sylvia had forced her to. In the last few days, she had made her sit at the bedside as their mother mostly slept. Annabelle would sob and beg, because she didn't believe what Sylvia was telling her; the talk of funerals, and relatives coming, and their father needing them to be strong – how could it be true? Their mother had been lively and talkative and busy, much more like Annabelle than Sylvia. And this faded version, about to be gone from them, didn't fit with any kind of new reality that Annabelle could fathom. Annabelle was lost and rudderless, while Sylvia just felt dead inside.

It was Dan who had saved Sylvia then. His love for her. But after that, he had failed her. She didn't want to think of the terrible ways he had let her down. Sylvia had worked hard to evolve spiritually over the decades, but still, she had locked some things away in the blackest, murkiest corners of her psyche. Some things were untouchably painful. Which was why all these years later she was appalled at her own weakness. Dan had promised that his marriage to Annabelle was a hollow void, so she shut her eyes, boxed up her self-loathing, and followed him into the abyss.

She shuddered. She could see her mother's face as she stared into the flames of the fire.

'I'm sorry, Mum,' she whispered. 'I'm a terrible sister.'

Sylvia put down the diary she was reading and randomly picked up another: 1995. There were a few cursory notes about the weather, and Lillian's daily art-making, and various issues involving people in the town. She turned the pages slowly, then stopped.

> 18 June: Annabelle very low. The loss of this baby has hit hard. The other losses were much earlier. Her morning sickness was terrible until the bleeding, so it made her think this one would make it. Something called a 'molar' pregnancy – she is convinced that she will get cancer

now because of something the doctor said. Poor soul.
Dan out and drinking most nights. She swears this was
their last attempt. She was sobbing tonight – says she
can't go through it again, even though she so wanted to
give him a child.

Sylvia stared at the words, a thick, heavy feeling in her chest.
She had never known this. Annabelle had never talked to her about
trying to have children. Of course she wouldn't have, though.
Walls had been erected. Annabelle's marriage to Dan had driven
an unspoken wedge between them.

A molar pregnancy. Sylvia knew what this meant from her nursing
training. She felt terrible at what her poor sister must have gone
through. A hydatidiform mole – a sickeningly malformed foetus
– grew in the womb instead of a baby. Sometimes it could leave
behind deadly malignant cells that caused cancer. Poor Annabelle.

She stared at the entry again. *She so wanted to give him a
child.* Sylvia felt the weight of the past settling in on her. The lost
opportunities. The choices made, then regretted.

The flash of a torch through the glass panel of the door pulled
Sylvia out of the past. She got up just as Indigo knocked and
walked in.

'Hi, Mum.' Indigo turned off the torch on her phone, then
held out a bottle of white wine.

'Oh, wine,' said Sylvia, taking the bottle and hugging her
daughter. She felt uneasy about the idea of alcohol on a week
night – at least now that Lillian wasn't here, demanding Scotch on
ice and a drinking partner. She'd almost gotten a taste for liquor
last year. This year she was back to being healthy.

'Chill, Mamma. It's organic, from that vineyard outside Launceston. Paid a fortune for a case of it on my way back on Sunday
arvo. Let's have a drink. It's been a weird day.' Indigo kicked off
her sandals and collapsed onto the couch.

'Weird how?' asked Sylvia. She pulled wine glasses from the cupboard and poured, wondering as she did how Indigo could afford expensive bottles of wine, the new car, the frequent trips to the mainland to meet friends – all on her cleaning and babysitting income and the occasional gym class she taught. She took a sip and flinched. The wine was tart.

'I had lunch with Willa today,' said Indigo.

'Wilhelmena? From England? How was that?' asked Sylvia. She handed the second glass to Indigo and sat down opposite on her favourite patchwork-covered armchair.

'It was nice. I ran into her in the street. I took her to Hero's. We had the new cauliflower rice dish.'

'I wasn't asking about the food. I mean, what about her? What's she really like? What did you talk about?'

'She's lovely. And we talked about lots of things. But mostly we talked about her idea that Lillian might have been her birth mother.'

'What? No!' said Sylvia. The words came out harshly. She could feel herself going pale. Her legs felt weak. She knew she sounded too defensive. *Wilhelmena was adopted?* Indigo was looking at her oddly.

'It's what she said. She was adopted in Tasmania. How do you know it's not true?'

'Well, Lillian… she would have told me if… if…' Sylvia couldn't seem to finish the sentence. She stared at the wine in her glass. She took a huge, disgusting gulp and forced it down.

'Mum, what's wrong?'

'When? When did she say she was adopted? Did she tell you her birth date?'

'Not exactly, no. But she has teenagers. She looks early forties at most, so she must have been pretty young when she had them. Don't you think?'

'I… don't know,' said Sylvia. She downed the rest of the wine and got up to refill her glass, but her head was spinning. She felt shaky.

'It's strange,' said Indigo, staring at Sylvia, her eyes screwed up. Sylvia remembered that look. She used to see it when Indigo was trying to do a maths problem at school. A focused intensity, like a dog with a bone.

'I mean, she looks nothing at all like Lillian, does she? No similar mannerisms, either. She's tall, and Lillian was short. She's got fine features – Lillian's were much thicker. She's pale, and Lil had that awesome olive skin.' Indigo took a sip of the wine, then swirled it around her glass and took another sip.

'I'm just going to the bathroom,' said Sylvia. Her stomach was churning. She walked into her bedroom and through to the small en suite. It needed updating, but she couldn't afford it. The tiles were brown and depressing and the small square shower unit had ground-in mould in the corners between the cheap metal frame and the white plastic of the shower base that no amount of her special organic cleaning products could remove. In the end, she had resorted to using bleach, but that hadn't worked either.

She pushed the toilet seat down and sat on the closed lid with her head in her hands. *Good grief. Willa was adopted in Tasmania around forty years ago.* She sat back up. Her heart rate was elevated. Her palms felt sweaty. Meditation. She needed to meditate. *Willa was the baby.* She scrolled through her mental index of the best stress meditations. *Such a tiny little thing.* She conjured up Jenoa Bay, the soft white sand, the green of the palm trees, the hammock strung between them. She transported herself there. The soft breeze on her skin. The rhythmic rush and froth of the ocean lapping and receding on the shore. She could taste coconut milk, feel the grains of sand between her toes as she breathed in the salty ocean air. In and out. In and out. She continued, letting the twitter of birdsong in the trees above calm her, the hum of distant traffic, the conversations of street vendors now on the beach chatting to tourists. She felt her heart rate slowing. Her breath came evenly. In and out. In and out. She felt calm.

Eventually she pulled herself out of the meditation. She felt stronger. More centred. She should go back to the lounge room and be a sensible, normal parent to Indigo. She washed her face and took some more deep breaths. She paused to regard her slightly lined face and fading blue eyes in the mirror. As she dried her hands she realised she must have been in the bathroom for more than fifteen minutes. Twenty at least.

When she walked back through to the lounge room, Indigo was bent over, reading.

'Sorry,' said Sylvia.

Indigo looked up. She had an odd, blank expression on her face. In her hands she held one of Lillian's diaries.

'You never told me you were with Dan first,' said Indigo. There was a definite accusation in her voice. It trembled with the injustice of it: that her mother had a sordid secret. A bizarre love affair with her Auntie Annabelle's husband.

Sylvia stood frozen at the end of the couch.

'I assume it's Uncle Dan that Lillian's writing about in here? It sounds like him,' said Indigo, pushing, probing. Like a dog with a bloody bone. She'd always been so forthright. So unwilling to compromise with the truth.

'Yes,' said Sylvia.

'That's…' Indigo looked up at her, 'just… I don't know. Weird. Totally *weird*.'

Sylvia picked up the wine glasses and crossed back into the kitchen. She put down the glasses and grasped at the bench top with both hands, peering out the window. From behind the clouds, a silver thimble of moonlight was catching the heaving swell of the ocean.

'We were in love.' She refilled the glasses to the top.

'Right,' said Indigo. 'So… how did Annabelle feel about that?'

Sylvia felt the crash of angry righteousness tumbling through her, bringing her back to her broken twenty-year-old self, lost and alone, pretending to be the grown-up while everyone around her went mad. *What the hell is it to do with Annabelle? I was with him first!*

'It was a lifetime ago. Let's leave it,' she said. Her head was spinning with the unfamiliar effects of the wine. 'They weren't together then. She was only sixteen when we broke up.'

'Is that why you left? Was it just after that?' asked Indigo. 'You told me once you left here when you were twenty.'

'Did I?' said Sylvia. She couldn't remember talking about it. She usually avoided the topic. But Indigo liked to probe people's emotional depths, and she had always found Sylvia to be an interesting psychological study. Sylvia was much happier confining herself to her own thoughts. It was less messy. There seemed to be so much pain everywhere you looked, if you probed too deeply.

'It was around that time, yes,' she said.

'I wonder if Lillian had the baby soon after that,' said Indigo. Sylvia could see she was doing mental calculations in her head.

'I told you, she didn't have a baby.'

'She could have had her after you left, Mum.' Indigo sounded so calm. So sensible. It was disturbing.

'She would have written. She would have told me,' said Sylvia.

'Everyone has secrets, Mum,' and Sylvia thought: oh, my clever darling girl, when did you get to be so wise? She wondered fleetingly what secrets Indigo herself was keeping, but then closed down the thought. She didn't want to know.

'Darling, you're right. But you have to remember, it was a different time. The secrets were necessary. Whole families' lives were at stake. Reputations meant something. Sometimes they were all that was binding us together.'

'Okay, sure. I get that,' said Indigo.

Sylvia pondered the casual flippancy, the condescending agreement. Indigo could never really understand. In 1977, the north-west coast of Tasmania had been a cultural backwater. News of the new law providing supporting mother's benefit hadn't made its way to the sparsely populated farming communities around Sisters Cove for a long time. Or if it had, there was little appetite to sign up for it in Sylvia's circles. A handout from the government was shameful when there was an honest day's work to be done. Pregnancy was no excuse either. An unmarried pregnant girl was an embarrassment at best, but she was a pariah if her family or the baby's father chose to turn their backs.

'If a baby had been born,' she said slowly, 'it wouldn't have been possible to keep her.'

Indigo looked at her carefully. She closed the diary, then got up and replaced it in the box.

'Whatever happened back then, Mum, Willa has to be helped. It's not fair to come between a child and her family. The blood ties, the search for identity. If she's looking now, if that's what Lillian was doing with this bequest, then she'll need your help.'

Indigo was staring at Sylvia with knowing eyes; an old soul. Sylvia remembered seeing that same look when her daughter was put into her arms twenty-eight years ago, as she lay in the birthing pool. A soul reborn, all-knowing, wise beyond words.

'Mum, she's going to need you to help her,' said Indigo again. And Sylvia thought: no. You have no idea what you're talking about. You have no idea what it is you're really asking me to do.

CHAPTER TEN

Willa

'How are you, darling? Really?' asked Hugo.

'I'm okay,' said Willa. Hugo didn't respond straight away, and she turned the question over in her mind as she pictured him sitting in their living room in Oxford with the fire burning, leaning back in his old leather chair. 'I really am, Hugo. It's lovely here. I've met some interesting people.'

'Great. Have you learned anything yet? About who the woman was?'

'Not for certain. No. I had lunch with her god-daughter yesterday, though. She hadn't heard anything about Lillian having a baby. But Indigo is only in her twenties. I suppose Lillian wouldn't have broadcast the fact if she'd given up a baby for adoption.'

'No, I imagine not,' said Hugo. 'You know, you could start the paperwork to get access to your birth records if you really want an answer.'

'I don't know,' said Willa. She stood up at the table. Through the glass double doors of the beach house, she watched the waves rolling and receding rhythmically across the fine white sand of the cove. A mother stood with her toddler at the shoreline, her jeans rolled up to her knees. The little boy was bouncing up and down, scooping up water and jumping around – whether in glee or fright, Willa couldn't quite tell. She slid the glass door open and walked onto the deck. The cool wind blew across her skin, bringing a fresh salt smell. She let the summer sun warm her. 'It seems… unnecessary in some ways. I'm just…' She let the unfinished sentence float. She couldn't quite articulate her feelings. Now that her mother, her beautiful adoptive mother – the only mother she had known – had passed away, she wanted to honour her memory. Digging up the circumstances of her birth felt strangely like a betrayal.

'Well,' said Hugo, 'is there anything in the house, perhaps, that might give you a clue?'

'I'm not sure,' said Willa. 'I haven't looked. I've signed some papers, but I don't have a key yet. I think there might be one final document to sign.'

'You could ask to borrow a key,' said Hugo. 'If nobody is contesting the will, it's probably pretty straightforward.'

'I guess so,' said Willa. She hadn't thought of that. For the past couple of years, she'd sometimes felt she was on autopilot, just moving from one day to the next, doing whatever she was expected to do. She'd relied on Hugo too much, and she'd known it couldn't go on like that.

But this morning, she had woken feeling rested. And in these last few days she had begun to feel like a different person to the woman who had sat on the park bench in Oxford, with Hugo, remembering their girl. Now she felt a hint, a glimmer, that some of the old Willa might be coming back.

'I will,' she said. 'To be honest, I'm not convinced I need to know who Lillian Brooks was.' But as the words left her mouth, she realised something was pushing her on. The need for a blood connection, a river that ran through her to her own children. To her daughter.

As the realisation settled around her, Willa said, 'It would be nice to look in the house again. It's gorgeous. Well, I think so anyway. You and Hamish would probably think it was a bit dingy and tiny. But Esme would have loved it.'

The word slipped through her lips like water. *Esme*. It was such a pretty name. So old-fashioned – as everyone had felt the need to tell them at the time, when she and Hugo had decided on it. So beautiful, she thought as she'd held her little Esme in her arms for the first time. *How could a mother give that up?*

Hugo was silent on the other end of the phone. She wondered what he was thinking. Perhaps he was surprised she'd said Esme's name so freely. She could feel the rolling, crashing tumble of the waves on the beach frothing through her. She had given everything to mourning Esme, but now she had to divert her grief or it would consume them all. She had lost the woman she once was; that woman had been buried beneath the cold English soil with her child. But the same part of her that had loved her daughter with such vehemence had also delighted in lively conversation with colleagues, in tasting strange foreign foods, in wandering with Kettles through parkland coloured and crunchy with autumn leaves. Her husband and son still needed that person.

'I'm sure she would have. I'm sure we'll all love it, darling. If you love it,' said Hugo.

'Maybe you should come over here for a week,' said Willa.

'I don't think I can just now. John Layton has asked me to stand in for him at the conference in London next week. Besides, Hamish has made it into Head of the River. There's a great bunch of boys in the crew. He was going to tell you.'

'Oh, that's wonderful, on both counts,' said Willa. For a moment she felt guilt and a longing to be home.

'Shall I put him on?' asked Hugo. 'He's studying in his room.'

'Don't disturb him. Tell him to call if he feels like a break.' She watched as the mother of the toddler scooped him up and wrapped him in a towel. She felt a longing to get her feet wet. To explore. 'I'd better go. I'll call you when I've had time to look at return flights. Maybe I'll stay a few more days, though,' she said.

'Are you really all right, darling? We miss you.'

'I miss you too. And I'm fine. I really am fine.' She was surprised to realise that this wasn't far from the truth.

Willa turned off the ignition and sat in the car on the empty dirt road, staring at The Old Chapel. A smile pulled at her lips. It was beautiful, and it was hers.

She turned to look into Annabelle's garden. Under an impressive grove of old elm trees, a floral arch had been constructed. A stout man in work wear was putting out white chairs in rows in front of it, leaving a wide path down the middle. Willa remembered that Annabelle hosted weddings. And today was Saturday, so it would make sense that there was one today. She looked up at the sky and the gathering clouds and hoped it wouldn't rain, for the sake of the bride.

She walked into the grounds of The Old Chapel and registered the floating calls of birdsong and the distant sound of the ocean. Without stopping to consider the overgrown garden and any wildlife it might be hiding, she skipped up the steps and fitted the key into the door. Ian Enderby had handed over the key with a smile, a bottle of champagne and a large wad of official paperwork.

Inside, the musty chemical smell hit her again. She switched on the light and the bulb threw a weak yellow beam across the room. She looked around for a moment, then took the steep staircase up to the landing. Sunbeams struggled through the dirty panelled windows. Boxes filled every available space. She squatted to avoid the sloped ceiling and pulled the lid off the first carton. Inside were old novels and works of non-fiction. She picked up a faded copy of a book called *On Photography* by Susan Sontag and flicked through it. The publication date was 1977. Her birth year. She wondered what the author would think of the fact that every single person now carried a camera on their mobile phone. She wondered if Lillian had owned a camera – if there were photographs of her life in one of these boxes.

In the next box she found letters, still in their original envelopes, with faded handwriting across the front. Several were simply addressed to *Lillian Brooks, The Old Chapel, Sisters Cove, Tasmania*. That had probably been plenty of information for the local post-master to deliver a letter back then. Perhaps even now. This place was so quiet and quaint. So removed from the bustle of city life.

During the week, Willa had walked the entire perimeter of Sisters Cove, marvelling at its untouched nature. She'd found a circular wooden hut in an overgrown garden above the surf club, housing a tiny café. The owner, a vibrant middle-aged woman with dreadlocks and dressed in a floaty dress and sandals, had sold tea and biscuits, healing crystals and home-made jam. She'd asked Willa which of the houses on the beach she was renting, then provided fifteen minutes of entertaining anecdotes about the house's owner. She'd then moved on to the village 'mayor' – a woman wandering the streets straightening up rubbish bins, clean-ing letter boxes and pulling out roadside weeds – and finished up with a description of the problems the locals were facing with a proposed new tourist development in the adjacent bay that she said was going to ruin the vibe of the place. Willa had paid three dollars for a cup of chilli and lime green tea that tasted like arsenic, and walked out feeling strangely refreshed.

She returned her attention to the letters. She was tempted to look inside, but resisted the urge. They were not meant for her. She wondered at her own moral compass – here she was digging through Lillian's life, yet there were still some boundaries she couldn't cross. She wondered if they would all be so clear-cut.

In another box were hospital letters and X-rays and medical insurance files. Willa looked through them and saw that Lillian had been diagnosed with breast cancer fifteen years earlier. She'd had a mastectomy, but it had returned in the other breast about three years ago. She thought of all the times doctors had asked her if she had any family history of disease, and all the times she had had to explain that she didn't know, because she was adopted. Mostly it hadn't seemed to matter, but now she wondered if it was something she should worry about. She felt uneasy, as if a time bomb might be ticking and she should at least take steps to see if she could defuse it so she didn't leave Hamish and Hugo without another family member.

In the next box was a collection of small framed photographs. She pulled one out and looked at it. The frame was old-fashioned, an ornately patterned tarnished silver. It was a man in work clothes standing next to a girl in front of a shed. As she replaced it, she noticed another photo, unframed, that was sitting loose in the box. In it, a young woman was standing near an older man in a wheelchair, in front of The Old Chapel. Next to them were a well-dressed middle-aged couple, seemingly caught in conversation with the man in the wheelchair. The young woman must have been Lillian. She was small and had a lovely open face and a generous mouth. Willa thought of the photo in the newspaper of Lillian aged around sixty in her lifesaver's outfit. In the features of this young woman, she found the resemblance.

'Hu-hoo! Hello!'

Willa looked down through the railings of the upper level, into the living room. Annabelle was standing in the doorway, smiling and waving.

'I saw your car!' she said.

'Hello,' said Willa. She uncrossed her legs and stood up slowly, shaking out the pins and needles that had settled in her foot.

'Would you like to come across for a cup of tea?' asked Annabelle.

'I brought herbal tea bags with me,' said Willa. 'And I noticed a kettle here the other day. Why don't you let me make tea for you?'

'Oh,' said Annabelle. 'Are you sure you wouldn't like to come across the road? It's no trouble.'

'No, I won't,' said Willa. 'I'm just getting started. And I see you're hosting a wedding today. Is that right? I wouldn't like to interrupt.' She began a slow descent of the stairs, still holding the photograph.

'Piffle,' said Annabelle. 'It's not till four. And my bit's nearly done anyway. The set-up and cottages. I have waitresses who offer the champagne and hors d'oeuvres after the ceremony. Then the guests all go off to the dinner venue, on a bus usually. It's easy.'

'That sounds like a lot of work, still,' said Willa. In the kitchenette, she rinsed out the kettle, refilled it and flicked it on. 'Are you sure you won't join me? I was about to have a quick break, so you're very welcome.'

'Oh, all right then,' said Annabelle. She took a tentative step inside the door, then stopped and looked around. 'Lillian used to come across to me for tea. There was never room in here, with all the canvases.'

Willa smiled at her. She picked up the photograph from the kitchen bench and showed it to Annabelle. 'Is that Lillian in the picture?'

Annabelle took a few moments to answer. 'Yes, with Constance and Andrew. And her dad, Len.'

Willa walked back to the kitchen and opened the cupboards. She found two mismatched mugs and held them up to the dim light of the window, then rubbed at some dust with the edge of her shirt.

'Andrew… Was that Dan's uncle who Ian Enderby was talking about the other day?'

'Yes.'

Willa looked up. 'He died on the cliffs?'

'Yes.'

Annabelle's expression faltered.

'I'm sorry. How insensitive of me. I was being nosy.'

'Oh, it's fine!' Annabelle held up the photo again and stared at it. 'He was very charismatic. Very… popular.'

'Well, I can see he was handsome,' said Willa. 'More like a movie star than a farm owner by the looks of that photo.'

'Yes, that's probably right,' said Annabelle. 'He was a much better lawyer than he was a farmer, I'm told. It was his tractor that caused Len to be in that wheelchair.'

'Oh? How so?' asked Willa.

'A farm accident. Len was the head farmhand at Merrivale then. He rolled the tractor and broke his back. Had a head injury too. There were rumours that the tractor was faulty, or something like that, and that Andrew had refused to fix it. Apparently Lillian didn't believe it, though. She and her father were both very loyal to Andrew over the whole thing.'

'What a sad story,' said Willa.

'Len was always very stoical, even though he was in constant pain. Not that I knew that back then, but over the years Lillian and I talked about him quite a bit.' Annabelle put the photograph down on the side table. 'He was a lovely man, Len.'

'It feels odd for me to be inviting you in here,' said Willa after a pause. 'You've obviously been here hundreds of times, even if you didn't stay for tea.'

'No,' said Annabelle. 'No, I never came in.' Her hand fluttered to her mouth, then slid down her neck. Her fingers clasped at a silver necklace that looked to have a cross on it. She was staring at the wood fire at the rear of the room. She looked pale, thought Willa. Less energetic than she had the other day.

'Are you all right?'

Annabelle's face sprang back to life as she moved her gaze to Willa. 'Yes! Yes, fine. I have been a bit off colour this week, actually. But apparently there's nothing wrong with me. Apparently I'm right as rain. Doctors know best, don't they!' She walked further into the room and stood in front of the couch.

She's stressed, thought Willa. Off balance. After their morning tea the other day, Willa had come away sensing something pent-up in Annabelle. Something grating. Today she could feel the same anxious energy, but also warmth and an odd sense of sorrow.

'Not always,' said Willa. 'Sometimes I think doctors are just poking around in the dark, doing their best.'

Annabelle deflated onto the couch.

Willa handed her a mug of tea. She sat opposite, sipping in silence.

'I had a bit of a hiccup this week. An episode,' said Annabelle. She was staring down into her lap, then she looked back up, a grave expression on her face. 'They think it's anxiety.'

'Oh?' said Willa. 'That sounds worrying.'

'It was. I thought I was dying,' said Annabelle. 'I still don't really believe that's what it was. Panic, I mean. I thought I'd been poisoned at first. Then I thought maybe it was a heart attack. That's how bad I felt.' There were tears in her eyes.

'It's truly awful,' said Willa. 'I've been there myself.'

'Really?'

Willa nodded. 'Did your doctor have any suggestions?'

'I have to see a psychologist,' said Annabelle. 'Apparently these episodes can just come on, just like that. If you've got a few worrying things on your mind.'

'Have you?' asked Willa.

'Well, I wouldn't have said so,' said Annabelle. 'The weddings are going all right. I've only done a few, but so far so good. Anyway, enough about me. What about you? What have you been looking for there?' She gestured to the upper level and smiled widely, and it was as if, thought Willa, looking at her face, she had completely transported herself to a new reality. One where everything was perfect in the world.

'I'm not sure. I didn't know Lillian. But I'm hoping to find something to link me to her.'

Annabelle's eyes were aglow with curiosity. Willa thought about telling her. She didn't usually talk about it, but sitting here, chatting about her health so openly, Annabelle just seemed sweet and guileless. And she'd already told Annabelle's niece, so what harm could it do?

'I do have a link to Tasmania, though.'

'Oh, how interesting!' said Annabelle. 'What is it?'

'I was born here.'

'Really?'

'I was adopted out at birth. Was Lillian ever pregnant, do you know?'

Annabelle's eyes widened. 'Pregnant? Yes... but...' She put down her tea and brought both hands fleetingly to her mouth, then dropped them into her lap.

'She was? When?' asked Willa.

'It couldn't be you,' said Annabelle.

'Why not?'

'She lost it. I was away, but that's what I was told. She... lost the baby.' Annabelle's face had collapsed.

'Perhaps she didn't,' said Willa carefully. She allowed a few moments to pass, but Annabelle just sat staring at the coffee table. 'Perhaps that's what she needed people to think,' she said a little more gently.

'No. Lillian wouldn't have lied like that. She wouldn't.'

They sat in silence for a minute.

'We all tell lies,' said Willa eventually. 'I told you the other day that I had two children. I let you believe they were both alive. But my daughter died almost two years ago.'

Annabelle looked up, aghast.

'I find it hard to talk about,' said Willa. A gigantic mass had wedged itself in her chest as she spoke, making it an effort to breathe. 'But sometimes you just have to do what it takes. You do the best you can.'

'I'm so sorry,' said Annabelle.

Willa could see that she was genuinely upset.

'What was her name?'

'Esme,' said Willa, and they both sat in silence, letting the name hang between them.

'Most people try to avoid talking about her to me,' said Willa. 'But sometimes I do really want to talk about her. She was such a darling. Sometimes I just want people to know everything about her. She was amazing.'

'Of course,' said Annabelle. 'How dreadful for you. It must be... terrible.'

'It is. Although sometimes it isn't. Sometimes I talk to her in my head and I picture her and I laugh at what she would have said back to me. Sometimes it's wonderful,' said Willa. 'On the days I can picture her clearly. Sometimes I can't tell the difference between good days and bad. They both make me cry.'

'Oh, my dear,' said Annabelle sadly. 'Well, you just go ahead and cry.'

'Thank you.' Willa wanted to get up and give Annabelle a hug, which was very unlike her.

'How old was she?' asked Annabelle.

'Fifteen,' said Willa. 'Nearly sixteen.'

Annabelle's eyes pooled with tears. 'That's a really hard age.'

'Yes,' said Willa.

'Was she sick?'

'No.' She wondered if she could bring herself to speak about it. Sometimes it felt like a betrayal of Esme, but mostly she was just angry and bitter that she hadn't heard her phone ring that night.

'I guess it was an accident,' said Annabelle, seeming to sense Willa's discomfort. 'I'm very sorry, Willa. I don't have children, but I imagine it's the worst thing that could happen to anyone.'

'Yes,' said Willa. 'I think it is.'

They both sat in silence. Willa looked across Annabelle's shoulder out of the window. She had a sudden urge to see the ocean and feel the breeze. She got up and went across to the little stained-glass window.

After a while, Annabelle spoke. 'Do you feel all right in here?'

'What do you mean?' asked Willa.

'Inside here. The Old Chapel? It doesn't feel creepy?'

'Not really.'

'Oh, well that's good.' Annabelle got to her feet and scooped up both cups, then headed across to the sink. She began washing them vigorously under the running tap.

'Why?' asked Willa after a moment.

Annabelle put the mugs on the drying rack, and turned to her slowly. She had a furrow across her brow, as if she was considering what to say.

'There was... an accident here once. I just... oh, I don't know. This place just gives me the creeps.'

'I heard about the little girl falling off the dog sled. The gravestone outside,' said Willa.

'Oh, no. I didn't mean that! And how insensitive of me to even... with your Esme dying. No, I... oh, I'm so sorry. I'm such an idiot!'

'It's all right,' said Willa. 'It's all right, I promise.' She wondered what was going on inside Annabelle's mind.

Annabelle wiped her hands on the tea towel and threaded it through the oven handle, taking care to spread it out evenly. 'Well, let's not talk about it. I shouldn't have said anything. Only... if I were you, I wouldn't sleep here. On your own. Being... sad, like you are. The energy in here is strange.'

'All right,' said Willa. 'I mean, I'm not sleeping here anyway.'

'I'm sorry. Please don't repeat any of this. It's silly. Dan would be angry that I said it.'

'It's fine,' said Willa. 'If you don't want to talk about it, that's fine.'

'No!' said Annabelle. 'Goodness, no! I don't know what I was thinking, saying anything at all. I… please forget about it.' She was clutching at the necklace again, rubbing the cross repeatedly with her thumb.

Willa stared at her and saw something disturbing in her eyes. It was fear, she realised.

'Annabelle, I promise I won't say anything. Whatever happened here, it's none of my concern.'

'Oh, Willa…' said Annabelle. She turned and walked towards the door, and without looking back, raised her hand. 'Thank you so much for the tea.'

She scuttled down the steps, and Willa watched her walk determinedly across the lane, open the gate and disappear through her flower garden.

CHAPTER ELEVEN

Annabelle

'Please just go to work, Dan.' Annabelle was perched on the edge of their bed in her dressing gown. It was eight o'clock and the sun was streaming through the window. The sky was a vivid blue and she could hear the birds singing outside in the walnut tree. Some attention from Dan should only have added to the perfectness of the day, except it wasn't the sort of attention she wanted.

'What did the doctor actually say, Belle?' asked Dan as he yanked at his shoelaces. 'It can't be anxiety. What could possibly be stressing you? You've got the life of bloody Riley, prancing about in the garden all day while I'm trying to earn enough to keep this place going. And you *look* properly sick.'

'Well the blood tests and thyroid and the ECG all came back normal. So it looks like you're stuck with a nutcase. Sorry about that.' Annabelle gritted her teeth. How *dare* he think she didn't have enough in her life to be stressed about?

When she'd seen Dr Collins, the woman had talked Annabelle through all the tests the hospital had done, and the further tests that had been done in her office. All clear. A perfectly clean bill of health, apart from a tiny elevation in her cholesterol and an admonishment about her weight.

'Is there anything that's been worrying you lately, Annabelle? Have you been irritable or not sleeping?' the doctor had asked, giving Annabelle a disturbingly empathetic look.

She was such a nice young woman. Pretty, too, with huge brown eyes. Took care of herself. She wore lovely make-up and had a nice dress sense. She should be treating properly sick people. Not people like Annabelle, who had every single thing they could ever have desired. A lovely home, the nicest garden on the north-west coast, an accomplished husband, an interesting – and probably soon to be wildly successful – new business.

'Not really,' said Annabelle. 'Everything's quite good.'

'Hmm.' Dr Collins' eyes flicked back and forth across Annabelle's face for a moment. 'Well, I still think what you experienced was most likely anxiety. A panic attack. It can happen when you have low levels of stress for a long period, then suddenly there might be a trigger – one you aren't even aware of – and your body releases lots of adrenalin and your brain is suddenly overwhelmed with physiological signals. It can certainly feel like you're dying, as you described. Your fight-or-flight response in overdrive, if you like.' She paused, waiting for Annabelle to comment.

Annabelle couldn't think of anything to say. Basically the doctor was saying she was insane.

'I know you're not convinced, but when you go home, I'd like you to log onto this website and fill out the anxiety checklist,' said Dr Collins, handing Annabelle a flyer for a depression and anxiety organisation. There was a pretty coloured butterfly at the top. 'The results will only be for your viewing, but there are lots of resources on there. And I'd also like you to make an appointment with a psychologist to discuss management, in case it happens again. Here are a few names, but look around and ask friends; it's important you have a good relationship with your therapist if it's going to work.' She was smiling patiently.

Annabelle had been making tiny rips in the corner of the flyer, without realising it. They both looked down at the shredded butterfly in her hands. She slid the offending corner beneath her palm. A *therapist*! How ridiculous.

'I'm not saying you're wrong, Doctor, but I just think it's unlikely,' she said. She folded the flyer and put it in her handbag. Her appointment time was over. She stood halfway up, then sat down again. 'I suppose while I'm here, I should get you to check a little cyst I have. On the side of my breast. I know it's nothing, but I feel bad about wasting your time with this other nonsense, so we might as well do some real medicine before I go.' Annabelle gave the doctor her best, most understanding smile. Nobody liked talking about mental problems, did they? A lump was much easier territory. It would make the doctor feel better about charging her for a long appointment.

On the examination couch, Annabelle removed her bra and fixed her eyes on the ceiling. Dr Collins' fingers probed her breasts, and when she got to the lump, she pushed and prodded it several times.

'Any pain?' she asked.

'No. None,' said Annabelle forcefully. *See, I am perfectly healthy!* 'I know I'm silly to even mention it,' she said. She wanted to get dressed. She'd only ever had one breast examination before – by a very pushy locum doctor several years ago, who had insisted on it, after she'd admitted she didn't bother. The whole thing was excruciatingly awful – to be nearly naked, with someone looking at her flabby belly and droopy breasts and touching her private bits under unforgiving fluorescent lights.

'All right, you can get dressed,' said Dr Collins, after she'd prodded a bit more.

Annabelle put her clothes back on and stood next to the desk, waiting to be dismissed. Dr Collins' fingers flew across her keyboard in a frantic tapping frenzy.

'Just sit down for a few minutes, Annabelle,' she said as the printer next to her computer hummed into life. She gave a crooked half-smile, and Annabelle thought: what a difficult woman you are.

'I'm afraid it's very unlikely to be a cyst. The lump is hard, and it's not moving around under the skin when pushed. I'm afraid it might be a tumour of some kind, and we will need to get it checked out quickly to see whether it's benign or not. I've typed up a referral to the breast clinic in Launceston. You'll need to spend most of the day there, probably. They'll do a mammogram and an ultrasound, then if they think it's possibly malignant, they'll do a fine-needle biopsy of the tissue in the lump on the same day. The results will all come back to me.'

She was staring directly at Annabelle with her silly bug eyes all gloopy with concern, and Annabelle was cross that she'd gotten herself into this ridiculous situation. How could the woman be so sure it wasn't a cyst? She didn't have time for a whole day in Launceston.

Dr Collins handed her the paperwork.

'Right. Thank you,' said Annabelle.

'You need to ring them today, Annabelle. It's not the sort of lump I like to find. It's very concerning.'

'Goodness, you're a worry-wart!' said Annabelle. She really didn't have the time for this today. She had to get to the farm co-op to pick up food for the chickens and two bags of fertiliser and several trays of new herbs to plant in the kitchen garden so they'd have time to grow before the fete. Then she had to repot the hydrangea cuttings into individual pots for sale at the fete, oversee the cottage cleaning and source a dozen new chairs for this weekend's wedding, which was bigger than any of the previous ones they'd hosted. *One hundred and twenty people!* Only sixty would have chairs, though. The others could stand and mingle.

She gave a little laugh to placate Dr Collins, but the woman pursed her pretty lips and leaned forward as if she was about to talk to a toddler.

'Please, Annabelle. I'll try to ring you this evening to find out your appointment date. If they can't fit you in by the end of next week, I'll ring a friend of mine who works there. I don't want a delay.'

'Oh,' said Annabelle. She could feel her heart thumping. She really, really hated anything medical, and Dr Collins wasn't giving her enough space. The idea of a big fat needle going into her breast sent little shivers through her.

'And I'd really like you to ring a psychologist today too. I imagine this lump has been adding to the anxiety you've been feeling. It may have triggered something.'

Now, in the bedroom, with Dan hovering about with a face like thunder, Annabelle sighed heavily. She wondered again whether the lump was anything to do with her having this so-called anxiety episode. Probably not; there were lots of other things that might have been playing on her mind. The new wedding business, for a start, which was really very exhausting if she was honest. Plus there was Dan complaining about their finances all the time. And Willa. Willa's appearance was very unsettling, but Annabelle didn't really want to think about it. She knew she should just be able to cope with all these little things, but lately she wasn't sleeping well, and she was just so incredibly tired.

'All right,' said Dan. 'Well, I'm heading off. A psychologist seems like a waste of money to me, though. What's he going to say that you don't know already? Stop being such a stress-head and get on with it. It's not bloody rocket science.'

Annabelle looked down at her feet. She hadn't told him about the lump yet. One thing at a time. The silly psychologist was bad enough. She was probably only going to teach her how to do a relaxation exercise or something useless like that. The woman had promised to let her know if a cancellation came up. She wished Dan would just go to work.

'I have a meeting at the golf club tonight. I'll probably be home around ten or so.'

'Okay,' said Annabelle.

'Don't save me dinner. I'll get something in town. Unless you need me to come home… if it turns out you really are sick or something.'

'I'm fine. I've got heaps of work to do. It will be good if I don't have to cook.'

Annabelle felt heavy. She didn't know what to do. She still hadn't called the clinic in Launceston. Every time the phone rang, her heart raced at the thought that it would be Dr Collins checking up on her. Somehow the idea of a psychologist was so much more inviting than the breast clinic. At least she could lie down and close her eyes in therapy. Wasn't that what people did? She'd seen it in Woody Allen movies. It looked quite relaxing.

Annabelle finished writing and propped the beautiful hand-printed card against the bottle of red wine. A local artist had given her an excellent discount on the cards, which were on lovely heavy stock and featured coloured tulips and other flowers from the area. Her guests appreciated the personal handwritten note. She was sure it helped when they considered their stay in the cottages. They left her excellent reviews on the accommodation website.

Annabelle is a truly delightful host!

We couldn't fault Annabelle's place – pristine and stylish!

Do ask for a tour of the orchard. Annabelle is dynamite!

She liked the ones with exclamation marks the best. They were decisive. *I am committed to the content of this review and I am not afraid to use emphatic punctuation to show it!!*

She closed the door of the cottage and left the key in it, ready for her guests checking in tomorrow. There was no need to lock doors around here, and it made the check-in process so much easier if she didn't have to think any more about it after the cottage was clean and ready.

She'd already had dinner, and it was late, but she'd been restless in the house and knew the best way to cure that was to find something to do. The cottage and the garden had called to her, and it was such a lovely evening. The sun was setting over the hills towards town, and beyond the cliffs the ocean was greyish-pink with tinges of orange. It reflected the swirling colours of the clouds that hung low over the cove in billowing puffs and streaks. It would be a clear day tomorrow, by the looks of those colours.

At five minutes to five, Annabelle had finally telephoned the breast clinic. She had an appointment at nine a.m. the following Friday. Seven days away. Seven long days with nobody to confide in. An image of her mother running in the paddocks behind the dairy kept appearing to her. Darling mum. Such a fun person. Annabelle was sorry she'd been so clueless back then, when her mother was dying. So completely separate from the whole thing. She could hardly remember it really – just that Sylvia had been bossy, and their father had been quiet, and whenever Annabelle looked back into her childhood it was through a painful veneer of guilt.

She should have read to Mummy; sat with her and told her stories. Instead she'd been doing what you did at that age: hanging around with friends, riding bikes, going to the beach, slathering herself with coconut oil and baking on the best tan possible. She shuddered at the damage she'd probably done to her poor skin cells. A thought settled through her, sharp and sinister. What if this lump *was* cancer? What if her breast was misshapen after treatment? Or she had a big scar? Dan *loved* her pendulous breasts. She had once been quite proud of them herself, back when they were still perky and evenly balanced and hadn't been competing for attention with her ever-growing belly and thighs.

She walked across the garden, stopping to pull some weeds that had grown through the mulch beneath a newly planted Japanese maple. The same image of her mother appeared in her mind as she squatted down – happy, carefree, beckoning to Annabelle as she ran backwards in her trousers and a bright red woollen jumper. A pain caught her in the chest, the kind she hadn't felt since she was a child. *I want my mum.*

Sylvia had stayed for a couple of years to raise her after their mother died, but she was distracted, busy, still in training as a nurse and out with Dan the nights she wasn't rostered on a night shift. She'd tried her best, but Annabelle had had a special bond with her mum. She'd felt abandoned by everyone after she died.

She supposed her mother was trying to tell her something now, appearing like this in her mind. *Go and chat to your sister.* And now that she thought about it, Sylvia might have a herbal remedy to make the lump go away. Or there might be some sort of cream she could recommend to rub on it. Lately Sylvia had been talking a lot about the ancient medicine of Ayurveda, and she seemed to have a powder or a herb to cure anything. Then another thought occurred to Annabelle. There might be a special Ayurvedic tumour-reducing diet she could go on! Lose some weight in the process as a bonus. She smiled to herself.

As the darkness fell, a strange sense of calm came over her. That *was* what her mother had been trying to tell her. In the house, she grabbed her car keys, stopping only to apply a quick swipe of lipstick, pull on a better cardigan, grab a small chocolate bar from the pantry and swap her garden boots for a pair of slip-on loafers. She was still in her gardening pants, but they were her best pair, and it was only Sylvia anyway. She would see no one else out that way at night.

She drove down the main road, then took the turn-off to the beach road, her headlights cutting bright swathes through the blackness. The road narrowed as she approached the top of the incline that hugged the hill. Stars were sprinkled through the sky like powdery gems, and out to her right, the ocean was a black mass of nothingness. It was now completely dark, and Sylvia's long, potholed driveway had no lighting at all and hardly any space to turn the car around when you got to the house – unless you were an excellent driver or owned a Mini. Annabelle had a very nice Lexus. Mid-sized. And she sometimes misjudged things, which meant she had already had two scrapes this year. Dan would be furious if she got a third one. She would park in the little lookout parking bay further along the road and walk back.

The more she thought about Sylvia's herbal cures as she sat looking out over the black ocean, the more the lump began receding as a problem in her mind. She turned on her phone torch as she got out of the car and listened to the scramble of something close by in the bushes. She swung the torch around to the noise and two bright red eyes glared at her from a low-hanging eucalyptus branch. A little possum.

'Hello, lovely thing,' she said. 'You gave me a fright!'

The possum turned its head and scampered up the tree trunk into the blackness. She took a deep breath and let the background swishing sound of the ocean calm her.

A chill had landed in the air, and around her the bushland vibrated with the constant high-pitched hum of crickets. She heard a mopoke call out from further into the bush, a throaty double trill that pulsed and echoed like a warning call. She shivered. *How silly! It's just a silly owl!*

She set off tentatively back up the hill on the unlit road, wondering if they would ever put street lights on this part. It was dangerous for pedestrians at any time of day, as there was barely any verge at all before the hill fell away. At night-time, it felt treacherous. When she reached Sylvia's driveway, she made a mental note to tell Dan to come over at the weekend with a trailer full of dirt to help Sylvia fill in the holes. They were dreadful.

Ahead, at the end of the driveway, she could see a dim light in the front room. When she reached the house, she tapped on the door. Nothing. She peered through the glass side panel, but there was no movement. To her left, at the front of the house, the windows were open. She must tell Sylvia to close them to keep out the cold ocean damp, or she'd catch a chill. She turned the handle of the door and put her head inside, calling out gently, so as not to startle her sister, 'Hello? Syl?'

Nobody answered. She closed the door behind her and walked into the kitchen. It was open to the living room, which was filled with an ugly patchwork chair and an old couch littered with various ethnic throws and scattered with woven cushions in muted colours that had seen better days. On the walls were abstract artworks and a very nice landscape painted by Lillian decades ago. A free-standing lamp beside the fire was turned on, throwing a faint warm glow across the room.

'Sylvia?'

Still there was no answer. Annabelle moved across the kitchen in the dim light. Instinctively, she walked towards the sink to take in the view through the window of the ocean and the stars, and of course, there was Sylvia, sitting outside on the deck enjoying the view too. It was such a lovely night. She was facing out to the ocean, and her back was to Annabelle. As Annabelle's eyes adjusted, she realised that Sylvia was sitting with someone else. Perhaps it was Indigo. Although they were sitting very close. Right next to each other, in fact, with no space between them at all. She squinted. It seemed to be a man, taller than Sylvia anyway, but facing away so she couldn't get a good look. Their heads were together, relaxed, in tune. She has a lover, thought Annabelle. Good. Good girl. They were hard to find in a small town like this. She felt a swell of happiness for her sister.

She turned and tiptoed back through the kitchen, closing the front door behind her. As she stood on the porch and got her phone out to light her way, she pondered this discovery. She wondered when Dan would be home, and if she should tell him about it, or if Sylvia would want her to keep it quiet. She always found this bit hard – navigating the divide between Dan and Sylvia. The awkward history.

As she was swiping to turn on the torch, her phone buzzed silently in her hand. It was Dan.

'Hi,' she whispered.

'Hi,' said Dan. 'Just ringing to say I might be a bit later than usual. A few of us on the committee are going to have a game of pool and a beer at the pub.'

'Oh, right,' whispered Annabelle, staring up the driveway into the pure blackness.

'Why are you whispering?' asked Dan.

Annabelle squinted, then half turned and noticed movement through the opaque glass side panel of the door. Damn. She'd disturbed them.

'No reason,' she whispered. She took a step further out into the blackness and away from the faintly lit porch. Dan was silent for a moment.

'Belle?'

'Mmm.'

'I'll probably just see you in the morning. Don't wait up. Okay?'

Something felt strange. The sound. The words. She could hear them in two places. She could hear *Dan* in two places. She stepped back into the porch and peered through the pattern of etched flowers on the glass. It looked like Dan. It *was* Dan. He was in Sylvia's kitchen, with his phone to his ear.

He was telling her not to wait up. From inside Sylvia's house.

'Annabelle?'

She felt something inside her plummet. A swift, violent realisation. She felt the dizziness coming. Her hand dropped to her side still clutching the phone, and she stumbled forward out into the blackness. Then, without any light at all to guide her, Annabelle began to run.

CHAPTER TWELVE

Sylvia

The long wail of the siren was interspersed with a maniacal whirring trill, and it was getting louder. The emergency vehicle sounded like it was coming down the beach road. Sylvia got up from the couch where she and Dan had just sat down. At the window, the rolling flash of red and blue lights was showing though the trees. An ambulance. It stopped just as it passed her driveway. She went into the kitchen and from the top drawer she took out her torch.

'I'm going to have a look.'

'Okay. I'd better stay here,' said Dan.

Sylvia picked her way up the rutted driveway, following the torch beam. As she neared the road, Rita Perotta, her neighbour opposite, almost collided with her. She was dragging her mad Border collie on a leash.

'Sylvia! I was just coming to see you. Annabelle told me not to, but I don't think she's making sense.' Rita was breathless, speaking in a fierce whisper.

'What is it?' Sylvia felt a prickling sense of dread moving down her arms.

'Annabelle – she's sick. I found her collapsed on the road. She couldn't breathe properly. I thought she was having a stroke or something. I called the ambulance and waited with her.'

The paramedics were talking to Annabelle in low tones about fifteen metres further along the road. She was sitting on a stretcher that had been lowered to ground level and was facing the other direction.

'Is she all right?' Sylvia tried to ignore the sinking feeling of guilt that had gripped her. She took a step towards the ambulance, but Rita held her arm.

'She's really agitated. When she stopped hyperventilating, she started sobbing. Told me not to bother you. Insisted I didn't.'

They both stared at Annabelle's back, listening to snatched words from the paramedics, until Rita's dog began scratching at something in the dirt and then bucking and bouncing like a rodeo bull. She jerked him sideways onto the road. 'Stop it, Biscuit!'

'I should check,' said Sylvia, as the dog settled momentarily.

'Just let her have a few minutes with them,' said Rita decisively. 'She seemed a bit out of her mind, actually.'

'What did the paramedics say?'

'Nothing much. I just told them how I found her and they suggested I step back for a bit. They're taking her blood pressure, I think.'

Sylvia felt her own pulse racing. Annabelle would need Dan, but she could hardly go back into the house and get him now. It would be bad enough with a normal neighbour, but Rita was an intolerable gossip. Cold fear whispered at her consciousness. *What if Annabelle had seen them?* She pushed the idea aside.

'I heard she collapsed at the garden meeting last week too,' said Rita.

'Did she?' asked Sylvia.

A scurrying sound emerged from the bushes on the hill, and Biscuit began pulling violently at the leash, whimpering with excitement.

Rita heaved him back with both hands. 'Yes,' she panted. 'Had a turn or something. Didn't she tell you?'

'No,' said Sylvia. She had banned Dan from mentioning Annabelle when they were together. She knew she could hardly take a moral stance on anything, but the whole thing felt worse, even more traitorous, if her sister's name was mentioned between them.

'Carted off in an ambulance. Hellie Beacher told me. Biscuit! No, boy!'

'I'll go in and ring Dan,' said Sylvia, sighing. She turned the torch back towards the house and shone it at the driveway, wondering what on earth she was doing. She should have insisted on speaking with Annabelle, checked she was all right, but something strange was going on. What was Annabelle hiding from her? What had caused this? Why was she sobbing? Surely she couldn't have seen Dan inside the house. His car was parked down at the surf club behind the toilet block, so she couldn't have spotted that either. Sylvia needed to think. She needed to speak to Dan.

When she walked back into the house, Dan was sitting on the patchwork chair, fiddling with his phone.

'What's the emergency?'

'It's Annabelle. She's had some sort of turn. Collapsed and hyperventilating. Down on the road.'

Dan was quiet for a moment, then he let out a huge, heavy sigh.

'Rita Perotta found her,' continued Sylvia. 'Said Annabelle didn't want to disturb me. Said she was sick last week, too.'

Dan brought both his hands to his head and slid them through his hair. He stared at the floor in silence.

'Rita said she went to hospital during a garden meeting. What was that about?'

Dan stood up and put his phone in his pocket. 'Doctors said it was a panic attack.'

'What? She doesn't suffer from anxiety, does she? Well, apart from the usual…'

'I don't know. Sounded like crap to me, but the doc said she had to see a psychologist.'

Sylvia flinched at his offhand tone. 'How did that go?' she asked.
Dan didn't say anything.

'Dan?'

'I don't know. Look, I'm going to head down along the beach and get the car. I'd better go home. Maybe it *is* panic attacks.'

'Poor Anna. Maybe she…' Sylvia shook her head, barely able to finish the thought.

Dan said, 'Hopefully she didn't work out that I was here, but if she did, I'm not going to lie about us.' He came across the room and placed a finger under her chin. 'Syl—'

'You'll have to drive past her on the road to get out. I *really* don't want her to find out you were here.' Sylvia's whole body was rigid with fear.

'Syl, I'm yours. I'm only keeping this secret because you want to.'

She flicked his finger from her chin with an irritable swipe.

A loud knock startled them both, and Sylvia spun around to face the door. Dan took a step backwards, just as she whispered, 'I'll ignore it.'

'Your car's there, and it's probably Rita,' said Dan quietly. 'I'll wait in the bedroom.'

The knocking sounded again, more forceful this time. Dan walked into the bedroom and closed the door. Sylvia took a deep breath, then went to open the front door. A paramedic was standing there, the bright white of his shirt stark against the night. He was holding a powerful torch.

'Sylvia?'

'Yes.'

He took a step sideways and turned back to face the driveway. Behind him, in the dark, the second paramedic was supporting Annabelle.

'Your sister felt unwell. We didn't think it was wise for her to drive just yet. She's going to be all right, though.'

The second paramedic walked forward holding Annabelle. In the light of the porch, she looked pale and shaken. She was staring down at the ground, and when she looked up at Sylvia, there was such a raw, desperate pain in her eyes that Sylvia wished a crack would open up in the earth and swallow her. Annabelle *knew*.

'Come in,' she said.

The paramedic brought Annabelle inside and took her to the couch. Annabelle sank into it and looked up at the men. 'Thank you. I'm so sorry to have wasted your time.'

'No trouble, love. It wasn't a waste at all. You make sure you get to the doctor tomorrow, okay?'

Annabelle nodded, and a tear rolled down her cheek. She swiped it away and stared at the floor again.

As Sylvia showed the paramedics to the door, she thought: please don't leave. This is the end of something. The beginning of something else. I'm not ready.

The scene felt strangely familiar, and yet it had been more than forty years ago that the whole thing had played out in reverse. She still remembered the jumpsuit she'd worn to Alice Tarraby's hen's night. Its plunging neckline and flared pants with a huge belt – a bright yellow outfit to celebrate the beginning of how things were going to be. The weddings amongst her friends were starting, and she knew Dan was keen for them to be next. He was older, twenty-four, and ready to settle down. They'd been together now for nearly three years and she'd been waiting for her father and Annabelle to be ready to manage without her before she let Dan propose to her properly.

Annabelle would leave school soon, get a job probably. Maybe at a dress shop. She wasn't as academic as Sylvia, but she adored people. She cared about making them happy.

Everyone knew Dan was a catch, but what they didn't know was how much he and Sylvia needed each other. It hurt them to be apart. He was so smart and so devoted to her. Which was why, when it happened, it felt like the whole world had collapsed on top of her in great piercing shards of rubble.

She'd been out with Lillian at the party. They'd taken Lillian's car – a slightly battered Kingswood that Lillian treated like a pet. She renamed it every week or so, depending on her mood. They had been drinking at the party, glasses of Porphyry Pearl, but not so much that she couldn't remember what happened afterwards, in all its hideous, crushing detail.

Lillian had dropped her home and she had dashed across the front of the garage trying to avoid the rain that was pelting down. Mud splattered up her boots and clung to the hem of the jumpsuit. She let herself in the front door. In the hallway, at the rear of the house, she stopped. From the light of the bathroom, she could see that Annabelle's door was wide open.

'Anna?' she whispered into the gloom of the bedroom. It was late, and usually she would have crept past, but Annabelle had always slept with the door firmly shut since their mother had died. At first it was probably so she could cry herself to sleep in private. But after the first few months, Sylvia decided it must have made her feel safer.

From the glow of the bathroom light, she could see that Annabelle's bed was empty. The bedspread looked as pristine and neatly made as Annabelle left it every morning when she got up.

'Annabelle?' She said it more loudly, but there was no answer. She flicked on the bedroom light. There was nobody there. She walked further down the hall to their father's room. Through the crack in the door she could hear his irregular grunting snores. She walked into the lounge room, flicking on the light as she did.

'Anna?' The house remained silent. Sylvia sat down in her father's armchair. It was past midnight. She took a cigarette out of the packet on the mantelpiece and lit it. Where could Annabelle be? She wasn't allowed out to parties. Soon it would be different, she kept telling Sylvia. Soon she'd be sixteen! She would twirl around the kitchen hugging herself and imagining the glorious life that lay ahead of her – boys, parties, beautiful dresses. Sylvia wished her little sister wasn't so extremely pretty, and so trusting. It hurt to watch her dream like that. Annabelle's nature meant that people would take advantage of her – she just wanted to please everyone, and that was a dangerous thing.

Sylvia took a drag on the cigarette and blew the smoke towards the fireplace, drumming the fingers of her other hand against her knee. Where was her sister? Worry began to gnaw at her. Should she wake her father and ask? Or had Annabelle slipped out with friends after he'd fallen asleep? There were no neighbours for miles, so she wouldn't have been able to walk anywhere. But one of the Palfrey boys might have come to pick her up. Or Eadie Bentley. She'd got her licence last month and was getting around in one of their family's farm utes. Annabelle had wanted to go roller skating in Burnie with Eadie tonight. Maybe she'd managed to persuade their father to let her, but it was doubtful. He worried about her going in cars with other kids. And anyway, it was way past any curfew he would have set.

Sylvia finished the cigarette and flicked the butt into the fireplace. She turned off the light and went into the kitchen. When she opened the fridge, the smell of something sour hit her. Ignoring it, she pulled a huge jug of milk from the top shelf and poured some into a glass, then turned off the kitchen light and sat on the window seat sipping the milk and wondering what to do. *What would Mum have done?* She wanted to phone Dan, but it was late. He had been stressed all week. Work stuff seemed to be getting on top of him; he had an urgent matter in court on Monday and needed to spend the weekend preparing for it. This had been good news for Lillian, who had pressed Dan into sitting with her dad for the night so she could go to the party with Sylvia. Len needed help getting out of the wheelchair, and occasionally he had seizures.

Sylvia wondered how Dan had managed tonight with Len's nightly routine. She'd done it a few times herself, when Lillian had things to go to. Len was quiet, but he was kind and had a wicked sense of humour. He'd joke about the pills he had to take with dinner that made his arms feel like liquorice and his head go fuzzy. Then he'd joke about the whisky he wasn't meant to be drinking on top of it, which all added to the difficulty of getting him out of the wheelchair and onto the bed when the time came. Sylvia didn't mind sitting with him. He was a good listener and he didn't waste time feeling sorry for himself.

Sylvia settled into the soft surface of the old window seat. She put a cushion behind her head and lay back, resting her eyes. Annabelle would be all right. She was just wanting to grow up too fast. That was all. She saw what Sylvia had with Dan and she wanted that too. When Dan slung his arm around Sylvia and drew her close – if they were washing up in the kitchen, or mucking around in the dairy helping to milk the cows at the weekend – Annabelle looked so wistful. She was like a puppy dog wanting to join in with its master. She adored Dan. It was sweet that she was so devoted to him.

Sylvia let herself relax. She wished Dan was here, holding her. He had been a bit grumpy this afternoon, she had noticed. He was busy and really didn't have the time to go and sit with Len, but he could squeeze in some work over there, and he wouldn't refuse Lillian. They were old friends as much as work colleagues.

She noticed the occasional set of headlights along the main road in the distance as they curved around the headland towards Sisters Cove. It was so quiet here; so removed from the world. One day she would travel. She hoped she could persuade Dan to go with her, but he seemed to want to stay around here, practise law, settle down. She knew she could change his mind.

She let her eyelids drop closed, and as she was drifting off, she had a fleeting thought. Perhaps Annabelle had told Dan her plans for tonight. Dan had been sitting at their kitchen table with her dad, finishing his cup of tea, when she and Lillian had left for the party. Annabelle had been dancing around the kitchen, chattering about something of little importance. *Perhaps Dan will know where she is.* Her eyes were heavy and her mind was thick from the wine.

Sylvia must have been asleep for a while when the crunch of tyres and headlights sweeping through the kitchen window woke her. Her neck was stiff and her mouth was parched. She straightened up and looked outside, rubbing at her eyes. The moon had emerged from behind the blanket of clouds and she could see that the car that had pulled up was Dan's. The headlights went out and she was momentarily blinded in the blackness.

She got up and crossed the kitchen to the front door. She wasn't sure what stopped her from going outside to meet him. Perhaps it was the cold that had set in during the afternoon and plummeted further while she was at the party. She was shivering in her jumpsuit, even though it was still late summer. She stood at the window inside the closed-in porch that faced the driveway. As her eyes adjusted, she could see Dan's silhouette in the driver's seat. The rain had stopped and the moon was bathing everything outside in a deep navy-black light. Another figure was sitting in the passenger seat. Waves of hair were silhouetted around her shoulders, and Sylvia could see it was definitely a girl. They were facing each other. Talking. She moved closer to the hat stand that was obscuring her view and ducked in behind it, leaning against a bed of coats.

Suddenly Dan leaned over and took the girl into his arms. Sylvia's stomach plummeted. *No.* After a minute, he straightened up, but they sat in the car for another five minutes or more. Sylvia lost track of time. She was cold, transfixed, turned to stone. What were they talking about? After a while, Dan leaned over again and the two heads came together – a terrible, faithless silhouette. Dan sat back after a moment and raised his hand to the girl's face, caressing it, touching her. Sylvia wanted to scream.

Without warning, he sat up. The girl opened her door a crack and the interior light came on. Sylvia thought her eyes must be deceiving her. She stared, but it was as if she was watching a film. It was a joke, surely? Annabelle swivelled and got out of the car. Dan stood too, but stopped at his door and said something that Sylvia couldn't hear. She stepped backwards, and the hat stand swayed madly. She grabbed at it, righting herself, then stumbled into the kitchen. Her whole body was shaking. As she headed towards the hallway, hot, angry disbelief was pulsing through her head. *How dare they? How could they? Cowardly, treacherous bastard!* And with her sister. Her own sister!

She heard the latch move on the front door. Her chest swelled with the enormity of the betrayal. She leaned on the dining table for support. Annabelle hadn't turned on the light. She must have been hoping to sneak back in without waking anyone. Above the pounding of her heart, Sylvia could make out soft footfalls, and saw a silhouette against the window in the moonlight.

'You little slut!' The words came out like hissing bullets.

Annabelle froze.

'Sylv—'

'Don't!'

'Syl, I—'

'How *could* you? I've been sitting here for hours, worrying about whether you'd driven off a cliff with Eadie, and then I…' Sylvia felt a rush of pain.

'Dan was just driving me home—'

'If you say one more word about Dan, I swear, I will strangle you with my own hands.' Sylvia felt herself becoming completely calm. The white-hot anger was bubbling beneath a blade of perfect clarity. She was now the carer, the mother. She was supposed to teach Annabelle right from wrong. She had failed, but so had Annabelle. She couldn't think about Dan now.

'Please, Syl.' A sob escaped from Annabelle, echoing in the night-time quiet.

Sylvia turned on the hallway light. Tears were running down Annabelle's face. She was flushed and dishevelled. Of course she was. And she was wearing Sylvia's favourite platform shoes. *Little slut.*

Annabelle put her fingers to her eyes to shield them. She spoke in a whimper. 'Don't be angry at me. Please, Sylvia, I didn't mean—'

'Go to bed.' Sylvia's voice was icy. 'We will never speak of this. Do you hear me, Anna? We will never, *ever* speak of this again.'

Sylvia dragged herself out of the distant memory. It was as clear as cut glass. Now, Annabelle was still bent forward on the couch, looking at the floor. Sylvia sat down in the patchwork armchair, her head spinning.

'Annabelle, are you all right?'

Annabelle looked past Sylvia, to the wood stove. Her face was vacant. Her make-up was ruined, and black smudges pooled in the creases under her eyes. She's aged, thought Sylvia. Annabelle was fifty-eight, but strangers usually guessed her to be early fifties. Tonight, though, she looked like an old woman.

Annabelle fixed her eyes on Sylvia. They were a piercing blue. There was something in them that made Sylvia blanch. A steely determination. Despite her blotchy skin and the mess of her face, there was something in the way she looked at Sylvia that cut into her soul.

'Anna, I'm sorry. It's unforgiv—'

'No.'

What did that mean? Sylvia *needed* to make this right. The past didn't excuse what she was doing with Dan. Nothing excused what she was doing. She needed to let her sister know that she was sorry. That she would go away. That she had no place in this town.

'Anna, please, I know—'

'I have a lump,' said Annabelle.

'What?'

'In my breast. The doctor seems to think it's cancer.'

'No. That's awful… That's—'

'And I need some of your herbs. Some powders or whatever. I came to find out if you have something that might help.'

'Anna, if you saw—'

'Yes. I saw the doctor. She said I needed to go to the breast clinic for the tests. And I will. But I thought you might have something herbal, maybe something from that Ayurveda thing you talk about.'

Sylvia stared at her, mute.

'Well, do you?'

'I suppose so. But you'd only take them after your other treatment. You need meditation and yoga now. Maybe I can order you some incense and oils, but—'

'Fine. Let me know when they arrive. I need to be getting home. Dan will worry if he gets back from his meeting and I'm not there.' Annabelle caught Sylvia's eyes and held them.

Sylvia forced herself to speak. 'Anna, the ambulance guy… he said you shouldn't drive.'

Annabelle stood up. She wobbled slightly and steadied herself on the edge of the couch.

'I'm fine.'

Sylvia stood too, but Annabelle held up her hand.

'No need to see me out. I have my phone for a torch.' She lifted her chin and walked towards the door. She opened it, letting the cool of the night air blow into the house. 'I'll see you soon. For the oils or whatever.'

'Okay,' said Sylvia.

'And Sylvia, please don't talk about what's gone on tonight. I couldn't bear it.'

Sylvia felt the guilt spreading hotly through her stomach.

On the porch, Annabelle turned back. 'You've probably forgotten what it's like to live in a small town. But I've lived here all my life. If you tell people about my little… episodes,' she paused and took a deep breath, and her voice wavered, 'it will make things difficult. For ever. It wouldn't be good for Dan either. And I won't let anything bad happen to him. He's my husband, Sylvia. If you talk about this, any of…' – she glanced back into the house, her eyes landing on the bedroom door – 'this, it could ruin us. Do you understand?'

Sylvia looked down at the ground, framing her next words.

'Sylvia, did you hear what I said?'

She opened her mouth to speak, but Annabelle cut her off.

'Be careful or you'll ruin everything.'

CHAPTER THIRTEEN

Willa

Willa sipped her coffee and looked out through the window at the children's playground at the top of the beach. A trio of children were circling each other at the base of the slide, running and ducking in a game of catch. She had started coming to the surf club coffee shop in the mornings. It was energising. She could sit and watch people and enjoy being a stranger, without having to worry that people might want to talk to her.

Later in the morning, the Sisters Cove surf lifesavers would come out of the shed at the other end of the building and walk down to their seats between the swimming flags. The fire-engine red and canary yellow of their uniforms contrasted beautifully with the perfect blue of the water and the powder-white sand. It was ridiculous, really, just how beautiful this place was. It was a crime that there were so few swimmers or sailboarders. Although, to be fair, the water was frigid.

Yesterday, for some reason she couldn't fathom, Willa had bought a swimsuit at the local boutique. It was hot pink with green stars on it – not one she would ever have chosen if there had been options. The lady in the boutique had been thrilled to have a sale.

'Gorgeous! I adore that costume. Going for a swim?'

'Yes,' said Willa.

'At Sisters?'

'Yes, I'm staying there,' said Willa.

'Brilliant!' said the woman. 'I hope you've got a wetsuit. You'll freeze to death if you don't!' She delivered the warning with irritating glee.

'I'll have to manage without one, I'm afraid,' said Willa.

'Good luck with that.' The woman shook her head smugly. 'Those waters are straight from Antarctica.'

Willa had left the shop nursing a grudge that she'd spent a small fortune on the world's ugliest bathing suit, and a renewed resolve to use it. Esme would have. But later, when she had braved the water, she realised the woman had been right. She had inched forward until the water was lapping painfully at her thighs, and when she dived under, she'd been rewarded with an immediate splitting headache and total body numbness.

Now she took another bite of her croissant and opened up her laptop. Despite the pain at the time, she wondered if the swim yesterday had done something to her metabolism. She felt more alive today, as if the water had woken her, washed away the cobwebs in her mind. She clicked on the airline booking site. She should go home. She missed Hamish and Hugo. And the anniversary was coming up. She looked out of the window again at the sparkling ocean, and sighed. The second anniversary of Esme's death had been a dark cloud hovering over her since Christmas. But now, in this perfect place, it felt like it might be a day she could manage.

She closed down the booking site and looked across at the barista, who was frothing coffee for a customer, the machine giving off a buzzing background whine.

A tanned, energetic-looking man in his fifties smiled at her from a neighbouring table. He had been here every morning for coffee too, and earlier she had spied him getting a paddle board out of one of the colourful beach huts that lined the shore. She wondered what his story was. A scientist? A retired business magnate? Sad and single since his wife had left him to find herself? She smiled back at him and wondered if he too was avoiding the hard bits of his life by coming here.

There were boxes and boxes in The Old Chapel that she hadn't dared to look in. They had all been left to her. The entire life of a woman she didn't know had been gifted to her. Perhaps she was meant to know something about this woman. Perhaps looking in the boxes was something she was supposed to do. It was like standing on the edge of a cliff strapped to a hang-glider, even though you'd never wanted to fly. Some idiot had given you a gift voucher for an extreme experience, and here you were, being told to step off a cliff. *No. No thank you! What if I plummet to the ground in some remote gully and they can't locate my remains?*

She sighed. What would her mother have said? *Stop avoiding it and get moving*, probably. But what if she *did* find out that Lillian was her birth mother, and then felt some sort of obligation to find the rest of her blood family? What would that mean? Perhaps it was what was stopping her from opening the boxes of paperwork. The idea of hurting someone. The memory of her parents.

'Hi, Willa.'

Willa jumped in her seat. Indigo was grinning at her. She was wearing denim overalls over a black T-shirt and her hair sat in two long, messy pigtails beneath her ears. Willa noticed that her arms were toned and lovely. Beneath the sloppy outfit, she probably had a beautiful figure.

'Indigo. Hi.'

'Can I join you?' asked Indigo. Without waiting, she sat down on the couch opposite Willa, and took a sip from the reusable coffee cup she was carrying.

'Sure. Of course,' said Willa. 'What are you up to today?'

'I'm off to my nannying job, unfortunately,' said Indigo. She raised her eyebrows.

'Why unfortunately?' asked Willa.

'The little boys are cute, but the mother's mental. Last week she sacked me when I got the nappy bucket and the bread bucket mixed up. Why would she buy the same colour buckets? It's just dumb.' Indigo shook her head.

'I'm not sure I follow,' said Willa.

Indigo sighed. 'Long story, but this woman is a try-hard hippy. Moved here to be organic and away from commercialism. Which is funny, because she's actually rich and drives a brand-new Tesla. But she tries to make herself feel less guilty by making her own bread.' She took another sip of her coffee. 'Anyway, so she kneads the bread dough in one of those huge wide soft plastic buckets. She also doesn't use disposable nappies, so the cloth nappies get soaked in an identical bucket. Apparently I mixed up the poo bucket and the dough bucket last time. She went tribal on me.'

'Tribal?'

'Super-angry.'

'Oh dear,' said Willa, smiling.

'But she rang and apologised. Asked me to come back. She can't manage those kids on her own. Needs to have a nap in the afternoon 'cos she's so exhausted from growing veggies and making her own soap. I keep telling her there's an organic produce shop down near the co-op.' Indigo grinned again and wriggled her bottom further back into the couch like a child.

Willa smiled. 'Well it's good that you'll have the income, I suppose.'

'The pay's pretty bad compared to my weekend job.'

'Oh, what's that?'

Indigo smiled uncertainly. 'I'm a dancer.'

'Really?' said Willa. 'And that pays well?'

'Yeah, well, the kind I do anyway. If the tips are good.' Indigo leaned forward, her voice low. 'I'm a pole dancer. At a men's club.'

'Wow,' said Willa. Her mind went into freeze-frame. *Don't judge, face neutral, open your mind.* 'How interesting.'

'I don't usually tell people. Mum thinks I teach fitness classes when I'm in Launceston. I do sometimes. Pole classes at the gym. It's pretty mainstream now.'

'I didn't realise that,' said Willa. She smiled as her initial surprise gave way to curiosity. 'So, are you also a… stripper? I mean, is the pole dancing done naked?'

'Sort of, to a point.'

'Is it… all right?' asked Willa.

Indigo chewed her lip. 'There's a darker side. Most nights there's at least one or two dickheads to deal with. They're not allowed to touch us, but try telling them that. They're like, "why have you got your bum out if you don't want it slapped?" Which makes my head explode sometimes. But usually it's fine.'

Willa asked, 'Why haven't you told your mum?'

'Dunno. She's funny sometimes. Open-minded, until it comes to me, then she gets all weird about things.'

Willa had some empathy for Sylvia. Most mothers would be terrified at the idea of men leering at their daughter as she writhed semi-naked around a pole for tips.

'So anyway, how about you? What are you doing today?' asked Indigo.

'I'm not sure,' said Willa, dragging herself away from the bizarre pole-writhing image. 'I was thinking of booking my flight home, but maybe I'm not ready.'

'I thought you were going to stay until you found out about whether Lillian was your birth mum. Or have you already worked it out?'

'No.' Willa looked down at her hands. 'I'm really tempted to go through the rest of the boxes, but something is stopping me.' She wondered why she was burdening Indigo with this.

'You're amazing,' said Indigo. 'I would have dug through every last scrap of paper by now. If she left it all in the house for you, there must have been a reason. Don't you want to know what it is?'

'Not really,' said Willa.

Indigo was staring at her, head cocked, a puzzled expression on her face.

'Well, maybe I do,' said Willa, 'but what if she *was* my mother? I keep feeling really angry about that. What if she was, and she was so gutless that she didn't want to meet me in real life? She knew I would have had questions, but she decided to disrupt my life when she was going to be completely unavailable to ask her things. That just feels like something a really selfish person would do.'

'You reckon?' said Indigo. 'I dunno. In my experience, most people are just a bit confused.'

'Sorry,' said Willa. 'She was your godmother, I know. I feel terrible for thinking those things. And you're probably right. I'm sure she was a really lovely person who had all sorts of reasons for doing what she did. It wouldn't have been her fault, and it must have been so awful for her to have to give up her baby girl.' Willa felt tears threatening at the back of her eyes, and focused hard on sucking her lips against her teeth to distract herself.

'Yeah.' Indigo sat back and frowned, her face a study in fierce contemplation. 'That's what Mum said.'

'Sylvia? You told her?'

'Yeah. I mean, at first she said Lillian didn't have a baby. But then she sort of said that if there *was* a baby, she couldn't have kept it. So I don't know – but something went on that she doesn't want to talk about.'

'Annabelle too,' said Willa, staring out of the window again.

'What?'

'Oh.' Willa shook her head. 'Probably nothing. Annabelle... she's lovely, isn't she?'

'Yeah. She's a good 'un. When she found out I was stripping, she was totally awesome. Just worried about me, but not judgy or anything.'

'How did she find out?'

Indigo raised her eyebrows. 'Dan told her that one of his friends saw me.' She raised her fingers into quotation marks around the word 'friends'.

'Oh,' said Willa.

'He came into the club one night. You should have seen his face when he spotted me. I almost wet myself laughing.'

'Oh dear,' said Willa, slotting the information about Dan into her mental file.

'Anyway, I'm due up at Merrivale after my babysitting to help her in the garden. She's getting frantic about this open garden thing for the festival that she's hosting in a couple of weeks.'

'Perhaps I can come and help you out,' said Willa. 'I've always thought I'd like to learn to be a gardener, but I was caught up with work and kids.'

'What sort of work do you do?' asked Indigo.

'I'm an event planner,' said Willa.

Indigo looked at her blankly.

'You know, organising big expos and product launches, corporate gatherings, that sort of thing. Although I haven't worked since my daughter died.'

Indigo's face dropped. Willa kept talking to smooth over the awkward pause.

'It's been two years nearly now, so I was thinking perhaps I might look for work again soon.'

'Oh, that's totally bad. Sorry, Willa – about your daughter,' said Indigo.

'Thank you.'

'Do you want to talk about it?'

Willa was surprised by the question. Nobody had ever asked her that before. Well, nobody apart from Dr Lee, and he was paid to ask her, so that didn't count. People already knew what happened – they'd heard a hundred different versions. There had been an inquest last year. And for those who hadn't known before, the coroner's findings had been reported in the media. It was so awful that nobody ever imagined she would actually *want* to talk about it.

'I mean, you don't have to,' said Indigo, looking straight at her. It was an interested sort of look. Indigo seemed to exist halfway between a child and a wise old woman, with her sweet, open face and serious eyes.

No, thought Willa, I don't really want to talk about it. But maybe I should. Since you asked, and I can be with Esme for a few minutes. So… maybe I do.

'She was at a party,' she said. 'It was her first proper party.' Willa stared off at the horizon. The beach was so perfect. Esme would have had so much fun dipping her feet in the water here. She wouldn't have cared about the cold. 'I'd checked with her friend's mother. Who would be there? Would boys be coming? Were they supervising actively? What time should I collect her and so on.'

She looked back at Indigo with a small smile. 'Esme was so sensible. It didn't occur to me that she'd be in any danger. We'd talked about things to be careful of, and she really didn't seem interested in the idea of alcohol or sex or drugs. In reality, I thought those things were still years into the future, but the books said to talk about them, so we had. We did.'

Willa had approached parenting as if it were an ongoing event, critical to her core business success. She planned, coordinated, read all the latest articles as her children changed stages. She monitored Hamish and Esme's social media and made sure they had open lines of communication. She was a particularly involved, very protective mother. Her own mother had thought she was *too* involved.

Willa realised she had been silent for a while. She was staring into space, still surprised that she was confiding in Indigo.

'What happened?' asked Indigo. She put her empty KeepCup on the table and was leaning forward, her hands between her knees.

'The girls were drinking a sweet cider-type drink very early on at the party. One of them smuggled it in. It was really strong. Almost the strength of vodka. But it tasted like cordial. A couple of them drank a lot, including Esme.' Willa felt a buzz of the old anger coming back. Anger at the parents of the party girl, who were inside the house with their friends, drinking, listening to music and joking about what the teenagers might be getting up to downstairs. Anger at the girl's brother who had bought the alcohol. Anger – pure white-hot *rage* – at Esme's friends for leaving her alone. The lovely, smart girls that Willa had known since they were toddlers. Girls she had loved.

'Sounds like lots of parties I went to when I was a teenager,' said Indigo.

'Esme felt sick and tried to call me, but I didn't hear my phone. She left me a message asking me to come and get her. We had a deal, that if she ever got into trouble and needed me, she should call and I would come straight away and not ask questions. I would just sort out whatever happened and nobody would get into trouble. We once heard a parenting expert talking about how important that was.' Willa felt her energy sagging. The noises in the café were receding into the background, and all she could focus on were the leaves on the potted succulent on the coffee table in front of her.

'That was smart,' said Indigo, and Willa realised the girl had been waiting patiently for the end of the story.

She reached across and pulled a little piece off the plant and dug her nail into the smooth green leaf. It left a dark, satisfying moon-shaped mark.

'It was still quite early in the night, so I wasn't expecting her to call until later. I'd forgotten to turn my phone volume up.'

'Willa, you can't blame yourself for that.'

Willa turned her mouth up at the corners, just a fraction: *thank you, but there's no need to try to make me feel better. I can and I do blame myself.*

'After that, she went into someone's bedroom to lie down, and she vomited. None of her friends checked on her. Not until the end of the night.' Willa's head was still spinning about that. 'She'd choked. Suffocated.'

'I'm so sorry, Willa.'

'Yes. Me too.' She dug her nail into the leaf over and over until it was sticky green pulp in her fingers. 'She was gorgeous. Sometimes it floors me – that I'll never see her again. It hurts so much that sometimes I forget to breathe.'

They sat in silence for a while, soaking up the chatter of the café patrons around them. The little girl from a table across the room wandered across, and hesitated before reaching for a sugar packet from the tumbler on their table and depositing her half-eaten Vegemite sandwich in return. Willa guessed she was about three years old. They smiled at her, then Indigo spoke. 'You're really strong, Willa. If you've survived that, I bet you can survive anything.'

Willa didn't reply. She leaned over and put the sandwich remnant onto a serviette and handed it back to the child. 'That looks yummy. My little girl liked Vegemite sandwiches too.'

The girl looked away shyly; then, after a moment, she looked back and smiled, and took the sandwich before toddling back to her table.

Willa stood up and Indigo came around the table and lifted her into a huge hug. Willa flinched, then sagged as the remaining energy in her body evaporated. She let herself be hugged. It was quite nice. Indigo was nice.

'Well, I'd better get going,' said Willa, stepping back. 'I think I'll go to Lillian's house. My house, I suppose now,' she added, wryly. 'There are things I guess I should know. Some boxes to consider.'

'Want me to come with you?' asked Indigo.

'No, it's fine. It's my closet. My skeletons. I can deal with them. I'm quite practised.'

They both gave a little chuckle, which seemed inappropriate but it made Willa feel much better. She would look in the boxes. And then she would put this mystery to bed. She really needed to be getting back to Oxford, but she might as well find out the truth before she left.

CHAPTER FOURTEEN

Annabelle

1977

Annabelle stared through the window. Sylvia was getting into the passenger seat of the old Kingswood. Her bright-yellow jumpsuit was jarring against the mucky red-brown of the driveway and the low grey sky. Lillian started the car, and as it retreated down the driveway, Annabelle rubbed absently at the teacup with the dish towel. Drizzle was sliding down the window pane.

Why had Sylvia been such a toad about not wanting her to go roller skating with Eadie tonight? Dad was fine on his own and Annabelle didn't have much homework to do over the weekend. Sylvia was always bossier when other people were around, as if she was acting out of a handbook about how to be a good mother, even though she wasn't the mother.

At the table, Dan and her dad were talking about the rain, and how the cows might not get back over the river if they had another big downpour. Dad was due down at the dairy soon to start the second milking, and Sylvia had instructed Annabelle to make sure she had his tea ready at 6.30 on the dot, because he was still feeling a bit off colour after last week's flu.

'How about a top-up, love?' he said. He was holding out his mug.

Annabelle lifted the woollen cosy off the teapot and brought it over to the table. She refilled her dad's mug and felt guilty as she looked at the strain around his eyes. Last time they'd had big rains there was so much mud that lots of the cows got mastitis and their milk production slowed and Dad had been worried about the bills. She hoped it wouldn't be like that again.

'Thanks, love.'

'Want another one, Dan?' she asked.

'No. I'm okay.' Dan grinned at her and Annabelle felt her heart flutter. Why did Sylvia get to have him? He was the nicest person Annabelle knew, apart from her dad. The weather was cool this afternoon, and Dan was wearing a patterned blue shirt that hugged his chest. There was a zip at the front, pulled down just enough so that Annabelle could see pleasing little swirls of his chest hair. She noticed how his jaw moved when he spoke to her dad, and how his sideburns curved perfectly under his cheekbones and were just a shade lighter than the shaggy mop of hair that curled around the base of his neck.

'What are you up to tonight, little Belle?' He half turned his chair to include her in the conversation. He was thoughtful like that. She felt her neck getting warm with happiness.

'Nothing. I can help you if you like,' she said. The thought had only just occurred to her. Dan had been railroaded by Lillian into sitting with Len tonight. But he had just finished telling Dad how busy he was at work, and how he didn't really have time to be sitting around minding Len. She *could* help him. She could get Len's dinner and his pills and whatever else he needed. Len was nice. Last time Annabelle had gone to visit Lillian, Len had started teaching her how to play gin rummy. She could bring her cards! It would be no trouble at all to sit with Len and Dan.

'No need. I'll be right,' said Dan.

'Please? I want to. Dad, that'd be all right, wouldn't it? Len was teaching me to play cards a couple of weeks ago. He'd love it if I came too.'

'I don't mind, love. Whatever suits Dan. But only if he can drop you home later.'

'Dan? Can I?' Annabelle was bouncing up and down on her toes, thrumming with excitement. 'Pleeaasse! I'll do all the boring bits. Promise!'

'Jeez. How could I refuse that offer?' said Dan. He was shaking his head, but his eyes crinkled. Then he laughed, and Annabelle twirled around the kitchen, her short checked skirt flapping against her legs.

'You'd better get ready, though, 'cos I'm going to drive home now to get some files sorted out before I head across to Len. Lil said he's fine for a couple of hours on his own, but it'll be time to check in on him soon.'

'Off you go then, love,' said her dad. 'And take a jumper. It's going to come in cold, I think. I've got to ring Ray Crassock about the fences before I go down to the dairy, so I'll say goodbye now, Dan.' He got up from the table and picked up the phone cradle.

Annabelle felt herself smiling, grinning. She bounced across to him and gave him a hug.

'Go on with you, girly,' he said gruffly as he slid the plastic toggle up from the bottom of the Teledex and pushed the button. He pretended to shoo Annabelle away, but she saw the ghost of a smile on his lips.

'Quick sticks then, Belle,' said Dan. 'I'll wait for you in the car.'

'Okay.' Annabelle pelted up the hallway and into her room. She grabbed a bag from inside her cupboard and threw in a pack of playing cards and a cardigan. At the mirror, she stopped and grabbed her hairbrush, running it through her hair in thick swiping motions. She looked at herself again, then frowned and ripped off her old shirt and ran into Sylvia's room. In the cupboard, she flicked through the hanging clothes, hesitating before lifting up the olive-green top that Sylvia had bought last year in Myer when they went to Launceston. It was Sylvia's best top, but she would never know. She flicked it off the hanger and pushed her arms into the sleeves, then buttoned it up, leaving the top two buttons undone. She knew it looked better on her than on Sylvia. Green was her colour, and her bust was much bigger than her sister's.

As she closed the cupboard, she noticed that Sylvia had left her make-up out on the dressing table. She picked up the pale-blue eyeshadow and squinted into the tiny mirror on the ledge. She rubbed a little eyeshadow across her lids with the pad of her finger, then picked up the mascara and swished the brush carefully against her lashes before replacing them both exactly where she had found them. As she was leaving, she spotted Sylvia's brown leather platform wedges lined up neatly against the wall with her other shoes. She took a deep breath, then pulled off her own sandals and wiggled her feet into the platforms, thrilled at the sight of her toes peeping out elegantly at the front. She wobbled as she let go of the bed. They were so high. She had an immediate feeling of being older, glamorous.

She picked up her bag and walked carefully into the hallway, stopping in front of the full-length mirror in the hall. Her lips parted in wonder, and she felt a shiver run through her. The green top strained across her breasts, her cleavage on perfect display between the two wing-like lapels. She leaned forward, entranced by the effect of the mascara. Her eyes looked huge and pretty. Although she wasn't tall, the shoes made her legs look longer, thinner. And her new checked skirt was the absolute best. Sylvia's snipes about it being too short were just jealousy. She ran both hands through the waves of her hair, and as it settled across her shoulders and spilled down onto her chest, she took another deep breath and considered the entire effect. Gorgeous.

As Annabelle walked down the hall, mindful of each footstep in the heavy, awkward shoes, she felt something changing inside her. She would be sixteen next week, and she was no longer a child. Lately she had been noticing the looks the boys at school gave her. And men in town, too. Appreciative, knowing looks. She understood that she was pretty, but there was something else in the way they stared at her, and in her most private, restless moments, when she allowed herself to think about what it might be like to kiss a boy deeply, or to go even further, she sensed that what she had – what was within her – was something profound and intense. Something that not everybody had. It would be unthinkable to ever voice it, or to even think of it in the same universe as when she longed for one last hug from her mum, or massaged her poor dad's shoulders at night, or fought with Sylvia about doing chores, but if she was being honest with herself, in those small snippets of the night-time as she drifted off into the simmering thickness of sleep, she wondered if what she possessed innately, in the way she smiled and talked and walked, was something *sexual*.

She opened the door of Dan's car and slid into the front seat, staring straight ahead.

'Let's get going,' he said.

Annabelle darted a look in his direction and their eyes met for one brief, excruciating second. She saw surprise and wariness, and then, in the final millisecond before he let the clutch out and took off down the dirt driveway, something else. She wondered, as she squeezed her eyes shut against the thought, if it might have been regret.

The silence, except for the rumble as the car navigated the uneven driveway, and the sound of the indicator as they reached the main road, was too much for Annabelle to bear. 'Can you play gin rummy, Dan?'

'Yep.'

'Maybe we can play later,' she said. They turned onto the main road and headed towards Sisters Cove.

'Maybe. I've got heaps of work to do before Monday, though. A big case starting in court. Maybe you and Len can play.'

'Oh. Okay. I can stay there on my own if you need to go back to your place and work.' She flushed with the knowledge that she'd overstepped the boundaries with the shoes and the make-up. She could feel him retreating from her, when all she wanted was to be helpful.

They drove the rest of the way to Dan's house without either of them speaking, Annabelle clutching her bag against her chest. She felt the silence like a heavy cloak. When they turned off the main road and headed towards the lighthouse, she spotted the lush green copse of old trees that surrounded Merrivale, just across the paddocks. To Annabelle, the big, beautiful house was the closest thing she knew to a mansion, except it wasn't made of stone like the ones in her mum's old English magazines. She wondered how rich Dan's Uncle Andrew and Aunt Constance were.

They pulled up out the front of Dan's house and he said, 'Wait here. Back in a tick.'

He dashed into the little orange brick building. The house block was bare apart from some patchy grass and a single old sycamore tree that stretched across the yard towards the clothes line. Sylvia had told her that the house was part of the Merrivale estate and that Dan rented it cheaply from his uncle. She looked around. In the paddock next to her, neat rows of bushy green potato crops extended out towards the deep green-grey of the ocean beyond the cliff. The crop was starting to brown off in patches, signalling that the potatoes were only a month or two from picking time. Sylvia had climbed through the fence and dug out a few when they'd had a barbecue here after Christmas, but they were small and pale then, not ready for proper harvesting.

Annabelle was distracted by a swirl of storm clouds moving across the sky. She jumped as Dan opened the car door and dumped a cardboard box on the back seat.

'We won't walk,' he said. 'Those shoes you're wearing won't like it, and the rain's coming back, I reckon.'

He started the ignition and backed out. Within a minute, they had passed the entrance to Merrivale, marked by an avenue of old trees. Dan drove for another fifty metres and swung the car into the driveway of The Old Chapel, opposite the big house.

Annabelle opened the car door and put her feet carefully on the muddy ground. The mud squelched thickly and her heart sank as it oozed up the side of Sylvia's shoes. She avoided looking at Dan in case he sensed her shame, her stupidity.

Dan gave two loud knocks on the door of The Old Chapel, then opened it. She hurried to follow him.

'Len?'

'G'day, Dan.'

Annabelle wiped her shoes on the mat and followed Dan inside. She was pleased to see Len's face light up when he saw her. He took another drag of his cigarette before speaking.

'Hello, Annabelle pet. How did I get so lucky?'

'Annabelle needed entertaining,' said Dan.

'Hi, Len. Thought you could give me a game of rummy.'

Len balanced the cigarette between his fingers and deftly wheeled his chair out of the little kitchen with the heels of his hands.

'Not unless you want to be whopped,' he said, winking.

Annabelle put her bag on the bottom tray of a wooden drinks trolley, out of the way of Len's wheelchair. On the top shelf of the trolley sat a decanter of whisky and two dirty-looking glasses. Behind it was the free-standing candlestick-style ashtray Lillian had given Len for Christmas. It was exactly the right height for him in his chair. The base was made of some kind of heavy stone so he couldn't easily knock it over. He tapped his cigarette on it.

'Brought a bit of work along,' said Dan, putting his box of files on the tiny dinner table. 'Annabelle reckons she'll keep you entertained, though, so I might head home for a bit later if she's going to chat your ear off.'

'Dan! I will not,' said Annabelle. She smiled nervously at Len.

Len laughed. 'No worries, love, it'll make a nice change. Lillian's always at those paintings after work. Barely get a word out of her these days.'

'Righto,' said Dan. 'Let's see what the boss has left us for tea.' He walked into the kitchen area, and Annabelle followed. This was her chance to make good. On top of the cooker there was a pot with peeled potatoes and carrots floating in some water, waiting to be boiled. On a tin plate there were four lamb chops sitting out. Dan picked up the plate and moved it across to the cooker.

'You can have one of my chops, pet,' Len told Annabelle.' And there's some peas in the fridge that Lil picked yesterday. We'll do some of them. Peel another few spuds, will you?' He wheeled himself across to the trolley and poured a Scotch that filled up nearly half the glass.

'Len, Lil told me you're not to have that before your pills and dinner,' said Dan, pretending to be stern. 'And then only half a nip.'

'Go on with ya,' said Len. 'This is my chance to have a good night.' He brought the glass to his lips and closed his eyes as he sipped.

'That daughter of yours does know how to keep us boys in line, I'll give her that,' said Dan. He bent down beneath the sink and pulled out two dirty potatoes from a basket, handing them to Annabelle. 'You said you'd do the boring bits.'

While Annabelle cooked the dinner, Dan went to the table and started going through his papers. After they'd eaten, and Dan had made sure Len had taken all his pills, she and Len sat watching the television and Dan carried on working. Len began nodding off, so Dan wheeled him into the bedroom. Annabelle could hear the faint murmur of voices. She wondered how Dan was getting him into bed and how he'd use the toilet, but she was too scared to ask. She did the washing-up and left the dishes to drain on the rack.

The night had turned cold, so Dan had lit the little woodburner in the corner of the room and it warmed the kitchen area nicely. Eventually he came out of the bedroom.

'You happy to be here for a couple of hours if I head home to finish some work?'

'Okay,' said Annabelle.

'Lil said he shouldn't need anything, but maybe pop your head in now and again, just to check he's okay. He hasn't had an episode for a few months, but you never know, I s'pose.'

'An episode?'

'An epileptic fit. From the head injury when the tractor rolled.'

An awful image of Len formed in Annabelle's mind; his face contorted, mouth frothing.

'Oh, okay,' she said. 'What if he does, though?'

Dan pointed to a padded wooden spoon in a cup on the bench. 'You put him on his side and stick that in his mouth so he doesn't bite his tongue. Then run and get me. Or get Constance, she's closer. They don't have a phone here, so you could use hers to call me.'

'Oh,' said Annabelle.

'Don't worry. It won't happen.'

Annabelle stood straighter. She was almost grown up. Of course she could do it. It was just that she felt a bit terrified at the idea, now that she was faced with being on her own. She saw Dan glance downwards. Maybe he was appreciating her cleavage. The thought made her happy even though it shouldn't.

He looked away. 'Just say if you need me to stay.'

'No, I can do it.'

He picked up his files. 'Good. I'm snowed under.'

'Dan, what if he needs to go to the toilet?'

'He's got his little urinal thing next to the bed. He'll be all right on his own with that.'

'Oh, okay.'

'I'll be back in a couple of hours, or when I see Lil's headlights go past my place. I'll drop you home.'

'Thanks.'

Annabelle watched him hurry to the car. The rain had started again, just lightly, and the day was finally receding into twilight. The summer evenings were long, and usually Annabelle loved them, but tonight the fading light felt like a betrayal. She looked down at Sylvia's shoes, the sides still caked with mud, and knew she'd have to work hard to clean them tonight before she went home.

Out the window, Dan's car had slowed outside the Merrivale gardens. A tall man in a black raincoat was holding a dog on a leash; a boxer she thought, but she didn't know if that was right. The hood of the raincoat was obscuring the man's face. Dan was talking to him. It must be his Uncle Andrew.

Annabelle had spoken to Andrew Broadhurst once, when she'd stopped in at the law firm where Lillian and Dan worked with him on her way home from school. She'd been there to pick up an envelope for her dad. Andrew had come out of his office while she and Lillian had been talking, and had made a special effort to come over and say hello. He looked like a film star – like her mum's favourite actor, Cary Grant, from the old films in black and white.

He'd smiled at her that day, when Lillian had introduced them. Of course, Annabelle had seen him around town plenty of times over the years – he was hard to miss – but he'd never taken any notice of her until then. He'd been really nice, and Annabelle wished she hadn't been wearing her school uniform, because she'd felt like a kid, and he was such a strong, good-looking man. A proper man. Several people had come in and out of the office while she was there, and it was as if he had this magnetic force around him, where people waited for him to say or do something before they could move. Carol Hines from two years above her at school had just got a job on the reception desk, and she had been almost breathless when he stopped to ask her about a client before heading back into his office. He had given Annabelle a genuine smile before he left, and shaken her hand, saying he was pleased to meet her; he'd looked at her like she was really someone, not just a kid, and inside she had melted.

Annabelle pulled herself out of the memory as the sound of a raised voice penetrated the small gap between the sill and the window. The man in the raincoat wasn't leaning down amicably towards Dan's car window any more. He was posturing, waving his hand, as if he was angry. Annabelle looked around, fearful that Len might wake, though she knew it would be hard to hear the noise from inside the bedroom. She leaned against the window frame and raised the sash another inch. The voices got louder, and the man slammed his fist on the top of Dan's car before striding off down the lane, towards the lighthouse, pulling the dog after him.

Annabelle pondered this exchange for a moment, then she closed the window and went across to the sink and found an old cloth. She bent down and carefully pulled the shoes off her feet and put them on the bench, having an immediate sense of regressing into her smallness, her childish self. She felt her mood deflate. *Blow!* The mud was everywhere. She wetted the cloth and began rubbing at the stains. If she didn't get the shoes back to being perfect, her life wouldn't be worth living.

A loud knock at the door startled her, making her heart jolt. Who would be out here, so far from anywhere? And in this weather? She glanced out of the window. The raincoat man was nearing the far end of the lane, the dog trotting beside him. Perhaps it was Dan's Aunt Constance at the door. Leaving the shoes on the bench, she slipped across the room and opened the door.

'Hello, Annabelle.'

She blanched as the huge young man leaned forward and the smell hit her. His clothes were layered with dirt and the look in his eyes wasn't quite right. He held out his hand and offered her a jar.

'Need to give this to Len.' His voice was nasal, and dragged with the sloppy, unformed movements of his mouth.

'Tippy.' She let out her breath in a rush. She'd always been wary of Tippy, even though Sylvia said he was harmless. She knew he did jobs for Dan and his Uncle Andrew sometimes, and if she ever ran into him, he would stare at her, his mouth hanging open, his head moving in line with her wherever she went. Once he'd left her a scrawled note on muddy paper, almost indecipherable, in the letter box after he'd delivered some honey to her house: *I luv yoo Anabel. Yoo pritee. From Tippy.*

'Honey? Thanks, I'll give it to him,' she said.

'Constance said I gotta put it away for him. Have to come in.'

'Oh,' said Annabelle.

As soon as she stepped back, Annabelle knew she'd done the wrong thing. She was always too nice to people. That was what Sylvia told her. But she never wanted to offend them, and now she'd let a huge, simple-minded man into the house, a man who'd been watching her weirdly for as long as she could remember. As he stepped past her, a sick chill ran down her spine.

Tippy lumbered over to the kitchen and put the honey in the pantry cupboard. Then he turned around and stood with his feet planted apart. She flicked her head around to look back out the door, letting her face scrunch up for a millisecond: *just go, please please please.*

'You're my friend, Annabelle.'

'Thank you, Tippy,' she said. 'You'd better go now. You don't want to wake Len up.'

'He never wakes up at night,' said Tippy.

Fear began to pool in Annabelle's stomach.

'You need to go, Tippy.'

He walked towards her and stopped, his arm pressing up against hers at the doorway. The thick, sour smell of him made her want to gag.

'Please, Annabelle. I just gonna stay for a little while.'

'No, Tippy.' Annabelle put her hand on his arm and nudged him towards the door. Tippy stood like a solid concrete statue. Then he took two steps back into the house.

'We're friends,' he said. He pointed towards the couch. 'We can play.' Annabelle gulped, her mind racing. He reached forward and clasped her arm. 'Please, Annabelle. Won't take long.'

She felt his grip tighten on her arm. Scream, she thought. All I need to do is scream. But when she opened her mouth, no sound would come out.

CHAPTER FIFTEEN

Sylvia

Sylvia sat in the car park of the retirement village, contemplating the fragrant oils for Annabelle that had been sitting on her kitchen bench for two days. She had also dug out the booklets about managing cancer through lifestyle change she'd ordered for Lillian.

Hopefully Annabelle's lump wasn't actually cancer. It could be anything really. Her doshas were clearly out of balance. Aggravated. The trouble was that Annabelle needed a whole-life overhaul, not just herbal remedies and oils. The hormone tablets she was taking were bound to be adding to the problem too.

Sylvia should have been up to Merrivale already to give the oils to her sister. She should be making her a nice pot of kitchari every day too. The lentils would be nourishing for Annabelle's body and soul. But it felt wrong to act like she cared, even though she did. Especially when her own terrible behaviour with Dan was no doubt part of the cause of whatever toxins Annabelle's poor body was dredging up. Sylvia knew that these things were always holistic, and on some deep unconscious level, Annabelle had probably sensed something was awry months ago.

Perhaps it was fear that was stopping Sylvia from taking the oils up to her. Fear of facing up to her own little sister. Yes, that was it, she realised. She was officially a coward. A miserable, fickle, shallow coward. How sad, to discover this about herself at the age of sixty-two.

She sighed. Across the lawn, a woman was wheeling an elderly man out of the front door of the main building. She pushed him along the path until they passed a birdbath surrounded by lavender bushes. Every time she arrived at Annarbee Lodge, Sylvia felt a niggling sort of guilt tapping at her conscience. It was the same as when she occasionally ate bacon or stuffed a plastic container in the rubbish bin when the recycling bin was full. *Be a better person.* But who was counting?

She supposed the guilt about old people stemmed from leaving her father on the farm when she was twenty, just when he needed her support. Leaving him with Annabelle and her wild moods. He was ageing and he had needed her, and she had left. Then she was too poor to afford the flight home for his funeral ten years later. She was barely surviving in an ashram in Israel, getting by on basic rations and meditation. So this was her penance. Old people. They made her squirm with inadequacy. But she refused to run from it, which was probably why she'd agreed to teach this yoga-for-seniors class when they'd asked her. There were plenty of other yoga teachers on the north-west coast. But they had asked her, maybe because her silvery-blonde hair made her less threatening to the class.

Dan had pointed out to her a few weeks ago that technically she was almost old enough to be admitted to Annarbee Lodge herself. Later, in bed, she had tensed her pelvic floor around his penis and he had widened his eyes, and she had said, 'I bet nobody in Annarbee Lodge could do *that*.' He'd laughed and kissed her neck and she had thought: I really am a bad person.

The minor bacon-eating guilt would have been welcome today, though, if it could have replaced the real guilt she'd been feeling since Annabelle had been delivered to her door by the paramedics. It was eating at Sylvia's insides.

Her phone buzzed and Dan's number appeared on the screen. She'd spent the last few days ignoring his calls, but they were coming every few hours now, messages pleading to see her after she had specifically told him not to contact her. She sighed again. *Be real, Sylvia.* Why would he take her seriously this time? She'd always given in before. She was her own worst enemy.

But Dan hadn't been able to hear the conversation she'd had with Annabelle in the living room the other night. So how could he understand that this time, things really did have to change? He hadn't seen the betrayal written in Annabelle's eyes.

A surge of irritation made her answer the phone. 'Stop calling me.'

'Syl, stop avoiding me. I need to see you.'

'No, Dan. No way. It's over. I'll be leaving Tasmania as soon as I get myself sorted.'

'Please don't. I'm leaving Annabelle. I need to be with you.'

'You can't leave her if she's about to start chemotherapy, Dan. That would make you a prize arse.'

'What?'

'Her breast lump. Did they confirm it was cancer?'

'What are you talking about? She hasn't told me about a lump.'

Sylvia hadn't talked to him about Annabelle's lump the other night. When he came out of the bedroom, he'd left with barely a word being spoken.

'Well you should talk to her. And don't call me again.'

'Syl, don't do this. You know as well as I do that we're meant to be together. I'm not taking no for an answer.'

'Bugger off, Dan.'

'Don't speak to me like that,' he said angrily.

'I'm not your wife. You don't get to boss me around.'

'I'd have you as my wife! You know I would. I'd have you between my sheets every night if I could.'

Sylvia cringed. Was it only about the sex for him? How typical. How tedious. 'Well you already have a wife, in case it slipped your mind.'

'You're the one I would have married if you hadn't left. I wouldn't have bloody been in this marriage hell if you hadn't disappeared off the face of the planet. She's a twit, Syl. I know she's your sister, but seriously, the woman is a moron. And she spends my money like it's water! I've been planning to leave for years, but divorce is bloody expensive.'

Sylvia was shocked into silence. Regret wormed through her. How could she have been so stupid? So blind?

'Poor, poor Dan,' she crooned. 'Can't possibly leave his wife in case he has to give up his mansion and his hundred-thousand-dollar car in the property settlement. And how *dare* you talk about my sister like that?' *Idiot.*

'What the hell's the matter with you?'

'I've risked my family for the sake of a mercenary arsehole without an ounce of compassion. Hmm, now let me see, what could possibly be the matter?' Sylvia took a breath. 'I mean it this time, Dan. Don't *ever* ring me again.'

'You can't get rid of me just because you feel like it, Sylvia. You forget what I know about you.'

Sylvia felt the menace leak down the line. She pulled the phone away from her ear and stared at it mutely for a second.

'You're unbelievable,' she said quietly. 'What I did back then was terrible, but if it came out, it would bring you down too.' She ended the call, then in one swift movement got out of the car and slammed the door. She stood, unseeing, in the lush old garden. Fool, she told herself. Silly, weak fool! She felt dumb with surprise, but it should never have surprised her. She shook her head, as if trying to flick off the grimy remnants of the conversation.

She'd seen him like this before. Heard that same threat in his voice. It had kept her awake back then, tossing and turning for nights on end, until she knew she had to leave him. *Leopards don't change their spots, Sylvia. You* know *that.* Why on earth had she trusted him this time?

The wind picked up in the trees ahead of her, a swirling, rushing canopy of movement. She closed her eyes, remembered her decades-old anger at Annabelle after she had stood in the kitchen that night trying to deny she'd been kissing Dan in the car. Then the rage that had burned and built after she had sent Annabelle to her room. The rage at Dan.

It had been after four a.m. when she had finally thrown off the covers, pulled on a coat over her pyjamas and driven the ten minutes to Dan's house at Sisters Cove through the wet black night. As she drove, she listened to the angry voices in her head: the words she would say to him, the excuses he would give, and her answers, ready in return. She pulled up on the deserted road outside his house, surprised that the lights in his living room were blazing.

She walked across the lawn and peered through the window. Dan was dishevelled. He was pacing, ending each small lap of the room at the dining table, which was covered in papers. He sat, then stood, running both hands through his hair in a rough, angry movement. The room was small, so Sylvia – cloaked in the blackness of the starless night – could see him perfectly. Mostly his back was to her, but when he turned and approached the window, her heart skipped. His shirt was mud-flecked and his face and neck had blood smudged down one side. She pulled back, shocked.

After a moment, she stepped towards the front door, knocked quietly, then opened it. She stood in the entry to the living room, and when he saw her, Dan let out a guttural moan.

'Dan?'

'Syl, I'm sorry.'

'You should be. She's my sister!'

He looked at her wild-eyed, uncomprehending. Then he shook his head. 'What? No. Andrew. He's…' He looked away, holding up both bloody hands, staring at them. 'Fuck. I can't believe it came to this.'

Sylvia's anger morphed into fear. 'Dan, what's happened? What have you done?'

She shook her head now to banish the awful, ancient image. Ageing memories, ageing people. Why had she agreed to take a job in this place of decrepitude? She turned and strode past the rows of old lavender bushes, past the woman and the man in the wheelchair, and hurried into the Annarbee Lodge reception to sign in. The foyer was painted a beige tone and the waiting-room chairs were an ugly shade of maroon, contrasting with the bleak grey-brown of the carpet. It was all terribly depressing.

The nurse at the front looked up at her briefly, then back down at her computer. Sylvia signed the book and hurried on. Her class would begin in ten minutes, and she didn't have time to think about Dan and his threats. The oldies liked to come in and get their chairs set up early and chat before it started. Most of this age group were too frail for working on mats.

'Sylvia, how are you today?'

Sylvia was unlocking the storeroom that held the plastic chairs. Delia was standing in her pale-pink velour tracksuit, hands on hips, bending stiffly to each side.

'I'm well, thanks, Delia. How about you?' She half listened as the older woman began moaning about the corns on her feet, and her arthritic hands.

Out of the corner of her eye, she noticed a trickle of people enter the room, one being Constance Broadhurst, dressed as usual in smart black pants and a beautiful, expensive-looking blue shirt that flowed down to her hips. She wore large pearl studs in her crinkly ear lobes and peach-coloured lipstick. Dan's aunt had once been an attractive woman. Her face still held a certain strength, a pleasing symmetry despite the sagging and the lines. Constance rarely spoke, and never gave any indication that she knew who Sylvia was. But then, they had only met a few times, forty years earlier, so it wasn't surprising. In any event, Annabelle had told Sylvia that Constance's memory wasn't perfect these days.

Sylvia took the class through a series of gentle moves, ignoring the chatter from some of the more vocal women at the front. She knew this was as much about social time as exercise, but sometimes their need to comment on the moves got on her nerves.

'Now, raise your right leg to the front, drawing up your belly button at the same time to support your back with your core muscles,' she said. She watched them follow her lead, some only bringing their feet an inch or two off the floor. 'Now flex your toes, backwards and forwards.'

'Oh, I hate this one,' said Penny Pancini. 'My legs cramp.'

Sylvia smiled. 'Just do what you feel your body can handle, Penny, and stop if it cramps.'

'My body's pretty good. It's just this silly pose that gets me.' The woman sniffed and lifted her foot higher.

'For goodness' sake, Penny, just button it.' Mavis Riley, a no-nonsense octogenarian with cropped white hair and a stern face, was glaring at Penny's back. Sylvia stifled an urge to laugh.

'Now, put your feet on the floor and we're going to twist around to the left side, putting one arm towards the back of the chair if you can. Inhale, bringing the breath down through your body. A nice deep breath. Now release.' Sylvia demonstrated. 'This is wonderful for your spine and your shoulder blades,' she said.

At the right side of the room, she noticed that Constance was still sitting facing the front on her chair. She looked pale.

'Now move back to centre and take three deep breaths, down into your body.' Sylvia got up and moved across the room to Constance.

'Are you all right there, Constance?' she asked quietly.

'Yes thank you.' Constance gave her a steady stare.

'Right, well just take your time. Don't overdo it.'

'I won't.'

At the end of the class, Sylvia encouraged everyone, as always, to practise their stretches through the week. The ladies trickled out of the room. Constance was slow, still sitting on her chair when most of the others had left. Sylvia had just reached down and pressed the home button on her phone to check the time when she became aware that Dan's aunt was standing beside her, small and frail, the last person left. A newly scanned photograph of Lillian and Sylvia taken decades ago in front of The Old Chapel was lighting up her phone screen, and Constance was staring at it. They both looked at the photograph until the phone went to sleep and turned black.

'I knew your friend, even then,' said Constance.

'Yes. I know. My sister is Annabelle. She lives at Merrivale – she's married to your nephew.'

Constance didn't seem to register the comment, and Sylvia regretted saying it. Regretted having brought Annabelle's marriage into public discussion, as if she had a right.

Constance looked off into the distance. 'He always said he didn't mean it, you know. And I suppose I thought it didn't matter, that I could endure, as long as it was just me.'

'I'm sorry?'

Constance was staring, blankly. 'But on the night he disappeared, the Lord revealed the truth. There were others. He sent the rain for a reason that night. So much rain.'

Sylvia went cold. 'Do you mean Andrew?' The thought of Constance's dead husband made her stomach turn. Sisters Cove and the surrounding towns and villages had been awash with speculation for days after he disappeared.

'For two days I prayed for deliverance. For two days the Lord kept me waiting to know my fate.'

Sylvia remembered all too well. It had certainly rained on the night he went missing, and she could hardly forget the fear that had overtaken her when she heard that his bruised and battered body had been found washed up by the tide around the headland two days later.

The town had talked about nothing else for weeks. *Could he have jumped? Why was he out on such a terribly rainy night? And so late! Why near the cliffs? Was he in some kind of trouble?* But the thoughts tumbling through Sylvia's mind had been far different.

'He wouldn't have been able to see in all that rain,' said Constance. 'It would have been slippery, too. And he loved that dog. More than he loved me, I think.'

'I'm sure he loved you,' said Sylvia, although she wondered why she said it. She'd hardly known him. Hadn't liked him much either. Behind the handsome face and the simmering charm, there had been something slick about Andrew Broadhurst.

'You should read the Bible, my girl.' Constance's eyes had become steely. 'Ezekiel Chapter 18, verse 20.'

Sylvia had the urge to put her hand to Constance's cheek. To comfort the poor, confused woman.

'I'm not religious,' she said.

'"The son shall not suffer for the sins of the father, nor the father for the sins of the son. Each shall bring wickedness only on themselves." That's what it says.' Constance held Sylvia's eyes steadily, and eventually Sylvia looked down, embarrassed.

'You must be good to them. They suffer,' said Constance.

'Who?' asked Sylvia.

Constance turned without answering and began to walk slowly to the corner of the room. She picked up a walking stick that was leaning against the wall and half turned so her face was in profile. 'I know who you are, Sylvia.'

Constance stood eerily still, ghost-like, and Sylvia's mouth went dry.

'You shouldn't have done what you did. It was wrong,' rasped Constance.

Sylvia felt a creeping dread crawl over her skin. 'I don't know what you mean,' she said, but guilt butted up against her conscience.

'You were young. You will still be welcomed by the Lord, if you only ask.'

Then Constance moved her stick forward and began her slow walk through the automatic glass doors and down the hallway.

Sylvia snapped the lock shut on the cupboard and reminded herself to breathe.

CHAPTER SIXTEEN

Willa

There was a familiar electronic *whelp* sound as the FaceTime link brought up Hamish's face on Willa's laptop. She felt longing, sadness and pleasure all mixed together.

'Hello, sweetie.'

'Yo, Mamma. 'Sup?'

'What on earth are you saying? Please don't tell me you've turned into a rapper.'

Hamish put his head to one side, bent his wrist and flicked his fingers in a strange motion. 'It all bomb diggity here, lady.' He did a remarkably good American accent.

Willa must have looked shocked, because Hamish burst out laughing. 'Chill, Mum. I'm just playing with you. What's going on down under? Do I need to come over there and get you?'

'No. Don't be silly. I miss you, though.'

'We miss you too. Dad's cooking is killing me. I think he was sick of steak and chips, so we've had two nights of bacon omelette. Don't think I can do three in a row.'

'It's only been two weeks, Hame. I'll be back soon. Tell him to pick up a lasagne from the Ville.' Willa felt a niggle of guilt. They needed her there. And the need for them to be together for the anniversary of Esme's death was pricking at her like a thorn in her shoe. It was next week. It would be weighing on Hugo and Hamish too.

She asked about Hamish's rowing and what was happening at school and what the weather was like. Hugo had already left for work. Hamish turned away from his laptop to put his bowl in the sink, then began stacking his books. He needed to get going, so Willa ended the call.

She looked around at the mountain of cardboard on all sides of her, and sighed. For the whole morning and part of the afternoon, she had successfully avoided the boxes. After chatting to Indigo in the coffee shop this morning, she had decided to drive to the small coastal town of Stanley an hour away and walk up an intriguing rectangular mountain called the Nut. It was like a mini version of Uluru. There was a chairlift down from the summit that gave her a wonderful view over the ocean and the heritage cottages that dotted the waterfront of the charming fishing village. Later, she had strolled into a delightful craft shop, where she had purchased a knitted beanie for Hugo, then she had found a pretty café and sipped tea while watching the tourists wandering past.

But now the sightseeing was over and she was back in The Old Chapel, surrounded by Lillian's boxes. So far all she had discovered were some old books and art paraphernalia. Annabelle had told her that plenty had already gone to charity. When Lillian knew the end was inevitable and she still had some energy, she had begun decluttering, and Sylvia had been tasked with taking carloads of junk to the charity shop. According to Sylvia, Lillian had insisted on packing and taping up some of the remaining boxes herself.

In the rear corner of the little mezzanine level, Willa started untaping another box. When she removed the lid and saw old photograph albums, she felt an uneasy anticipation. She picked them up, one by one. They were marked with the years that the photographs within had been taken, and each one covered a period of around five years.

She started with the most recent ones and worked her way backwards, seeing Lillian as a sixty-year-old, then regressing through time until she was young and fresh-faced. She had a nice look about her. Warm and welcoming. As an older woman, her face was very lined and sun-worn, but as Willa went back through the albums, she could see that Lillian had been attractive in a wholesome sort of way. She had lovely tanned skin, and though short, she was athletic-looking. She had generous lips and large brown eyes and curly black hair that she had cut very short as she aged and it had gone grey.

If Lillian was her birth mother, Willa must have taken after her father. Willa was much taller, and had a different, leaner body shape and facial features.

Going back through the decades, looking at photographs of Lillian with people Willa didn't know, she imagined her to be a lively, interesting sort of person. She stopped at a photograph of her skiing, standing in a line of four friends on what looked like little more than a snow-covered hill with patches of brown gorse showing through. The group wore knitted beanies over long hair, and two of them were only in jumpers and jeans, which seemed an odd choice for skiing. Lillian was the smallest, and she was smiling straight at the camera.

The notation at the bottom of the page said: *1979 – Cradle Mountain with the Bellinger boys and Pip Radley.* Willa would have been two years old then, and here was her birth mother, off skiing with a gang of friends, carefree. Child-free. She would have been twenty-two, and Willa would have been a toddler living in Sydney with her doting parents. She wondered if one of the Bellinger boys was her father. She peered closely at their faces – young men with sideburns and shoulder-length hair, smiling and squinting into the sun. She felt nothing, and thought that was probably a good thing. Unless she found her original birth certificate, and it actually listed a named person as her father, she knew she would never know. Did it matter? She wasn't sure.

Willa picked up the next album and began flicking through it. This one included photographs from the year of her birth, and she felt the tension increase in her shoulders. There were barbecues by the river, old cars parked under trees, bikini-clad girls on sunloungers woven from thick bands of contrasting plastic, young men and women in flared jeans and roll-necked jumpers. There were photos taken at the beach, with the Sisters Cove playground and café already there, a familiar, anchoring sight. A group of bare-chested young men outside the surf club in high-waisted tight shorts, with gangly bodies and ridiculous moustaches.

She turned page after page, seeing Lillian's life unfold before her, faded images of a time gone by. There were none of Lillian looking particularly pregnant, although she was wearing loose-fitting clothes and baggy jumpers in some of the shots. It was possible that she might have been. And with a first pregnancy, some people didn't really show much until right at the end.

There were very few photos taken at the end of the year, apart from a group shot labelled simply: *Christmas Day 1977*. It had been taken in the garden at Merrivale, the house painted freshly white then, and the garden looking lush and full of summer flowers. A swing hung from the elm tree in the foreground. There were half a dozen people sitting around on chairs in T-shirts and sundresses, enjoying the warmth of the day. A formally laid table ran along the front of them on the grass, obscuring much of the detail. Willa couldn't identify a single person.

When she turned the final page, a large envelope slipped from the back of the album. The paper was yellowing with age. Nothing was written on it. She prised it open. The sticky residue on the flap was brittle and dry and gave way with the gentlest force. She tipped the envelope up and a photograph slipped out. When she picked it up, Willa heard her own sharp intake of breath. Reflexively her thumb and finger parted and the photograph dropped to the floor. She hesitated, then reached down and picked it up again by the corner, staring at it in disbelief. It was her parents. Much younger, but undeniably them.

They were sitting in a living room with a group of people, and nobody in the photo was quite facing the camera. There were two couches in the room, at right angles to each other. On the first couch sat her mother. In her arms was a tiny baby with a white knitted cap on its head. Her mother was beaming. She was dressed in a pretty white sundress and sandals, showing off her summer tan. Her hair was loose and long. Next to her sat Willa's father. He was wearing knee-length shorts with long socks and lace-up leather shoes. It was his casual look that Willa remembered from her childhood. He was looking down at the baby seriously, his greying temples already giving away the signs of middle age.

Further back in the room, standing at the end of the couch, small and pretty, was Lillian, her sweet twenty-year-old face staring not quite at the camera, her dark curls falling messily about her shoulders, the barest ghost of a sad smile on her face. Willa gazed at her for a long moment, trying to decipher the strange expression. Next to Lillian, an attractive middle-aged woman was perched on the edge of the second couch, looking across at the baby. She had one leg bent in front and across the other and her hands were clasped in her lap, as if she were royalty. She wore a tailored floral dress to the knee. It had long sleeves with white cuffs and a high neck that accentuated her slim figure. Her fair hair was pulled back in what looked like a chignon. To the side of her, slouched at the other end of the couch, was a girl of perhaps fourteen. She wore a headband and a dark pinafore dress, and she was looking away from the camera, her arms crossed in front of her in a typical teenage pose.

Willa turned the photograph over. On the back it read: *19 December 1977. Baby Bee-Bee and her new family. Launceston.*

A shiver ran through Willa. She knew the baby could only be her, but her tiny, scrunched face looked just like Esme's as a newborn. Baby Wilhelmena would have been just nine days old in the photograph.

She stood and placed it on top of a stack of boxes as she stretched her cramped legs. She wondered about the identity of the unknown woman and girl in the photograph. Perhaps they were extended family members. Or friends. Or the woman might be from some sort of adoption agency. She knew from talking to Annabelle that it couldn't be Lillian's mother, because she had died when Lillian was young, and she didn't have siblings.

Willa looked back at the photo. She had always known she was adopted, but she had never talked to her parents about the early days of her life. If Lillian was her mother, then the photograph proved she had met Willa's parents, and must have known them a little. Or perhaps more. But Willa's parents had never admitted to knowing her birth mother, and somehow Willa now felt cheated – betrayed that her adoption might not have been the scenario she had always imagined: her parents receiving a phone call from a faceless social worker or administration officer saying a baby girl was available to pick up at the hospital. All parties anonymous to the others.

Now it seemed that her parents had owned a key to Willa's identity that they had kept hidden. She'd always assumed that seeking out her heritage would be a bureaucratic nightmare, with endless forms and applications, red tape and rights of veto and waiting periods. And then the emotional pay-off might not be worth it. She had a friend who'd been adopted and then traumatised by the hostile reactions of her birth parents. She thought she might not have had the strength to navigate such a situation; what if all she found was an unwilling stranger at the other end who resented her for her troubles? But if the hurdles weren't there, and the truth had been just a conversation away, it mattered. Especially now that neither her biological nor her adoptive parents were here to tell her how it had all happened.

She put the photograph back into the envelope and squashed the flap closed, then flicked through the last two albums. One contained photos of Lillian in her teens, some taken with her father standing next to her, then later sitting in a wheelchair. In those, Lillian looked much older, as if her father's accident had added a decade of maturity around her eyes. The last album held photographs of her childhood, some taken with her mother and many with familiar background scenes around Sisters Cove and The Old Chapel. A sadness seeped through Willa as she replaced the albums and closed the box. She needed to get outside. To walk. To think.

At the end of the lane, she turned left, the lighthouse beckoning in the distance. The day had become grey and cool, and it suited her mood. She was wearing her leather walking shoes, and she stepped up the pace, wanting to force her brain into a busy rhythm, her breath to come faster, her heart to pound. Before she could make sense of it all, she needed to clear her mind.

It was windy, and she enjoyed the noise of the wind sweeping through the crops and the background pounding crash of the ocean on the rock face at the base of the cliffs. Ahead of her, the lighthouse loomed, an enormous white apparition against the sky. Its base was fenced off, and as she reached the gate, she noticed it was locked. She stopped for a moment, taking in the paddocks, then the majestic scenery of the vast ocean extending off into the distance, scrubby trees clinging to the cliff faces as far as she could see. She walked around the lighthouse. At the front, a bush track opened between trees. The wind was whipping off the cliff face now and the barest hint of salt spray swirled through the air.

She followed the path down towards the face of the cliff, and as she neared the edge, a clearing emerged. Trees had been chopped back and a brilliant vista of the ocean opened up. A wooden seat had been installed. On the seat sat a woman in a patterned raincoat, her hood pulled up. She was completely still, with her back to Willa, staring out towards the ocean.

Willa was unsure whether to continue down the track. She watched the woman for another minute. It was as if she was a statue, frozen by the sheen of the ocean. Then something must have alerted the woman, because she turned, and her face creased into a huge smile.

'Willa!'

It was Annabelle. She pulled the hood from her head and bustled across, greeting Willa as if they were long-lost friends.

'Oh Willa, I'm so glad to see you! What a coincidence. I was just thinking to myself how lovely it would be if you could spend some time in the garden with me. Indigo was saying you want to learn, and I have plenty of tips if you can bear to listen. I *love* gardening.'

'Oh,' said Willa, startled by the sudden onslaught. 'Yes, that would be nice. Thank you. I'm only here for a few more days, though.'

'What a shame you can't stay for the garden fete. It's in two weeks – first weekend of autumn. Thankfully I don't have any weddings booked for the next month, so we're free to concentrate on it.'

'I'm sure you'll love every moment. That garden of yours is wonderful,' said Willa.

Annabelle was thoughtful for a moment. 'Do you think your husband and son could manage without you a bit longer if you stayed on? I promise you would love it. We have a petting zoo for the children, and market craft stalls and food stalls and of course lots of pot plant stalls. We've been striking plant cuttings for a year!'

'I'm not sure,' said Willa. She knew she couldn't stay. She needed to be with her family for the anniversary, but it didn't feel right to quash Annabelle's enthusiasm by mentioning Esme.

'Well, anyway… you decide. If none of us can persuade you to sell The Old Chapel to us, then I suspect we'll be seeing more of you in the future anyway. Neighbours. Only occasionally, I suppose, but still. Won't that be nice?' She smiled with delight, as if Willa turning up every couple of years for a holiday at Sisters Cove would be the most wondrous thing that could possibly happen.

'Yes, lovely.' Willa looked across at the seat. 'I'm sorry to disturb you. You looked as though you might be meditating.'

'Oh gosh. No. I don't really know how. Well, Sylvia's told me how, but it's impossible to just let your thoughts go blank, isn't it? I mean, you tell yourself to empty your mind, but it's like that thing where they tell you to not think of a pink elephant, and of course all you can think of is the darned pink elephant!'

Willa smiled. 'I've never quite got the hang of it either. I have a wonderful phone app, though – it's great for getting you started. It gives you little five-minute meditations to help you focus. I can show you if you like.'

'Really? That sounds good. Anything that helps sort out the million silly things that are always zinging through my head.' Annabelle paused, and seemed to be turning something over in her mind. 'I was just thinking about a bit of a problem I have, you see. I don't know what to do about it. I thought about telling Indigo when we were gardening, but she's too young to burden with these things. And anyway, it's not something she needs to know.' She stared past Willa's shoulder for a moment, confusion flitting across her face in the tiny movements around her eyes and mouth.

'If you need someone to talk to, I'm a very good listener,' said Willa.

'Oh!' said Annabelle. 'Really? You'd listen to my silly problems?'

'Shall we sit down?' said Willa, immediately regretting her offer, but at the same time craving the distraction of other people's much more manageable problems.

'Well, since you're not a local, perhaps it would be a good idea to get things off my chest to you.' Annabelle laughed, as if at some secret joke she'd just made.

They sat on the bench and looked out to the ocean, and Annabelle was strangely silent. Willa resisted the urge to look across at her. The ocean was soothing in its own, vast way.

'I was thinking of Dan,' Annabelle said eventually. 'He never loved me like he loved Sylvia. He only married me because I followed him around. I chased him. For years, until he gave in really. Sylvia ran away from him, you see, to Melbourne, then overseas, and I… I adored him. Always have. And of course, I suppose in those days I had certain charms. I could host excellent dinner parties. I was an asset as a wife because I could talk to anyone. And I was pretty and curvaceous and men liked to look at me. Back then, at least.'

Annabelle had turned towards Willa, as if to emphasise the notion before looking back to the ocean.

'And Dan adored my breasts. He would say it all the time. "You have the most *spectacular* breasts, Belle. I could live in those breasts!"'

Willa felt herself reddening under her collar. She wanted to put her fingers in her ears. In her head she could hear herself running interference. *La la la la la la la la.*

'But now the doctors say that all the tests show I definitely have breast cancer and that I might have to have one chopped off. And I don't really want to. But I keep saying to myself, what does it *matter*, though, Annabelle? Dan is sleeping with Sylvia anyway. He doesn't love you, he never has, and now he won't love your breasts either.'

'Oh, Annabelle…' said Willa, turning to her.

Annabelle had tears running down her cheeks.

Willa reached down and placed her hand on top of Annabelle's hand. She couldn't think what to say, so they sat in silence, her hand warming Annabelle's cold one underneath.

After a few minutes, Annabelle said, 'Thank you, Willa. For not jumping in to tell me it will be all right. I know I'll manage. I always do.'

Willa squeezed her hand. 'Somehow I think you will.' Underneath Annabelle's frippery, she sensed a steadfast resolve.

'Please don't mention this to anyone, will you?'

'I wouldn't dream of it,' said Willa. 'We all have things we want to keep under wraps.'

Annabelle wiped her eyes again. 'Thank you. And sorry – you're probably out here for your own thinking time, and here's me wittering on as if I have the biggest problems in the world.'

'They're not small problems. And really, it's fine.'

'Are you sure?' asked Annabelle, drawing her eyebrows together and pondering for a moment. 'Because you do actually look a little sad today, Willa. I know it might be because of Esme, but is there anything else?'

Willa hesitated. She hadn't planned to say anything, but Annabelle had trusted her, and she sensed they were allies now.

'I was in The Old Chapel just now, going through documents and so on. I found a whole heap of stuff, including a photograph of me as a baby with my parents and Lillian. I'm pretty certain now that she really was my birth mother. And I somehow feel cheated; that my parents lied about things.'

Annabelle stared back at the ocean and was silent for a while. 'Lies. So many lies.' She sounded tired and sad, and Willa regretted adding to her worries.

Annabelle spoke again. 'They told me Lillian miscarried. Late in her pregnancy. I wasn't in Sisters Cove at the time, you see. She had decided to keep her baby and raise it herself. She didn't need a man or permission to keep it; so she said, anyway. She didn't care what anyone thought – she was a feminist. We were quite unalike in that regard.' She glanced at Willa and gave her a small, sad smile. 'But if you've found proof that she adopted you out, then she lied, and I'm not sure why she did that. I would have understood. It would have been a comfort to me, to know that her baby had lived; that she hadn't suffered that loss.'

'Yes,' said Willa.

They both fell silent for a moment, then Willa said, 'What about my biological father? Did you know him?'

'Oh Willa, I'm sorry, but he passed away. And I can't tell you his name because it would be betraying someone who trusted me. And he wasn't really… well…' Annabelle's glance was awkward. She looked down at her hands and paused. 'He wasn't really worth knowing, if you take my meaning. But if it helps you, I think Lillian loved him, for a time at least.'

Annabelle brought her hand to her mouth briefly, then let it fall to her neck, where she caressed the cross on her necklace in restless, repetitive motions. 'We love whom we love, don't we? Men aren't perfect. Sometimes they're just plain horrid. But our hearts can be blind. *We* can be blind. Blind and stupid.' She turned to Willa, and there was a desperate sadness in her eyes. 'But the love is real, Willa, so what's a girl to do?'

CHAPTER SEVENTEEN

Annabelle

'I just met Wilhelmena Fairbanks,' said Dan, coming through the door. 'She's over in The Old Chapel garden.' He pulled a beer out of the fridge and sat down at the table.

Annabelle was busy making fig paste to sell at the garden fete.

'Mmm,' she said, steeling herself to keep her voice even. Every day it became a little bit easier to swallow the hurt. 'She's lovely, isn't she? She was going to go home a few days ago, but her husband and son surprised her by turning up.'

Dan raised his eyebrows, then turned to stare out the window. Annabelle wondered what he was thinking. Perhaps he was worrying that if Willa's family had come all the way from England, they must want The Old Chapel for themselves. Perhaps they wouldn't sell it to him.

'I didn't spot the husband,' he said. 'Leandra Pickle was helping her do some mulching.' He took a swig of his beer. 'That woman is a total pain in the arse.'

'Dan!' said Annabelle. It was true that Leandra was very annoying, but he didn't have to say it so forcefully. Especially when she was just across the road. What if she popped across to borrow a rake or some pruning shears?

Annabelle pondered Dan's recent foul moods as she stirred the fig paste and tried to decide if she should let it thicken a bit more. It had been on the stove top for nearly three hours and she needed to use the last of the evening sun to finish deheading the geraniums and weed along the northern boundary.

'What's for dinner?' said Dan.

'I don't know,' said Annabelle. 'Whatever you're cooking, I suppose.'

She caught his eye and noticed the look of annoyance. Dan hated cooking, but there was still so much to do this evening, and really, it was about time he took a turn.

He put down the beer and opened the fridge, and stared for a long time at the shelves. 'Not much in there.'

'I haven't had time to shop.'

'I'll head down to the surf club and get some fish and chips.'

'That's not very healthy.' Annabelle picked up the pot and began pouring the thick figgy sludge into the first of two large rectangular dishes to set overnight in the fridge. Tomorrow she would cut the hardened mixture into small squares, wrap them and label them, ready to sell each one for five dollars at the fete.

'I'll eat the chips and you just have the fish.'

'They only do battered, Dan. I'm not eating it.'

Annabelle had told him about the lump a week ago. She'd also told him she was only eating healthy low-sugar and low-fat food from now on to deal with the cancer naturally, until she started treatment.

Dan breathed out a heavy sigh. 'Christ, you're hard work sometimes. What if I defrost some lamb chops?'

'Perfect,' said Annabelle. 'What about greens?' Dan wasn't a fan of vegetables, but she had been forcing him to eat them for nearly forty years now. Every night he'd leave half of whichever one he didn't like, and as she scraped it into the chicken bin, she'd console herself that at least he'd had a few mouthfuls of vitamins and fibre and antioxidants. She wasn't going to let him die young if she could help it.

'Spuds?' he asked hopefully.

Annabelle stirred the remaining fig paste in the pan and waited.

Dan spoke again. 'I suppose I could make a green salad. Is there still rocket in the back veggie patch?'

'Yes,' said Annabelle, and she felt a hot stinging behind her eyes. She blinked it away. It was just that she was tired. So tired. 'That sounds lovely.'

He dug around in the freezer for a few moments before pulling out an ice-covered bag, then began looking in the fresh-produce drawers of the fridge.

'I asked Wilhelmena if she'd considered my offer to buy The Old Chapel, but she fobbed me off. Did you get any further with that?' asked Dan.

'No. I didn't.' Annabelle felt herself tense. She jabbed the wooden spoon into the pan, making thick, sticky lines on the bottom of the pot.

'I don't know why she's being so difficult. It makes no sense to have a holiday house here if you live in Oxford. It's nearly forty hours of travel to get here. She's *got* to be thinking about selling.' Dan pulled a couple of tomatoes and a cucumber from the drawer. Then he looked at the empty knife block on the kitchen bench for a few seconds, a blank expression on his face.

Annabelle tried to ignore him. She'd mollycoddled him for too long. What if the cancer took her? What would he do then when he needed to find a kitchen implement? *Sylvia would move in.* Annabelle felt a sharp pain snake across her chest. She dropped the wooden spoon against the pot and took hold of the bench, pretending to look out the window. She took some deep breaths and squeezed her eyes shut against the hot, hateful thought. Sylvia would move in and make him eat lentils and brassicas. And that would jolly well serve him right.

Dan pulled out the implements drawer and began digging through it with rough, noisy movements, picking up and discarding peelers, stirrers, salad servers, upsetting Annabelle's system. Annabelle flung open the dishwasher and pulled out the top rack. Three chopping knives sat across the tray, gleaming.

He grunted, taking one and not looking up. 'Maybe you could have another chat to Wilhelmena this week about it. She seems to like you.'

'Dammit, Dan! No! I am not doing your bidding. I don't even want that horrible little place!' Without warning, tears began running down Annabelle's face.

Dan stared at her, his lips parted. She wanted to curl up and hide in a dark place, but the fig paste would be ruined if she didn't finish with it now. She swiped at the tears with the tea towel and turned her back to him.

'All right, all right,' said Dan. 'No need to get so emotional about it.'

Annabelle could feel her face getting prickly and blotchy, but she stayed silent. She couldn't speak in case the seething mass of bitterness inside her accidentally came out.

Dan put the chops on a plate and put it in the microwave. 'How long do they need to defrost?'

'Give them one minute but keep an eye on them,' said Annabelle, squeezing her eyes shut again.

'On the topic of radiation,' said Dan, as he pressed the start button, 'did the oncologist give you a treatment start date yet?'

Annabelle swallowed. She felt that awful dizzy feeling wavering just at the edge of her brain, as if she needed to hold on and plant her feet in case everything began to spin. It had been happening quite a bit lately. Probably a part of her anxiety symptoms, according to the therapist woman. Lena. She was a very herbal sort of person and quite boring and not very helpful either. But still,

Annabelle knew she needed to try harder. It wasn't Lena's fault that she couldn't seem to talk about things properly.

She was suddenly back in the therapy room, Lena leaning forward, her purple gypsy earrings jangling around her face.

'Before we talk about the anxiety episodes or the cancer, Annabelle, it helps me to understand a little more about you if I know about events from the past that might have shaped you and your ways of coping.'

Annabelle had swallowed and shifted in the armchair. It was deep and squishy. Too deep. She felt like she was trapped in the silly, airless room. As if the chair was designed to trap her into relaxing. Into saying something she might regret. 'All right.'

Lena smiled at her, crinkly lines forming beside her eyes. She spoke with a slow aura of calm that sounded just a teensy bit fake.

'Do you ever recall being faced with a distressing event in your past – an event that may have made you question yourself or your future, perhaps?'

'I…' Annabelle felt her heart rate speeding up, as if she was heading up to the peak on a roller coaster, ready to fly back down the other side amid screams and wind and terror. She was holding her breath, and after a moment she let it out with a little cough.

'No. No. I… don't think so.'

'Perhaps a situation where you felt a lack of control?'

'I… well, no. Not that I can think of.' Annabelle felt herself rubbing at the cross on her necklace and forced her hand down onto the chair. She closed her eyes briefly, then opened them and smiled. 'My mother died of cancer when I was a young teenager, but I had my dad and my sister. I was all right.' She gave Lena a smile that said: *sorry, I know I should be more interesting, but I'm really just so normal and boring.* She wasn't about to disclose her most awful secrets to this dippy woman after knowing her for five minutes.

Annabelle realised she had been staring at the kitchen floor, cringing at the memory of her therapist. She looked up. Dan was watching her, waiting for an answer. 'They wanted to do the surgery next week, then chemotherapy after that,' she said.

'Do you need me to drop you at the hospital or something?'

She shook her head. 'Obviously I can't have surgery yet. I've told them I'll book it in a month or two. After the fete. And I've got three big weddings coming up after that too – I need to source all sorts of things for those.'

'What?' Dan stopped chopping and scrunched up his face as if she'd just spoken to him in a foreign language .

Annabelle sighed. The dizzy feeling had slipped away and she just felt tired again. She turned off the pan and lifted it up and began pouring the remaining fig paste into the second dish.

'What do you mean, what?' she said.

'Are you seriously telling me you're delaying treatment for a big cancerous lump because of a *fete*? What's the *matter* with you?' Dan picked up his beer and drained it. He put the bottle down on the bench and got another one out of the fridge.

Annabelle noticed a wet ring where the bottle had been.

'The ring,' she said, pointing at it.

'What?'

'Wipe up the ring. And put the beer bottle in the recycling. Please.'

Dan looked at her for a long moment, as if he was trying to decipher a puzzle. Then he made a huffing sound, picked up the bottle and put it in the bin under the sink and gave a swipe with the dishcloth over the ring.

'Well?' he said. 'A month could make a difference. It might spread.'

'I doubt it.'

'You're being ridiculous. Just go and get it sorted out.'

'Don't be so bossy,' snapped Annabelle.

The microwave pinged, and Dan leaned over and pulled out the chops.

'Anyway,' she said, 'who's going to do everything that has to be done for the fete if I start treatment? They said I'd need several weeks of recovery time, and that's just the surgery bit.'

It was a swipe at Dan, and she knew it was rude, but she was at the end of her tether. Seriously, what did he expect her to do? He wasn't the one hosting the entire north-west coast at this damned garden fete. He was barely lifting a finger to help, and she could feel the rage building inside her whenever he came home late from work, or popped out in the evening just as she needed him to do something. She was falling into bed just before midnight and was up again at dawn trying to fit everything in.

'Jesus, Belle. Get the garden club biddies to set up the stalls for the fete. They live for that stuff. What else is there? I can do anything you need me to. I keep saying, just give me a job.'

'That's not true! All you've contributed so far is a promise to mow the lawn the day before the fete and a half-hearted effort to hang my lobelia baskets after I asked you a hundred times!'

Dan stared at her for a moment, then turned and walked out the door and into the garden. He let the screen door bang behind him, making Annabelle jump.

She placed the second dish of fig paste carefully across the first and carried them both out to the back fridge. She wondered if Dan was picking some rocket or whether he'd gone off in a huff somewhere instead. She was wiping her hands on her apron when she heard a knock, and looked up to see Willa standing at the screen door with Leandra Pickle.

'Hello!' she said. 'Come in. Please, ladies! Don't stand on ceremony. Come on in.'

'Sorry,' said Willa. 'I don't mean to intrude. I know it's late.'

'Fiddlesticks,' said Annabelle.

Willa and Leandra pulled off their gardening shoes and came into the kitchen.

'Annabelle, you look absolutely exhausted,' said Leandra, who was in grubby gardening clothes, her wild grey hair pushed up under a faded cloth hat, and not looking all that glamorous herself.

'Do I?' said Annabelle. She wondered if the tears earlier had smudged her mascara. She always wore make-up, even at home. There was no need to let standards slip just because you might not expect to see anyone during the day. She'd always liked the French attitude that her mother had explained to her as a girl – one's appearance was a favour to other people. They were the ones who had to look at you, so you should make an effort as a sign of courtesy. You could never be sure who might drop in.

'You're running yourself ragged over this fete, old girl. You mustn't!' exclaimed Leandra, and Annabelle wondered why she felt qualified to make such pronouncements if she wasn't offering to help. There was a patronising edge to the comment. Also, the term 'old girl' was offensive.

Annabelle smiled thinly, then turned her eyes to Willa and her smile became genuine. She had developed a weakness for Willa. Such a reserved slip of a girl, but there was something achingly endearing about her. It felt like a privilege whenever she opened up.

'Leandra has been helping me after I agreed to let The Old Chapel garden be part of the fete,' said Willa. 'That's all right, isn't it? If people also wander over there?'

'Of course!' said Annabelle.

'That's good. I should have checked earlier. It's just that Sylvia asked me and…' She had a distracted, distant look in her eyes, as if it had just occurred to her that she might be offending Annabelle in some way.

'Annabelle doesn't mind,' said Leandra. She walked across to the sink and began washing her hands. 'It's a community fete – more offerings mean more money for the charity, and Lillian's garden has some fabulous old specimens. Better than yours even, Annabelle.

Have you seen that gorgeous old macrophylla? I think it's a Prince Henry. Fabulous variegated petals. We should get people to put another gold coin in the pot to get into The Old Chapel garden.' Leandra had squirted soap on her hands and was lathering them vigorously. Then she began using the dishcloth to clean around her fingernails. She seemed oblivious to Annabelle and Willa's stares.

They listened to the soupy sound of Leandra giving one last lather to her hands, then Willa said, 'I just popped over because I wanted to ask you if you'd like to meet my husband and son. Perhaps for coffee at the surf club tomorrow? Around eleven?'

'He's a total dish, that hubby of hers!' said Leandra.

Annabelle glanced across at her.

Leandra was grinning. 'And the son, absolutely gorgeous. Must be all that rowing. He's all muscles!'

Compared to Willa's gentle voice, Leandra's was sharp and loud and Annabelle pushed her fingernails hard against her palm. 'That sounds lovely, Willa,' she said, just as a motorbike approached with an explosive roar. It pulled into the driveway at the front of the kitchen. Banjo began barking in the garden, and they all looked out the window as Dan got off the bike, kicked the stand into position and slung his helmet onto the seat. They stared as he walked towards the kitchen door. He obviously wasn't expecting company, so when Leandra spoke, he looked momentarily startled.

'Dan Broadhurst! I thought you got rid of that midlife crisis of yours years ago! And you're still in your work suit. Hardly the right gear for bike-riding, is it? Still, we should be thanking the Lord that at your age we don't have to see you in leathers!'

'Leandra. Hello,' said Dan.

Why can't you just try a little bit harder? thought Annabelle, flinching at the sneer in his voice.

He turned to Willa. 'Hello again.'

'Dan was just getting rocket for dinner from the garden,' said Annabelle, although she realised he must have been up to the top shed to get the motorbike instead. There was an awkward moment of silence as everyone looked at his empty hands.

'I'm just off to get it now, actually,' said Dan, but he made no immediate attempt to move, and Annabelle began thumbing her necklace, wondering what to do next. Usually she'd invite the visitors to stay for a drink, but Leandra was likely to say yes, and Dan might say something rude.

'Actually, there was one other thing before I go,' said Willa.

Dan began digging around in the drawers, pulling out various plastic containers and assessing them, Annabelle presumed, for their suitability to hold the rocket.

'Yes?' she said.

'I found some of Lillian's diaries. Decades worth of them. Tucked away in a seat. I'm not sure what I should do with them. If I should read them. What do you think?'

Annabelle paused as everything began slowing and receding around her. Banjo's barking, the sounds in the kitchen, the warbling songs of birds in the twilight outside. She took a few slow, shallow breaths and forced herself to look normal.

'Diaries,' she said.

'Yes, I counted thirty-five. But there are about a dozen missing from the date range. They start in 1973.'

'Diaries,' said Annabelle again, her voice sounding small.

'How intriguing!' said Leandra. 'She played her cards close to her chest did our Lillian. I'd love to know what she really got up to inside that little place.'

Dan put a container down slowly on the bench. 'Leandra, this is a private discussion. It's probably best you leave us to it.'

Leandra's face dropped, and Annabelle flinched at his bluntness. This was Dan in work mode, the man who could negotiate settlement deals and win over a courtroom full of lawyers and a judge without quaking the way Annabelle would have done with all that pressure. She found it breathtaking just how quick-witted and cruel he could be sometimes.

Leandra looked at each of them defiantly, and Willa dropped her gaze to the floor.

'Well, if you think so,' she said. 'Willa, I'll be back in the morning to finish with the mulching. And I'll bring some thin stakes to hold up those wonky zinnias.'

'Thank you,' said Willa.

They waited as Leandra stopped at the doorway to put on her shoes then marched down the garden path. Banjo began to bark again. A blowfly started swooping around the kitchen, bashing itself against the window, making Annabelle conscious of the silence.

'Which ones are missing?' asked Dan.

'I can't remember,' said Willa.

Dan stood still and silent for a moment, staring past Annabelle's shoulder at the wall that held the painting of Merrivale. It had been commissioned by his Uncle Andrew in the 1960s. In the foreground of the garden a woman and dog were depicted. Andrew had loved his dogs apparently, much more than his women, Annabelle suspected.

'If they're part of Lillian's estate, they belong to you, Wilhelmena,' said Dan. He dropped his head while Annabelle thumbed the cross around her neck and felt her stomach clenching. Then he looked up. 'But there's something tawdry about dipping into other people's private lives, don't you think? Just because you can, doesn't mean you should.' He was staring at Willa now, and she at him.

Annabelle hated this. The still, loaded silence. The judgement as two people she cared about sized one another up. The psychologist had been teaching her mindfulness. To live in the moment, noticing what was happening to her. She registered the pull of her breath as her heart sped up.

Eventually Dan looked down at the container on the bench. Then, without picking it up, he walked out of the kitchen, letting the door slam, breaking the dreadful stillness. The motorbike roared into life and both women turned their heads as the noise filled the air then drifted into the distance.

Good grief, thought Annabelle. This is it. She tried to pull together the fraying threads of her mind. 'I'm sorry, Willa. He was very close to Lillian. Like a brother, really.' *Excuses. Obvious excuses.* She pushed on. 'They grew up together. Well, not together exactly, but he would come for summer holidays here, to stay with his aunt and uncle, and Lillian was just across the road there, so they were friends since childhood, you see.'

'It must be hard for him then, with her gone,' said Willa.

'He's all right. He's fine. But I understand why he doesn't want you going through her private life. It would feel like an intrusion into his own family.'

'Of course. And I don't think I'd feel right reading the more current ones anyway. But if Lillian was my birth mother, I just thought perhaps… well, that I could read the diaries from around the time I was born. To help me understand.'

'Nineteen seventy-seven?'

'Yes.'

'He really wouldn't want you probing through that one. It was the year his Uncle Andrew was killed,' said Annabelle. 'It was… awful. They couldn't find him for days. He… fell from the cliffs looking for Charlie. His dog. And Dan was left to look after his aunt, and Merrivale. It was a very difficult time.'

'You were around when it happened?' asked Willa.

'I… No. Well, yes, I lived around here, but I was only sixteen. I didn't really… well, I didn't really know Andrew.' Annabelle twisted her hands together. 'That was a shocking year, and dear Lillian would have suffered terribly.'

'Why? Was she close to Andrew too?'

Annabelle could feel her heart shuddering and shaking intermittently inside her ribcage. It was the strangest sensation. She lifted her hand and noticed that it was shaking too. 'Please, Willa. Don't go digging up her secrets now.'

'Secrets?'

'We all have secrets, my lovely. Lillian was a good person, but she was tortured by her past. I think that now she's gone, her soul deserves some rest.'

Willa nodded slowly and gave Annabelle a sad smile. 'Tomorrow at eleven then, for coffee?'

'Wonderful.'

Willa stopped at the door and turned. 'And... what you said. I don't know, Annabelle. The living have to live. The dead are already at peace. It's the not knowing – the not understanding – that breaks you.' Her voice had become thin and tremulous. 'It's the living who are tortured.'

There was a thread between them. Annabelle felt it. A glistening, unbreakable thread.

Willa broke it. 'Hugo and Hamish have come out because it's the two-year anniversary this week. Our beautiful Esme was still alive two years ago.' She was staring back out of the window now, to The Old Chapel and across to the ocean. With a quick motion, she turned her head and fixed Annabelle with a look filled with loss and longing. 'And if you tell me that not knowing things is better, you're wrong. It just prolongs the pain. I'll think about what you both said about the diaries, but I can't promise I won't read them. I'm sorry, but I just can't.'

CHAPTER EIGHTEEN

Sylvia

Sylvia woke to the sound of the ocean crashing onto the rocks. The window of her bedroom was slightly open and the sill was wet. It had rained during the night, but now the rising sun was throwing a weak silver glow across the rolling surface of the water. What was she doing back in this place?

In searching for her identity, her sense of home, she'd broken her family even further. She'd spent decades questioning her own stupidity, and living with the guilt that she'd run away all those years ago. She had still loved Dan then, but now she knew she'd made the right decision to leave. She'd spent all this time pining for a man who was deeply flawed. And it seemed he'd only gotten worse. She flicked her bare legs over the side of the bed, and in that one liberating moment, she realised that the hold Dan had had over her was completely gone. Hearing his anger on the phone, and his attitude to Annabelle, had made something inside her die.

Still, coming back to Sisters Cove had been good for Indigo. Given her a place to call home. And now Sylvia realised that Indigo would be fine whether she herself stayed or not.

She went into the front room and rolled out her yoga mat in front of the glass doors so she could see the ocean, grey-green and vast under the overcast sky. The froth and tumble of the waves calmed her. After her stretching session, she walked towards the kitchen to make spicy oaten porridge to pacify her aggravated vata. All this stress was terrible for her system.

Annabelle had laughed when Sylvia had tried to explain the principles of Ayurveda, and how her doshas were out of balance. It had been months ago, when they were chatting about her diet, but Sylvia remembered what she had said. *I'm all out of balance everywhere. Of course I am, silly billy. I don't need a funny name for it!* She had laughed and flicked her hand at Sylvia as if the Ayurvedic words – dosha, vata, pitta, kapha – were hilarious snippets of mumbo-jumbo. It had irritated Sylvia, but she was resigned to it. Her sister wasn't especially emotionally evolved. Still, Sylvia knew she didn't deserve to have an opinion on the matter. She was a little shabby in the emotion department herself.

The box of diaries caught her eye as she padded through the living room, and the feeling of peace that had descended during her stretching session vanished. The diary marked 1977 was on the top. She specifically hadn't opened that one. Couldn't face what she might find. She knew she had broken Lillian's heart too when she left, not just Dan's. Worse still, she had abandoned Annabelle when she needed her most, and broken the promise she made to her mother just weeks before she died; her promise to be there if ever Annabelle needed her. Sylvia couldn't bear to read Lillian's judgement – see her battered feelings – right there on the page. She was aware that her abrupt departure all those decades ago had been inexcusable, but she had felt there was no other way out.

Ginger tea. That was what she needed. Warm ginger tea to restore her balance. She opened the fridge and took out the knob of ginger. As she pulled a knife from the block on the bench, she heard the growl of a motorbike up on the road, and some sense of foreboding told her it would be Dan.

A minute later, there was a quick knock and she heard the door open. I could have locked it! she thought. Why didn't I lock it?

'Morning, Syl.'

She kept chopping the ginger methodically, not looking up. Not giving him the satisfaction. How dare he come in here uninvited?

He cleared his throat and remained at the door, presumably waiting for a welcome.

She put the ginger peelings into the worm bucket.

'I'm here because I want to talk about The Old Chapel.'

She let out a heavy sigh. *That* again. It felt so unimportant. So secondary, now that Annabelle was sick and knew about their affair.

'There's a thing called text, Dan. And anyway, I have no desire to talk to you. How dare you threaten me?'

'I don't understand why you won't... I love you, Syl, I—'

'The Old Chapel?' said Sylvia forcefully as she put the ginger pieces into the teapot.

Dan walked across the kitchen and stood with his hands in his pockets, as if he didn't quite know how to proceed.

'What if I buy it – I mean, if I can convince Wilhelmena to sell it – and let Indigo rent it from me? But really cheaply. I don't want to be at odds with you over it.'

'Why do you want it so much?'

He pulled out a chair from the kitchen table and sat down, staring out at the ocean for a moment. The familiarity irritated Sylvia. She deliberately remained standing as he ran his hands through his hair and nodded twice before he spoke, as if giving himself permission.

'A couple of years ago, I made some bad investments. One was a property development I've had to prop up. It's all having an impact now, Syl, and I'm at retirement age. I want to be able to sell Merrivale when I finally get the title. But I need to get a good enough price for it. And as you can probably imagine, the value is a lot less without waterfront access, especially if this wedding business venture takes off. If I owned The Old Chapel and could sell them together, it would at least double Merrivale's value. That ocean frontage is priceless, but only with Merrivale in the mix to add the scale to it. It isn't worth much on its own. Together, though, they'd be an amazing site for development. Much better than the site the council rejected the other day for the resort down near the beach. And more chance of getting development approval.'

Sylvia stared at him, processing this information. Property values, investments, developments. They were just so *uninteresting* to her.

'Is that why you didn't push for the other development? Because you had this in mind all along?'

Dan shrugged and gave her a wry smile. 'Well, you've got to admit it's a good idea. I assumed I'd have no trouble buying The Old Chapel. Until Wilhelmena came along.'

Sylvia considered him for a minute. She was flabbergasted that he would assume that the idea of transforming this beautiful little backwater into a tourist hotspot would appeal to her. Did he know her so little? But more importantly, what about her sister's life's work in that garden?

'What does Annabelle think?' *She* was allowed to mention Annabelle's name if they were together. It was her rule after all.

'I haven't really discussed it with her. You know what she'd be like about selling Merrivale. But the truth is, I can't afford to retire comfortably if I don't sell. Not with my share portfolio the way it is now.'

'I can't believe you'd even think about it.'

'It's just a house, Syl.'

'But it's been in your family for generations.'

'There is no next generation. Well, I guess there's Indigo, but—'

Sylvia waved him away and poured herself a mug of tea. She didn't want to discuss Indigo with him. Indigo had her own father. She was just fine on the father front, thank you very much. Not that Sylvia knew where the useless man was, or whether he was even still alive, but she was sure Indigo had his email address and could find out if she really needed to.

But a bigger thought had entered her mind now. She knew she should just blurt it out, but something made her pause. She hadn't yet read the diary and she knew it might clarify things, but really, what else would she learn?

She stirred her tea and took a breath.

'What about Willa?' She pulled the teaspoon out of her mug and watched the little bits of ginger floating in a whirlpool.

'What do you mean?'

'I suspect she's your daughter.' She looked up at him, perversely interested in how he would take this news if he didn't already know it. 'I don't know if Annabelle has told you, or if she even knows it herself actually, but… Willa – Wilhelmena, I mean – she's adopted, and I assume she's yours. Yours and Annabelle's.'

'What?'

'You should probably talk to Willa about it. I think she wants to know how it all happened. Talk to Annabelle too.'

'What on earth are you talking about?' His voice was strained, hard-edged.

Sylvia sighed and sipped her tea. Dan's face was creased with questions, and for a moment she saw him as a younger man, her lover, an ambitious man with twinkling eyes and a smile that could melt her heart. Then anger flared in her, so quick and unexpected that she swallowed too much tea and felt the ginger burn her throat. He had slept with her sister and gotten the poor girl pregnant, and all the while he'd been banging on about how Sylvia was the only woman in the world for him. She turned and looked out the window at the ocean, not trusting herself to speak. The rain began again suddenly, thin, sheeting waves of it, blowing across the face of the sea in powerful gusts.

She took a breath, raising her voice over the noise of the rain. 'When I tried to confront you about Annabelle that night, you were out of your mind about what happened with… well, about Andrew, and I didn't know what to do. The Andrew thing, it just seemed so much worse, and it took over my mind. But you never apologised about Annabelle. You never apologised for being a smarmy arsehole. She was so young, Dan. How could you do it?' The words had rolled around, boiling and spitting in her mind for so many years, and now they were out. Just a few little words, but they defined her life; defined everything she'd done since that night when she had seen Dan and Annabelle in the car, locked in that awful embrace.

'What?'

'Don't! Don't you dare. I deserve to know, Dan.'

'Sylvia, please.' His face was creased; pleading.

'You slept with a child, Dan. She was *fifteen*!' She spat the word at him, the hard sound of it vibrating in her throat. The accusation sounded worse now that she'd voiced it. Disgusting.

Dan stared at her. He got up from his chair, and shook his head at her slowly. 'No.'

Sylvia clenched the mug tightly, wanting to slap him. Annabelle had been days away from turning sixteen, and no doubt it had been consensual. She had been following him around like a lapdog for years before that. But the age of consent was seventeen in Tasmania. She'd checked, because she knew that the detail mattered. And she mattered too. She needed to know what had been going through his mind on the day he shattered so many lives.

He stopped in the middle of the lounge room, his back to her. Then he turned around slowly to face her.

'Are you telling me you walked out on me not because of the things we did that night... Andrew and...' he stopped, shook his head again, 'but because of Annabelle? And you think we had a child?'

'That must have been the night she got pregnant. Around then anyway. And no, it wasn't the only reason, but it was part of it. The whole thing was a nightmare. But the main reason I left was *you*, Dan. You really expected me to stay after what you made me do that night?'

She let her eyelids droop and close. She was tired of this already. Her emotions were like birds, gliding above the cliffs, then swooping down low to skim the cold blue water.

'Sylvia?'

'What else could I have done except leave, Dan? You betrayed us all, and now you have the gall to threaten *me* with exposure.'

Dan shook his head again and raised both hands to cover his mouth and nose. When he dropped them, Sylvia expected to see shame, but she didn't. In the squint of his eyes and the movement of the muscles around his mouth and nose, she saw something hard and disbelieving. She saw disgust.

'Why would you even think that? Annabelle's never had a baby. We couldn't have children,' he said, anger showing now in the flare of his nostrils, the clenching of his jaw.

'What would you know?' hissed Sylvia. 'What would you bloody well know? What you did was horrific, and Annabelle is the one who came off worst. I can't believe she cared for you, *married* you, after the way you treated her!'

He stood silent, breathing heavily, Sylvia's words hanging like daggers between them. Eventually he spoke, coldly. 'I know I made some big mistakes, but you were the one who abandoned her.' He opened the front door and began striding up the driveway.

'A mistake?' she screamed. 'Is that what they call it these days? A mistake!'

The rain had eased to a pattering irritation. Gum leaves were clumped, dark and slippery, on the driveway.

'Don't you dare walk away from me, Dan Broadhurst! You owe me more than an apology!' Every moment of Sylvia's broken life had boiled down into a delicious, hot, seething sea of rage. It was a revelation, this anger, the white-hot loss of control. It was something she never gave in to, but it felt so right! She was ablaze with the thrill of it. 'You're a cruel, dishonest man!'

He didn't stop, or slow, and she ran after him, barely noticing the water falling on her bare arms. He had parked in the little bay fifty metres down the road on the ocean side, and as he strode towards his bike, Sylvia followed. 'Answer me, Dan!' she screamed.

He ignored her.

'Go on, then, you coward. Run away! Screw me, then run back to Annabelle! There's a pattern there, you faithless bastard! Can't you see it?'

She stood panting in the middle of the road. As the noisy rush of anger finally quelled in her ears, she became aware of her surroundings: the bending of the trees in the breeze, the movement of surfers below the cliff in the pounding storm waves, the sound of a car idling behind her on the road. She turned.

Rita Perotta had pulled up at the entry to her driveway and was staring at Sylvia through the open window. A throaty revving suddenly filled Sylvia's head, and as Dan's motorbike roared past them, back up the hill, she folded her arms to cover her breasts, which were showing through the wet fabric of her fitted white singlet. Rita's mouth was hanging open in a comic display of disbelief. Sylvia looked down down at herself. Her eyelids fluttered closed. She was standing in her underpants.

CHAPTER NINETEEN

Willa

The banoffee pie sat in the centre of the table. Hugo had suggested it, so she had been into town yesterday to buy the ingredients. There wasn't a proper baking dish in the rental house, but she had found one in The Old Chapel, and yesterday she had spent a happy, dreadful afternoon baking. Because that was what Esme would have wanted. This morning she had taken the pie out of the fridge after breakfast and placed it on the table to make Esme the centre of their day.

She was tempted to take a slice of it now, even though she was afraid that when the caramel hit her tongue, she would break apart. But at least the grief would then be physical, and it would bring Esme back for a moment. That sickly-sweet taste that Esme had adored would be hers. And she would adore it too. She would eat it and adore it. Even though she would hate it.

Willa raised her finger and let it hover over the pie. Grief was a little bit like labour. It swept through you in waves. Sometimes she needed to hold her breath for fear of dying with the pain, and then it was gone and she was all right. She was fine. She felt Esme talking to her, walking with her, living inside her, and she was absolutely okay. And then it would come again the next day, or the next week. Or when she saw a girl with long blonde hair, or when she heard someone singing a song by Adele. Don't, she would think. Stop it! That was Esme's song. You have no right to sing Esme's song so tunelessly!

This morning, Hugo and Hamish were braving the frigid waters of Sisters Cove Beach to do some surfing. It had been raining earlier, but it had stopped now and the sky had magically cleared. The huge sea swells continued, though. Willa looked down through the picture windows of the house to the beach below. They were the only two in the water. Neither of them seemed to be able to stand up on the board for very long. Three years ago, all four of them had had surfing lessons when they were on holiday in Majorca, and yesterday they had sat down to watch YouTube videos about surfing techniques. Hamish had been confident that it would all come back to him. They had borrowed boards and wetsuits from one of the gorgeous little painted beach huts that sat on the sand next to the surf club. Annabelle knew someone who owned one, so she had arranged it for them. It was very sweet of her.

Willa pulled her eyes from the ocean and let her finger drop onto the centre of the pie. Once, she wouldn't have dreamed of dragging her finger through the cool, thick, creamy decoration, ruining her own hard work, but now she was tempted. She would wait to actually cut the pie and eat it with the boys for morning tea, because it was their special celebration of Esme, but the cream called to her now. These days she didn't really care what people thought. It was liberating. She scooped up a blob of cream and touched it to her tongue and closed her eyes. *Darling girl.*

Tears ran down her face and she let them. She scooped up another blob and smoothed it over her lips, then licked it off.

'Yoo hoo!' There was a tapping at the open door and she turned without wiping her face.

'Oh,' said Annabelle. She put down her basket and a large pot plant she was carrying. 'You poor, poor girl.' She crossed the room to Willa, wrapping her arms around her. Willa let her head fall onto Annabelle's shoulder.

'I just brought you some flowers from the garden,' said Annabelle, after Willa felt strong enough to raise her head. 'For Esme.' She pulled them out of the basket and handed them to Willa.

'Thank you,' said Willa. And she was genuinely touched. Most people tried to avoid the subject of Esme at all costs, and if they accidentally mentioned their own daughter and how well she was doing, or talked about a party their teenagers had been to, they would suddenly remember, and in their eyes Willa would see a split second of sinking terror. Then they'd stutter and stumble, and she would see the colour draining from them, or collecting in vibrant patches around their necks or cheeks. Sometimes she would help them – *Of course you must tell me about Amelia/Katie/Henrietta* – even though she didn't want to hear about their girls at all, or maybe she did, depending on the day, depending on how fragile she was feeling. Sometimes she'd just pretend not to have noticed and the conversation would be turned around without a word from her. But here was Annabelle with a huge bunch of hydrangeas, and she was smiling and bringing Esme right into focus.

Willa smiled back at her and wiped her sleeve across her eyes.

Annabelle hurried across to the doorway and picked up the pot plant, which Willa now realised was a rose.

'And this. To plant somewhere for her. I thought it might be nice to have something growing in Australian soil.' Annabelle plucked off a small black growth from the side of the plant, and tutted as if the sight of it offended her. 'It's an Esme rose. A bush variety. Quite hardy, apparently.'

'Oh. Thank you,' said Willa again, stunned at her thoughtfulness.

Annabelle gave her a huge smile as she put the plant on the table and looked across to the ocean.

'Is that them?' she asked.

Hamish was paddling out to meet the swell. A large wave began to crest, and he turned the board to shore right as it peaked and rolled forward, and Annabelle said, 'Go!' at the same time Willa said, 'I think he's missed it.'

But Hamish had just caught its surge. He balanced across the top of it, then in one miraculous motion pushed himself up into a squatting position, stood and rode the huge breaking wave right into the shore.

Annabelle clapped. 'Good boy!' she said.

Willa laughed. She felt off balance with the see-saw of emotion, but better all the same. 'Would you like a cup of tea?'

'That would be lovely,' said Annabelle.

Willa boiled the kettle, grateful for something to do with her hands.

'Did Esme like the beach?' asked Annabelle.

'Yes,' said Willa, then she added, 'She wasn't really a sun bunny, but she liked to try everything. If she were here now, she might well have been surfing with the boys.'

'They'll be missing her out there then, I imagine,' said Annabelle.

Willa poured the water over the tea bags then began searching through the cupboards for a vase. How to explain Esme? 'Perhaps. But equally, she might have been trying her hand at macramé right now, or painting the ocean, or building elaborate sandcastles. Then when she'd mastered those, it would have been something else. She liked to put her mind to things, just to see if she could do them. She was very talented.'

'She sounds extraordinary,' said Annabelle.

'She was,' said Willa. 'And the good thing is that now I get to say things like that and nobody minds that I'm boasting. I have a permanent leave pass to be annoyingly boasty.'

Annabelle chuckled. They both watched as the boys began walking back up the beach with their surfboards under their arms. At the base of the hill on which the beach house was built, they dropped the boards in the grassy area, rinsed under the outdoor shower and headed up the side path to the house. Willa waved to them.

'I should probably cook them something substantial before we have that,' she said, nodding at the pie on the table.

'I'll go then,' said Annabelle.

'No, please, you must stay. They'd love to see you again. And have some banoffee pie with us. It was Esme's favourite. It's our celebration of her.'

'Well, I'll stay for a cuppa at least,' said Annabelle. 'I'd love to see them again too, although I've got lots to do for this silly fete.'

'You're such a busy person,' said Willa. 'I do hope you're looking after yourself.'

'Oh, pfff,' said Annabelle, blowing out her lips.

'When will you be starting treatment?' asked Willa.

'A few weeks' time. After the fete. Anyway, I feel great. Some days I think the doctors don't know what they're talking about.'

Willa noticed the forced cheer in the set of Annabelle's jaw; the bright, brittle sound to her words.

'You're being very strong,' she said.

'Well, you've faced much worse, my lovely, so I'm taking your lead,' said Annabelle.

'But still,' said Willa, 'I always had Hugo to hold me up.' She glanced across at Annabelle, wondering if making space to bring Dan into the conversation was wise. But she knew that sometimes you needed to give people permission to talk about their problems.

'Yes,' said Annabelle. 'Well, I have Dan too. I've forgiven him. For the Sylvia thing. Well, not that I've told him I know about it. Some things are better left unsaid.'

'Right,' said Willa. 'I'm not sure I could be so understanding.'

Annabelle's face took on a perplexed look. 'He's my husband. We made vows. Till death do us part and all that. I'd never leave him.' She shifted in her seat. 'Did you decide to read the diaries?'

'I haven't yet,' said Willa.

'Well, that's all for the best, I should think,' said Annabelle.

Hugo and Hamish startled them, appearing on the front deck, towels around their shoulders. They dried themselves and Willa opened the door.

'Cold?' she asked.

'Nah,' said Hamish, shaking the wet strands of hair from his face. 'We went numb ages ago.' He grinned at her, and Willa thought: you're nearly a man. Look at you, all muscled and tall.

'Hello!' said Annabelle. 'Goodness, you are brave! Dan likes surfing but he hasn't done it for ages. Too busy. He'd be jealous if he saw you now.'

'Hello, Annabelle,' said Hugo. 'How lovely to see you again.'

Willa smiled at her handsome husband, the perfect English gentleman. She could see Annabelle melting. People did that around Hugo. She did it too sometimes.

'I hope you're staying for brunch,' he said.

'Oh, no, I… I can't really, I'm… I'd hate to impose.'

Willa watched the colour rise in Annabelle's cheeks as she mentally discarded all the reasons why she needed to go. It would be nice if she stayed. It might help them get through the next little bit of the day.

Hugo leaned down to Willa and kissed her cheek.

'Mum does a really good bacon sandwich,' said Hamish, smiling at Annabelle, and Willa saw then that sometime in the last two years, when she hadn't been looking, he had developed his father's charm.

'Oh, well, I was going to stay for a cup of tea,' said Annabelle. 'But I'm on a health kick. No bacon for me!' She gazed at Hamish adoringly.

Hamish began digging through the fridge and brought out a huge packet of bacon. Willa took it and began searching in the drawers for a knife.

'Hamish, could you show me how to do that Instagram thing again?' asked Annabelle. 'I tried to post a shot of one of the weddings on there earlier, but I'm hopeless with all these apps and things.'

'Sure,' said Hamish. He pulled on a T-shirt. 'Where's your phone?'

Willa pushed the hissing bacon around in the pan and listened as Hamish explained the functions of Instagram again and they discussed the best hashtags to use to get more brides to follow Merrivale Garden Weddings.

After that, the bacon sandwiches were demolished in minutes. They sat sipping tea, until Hugo said, 'I'd love a piece of that special pie.' He reached across and took Willa's hand.

She nodded.

Hamish picked up the knife. 'You would have liked my sister, Annabelle. She was much better at social media than me. She'd have loved all that wedding stuff.' He began putting pieces of the pie onto plates and handing them round with the spoons.

'You must try it,' said Willa, as Annabelle's hand faltered above her plate. 'We feel very lucky to be here in Australia with you, remembering Esme.'

Annabelle nodded gravely, and after a moment, she leaned over to Willa and said, 'I do hope you keep The Old Chapel for yourself, Willa. Then you could come back every year.'

'Yes,' said Willa, warming to the idea.

'Come in the spring,' said Annabelle. 'We have a wonderful tulip festival. The farm down the road is glorious when they're in bloom. Come for your birthday.'

'My birthday's in the Aussie summer,' said Willa. 'December the tenth. So we would have to make it a lovely long stay for Christmas.'

Willa brought a portion of the pie to her mouth and closed her eyes as the caramel melted across her tongue. When she opened them again, she noticed that the colour had drained from Annabelle's face.

'Annabelle?' she said. 'Are you all right? Are you sick?'

Annabelle gave a tiny shake of her head.

'What's wrong?'

'December the tenth,' said Annabelle, her voice a whisper.

'My birthday? Yes,' said Willa.

'But you must be in the spring,' said Annabelle. 'Lillian's baby would have been born in early spring. September, or… even earlier.'

'Oh,' said Willa. Suddenly her whole body was encompassed by a swoop of sorrow as another door closed on her identity. She slumped, drowning in the sensation that Esme should be here, and that if she was, none of this would matter at all. Just last night she had confided to Hugo that she believed she'd gotten to the bottom of who her parents were. It made sense that it was Lillian and this unknown man, this dead man that Annabelle didn't want to talk about. The man Willa would gather up the courage for soon – the courage to read about him in the diaries. Both her biological parents were dead, so there was no hurry. And for that moment, when she had been lying there last night with her head in Hugo's lap, listening to the waves and drinking wine, it didn't feel important, because Esme was more important and there was only so much loss you could carry, and tomorrow it would be the day to think about Esme.

Hugo squeezed her arm. 'Darling?'

She didn't respond. She just felt so tired.

Hugo looked from Willa across to Annabelle, who sat ashen-faced in her chair, clutching hard at the edge of the table as if the room was spinning.

'What is it? What's wrong?' he asked.

Annabelle lifted her head and seemed to consider the remaining banoffee pie in the centre of the table.

'I'm sorry,' she said quietly. Her chair clattered noisily across the timber floor as she stood, then she picked up her basket and walked out.

CHAPTER TWENTY

Annabelle

Annabelle sat in her car, clutching the steering wheel. She could do it. It wasn't hard. Press the ignition button, put it in gear, foot on the pedal, drive up the hill. But the fear was grasping at her throat, punching at her insides. She squeezed her eyes shut. *Stupid girl, stop fussing, just drive the darn car home!*

She pushed the button and reversed out of the driveway, refusing to look at Willa and Hugo, who were standing on the porch looking at her with puzzled faces. As she drove up the wet, winding cliff-side road towards Merrivale, she thought, push your foot down hard, woman. Go over the edge. *How much better, to be at the bottom of the sea.* And yet the cold tip of something enormous was pressing at her. An iceberg of realisation. *No, I might be needed. What if I'm needed?*

She pulled out onto the main road, taking slow, deep breaths that didn't seem to be having the slightest effect on the heavy sense of dread that had settled on her chest. She turned down the road towards home, and at her driveway, she stopped as a woman waved to her.

She let her window down and the woman leaned towards the car.

'Hi, Annabelle. I thought I'd come and help with repotting all those rosemary cuttings we put in the back shed.'

Annabelle stared at her. She began counting in her head – *ten, nine, eight, seven, six, five* – hoping the woman's name would come to her. She knew her. Yes, she was certainly someone well known to her. But Annabelle's head was spinning. 'Right,' she said. She realised she was staring at the woman, and so she put her finger on the window button and the window moved up noiselessly. *No. That looked even more odd.* She wound it back down again. 'Cuttings.' She heard the word come out of her mouth, not sure where she had been going with the thought.

'Are you all right?' asked the woman.

'Perfectly,' said Annabelle.

'You don't look well. I actually came up here because I thought you might need some moral support.'

'Really?' Annabelle wondered how the woman could read her mind.

'Rita Perotta was mentioning this morning at the café that Sylvia seemed a bit off balance. Rita was spouting stories. Silly untrue gossip, no doubt. About… Sylvia and Dan. And Sylvia being in her underpants when he—'

'Mira!' It was *Mira* she was talking to. The relief at remembering her friend's name had made Annabelle bark it out. Mira from the garden club. Why did Mira think she wanted to hear the town gossip?

Mira looked at her oddly. 'I didn't want people to be talking about it behind your back. Thought you should hear it—'

'Yes! Yes.' Annabelle took a quick breath and put her shaking hands back on the steering wheel. 'Let's do some repotting. I'll just get changed.' She wound up the window again and drove the car into the garage. She felt a pang of relief as Mira headed off in the direction of the shed instead of following her in.

She didn't have time to think about repotting, or cuttings, or Rita's stupid gossip. She needed Lillian's diary urgently. The one from 1977. Willa must never be allowed to read it. Making sure Mira was safely out of sight, she ducked around the side of the main house and crossed the lane into The Old Chapel garden. She looked left and right, but the lane was deserted. Across the paddock, the ocean was a deep grey-blue. She rattled at the door handle and was annoyed to find it locked. She ducked back down the two steps and skirted the house, hoping she could push open the kitchen window. She stood on tiptoe and placed her hands against the dirty glass, but the swollen timber and old paint held it fast.

Annabelle's mind ticked over frantically. She needed a ladder. Yes, a ladder would get her in one of the windows – she'd try a far-side window, though, so she wouldn't be spotted from the lane or from Merrivale's gardens. She hurried back across to the shed, and as she crashed through the door, she was startled to see Mira. How could she have forgotten about her already? She cursed her silly brain. It was like a piece of Swiss cheese.

'Er, I just need the ladder for something. Something up high. A high item… on a high shelf,' she panted, her curls sticking to her face as she began to sweat. 'I'll be back soon to help you with those lavender cuttings.'

'Rosemary,' said Mira.

'Who?' said Annabelle.

'Not who. What,' said Mira.

'What?' said Annabelle, scrunching up her face.

'It's rosemary, not lavender!' said Mira.

Annabelle shook her head. Who *cared*? The woman was being obtuse. She pushed past her and found a screwdriver, which she shoved into her front pocket. Then she picked up her favourite lightweight ladder from the back corner and hurried out and across the garden with it. Light as a feather was her ladder, although frightfully unstable. But good for middle-aged ladies like herself who couldn't lug those dreadful heavy contraptions around every time they needed a pot of pickled walnuts down from the very high shelf in the laundry.

Around the back of The Old Chapel, she extended the ladder and pulled the legs apart, balancing it against the house on the rough grass. She tested it for stability, then climbed up it, clutching at the side of Lillian's house with one hand. Paint flecks broke away beneath her touch. When her feet were two steps from the top of the ladder, she swivelled and took a moment to gain her balance before retrieving the screwdriver from her pocket and levering it carefully under the window latch. With a few sharp bangs on the handle, the latch rattled and gave way. Success!

She stopped and considered what she'd done for a moment, then gave a mad little laugh. *I'm a burglar!* But it didn't matter. She needed that diary, and a tiny bit of law-breaking was perfectly understandable in the circumstances. Necessary, in actual fact.

She dropped the screwdriver onto the grass below and pushed up the little sash window as high as it would go, which was only halfway. She peered at the open window sceptically. It wasn't a large opening, and she hadn't really seen any results from her health kick yet. Her hips and belly were still annoyingly large. Still, she could probably wriggle through. Inside, beneath the window, was a sideboard, so if she lost her balance, she wouldn't fall far.

Annabelle swivelled again to hold onto the ladder, then put one leg through the window and lowered herself down just a fraction until her foot felt the sideboard. She put the other leg through and pushed her bottom in. She slid backwards and tried to move herself sideways, so she wouldn't fall off the end of sideboard. A sharp jab at each side of her hips made her stop. Her hands wobbled on the ladder. She moved her leg slowly behind her, trying to find traction, but all she could focus on was a sharp pain where her knee was digging into timber. The noise of a car engine approaching, followed by the slamming of a door, made her stop. Her breath quickened. She wiggled further backwards, and as she peered to her left down the side of the house, her hand slipped. She grasped wildly at the ladder, but instead of holding it, she knocked the silly thing away.

For a heart-stopping moment, it teetered on two legs before crashing, lightly, to the ground. Annabelle swore. She was bent forward, chest heaving, arms pressed against the exterior of the house. She was stuck.

Behind her, from within the house, she heard the rustling noise of a key, then a door squeaking, then footsteps. She couldn't turn. Couldn't see. She was sweating; panting with the exertion of keeping herself balanced.

'Annabelle?'

Sylvia. Annabelle felt her insides plummet. She imagined her sister staring at the enormous pink floral moons of her bottom. She clenched her pelvic floor – a habit she'd gained after a Pilates instructor once told her it would make her look slimmer when naked. She *felt* naked.

'What are you doing?'

'I could ask you the same thing! I'm looking for something,' said Annabelle tersely. 'Help me down! I'm stuck.'

She heard Sylvia's hurried footsteps, then felt a hand on her thigh and another on her back.

'You do seem to be quite stuck,' said Sylvia after a moment. 'What are you looking for out there?'

'A spider!' spluttered Annabelle. 'I was chasing a spider and it ran out here and I tried to swat it.' She would have congratulated herself on her own quick thinking, but the window frame was digging painfully into her sides.

'Let me hold you tight around the legs and see if you can shuffle backwards,' said Sylvia doubtfully.

Annabelle made a huffing sound, then did as she was told, but she knew she was just getting more wedged in. 'You'll need to go outside and stand the ladder back up for me,' she panted.

'Why is there a ladder out there?' asked Sylvia.

'I told you!' said Annabelle testily. 'I was cleaning spider webs. Just hurry up and do it.'

After a moment, Sylvia appeared on the grass in front of her and lifted the ladder, and Annabelle was able to wriggle out and clamber back down. She brushed herself off, and Sylvia stood with her arms crossed and watched her, before bending down and picking up the brass fixture that had fallen off the window when Annabelle broke in. She held it up.

Annabelle ignored her. She hurried back around to the front and let herself into The Old Chapel. Her hips throbbed. Her whole body was taut, sweating, but she pushed on, moving from one box to the next, lifting lids, checking if they held anything that looked like diaries.

'What on earth are you doing?' asked Sylvia, appearing next to her.

'Don't be such a busybody,' said Annabelle, brushing past her. She pulled the tape off a sealed box and was disappointed to see only files inside.

'That is possibly the most ridiculous thing that has ever come out of your mouth,' said Sylvia.'

'There's no need to be rude,' said Annabelle. She was so hot and flustered, she felt like her feet were sweating. It was an extremely odd sensation.

'You were breaking in!' exclaimed Sylvia.

Annabelle moved to the next box, flipped the lid. Flicked through the books.

'Annabelle, these are Willa's things. You have no right to be going through them!' said Sylvia sternly.

'She wouldn't mind. She doesn't mind,' said Annabelle. 'I need something urgently. Where did you put Lillian's... personal papers?'

'If you're looking for the diaries,' said Sylvia, after a moment, 'there are a dozen of them in the box I just put by the door.'

Annabelle looked up.

'I took them home by mistake.' Sylvia was glaring at her.

Annabelle said, 'What about the one from 1977? Is that one in there?'

Sylvia regarded her for a moment. 'Willa is your baby.'

Annabelle felt the wind go out of her. She took a step forward and slumped onto the couch. 'I just need the 1977 one,' she said quietly. 'I don't want her to read about it.'

'There's nothing in it,' said Sylvia. 'Nothing interesting, anyway. I checked.'

'Oh,' said Annabelle, letting out a sigh of relief.

'Why don't you want her to read about it?' asked Sylvia. 'Would it be so bad if she found out you were her mother?'

'No. Yes! No… it's… oh! Just mind your own business,' snapped Annabelle.

Sylvia sighed. 'Have you known for a while? About Willa?'

'I only just found out,' said Annabelle tersely. Then she sighed and looked out the window. 'I only just found out her birth date. She doesn't even… look like me.'

'Are you kidding?' asked Sylvia. 'There's a definite resemblance in the eyes. And the way she laughs.'

'Is there?' said Annabelle. She felt a flutter of something in her chest.

Sylvia said, 'I'm sorry I left you, Anna. To have her on your own. But that night, when I saw you with Dan, I thought – later… when I found out you were pregnant – well, I thought the baby was Dan's. He says it wasn't, but—'

'She's not,' said Annabelle. 'Of course she's not.' The way Sylvia was looking at her, the doubt in her eyes, it was monstrous.

'Did you have a boyfriend?' asked Sylvia gently.

Annabelle ignored her. How dare Sylvia think she had any right to be having this conversation, the way she'd been gallivanting with Dan.

'Anna? Who was the boy?'

'It's none of your business!' said Annabelle.

Sylvia sighed again. 'Why on earth would Lillian leave the house to your daughter? It makes no sense.'

'Go away,' snapped Annabelle. 'Just leave.' She looked down to avoid Sylvia's glare.

'No, thank you very much,' said Sylvia. 'I'm the one with the key.'

'Oh, don't be so immature!' said Annabelle.

'Well, that's the pot calling the kettle black. You're the one who got your bum stuck in the window in the middle of a robbery.'

'Oh, pooey poo poo!' shouted Annabelle. Where on earth had those words come from? They sounded so childish! She felt herself welling up with laughter.

'Hello?' A voice at the door made them both jump. Mira was peering nervously into The Old Chapel. No doubt she'd heard the angry voices.

Annabelle caught Sylvia's eye and saw the glint of shared mirth, waiting to burst out.

'I just thought I'd pop in to say I've finished repotting the rosemary,' said Mira. 'I, umm… Annabelle,' she glared at Sylvia, 'did you want me to stay and keep you company?'

'No,' said Annabelle. A gushing, snorting noise escaped from the back of her throat. Her hand flew to her mouth to stop the laughter coming out.

'Really?' asked Mira, peering at her worriedly.

'Absolutely not,' said Sylvia.

Mira ignored Sylvia. 'I know you're probably feeling a bit hurt right now, Annabelle, but if you want any support, I'll be just over at your house.' Mira hesitated, looking between them. Then she turned reluctantly and left.

Annabelle looked down at her feet, trying to regain her composure.

Sylvia said, 'Sorry. It's none of my business who Willa's father is. And I'm sorry, too, about Dan. That's what Mira would have been meaning, with that comment. I guess you've heard about me being on the street yelling at Dan in my undies this morning. It wasn't what it looked like, by the way. I mean, I had been seeing him previously – you knew that, the night you had the panic attack – but not since. And I'm sorry. Can we talk about it?'

'You were wearing your underpants on the street?' said Annabelle, confused.

'I disgust myself.'

'Yes. Well, I'm not surprised,' said Annabelle.

Sylvia let out a little cough of a laugh. 'Anyway, I'm sorry that I've embarrassed you. There'll be gossip.'

'Yes,' said Annabelle. 'Dan will be cross.'

'Screw Dan! He's not worth the mat you wipe your feet on,' said Sylvia angrily.

Annabelle bristled with indignation. That was so unfair! Just because Sylvia had managed to lure him back into her bed after all these years. There weren't many men who'd be able to withstand Sylvia's confidence and her beauty, if she set her hat to them.

'I don't need your opinion on my husband, thank you very much!'

Sylvia's shoulders slumped a little. There was a long silence before she said, 'Anna, in the diaries, there's... I don't want to break your heart, but Dan hasn't ever been a faithful husband. Apparently Lillian called him out on it a few times. Each time he promised he'd stop, but he didn't. I'm just the latest idiot to fall into bed with him.'

No, no, no, no, no, no, no, no, no. Annabelle's head dropped and she felt the energy leaking out of her. She didn't want to know this. Didn't want her whole life to be a lie.

Sylvia said, 'It's not your fault. He's always been a narcissistic bastard. It's easy to get swept up by his charm when he turns it on.'

'But… he was my only boyfriend. The only man I ever…' Annabelle looked down again and noticed tears falling onto the floorboards.

'What about Willa's father?' asked Sylvia, uncertainly. 'When… Who was he?'

Annabelle turned her head towards the wall, wishing it would somehow swallow her up. Why couldn't Sylvia just leave this alone? She wanted to crumble and cry out for her mother.

Sylvia sighed. 'When I got the letter saying you were pregnant, Lillian said she'd already arranged for you to go to Launceston to wait it out, so no one would know. I felt terrible leaving you on your own, but I knew Lillian would look after you. And she said the couple who were adopting the baby were lovely.'

Annabelle felt all the decades of sadness dragging through her.

'I know I should have come back,' said Sylvia. 'But I was sick. Depressed. I couldn't face seeing him.' When she got no answer again, she said, 'I was so ashamed of what I did that night. Of the real reason I left.'

'What do you mean?' asked Annabelle, wiping at her eyes. 'Because you yelled at me like an evil banshee when you thought I'd been with Dan?'

Sylvia's hand shook as she pressed it hard against her mouth. Then she brought her other hand up so that both were covering her whole face. After a moment, she slid them down, so that now they were only covering her mouth. She gave a small shake of her head.

'No. Well, yes, of course. But there was something else. After that.'

Annabelle could feel her despair. She was inexplicably terrified by it. 'Syl, what did you do?' She got up from the couch, trembling.

'I can't…' sobbed Sylvia. She turned and walked to the open door, pulling the key out of the keyhole. 'I can't tell you, but I'm sorry, Anna.' She looked at the key, then dropped it onto the tiny round table in the vestibule. 'And I'm sorry about Dan, too. I can't tell you how sorry I am.'

Annabelle nodded. And as Sylvia walked away, the strangest thought popped into her head. *Maybe I knew that Dan wasn't faithful. Maybe I always knew.*

CHAPTER TWENTY-ONE

Willa

As she folded the last of her clothes into the suitcase, Willa pondered the phone call. Annabelle had sounded serious. Not at all like her usual self. Willa was suddenly nervous. Had she upset her in some way with the garden fete? Had she removed some important heritage plant from The Old Chapel garden? Leandra had been prattling on and on in the last weeks about the rarity of some of the specimens.

She wished Hugo and Hamish hadn't gone back to Oxford. She missed their company, but Hugo had lectures to deliver and Hamish had already missed a week of school. Willa had decided to stay on for a few days alone, as there were still loose ends she needed to tie up in terms of managing The Old Chapel after she went home. And she had friends to visit in Sydney, too. It might be a while before she made it back to Australia again, so she couldn't give up the opportunity to see them. She would miss being here in her homeland. The lifestyle was so casual and easy.

It had been nearly a week since the anniversary of Esme's death, and in those few days, Willa had felt a growing urge to know her birth heritage. To find something here that tied her to this soil. She had planted the Esme rose in The Old Chapel garden. She wasn't selling the place. Not yet. Maybe not ever. Esme would grow at Sisters Cove. She could be wild and free like the winds that buffeted the cliffs.

Willa had read some of Lillian's diaries over the course of the week, but they didn't seem to give her any clues to her parentage. Disturbingly, she'd read one entry about an affair Dan had been having with a young lawyer at his office in 1989. Lillian had been furious with him when she'd discovered an erotic love note on the woman's desk, among some files. Poor Annabelle. Willa wondered if she knew that Sylvia wasn't his first transgression.

She sat down heavily on the bed, thinking again about Annabelle's call. 'I have something to talk to you about,' she'd said. 'Can you come for a drink?' The request sounded odd, and Willa felt uneasy as she picked up her car keys and headed outside.

She parked the hire car at The Old Chapel and walked across the lane. Merrivale's garden was picture perfect. Most days Willa had been coming up to help Leandra in The Old Chapel garden, and each day she would see Annabelle and her helper, Pete, and sometimes women from the garden club; a busy bustle of helpers planting, preening, cutting and weeding; erecting garden arches and fixing dry-stone walls. As the fete drew nearer, Annabelle's stress levels were rising to fever pitch. Willa could see it in the way she walked and talked. It couldn't be good for her health.

Through the screen door of Merrivale's kitchen, Willa noticed that the table was set beautifully for two, with deep-blue linen place mats, white linen napkins and crystal wine glasses and water tumblers. It must be the way Annabelle always set the table, because she'd seen it like this the last time she was here around dinner time.

Annabelle stood at the stove, sweating, but otherwise smartly dressed in a top patterned with daffodils, tailored trousers and a pair of bright-yellow leather loafers.

'Oh, come in! Come in, Willa,' she said. 'What a pretty name it is, really – Wilhelmena,' she added, then appeared to mull over that thought. 'Would you like a glass of wine?'

'Yes please. White if you have it,' said Willa, after they'd hugged briefly.

'Right. Well you stir this, and I'll go and get a bottle from the cellar.'

Annabelle bustled off to the back area leaving Willa to stir a casserole pot that held some kind of beef dish. It smelled delicious.

She returned with two glasses of wine. 'I hope you like this one. It's a Chenin Blanc from New Zealand. I bought a couple of cases from a vineyard owned by the parents of a girl getting married here. I just *had* to order some when they told me. A bit of mutual business support!'

They both took a sip, and Annabelle closed her eyes as she swallowed. 'It was nearly fifty dollars a bottle, but don't tell Dan. He'd get cross,' she said with a laugh.

'It's really delicious,' said Willa.

'You're probably wondering what I wanted to talk to you about,' said Annabelle, after a moment.

'I'm intrigued,' said Willa. 'What is it?'

Annabelle sighed heavily. 'I wanted to know if you might consider staying on. Until after the fete. I… I need help, you see. Everything is getting out of hand, and I know how good at organising things you are. Just this week, I've heard you sort out so many problems whenever you popped over. The garden ladies think you're wonderful.' She picked up the wooden spoon and resumed stirring the pot. 'And I'd be so happy if you could be here to show The Old Chapel garden yourself, now that Lillian has gone.'

'Oh,' said Willa. 'Really? But I'm booked to go tomorrow to Sydney.'

'Could you possibly delay it? It would mean so much to me. To have a deputy. In the fete-organising department, I mean.'

Willa knew immediately that she would say yes. She'd been having the strangest sensation that her business here wasn't finished. But it was hard to know what she was waiting for.

'Of course I can stay,' she said. 'I'll ring the airline. Change my flight.'

'Oh goody!' Annabelle clapped her hands then looked up as Dan's Range Rover appeared in the driveway. Her hand fluttered at her neck. 'Ah, here's Dan.'

She's nervous, Willa thought.

'I'll just pop to the bathroom,' said Annabelle, as his car door slammed.

She left Willa in the kitchen, and after a moment, Dan appeared at the doorway, carrying a heavy-looking cardboard carton. He put it down outside the screen door and returned to the car to get another. When he had stacked four identical boxes near the doorway, he came inside, just as Annabelle returned.

'Perfect timing,' she said, handing him a bottle of red wine from the sideboard. 'Dinner's nearly ready.'

He took the bottle without speaking to her.

'Hello, Dan,' said Willa.

'Oh, hi,' he said, clearly surprised. He obviously hadn't noticed her in the corner. 'Aha, now let me see. You're here because you've changed your mind and decided to sell me The Old Chapel?'

'Dan! Willa's just here for a quick drink, not to be hassled.'

'Calm down. I was just kidding,' said Dan.

Willa looked at his furrowed brow and knew that he wasn't. 'Um, I might head off then, Annabelle,' she said.

Dan was now sitting at the table pouring himself a large glass of wine and scrolling on his phone. Willa found her dislike of him hard to disguise.

'You could join us if you like, for dinner,' said Annabelle. But Willa noticed the lack of enthusiasm in her voice. She clearly didn't want a dinner guest, and Willa didn't want to stay.

'Thanks, but I'll just see you tomorrow. We can make a plan of attack,' she said, and Annabelle looked unnerved.

'Wonderful,' she said. 'A plan. Good.'

CHAPTER TWENTY-TWO

Annabelle

As Willa walked out, Annabelle began steaming the broccoli to serve as a side to the beef. She knew Dan wouldn't eat it, so why was she doing it? Was she a *complete* fool? No, no. *She* would eat it, and she would get all the benefits of the free radicals.

Sylvia's revelation about the affairs had felt like a punch to the stomach. She could still feel the hurt in her solar plexus. But what could she do? She was part of Merrivale. This was her place in the world. The ocean, the garden, the house; she'd invested every single bit of her energy – every single day of her married life – into making it her home. Without children, without anywhere else that mattered, what was out there if she left him?

She drained the broccoli, then served up the casserole as Dan continued playing on his phone at the table.

'Beef stroganoff,' she said, putting the plate in front of him. She had chopped the mushrooms extra fine so he'd be forced to eat them in the mix. Mushrooms were full of vitamins. Important for her immune system. She had put more in than usual, and there was a good chance Dan would actually notice the flavour. Half of Sisters Cove knew by now that he'd been having an affair with Sylvia. She had been pondering this as she had chopped the extra punnet of mushrooms into the sauce. He deserved to taste the bloody things.

He grunted, not looking up.

'I've something important to tell you,' said Annabelle, fiddling with her napkin.

Dan began shovelling the beef into his mouth.

She took a breath and closed her eyes. This was it. The beginning of a new chapter. 'I'm Wilhelmena's birth mother. I had her when I was sixteen. She was adopted.'

Dan froze, his fork piled with beef hovering in mid-air.

'What?' he spluttered.

'I only found out that she was my baby a few days ago, and it's taken me a little time to work up the courage to tell you. I'm sorry,' she said, although she didn't feel sorry. She felt irritated and stomach-punched.

'But the doctors said you couldn't carry a baby to term.'

'Well I did. Once. It wasn't an easy birth. There were complications.'

'But… I would have known,' said Dan, perplexed.

'I went away, for six months, after Sylvia left.'

'But you went to boarding school. You hated it, that's why you came back.'

'Lillian told me to say that. And Dad. They thought I'd get a reputation if people knew.'

Dan stared at her in silence. Then he said, 'Yeah, well. You would have.' He refilled his wine glass, and grimaced. 'I can't bloody believe you never told me.' He chewed another mouthful, slowly now, and Annabelle could sense the anger rising in him. 'Who would have thought it, huh? That prim little miss I married.' His smile was cruel and he shook his head slowly, never taking his eyes off her. 'Who were you sleeping with?'

Annabelle ignored him and forked a small piece of beef into her mouth, barely tasting it. Barely breathing.

'Who was the bloody father?' demanded Dan.

Annabelle looked down at her hands.

'Have I been the laughing stock round town my whole life? A bloody cuckold? I was probably having beers at the pub back then, telling everyone I was marrying the Virgin fucking Mary, and the guys were all pissing their pants behind my back.' He pushed his chair away from the table.

'Don't be ridiculous,' spluttered Annabelle, barely able to form words.

'Don't be ridiculous? When Little Miss Perfect – who bloody chased me for years, begging for me, batting her eyelashes at me, throwing her virgin self at me and promising I was the only one ever – was screwing around all that time!' He thumped his hand on the table.

'You can hardly talk!' cried Annabelle, and she shuddered, forcing down a violent sob.

Dan stood suddenly, his chair crashing backwards. 'You buttoned-up bitch!' He glared at her, then stormed off towards the veranda door and yanked it open, letting it bang behind him.

Annabelle screamed, 'Don't be so cruel!' and raced after him, pulling the screen door open. 'I never—'

But the next sound from Annabelle's mouth was a loud screech as her foot connected with something hard. A stack of cartons had materialised from nowhere outside the door. She felt herself tipping, tumbling. She grabbed wildly at the top box, but it was too late. The box fell first and Annabelle's feet were swept from beneath her, and she landed with a shocking thump on the tiles.

For a moment, the pain in her wrist, in her whole body, silenced her. Her knees began throbbing. She pushed herself up, whimpering.

Dan appeared.

Jars of golden liquid had tipped out of the fallen box. One of the jars had cracked and a gooey, glistening substance was spreading over the tiles.

'Ow,' sobbed Annabelle, rubbing at her wrist.

'Bloody hell,' muttered Dan, picking up two stray jars that had rolled across the veranda.

'What are these?' cried Annabelle angrily. She sat up against the wall, the humiliation making her want to shrivel up.

'Honey for the damned fete. Tippy wants to have a stall so I offered to bring them up.'

'No!' cried Annabelle. 'You know I won't have that dreadful dirty man coming round here. How could you, Dan?'

'I'm sick of your bullshit, Annabelle! You're such a bloody snob! He's just a guy trying to make a buck like the rest of us. He can't help it if he was born with half a brain!'

Annabelle looked up at him, pleading. 'Please, no, Dan. Don't bully me into this. It's *my* fete.' Tears welled in her eyes.

Dan shook his head and kicked at the broken honey jar in disgust. As he stormed off towards the shed, he called back over his shoulder. 'If you don't want Tippy to come to the fete, you can bloody well tell him yourself.'

CHAPTER TWENTY-THREE

Annabelle

1977

Annabelle pushed herself away from Tippy. Her head was swimming with the smell of him, the huge, disgusting size of him. Scream! she told herself. Len would wake up, wouldn't he? But the idea of screaming, calling out even, seemed so dramatic. *Don't make such a fuss, Annabelle.* Most days her mother's voice was still warm and near. And Tippy wasn't really doing anything. He hadn't tried to touch her in a bad way, not really.

The rain began to fall, a sudden crashing noise on the tin roof, and Annabelle tensed with the sound of it, the sight of it, grey and thick through the window. Water was sleeting through the open door.

'Tippy, you've got to go home now. I need you to go outside and close the door.' Suddenly she wondered where he lived. How far he had to go, how he would get through the rain. Then she stopped herself. *Not your problem*, she could hear Sylvia saying.

Tippy stood at the edge of the little couch near the coffee table. He leaned down and picked something up. Annabelle was flicking her eyes around the room, looking for a heavy or sharp object to protect herself with. Her eyes fell on the knife block on the kitchen sink. When she looked back at Tippy, he was holding something out to her.

'Snap,' he said.

'What?'

'Play snap wiv me. Won't take long.' It was a pack of playing cards. 'My grandma plays snap wiv me. We can play.'

Annabelle let out her breath. 'I... Oh. Maybe another time, Tippy. It's just that...' She cast around for an excuse. 'It's just that I have to give Len his pills now, and he might get sick if I don't give them to him on time.' She held her breath.

Tippy's eyebrows drew together as he thought about this.

'You like Len, don't you, Tippy? You wouldn't want him to get sick.'

'Len's my friend too,' said Tippy. He put the cards back down on the table. 'My mum will want me home for tea. She gets cross if I don't get home for tea.'

'Yes!' said Annabelle. 'She's probably got your tea ready. You'd better go.'

'Got my bike out there,' said Tippy, and he looked proud, as if this news should impress Annabelle.

'Better pedal fast,' she said, trying not to let the relief show in her voice. 'Don't want your tea to get cold.'

'All right,' he said, sighing sadly. 'Bye.' He lumbered to the door and closed it carefully behind him.

Annabelle let out a breath. She moved to the window and watched him wheel his old bike towards the road, over the deep puddles in the driveway. He threw his huge body over the frame, wobbled a little, then set off down the lane, sitting up straight, seemingly unaware of the pouring rain. She ran to the door and flicked the latch, then sank down on the couch and covered her face with her hands, letting her breathing get back to normal.

After a while, she got up and forced herself to finish cleaning the shoes, then she sat down again and turned the television back on and watched a game show. The light was fading fast outside now, and the rain had eased, but she could still hear a steady patter on the roof. She sat for a while longer and watched the night shadows fall. Then she stood to get a glass of milk from the fridge, and as she passed, she picked up the shoes from the kitchen bench and leaned down to put them back on her feet. She practised walking, back and forwards through the tiny kitchen, faster each time until she wobbled less on the high platform heels. She twirled and dipped, pretending she was a dancer, a model on the catwalk, a film star, sliding her hand up her thigh, across her breasts, pointing a toe, dipping her chin, fluttering her eyelashes. Soon it would be her turn. *Soon.*

There was a faint flash of light through the window, and the crack of thunder that followed startled her back into reality. She should check on Len. She tiptoed into his bedroom. There was a night light on, and in the dim glow, she could see Len's chest rising rhythmically. She inched the door closed and walked back towards the couch. As she passed the window, another bolt of lightning flashed through the night sky. She froze. In the light, she'd seen a figure. In the garden. Her heart began pounding and she stepped back from the window, aware that she was completely visible through the glass if Tippy had come back to spy on her. Had he been watching her twirl around the kitchen? Watching her run her hands across her body?

She cringed and ducked down, crawling over to the light switch. She flicked it off, then forced herself to stand, her heart rocketing the blood through her veins. After a while, her eyes adjusted to the darkness and she crept back over to the window and peered through the corner, out onto the road. Through the rain and the blackness, she couldn't see anything much. There were no street lights and barely any moonlight through the thick cloud cover, but she knew she had seen someone.

There was a sudden sharp *knock, knock, knock.*

Annabelle jumped. It didn't sound like Tippy's knock. It was confident, forceful. An adult knock.

She crept towards the door, looked at the latch and wondered what to do.

'Hello?' she called.

There was no response. The rain was still loud. Perhaps the person hadn't heard her.

'Hello, Dan, is that you?' she said, louder now.

'It's Andrew. From across the road.'

Annabelle let out a huge sigh of relief. She looked down and smoothed out her skirt, then ran her hands through her hair. Then she flicked on the light, reached for the latch and slid it back. Andrew Broadhurst stood under the porch overhang, the hood of his black raincoat sitting around his shoulders. He smiled at her, and Annabelle felt her heart give a little jump. Up close, he was crazy good-looking.

'Hello,' she said, and she stepped back instinctively, allowing him entry.

'I've just come to see Len,' he said. He walked in, stopping only to pull off the rain jacket and hang it on a hook, his body filling the tiny vestibule, filling Annabelle's senses. He strode past her into the living room, leaving his jacket to drip fat raindrops onto Lillian's shoes.

'He's asleep,' she said. She closed the door. There was silence, and Andrew leaned down to the whisky tray and picked up a glass. He looked up at her. 'What a shame. I often stop in for a nightcap with him.' He smiled. 'But if he's asleep, why don't you join me?'

'Oh. I... I'm not... I mean...' She stopped, trying to think over the loud beating sound in her ears. 'I don't really drink.'

Andrew took a moment to sweep his eyes over the green top, the skirt, the shoes. She felt hot, flummoxed. She felt a flutter of excitement in her chest and hoped she wasn't turning red.

'You should try it.' He poured some whisky into the other glass, much more than the nips she poured for her dad, and handed it to her. Then he turned and sat down on the couch and crossed his long legs, settling back and taking a sip of his own drink.

Annabelle wasn't sure what to do. Her father would tan her hide if he knew she'd taken a drink. But Andrew Broadhurst was treating her like an adult, and she liked it. She didn't want him to think she was a stupid child who wouldn't even have one drink with him. She didn't want to be rude.

She perched herself on the edge of the armchair and took a tiny sip of the whisky, noticing that her skirt had ridden up her legs. She left it. She didn't want to look silly by pulling it down. The whisky burned her mouth and she swallowed it slowly, trying not to wince or gag. It was awful.

Andrew smiled at her, threw back his drink in one gulp and poured himself another. 'You're Lillian's friend I met in my office a while back, aren't you?'

Annabelle felt herself blush at the pleasure of this statement. 'Yes, I'm Annabelle. Lillian's gone out tonight.'

'Yes, I know. She told me about the party.' He smiled at her again, and everything in his face lit up. 'She's a good friend of mine too.'

Annabelle relaxed. This man was lovely. His eyes were round dark pools, and as she took another tiny sip of the whisky, she felt a little bit hypnotised by the way he was looking at her. As if she was the loveliest thing he'd ever seen.

'Sometimes Scotch tastes better with a bit of water,' he said, looking at the large nip still in her glass. He stood and took it from her hand, letting his fingers rest gently on hers for a moment, and Annabelle's face flushed. She felt a warm, sticky pleasure go all the way through her. He crossed to the sink and added a little water, then handed the glass back to her, looking at her expectantly. It was thoughtful, and she appreciated it.

She took a sip as he watched, and it did taste better. She took another, larger sip, to fill the silence. He was still standing over her, and she wasn't sure what to do. She dipped her head and took another sip. She still didn't like it exactly, but perhaps she did like the heat, the closeness of him standing right there in front of her, though she wondered what that meant, because he was a married man. A really powerful, popular man, and she wasn't supposed to have such feelings.

She closed her eyes and swallowed another mouthful of whisky, letting it slide down her throat and settle in her belly. When she opened her eyes, Andrew was squatting in front of her, his face close, right there, his breath warm. Annabelle felt suddenly unsure. This had gone too far, but she was embarrassed because there was nothing she could say, so she took a large gulp of her drink, and this time she coughed with the power of it.

Andrew chuckled, and suddenly she felt his hand patting her back, his other hand warm on her knee. 'Poor thing. You drank it too fast.' He began rubbing her back with slow, rhythmic motions, and Annabelle's head was spinning, but in a nice way. The whisky was making everything a little bit blurry-edged and calm.

'Sorry,' she said. She closed her eyes and let him rub her back and wondered, distantly, if Dan would come back soon, and then he could have the drink with Andrew and she could go to bed, because suddenly she was quite tired.

Andrew's hand slid from her back and rested on her cheek, and she kept her eyes closed because now she knew this was bad. What if he kissed her? What if Dan walked in and found him kissing her? Dan would be so angry with her. But she couldn't open her mouth to speak, because she didn't want him to look at her mouth and think about kissing it, because she could tell he liked her. She had encouraged him to like her.

From behind her closed eyes, with a sinking feeling, Annabelle registered that his other hand was still on her knee, and then higher, on her inner thigh, and although she didn't want to offend him, she pushed her legs together so he knew he couldn't do that. She heard his breathing getting heavier, could feel it on her face, and she thought: keep your eyes closed, keep your eyes closed.

All around her, Annabelle could feel the rain. It was in her ears, driving into her mind, washing around her head like a swirling field of fog. She felt his hand go higher now, and then his mouth was on her face, kissing her, then gobbling her, slithering across her teeth, heaving breath into her nose. She felt the chair recede from beneath her as he pulled her up, propelled her across the room, pushed her back against the sideboard cabinet.

'You like that, don't you?' he was murmuring. His hand was under her top, Sylvia's good top, and he was pulling at it, stretching it, ripping it, and Annabelle wanted to cry. She would be in so much trouble. This was her fault. Of course it was. The top was too tight on her, and Sylvia had told her the skirt was too short. And she'd drunk the whisky, and it had given him the wrong idea. He thought she was an adult. She needed to say something, to tell him she was a kid, but the words wouldn't form.

He was making strange panting sounds, and Annabelle opened her eyes. He was staring at her, then he grinned, and there was something distant and hard about it. She needed to speak. Tell him *No!* But she looked down and his pants were undone and fear froze the word in her throat, because he was pushing up her skirt, then pulling at her underpants. She told herself to scream *stop!* but still nothing came. She pushed her hand against his chest, but it was like a solid wall, and then his hand grasped her head. His fingers were iron prongs in her scalp, tugging at it, yanking her hair. The cabinet was digging into her back, and then suddenly she was overcome with piercing pain, which started down low but then was all the way through her, and terrible.

'You like that?' he was growling, grunting, over and over, thrusting into her, slamming her back into the cabinet. 'Hmm? You like that?'

Annabelle felt herself burning up, receding, melting into the driving clatter of the rain on the roof as the sound and the force and the smell of him drummed through her.

Then it was over. He pulled himself out of her. He must have moved away, because all she could hear now was her own breath, but she didn't dare to open her eyes, just in case. After a long stretch of time, with only the rain and her ragged breathing for sound, she forced her eyes open. Andrew was across the room doing up his belt, facing the kitchen. He picked up his whisky glass and started refilling it.

It took a moment – because of the noise of the rain, or perhaps because her mind had blocked everything but him – before she noticed Lillian. She was standing in the vestibule, completely still.

She caught Annabelle's eye, then her gaze dropped downwards, to Sylvia's shoes and the torn outfit. Annabelle felt shame engulf her. Her skirt was up around her waist, and her underpants were at her knees. She bent and yanked them up and shoved the skirt back down. Her bra was showing, but when she tried to fix the top, she couldn't cover herself properly because Andrew had ripped it at the neck and it was stretched where he'd pulled it down. She felt tears bubble in her eyes as she hunched her shoulders and spread her fingers to cover the place where the shirt should have been.

Andrew must have noticed Lillian, because he turned.

Lillian stepped into the room, closing the door slowly, carefully. 'What have you done?'

There was a strange look on her face, and Andrew glanced across at Annabelle, a fleeting, blank glance, before he said, 'Nothing. I just popped over to see you.'

'But you knew I wasn't here tonight.'

'I forgot.'

'It was obvious. My car wasn't here.' Lillian took a few steps towards Annabelle, and looked at the ripped top again, as if she hadn't quite taken it in the first time. Tears were running down

Annabelle's face now, and she thought: stop crying, just stop it. Lillian is so angry at you. Sylvia will find out. She pushed the back of her hand across her cheeks, trying to stem the tears, to get them off her face so she could just talk properly. So she could ask to be driven home.

'You hurt her,' said Lillian. 'She's a kid, Andrew.' She crossed the room to Annabelle and touched her arm gently.

Annabelle looked down to the floor and lifted her hand to her hair to smooth it. When she dropped her hand, thin strands of hair were caught in her fingers. She turned her palm upwards.

Lillian saw the hair too. She reached out and smoothed Annabelle's hair, then wiped her thumb across her tears.

'Don't be dramatic,' said Andrew. 'I'm going home.' He put the whisky glass down with a crack on the coffee table and walked across to the vestibule.

'Did you *force* her to have sex with you?' asked Lillian. There was breathy disbelief in her voice, and her hand had dropped to her stomach protectively. Up close, Annabelle noticed the swell of it, just a small bump in Lillian's usually flat tummy that she had missed before now.

'What?' Andrew flicked his raincoat off the hook and began threading his arms into it.

'Her top is ripped! You were doing up your pants, Andrew!' Cold, driving anger burned in Lillian's voice.

'You never complained when I took them down for you. Jealous, are you, Lil?' He laughed and opened the door and walked down the steps, and Lillian ran after him.

'She's fifteen, you callous bastard. *Fifteen!*'

Annabelle knew she should do something, but she wasn't sure what, because her body had begun to shake so badly she couldn't think. She understood from something in the way Lillian spoke to Andrew that they weren't like normal neighbours, and that he wasn't just her boss, and that maybe she'd upset the balance of something, but she couldn't think what it all meant. She stumbled to the couch and sat down, and listened to the clatter on the roof and felt her teeth begin to chatter inside her clenched jaws. The pain began surging through her, in her arms, her back, her scalp, between her legs. Tears were streaming down her face as huge sobs came from nowhere and she shook with them, and over and over the same thought came into her mind. *Now I've done it. Now, I've really gone and ruined everything.*

CHAPTER TWENTY-FOUR

Willa

Willa glanced around Annabelle's garden as the man in front of her tried to decide which combination of four baby succulents he would choose for his twenty dollars. In one direction black and white cattle grazed under a blue sky, but in front of her, over the ocean, a bank of grey-black storm clouds hung ominously. Yesterday had been perfect. Warm, no wind, billowing white clouds that hung like Cupid's pillows in the bright-blue sky. But today, the thirty per cent chance of a storm she'd seen on her weather app felt more like a promise.

It had been a frantic week, finalising details for the fete and getting the gardens in perfect condition. But Willa had relished the challenge and she was awakening each day feeling fresher than she had for ages.

The fete had become bigger than anything Annabelle, or the garden club members, had ever imagined. On Monday, the state tourist board had called and asked if they could bring a large delegation of Asian tourism operators through, because they had heard that the Merrivale garden was one of the best in Tasmania. They wanted lunch and formal photo opportunities. The newspaper had run the story – after Willa emailed them a press release – and numbers were predicted to surge. Hellie Beacher's gourmet sausage sizzle stand wasn't going to be enough. Annabelle had been bubbling with stress, but Willa had come alive. This was one of her favourite modes. Work mode. She was good at solutions. Good at seeing what needed to be done and finding creative ways to do it. She had missed this.

In Burnie, she had found a mobile wood-fired pizza van, which was now located near the garden entry, and then she'd found the Paella Pan Man who was currently stirring up huge vats of fragrant rice in an oversized pan in front of the open-sided marquee, where people could sit at crates-turned-tables and eat. Seating was provided by hay bales. Willa had spotted them in a local shearing shed on one of her walks and had sourced and washed blankets from the local charity shop to cover them. These were easy fixes, but Annabelle was overjoyed with the help, verging on hysterical. She admitted she hadn't been sleeping, and Willa could see she was teetering right on the edge.

Since word of Dan's affair had spread like a virulent virus throughout Sisters Cove, Annabelle's friends from the garden club had been rallying around her in suffocating hordes. There was head-shaking and tut-tutting, and when Dan had dared to show his face in the garden earlier, Willa had noticed Abigail Beddingham, walking on the arm of her decrepit husband, actually turn her head away in disgust.

The man in front of Willa finally decided on eight succulents, and she put them into a little carry tray and took his fifty-dollar note, digging around in her Tupperware container for change.

'Aren't they gorgeous?' she said, and the man smiled at her and agreed.

Across the garden, a teenage girl sat under the huge Irish strawberry tree strumming on her guitar and singing old tunes into a microphone. Next to her, six tents were lined up – some selling cuttings, others full-grown plants. There was a fresh lemonade stand and a craft stall that the women from the Sisters Cove craft group had put together, selling everything from hand-spun and woven scarves, felted soap covers and resin earrings, to tiny painted cards featuring scenes of the beach. Further down, near the orchard, bookings were being taken for guided tours of the garden every half-hour, and next to that, the local lily farm was selling closed-budded lilies for five dollars a bunch – a quarter of the price that Willa would pay in Oxford.

Groups of people meandered through, chatting happily. Mostly they were grey-haired and clad in floral blouses, sensible slacks and broad-brimmed hats, but there were plenty of families among them. Children ran and squealed and toppled on the manicured lawns in front of her, and she listened to mothers warning them about staying out of the flower beds and away from the man selling fire pits, whose hand-forged iron contraptions were lit for effect.

A woman walking with an old lady waved at Willa from over by the row of tents. She was wearing a huge floppy hat and jeans. The pair moved slowly across the lawn, the old woman lifting and dropping her walking stick with care. As they drew closer, Willa realised the younger woman was Indigo.

'Hi Willa.' Indigo grinned.

'Hello Indi. Can I interest you in a succulent or two?' Willa smiled.

'No thanks. I just wanted to introduce you to someone. Willa, this is Constance Broadhurst. This used to be her garden.'

'Hello, Mrs Broadhurst.'

'Constance, please.' The old lady gave her the hint of a smile. She was perfectly groomed, her white hair in a wispy bun, pink lipstick, a pale-blue blazer complementing her neat black trousers. A string of pearls sat around her neck, and the whole effect reminded Willa of an elegant storybook grandmother.

'What a wonderful legacy you've left here, Constance,' she said, then cringed, because that made it sound like the woman was already dead.

Constance nodded her head but didn't say anything.

'Annabelle is very grateful for the amazing specimens you've planted and for all your advice on the garden you've given over the years,' Willa began again. This was true. Annabelle seemed very devoted to Constance. She visited her weekly.

Constance nodded again, but still didn't speak.

'Willa's just inherited The Old Chapel from Lillian,' Indigo told her. 'She's the mystery beneficiary. Annabelle must have told you about her.'

Constance was peering at Willa, looking her up and down, studying her as if she was a specimen in a museum.

'Not such a mystery,' she said eventually. She pursed her mouth, averting her eyes now, as if the sight of Willa offended her in some way, and turned to the succulents on the table. 'Twenty dollars?' She shook her head in disbelief. 'Daylight robbery.'

'How about we head over to the house for a cuppa, Connie?' said Indigo.

'All right. Goodbye then,' said Constance. She gave Willa one last look, then turned with her walking stick and began to cross the lawn towards the house.

Indigo winked at Willa and said in a hushed voice, 'I would have liked to see you wangle twenty bucks out of her. Never spends a penny even though she's loaded. This place provides the least of her income.'

'Oh really?' said Willa. 'I thought Merrivale belonged to Dan and Annabelle.'

'Well it does, sort of. But Connie makes them pay rent. She has a life tenancy or something, then they get it when she goes.'

Willa raised her eyebrows.

'Dan wouldn't be the only one with an interest in Connie carking it,' whispered Indigo. 'There'd be plenty of distant relatives waiting in the wings for her loot.' She waved to someone behind Willa, then added, 'I like her. I hope she keeps them waiting for years.'

She winked and set off after Constance. She walked with the lightness of a dancer, and suddenly Willa felt a fierce protectiveness and pride. Pride in Indigo's good, kind nature. She watched her settle Constance onto one of the white plastic chairs that Annabelle used for the weddings. Willa had helped to bring out all the little desks and side tables from the house, so that people could sit down and enjoy Devonshire teas that were being prepared in the kitchen by the garden club committee.

A low rumbling sound made Willa look up. The storm clouds were sweeping in from the ocean, blocking out the sunshine and sending dark shadows over the lawn. Across the garden, Annabelle was bustling towards her. She was dressed in a bright pink linen shirt, white culottes and purple leather ankle boots. As she came closer, Willa could see that underneath her pretty straw hat she was red in the face, and her make-up was smudged around her eyes.

'Hello, my lovely! I don't suppose you'd like to sell these raffle tickets for me, would you?' She paused, holding up a book of tickets and a calico bag. 'I'm just a bit worried this rain is going to come in, and I think I need to move a couple of the open stalls under cover.'

'How about I find someone else to sell them and I help with moving the stalls?' suggested Willa.

'Good idea!' said Annabelle. She trotted off, leaving Willa with the tickets.

She's really wired, thought Willa.

'Hello, Willa, ready for me to take over?' Barney McIntosh, a charming white-bearded octogenarian who had been helping with fete preparations during the week, appeared as if by magic. He was rostered on to take over stallholder duties from Willa, and she grinned at him.

'Thank you, Barney. Just in time.' She held up the raffle tickets. 'Don't suppose you could sell these while you're at it, could you?'

'Not a problem, young lady.' He took the tickets, and Willa headed across the garden after Annabelle.

She deviated inside the house to use one of the bathrooms, which were off limits to the public. After the intense week of stall preparations and carting furniture to set up the fete, she had become very familiar with the layout of Annabelle's house. In the hall, she noticed that the door to Annabelle's study was partially open. Angry voices were coming from inside.

'It's none of your business, Dan,' she heard a voice say. *Sylvia.*

'Yes it is. I'm her husband! She married me after it happened. She never bloody told me a thing.'

'Well maybe she didn't feel right about telling anyone. Just stop feeling sorry for yourself, Dan. Have you ever thought how hard it would have been for Annabelle? Having a baby taken away from her when she was only a child herself?'

Willa felt her chest constrict. She was overcome by a strange distant feeling, as if she were a ghost.

The screen door to the veranda banged, and Willa looked down the hallway.

Annabelle appeared. She called back over her shoulder to someone. 'Tell him to go round the back! It's through the laundry. I don't want to see him. He absolutely stinks!' She looked around. 'Willa! Excellent, just the girl.'

Willa felt herself clench inside. *Annabelle had a baby and it was taken away.* She turned so her body was blocking the view into the study. She really didn't want Annabelle to see Dan and Sylvia talking. She could feel the storm swirling through her mind, seeping in through the walls.

'I was just coming to help you,' said Willa.

'Great. I need to set up a new stand. We have the local honey vendor just arrived. I was hoping he wouldn't come, but never mind. He has.'

'All right.'

'Dan encouraged him. It's infuriating. He's just so smelly.'

Willa looked at her, perplexed.

'He's simple,' Annabelle said, as if this was a complete explanation.
'Right.'

'Good, well I think there's another trestle in the back shed. Perhaps you could carry it. I just need to organise Tippy a towel for his shower. I've insisted he have one.'

'Right,' said Willa again. She couldn't trust herself to say more. Her whole body felt floaty and strange.

Annabelle walked towards her, heading for the door behind her, into the study. Willa sensed that everything was about to slide out of control.

'I just need to check the weather online,' said Annabelle. 'It's doing my head in. The uncertainty.'

Willa was frozen.

Annabelle walked around her, then stopped. Dan and Sylvia were looking at her, like deer caught in the headlights.

Sylvia held up her hands, as if surrendering. 'I've just come to say goodbye to you, Anna,' she said. 'I'm leaving. On tonight's ferry.'

'How thoughtful of you,' said Annabelle, and her voice had a sharp, quivering edge to it.

'Anna, really. I wasn't here to see Dan. I told you it was over,' said Sylvia urgently.

Annabelle crossed the room and sat at her desk, fiddling with the mouse until her computer screen jumped into life.

'Anna?' said Sylvia.

Annabelle ignored her. She typed something and the weather radar came up on the screen. As she manoeuvred the map, a dark patch of rain cloud hovered across the coastline.

'Who was the father, Belle?' demanded Dan.

Willa noticed he was holding a glass of whisky in his hand, and a half-full bottle stood on the side table.

Across the room, Annabelle stiffened.

Willa was still outside in the hallway, so that neither Sylvia nor Dan could see her. She felt a strange sense of recognition settle through her. It should have been obvious. Weeks ago. *Annabelle*. Annabelle was her birth mother.

Suddenly, a gentle pitter-patter sound began over their heads. It became heavier by the second. Annabelle looked up, staring at the ceiling. 'No!' she exclaimed.

A shadow fell through the window and Willa looked out. The bank of clouds that had been far out in the ocean not long ago seemed to have blown directly overhead. The rain began to thrum on the tin roof, and Willa felt her heart breaking for Annabelle, who had so wanted the fete to go off without a hitch.

Dan seemed oblivious. 'Annabelle, are you deaf? Who were you screwing? Who was Willa's father?' He tipped back his head and emptied his glass.

'Dan!' said Sylvia angrily.

'It's not a bloody trick question. She knows who he was. I deserve to know too.'

Annabelle turned around, avoiding Dan's glare. She looked into the hall at Willa. 'We need to help the Paella Pan Man. His food will be getting ruined.' Then she turned back to Sylvia and Dan. In a strange slow motion, she raised both her hands in front of her, then balled her fists. She shuddered, and her face screwed up into a terrible pain-filled mask. 'Willa is right there!' she said, pointing. 'How dare you speak like that in front of her? And just so we're clear, Dan, it is none of your business!'

She marched past them and stopped in front of Willa in the hall, taking hold of her hands.

'There is nothing I can say that will make this right. I'm so sorry you found out like this. I… I just can't talk about it right now.'

She hung her head, then dropped Willa's hands and walked out the screen door and into the rain without breaking stride. The door slammed shut.

Willa spun around as another movement caught her eye. At the other end of the hall, a huge hulking giant of a man stood in dirty clothes that had been plastered to his body by the rain. His grey hair and beard were matted and he looked at Willa with a shy, blank sort of expression.

'Annabelle said I gotta have a shower,' he said.

'Okay,' said Willa, as if this was the most reasonable thing she had heard all day. Her voice sounded remarkably normal. 'I was just on my way to the bathroom,' she said. 'How about I show you where it is?'

As she walked down the hall, the smell of something rotten wafted from the man.

He leaned down to her and said, 'You're pretty.'

'Thank you,' said Willa gently. 'It's very kind of you to say so.'

'Annabelle says I stink,' said the giant.

That is not an understatement, thought Willa. 'Perhaps,' she said after a moment, 'Annabelle was just trying to help.'

'Yeah,' said the man. 'Haven't had a shower for a while. My mum said it was time.'

Willa blinked hard.

'Yes,' she said. 'Mothers seem to know these things.'

CHAPTER TWENTY-FIVE

Sylvia

1977

Sylvia took a step towards him. The blood on Dan's face was from a cut near his temple. Two long, deep scratches started at his forehead and ran down the side of his face. His hair was matted with dried blood.

'Dan? What did you do? Were you in a fight? What do you mean about Andrew?'

Dan lifted a dirty, blood-streaked hand and swiped it across his jeans.

'I think he's dead,' he said. His voice was hoarse. He turned to the table and began flicking through some papers. 'It's a nightmare.'

'What's happened?' Sylvia tried to quell the hysteria that was rising up in her.

'He's gone over the cliffs. I've been helping the police search, but…' He shook his head.

'Why do you have all those cuts?' asked Sylvia.

'Jesus, Syl. Don't ask dumb questions. I've been out on the cliffs for half the bloody night, pushing through bushes with the search party.' He sat down at the table and began going through the papers. 'I've just been into the office to get his will. I need you to do something for me,' he added without looking at her.

'What?'

'If Andrew's gone, then we're all up shit creek. Me and you, Lillian. Financially, I mean.'

'Why?'

He gave a heavy sigh and stopped rifling through the papers. 'I found out that Andrew was taking money out of the trust account at work. To pay for his gambling. We fought, and I agreed to cover it up until he could get his hands on some of Constance's money to pay off the debts. I countersigned some documents. The trail will lead back to me if I don't sort it out now. God.' He balled his hands into fists. 'I'm so fucked.'

'Just tell someone. It wasn't you doing the stealing.'

'It's not that simple. And there's something else. He promised ages ago that he'd change his will in favour of me. At the moment, Merrivale goes to Constance if he dies. There's no provision for it to stay in the Broadhurst family if that happens. She could leave it to whoever she wants in her own will. He knew that wasn't right. It belonged to my great-grandfather, Syl. Even before all this, Andrew promised to change it.'

'Then why didn't he?' asked Sylvia.

'I'm not sure. I had Lillian type the new will up ages ago, but he kept putting off signing it. Constance has some sort of hold over him. Maybe she knew about the gambling or something.'

'What can you do about it now, though?'

'I need you to forge his signature, Syl. I can't do it. I've been trying all bloody night. He swiped angrily at a piece of paper on the edge of the table. It had dozens of lines of messy writing on it, one beneath the other.

'But that's fraud,' said Sylvia in a tremulous voice. 'And how can you do that to Constance?'

'It's not. Not really. He promised me he'd change it. His intentions are all in this new will,' Dan pushed the unsigned document across to Sylvia, 'Merrivale is left to me if Andrew dies, but Connie gets a life tenancy. It's not like we'll be turfing her out. She gets to live there still. And you know she doesn't need the money. She's got a huge trust fund of her own. She could buy half the state if she wanted to.'

'But Dan—'

'Syl, you *have* to. If this new will goes through, I should be able to borrow money against Merrivale and pay off Andrew's debts as well as put the money back into the trust account to cover his tracks. I'll be doing Connie a bloody favour. It won't look good if it comes out that her husband was diddling the clients by using their money when we were meant to be holding it on trust. Trust accounts are sacred, Syl. Untouchable.'

Sylvia blinked hard, trying to process what he was saying, hearing the angry, entitled edge in his voice.

'People won't believe that Lillian didn't know about it either – she's in charge of the books. A scandal like this would shut the firm down. I'd be tarnished by association. I could lose my practising certificate.'

Sylvia's whole body began to shake.

Dan pressed at her arm. 'Lillian would lose her job. You know she can't afford for that to happen. Len's depending on her.' He pulled her towards the table. 'Look, his signature's really swirly. Like that calligraphy you do. It's pretty. You'll be able to copy it.'

Sylvia looked at Dan's aborted attempts at Andrew's signature. Dan's handwriting was tiny, crude and squashed together. As far away from his uncle's elegant script as it was possible to be. She glanced up at his desperate face.

'I'll be taking on his bloody debts, Syl! It's the opposite of fraud. I'm doing him a favour. I'd be doing everyone a favour!'

Sylvia wondered, as she picked up the pen, about the blood. About the huge double scratch on his face, like fingernails.

What if there were no trust account debts? What if he was telling her that to convince her that changing the will wasn't so bad? Why would Andrew be out on the cliffs in weather like they'd had tonight, anyway?

What if he wasn't dead?

CHAPTER TWENTY-SIX

Sylvia

Sylvia let out her breath as the bang of the screen door echoed into Annabelle's office. She sighed with disappointment. She had been a terrible sister and she was still failing at it. This afternoon, she was planning to leave for Devonport to catch the night ferry, and after that, she supposed she wouldn't be back. She wouldn't be welcome in this house, anyway. Her heart felt dark with loss.

Dan was silent. He poured another glass of whisky, ignoring her angry look.

'Goodbye, Dan.'

She walked out, dragging the roaring silence of the room behind her. Outside, the rain was quickening. People were huddling on the veranda, holding coats over their heads and taking shelter beneath trees.

Across the garden, she saw Annabelle walking briskly towards the back shed. The Paella Pan Man had already moved his food stall inside the large open-sided tent.

She thought about the pain in Annabelle's eyes. It had been terrible. No doubt it was partly due to seeing her in the room with Dan, and partly also due to the presence of Willa. Perhaps that accounted for it, but she couldn't help feeling there was something she was missing. Annabelle's face had been pleading, distant somehow. Something was very, very wrong. Sylvia could feel it. She had known it for ever really. Her sister needed something from her, but she wasn't quite sure what.

She wished again that she hadn't come to Merrivale today. It was such bad luck that Dan had found her leaving a goodbye note for Annabelle in the office. Neither of them was welcome at the fete, but Dan's resentment at being publicly humiliated over their affair had made him cruel. And Annabelle was bearing the brunt of his damaged ego.

Still, it was clear to Sylvia now that he hadn't been lying; he wasn't Willa's father. But she had no idea who was. Dan had fitted. Thirty-nine weeks after that night in the car, Annabelle had given birth. Lillian had written, and the letter had left Sylvia cold. It was icy confirmation of Dan's faithlessness and Annabelle's betrayal. And yet it hadn't been that at all. But the dates meant that Annabelle must have become pregnant within a week or two either side of that horrible night. The night Andrew had disappeared. The night Sylvia had forged the signature on the will.

None of it made sense. Annabelle hadn't had a boyfriend back then, and she was rarely allowed out except under Sylvia's supervision. Sylvia had remained at home for nearly another two weeks after that night.

When she had returned to her bed, cold and terrified after signing the will, she knew she couldn't stay in Sisters Cove. She couldn't stay with Dan. But it took time for her fare to be arranged and a job to be found in Melbourne. And Annabelle hadn't left the house during that time for a single evening.

Sylvia had refused to meet with Dan that whole time, so she had been at home too. Annabelle had barely looked at her during those long days. Evening meals, when their father insisted they eat at the table together, were awful, silent affairs, the air as thick as rancid butter. It had left their father perplexed.

Could it have been a boy from school she'd met during the daytime?

There was a small voice inside Sylvia's head telling her that it was important she find out. Annabelle needed her to know. She followed her sister across the grass, the rain running coldly down her neck and squelching beneath her feet. By the time she reached the shed, the rain had soaked through her clothes. She opened the door.

'Annabelle?'

In the dim light, she could see Annabelle moving from one side of the shed to the other. She was pulling dusty old sheets of board away from the wall, craning her neck to see behind them.

'What are you looking for? Can I help?'

Annabelle ignored her. After another minute of searching, she turned back to the door, pushed past Sylvia and strode across the garden towards the little gate onto the road. Sylvia followed. Annabelle crossed the lane and reached The Old Chapel, but instead of going in, she walked through the garden and disappeared behind the house. The rain continued, a steady blanket of cold, beating through Sylvia's clothes. She passed the corner of The Old Chapel and stopped at the back of the woodshed, where there was a storage area. It was the only place Annabelle could be. She peered in.

Annabelle was panting heavily, turning from one end of the tiny dark space to the other with a look of disbelief on her face.

'What do you need, Annabelle?'

'A trestle, all right! I need a trestle table for Tippy's honey. Lillian always kept one in here. *You* cleaned up. What have you done with it?' Her voice was brittle with anger.

'Anna, there's no point setting it up. I don't think this rain is going to ease. How about you come inside?'

'Don't you dare tell me what to do!'

'I'm sorry. But you're shivering. I'd really like you to come inside and dry off. And I want to apologise, for everything.'

'It's a bit late for that, don't you think? You're leaving. You're leaving me again!' She was glaring at Sylvia, her eyes full and bright, her face taut.

'Yes, but I… I thought that would be the best thing to do. For you. I'm still your sister. And I know I wasn't there for you back then. I mucked things up. I'm still doing it.'

'Yes. You are! You always thought you knew best. So quick to judge. All the time. Your own daughter won't even tell you what she's doing with her life because you're so damn judgemental!'

'What do you mean? What about Indigo?'

'Oh, forget it,' hissed Annabelle. 'You ruined my life when you walked out back then, and now you're doing it again.'

Sylvia felt the bitter blame in the words, and before she could stop herself, she said, 'But you didn't help things either. You didn't tell me anything. If I'd known there was a boy on the scene, that you were pregnant, I would have supported you. Helped you to keep the baby if you wanted to.'

Annabelle came towards her out of the gloom of the shed. Her face was twisted with fury. 'Go away! Just go away!' she screamed.

Sylvia stumbled backwards. 'Anna, really. I'm so sorry I left. I was afraid. I was afraid that Dan had killed Andrew!' She blurted out the words in a rush of anguish. 'I was terrified. I ran away because I thought I might have helped him cover it up.' She put her hands to her mouth to stop the sob.

Annabelle stopped and squinted at her. 'What?'

'There was so much blood,' said Sylvia. 'On his face, his hands. Then he asked me to forge the will. I did it, but later, when they found Andrew's body… Well, they couldn't rule out foul play, because he'd been in the water for so long, near the rocks. But when I thought it through, I had this terrible niggling doubt. I could barely eat or sleep.'

'No,' said Annabelle bluntly.

'It's true,' said Sylvia.

'No. Dan didn't kill him.' Annabelle shook her head. 'I know he didn't.' She reached out and touched Sylvia's hand. 'There's something I should tell you.'

She took Sylvia's sleeve and pulled at it, and when Sylvia didn't move her feet, she dropped it and turned towards the ocean. Seemingly oblivious to the rain, she began walking past The Old Chapel. When she reached a small gate into the paddock, she stopped and opened it.

Sylvia hurried after her and closed the gate behind them.

'What?' she asked.

'Connie knows,' said Annabelle. Her hair was being swept back in the wind, and she was concentrating, looking straight ahead, walking fast.

'Connie knows what? About the will? That I forged his signature?' asked Sylvia. She stepped around a cowpat and stumbled as the grass grew rougher.

'Yes,' said Annabelle. 'Andrew had asked her that night, before he died. Asked her to pay off his debts. She said she'd do it because she was afraid of him. He was violent,' she added. 'Did you know that?'

Sylvia shuddered. The matter-of-fact way Annabelle was speaking was unsettling.

'Connie knew the debts were never going to end. That his gambling was an addiction. She was afraid of him. She knew she couldn't live like that any longer.'

'What?' said Sylvia. A sweet, sick sensation erupted at the back of her throat.

They were standing near the cliff face now. In front of them were three flimsy strands of wire. Waves were crashing into the rock face below.

Annabelle took Sylvia's hand and looked at her steadily. 'Constance knew that man deserved to die, long before he raped me.'

CHAPTER TWENTY-SEVEN

Annabelle

1977

Annabelle looked up at the rain coming in through the open door in the foyer. She needed to get up. Needed to do something. She pushed herself off the couch, dragging at a knitted blanket that was slung across the back. She wiped it roughly across her face, then glanced down again at Sylvia's ripped top, knowing she needed to cover it before Dan came back.

On the hook in the vestibule she spotted Lillian's gardening jacket. She walked across the room, each step making her grimace at the sharp, throbbing pain between her legs and across her back. She put on the jacket and zipped it up, then turned to look out the door into the blackness. Nothing.

She stepped outside and rain pitter-pattered coldly into her hair, its gentle tapping rhythm melding with the background rush and hiss of the ocean. After a moment, she caught the sound of voices. She crept towards them, peering around the corner of The Old Chapel. A weak glow of electric light came from the tiny window high up, and as Annabelle stood squinting, shaking, the clouds parted and moonlight moved across the garden, right onto little Maisy's headstone.

Lillian and Andrew were standing near the woodpile. The rain began to ease and the noise of the ocean receded. Lillian was shouting. 'Tell me! Just tell me!'

Andrew just stood and looked at her.

'You're a monster!'

'Stop it,' he snapped. 'It's none of your business who I sleep with.'

'That wasn't sex, you bastard. It was rape!'

Before Annabelle could register the shock of the words, Andrew raised his hand and hit Lillian hard across the face. Her head whipped sideways and she stumbled backwards, letting out a low cry. But she recovered almost immediately and threw herself at him, lashing at his chest, screaming, pounding at him.

Annabelle shrank and cowered, holding onto the building. She was stuck, completely frozen.

Andrew seemed momentarily stunned too, then with one sure movement, he grabbed Lillian and threw her backwards against the tin wall of the woodshed, slamming her head into the corrugations with a vicious clang. Then he raised both hands to her neck and lifted her off the ground. Lillian's feet were flailing, kicking metallic thumps against the shed that became weaker and weaker as Annabelle watched. There was deathly fear on her face, and soon everything was completely, terribly silent.

Annabelle stared until panic broke through her trance. She looked around, but there was no one there to help Lillian. Only her. She stumbled back up the steps of The Old Chapel, kicking off Sylvia's shoes as she went. Her eyes moved in small, jerky motions around the room. *Something heavy. Something heavy.* They fell on Len's ashtray, and she knew immediately that that was it. She grabbed it, and the little removable tray clattered to the floor, ash scattering over the mat. The cube-shaped marble base of it was a solid weight, heavier than she expected. She pulled it behind her and ran back outside, flying with the terror. At the corner of The Old Chapel, she stopped.

Lillian was on the ground. She was rocking on all fours, coughing and trying to say something through heaving sobs. The rain had become a fine mist, and Andrew bent down and said something to her. Then the rain petered out and everything went quiet, apart from the background sounds of the ocean and the whimpering coming from Lillian's mouth.

Annabelle stepped towards them, thoughts spinning. Should she help Lillian? Would Lillian want her to interfere? Would Andrew kill her? She felt herself shaking inside the thin coat, as if the cold was in her bones.

Andrew was speaking again, but she couldn't hear what he was saying, then Lillian turned her head and looked up at him. 'How could you say that? It *is* yours. But now I wish it wasn't.'

And in that moment, Annabelle understood. Andrew was a monster. He was a monster inside the body of a handsome, clever man, and he hurt women. With his words and his body and his fists.

'You loved every minute of it. Every single time, sweet-cakes,' he said to Lillian, then he flicked his head back towards The Old Chapel and said, 'And so did she.' He smoothed down his hair and straightened his jacket.

Lillian put an unsteady hand to the ground and pushed herself to her feet.

'You're insane,' she said, leaning forward, her voice wavering. 'She's a child.'

Andrew shrugged indifferently. 'Get over yourself, you silly bitch.'

He walked away from Lillian, then turned his head, and looked straight at Annabelle. A smile formed on his lips, and in a voice of pure authority, as if it was the absolute, certain truth, he sneered, 'You loved it.' Then he looked towards Merrivale, as if dismissing her. As if the whole night was nothing.

Annabelle took a step forward. 'Stop,' she said. Surprise, then amusement registered on his face. He shook his head as if she was an unbelievably naughty kid playing at being grown up. And she was. He was right.

In her hand, she felt the long, heavy pull of the ashtray, her fingers curled around the circular brass lip, its solid base resting in the mud.

An anger more pure and brilliant than anything Annabelle had experienced before surged through her, and without further thought, she twisted her body sideways and upwards and drove the ashtray with all her strength towards Andrew's head. The corner of it caught his temple with a thick, satisfying thud. After a flash of shock, he crumpled and tumbled forward. His knees hit the ground first, then his body and face planted straight into the mud. Annabelle dropped the ashtray and stared.

Lillian stumbled forward. 'Oh God.'

Small panting noises were coming from Annabelle's mouth. 'No,' she whispered. His vile, hateful words pushed at her, mocked her. *You loved it. You loved it. You loved it.* Something inside her was brewing, black and boiling. Her mind was expanding, heating up with the remnants of spent rage; swirling with awe at what had been done to her, at what she had done. Her words began as a stutter, but they ended in a roar. 'No I did not. I DID NOT!'

CHAPTER TWENTY-EIGHT

Willa

Willa stood at the top of the veranda stairs, wondering what to do. Across the lawn, Barney was helping someone to move craft items off the display stands and bring them under cover into the main tent. People were crowded onto the veranda, exclaiming at the downpour.

She had left one of the garden club women in charge of looking after Tippy.

'We needed this rain,' said a woman standing on the steps beside her. 'Just a pity it had to be now. Annabelle went to so much effort. We all did.'

'Yes,' said Willa. 'Perhaps it will stop soon.'

'Doesn't look like it,' said the woman, shaking her head.

Cars were pulling away from the paddock car park. Still, there were lots of people waiting under cover. Hopefully they would wait it out. Suddenly Willa wondered if people over at The Old Chapel gardens might need more shelter. She should probably open the house up and invite people inside. It should still be warm. She had lit the fire earlier to take the chill off, happy that she could have her own cosy base for the day. In the first week of autumn, Tasmanian weather could be temperamental.

Willa pulled up her jacket hood and bolted down the stairs and across the lawn, gasping at the cold rain. As she crossed the lane, she saw Indigo and Constance coming towards her, an umbrella swaying above their heads in the gusting wind.

'Come into The Old Chapel. It's closer,' called Willa as she neared them.

'Good idea,' said Indigo. 'This weather's a bugger.'

Willa jogged up the steps and unlocked the front door, then came back to usher Constance and Indigo in ahead of her. 'I might need to stoke the fire for you.'

She crossed to the fire in the corner of the room. The door of the slow-combustion stove was still hot, but the logs had burnt right down to embers. She threw some sticks and a handful of the tiny silver packets of instant fire-starters onto the smouldering remnants. After a few seconds, they burst into flames, and she added another log from the old copper bucket sitting on the hearth. She sat back, satisfied as the fire began throwing out heat.

'I'll just see if I can help move anything in from the stalls,' she said, smiling at Indigo. 'Make yourselves a cup of tea.' She motioned to the kettle.

Outside, across the ocean, the clouds were a thick, swirling blackish-grey. As she was about to turn towards Merrivale, she noticed movement. A slim figure in black was standing out on the cliff, and another person was just ahead of her. In pink. *Sylvia and Annabelle.*

For a moment, Willa was confused as to what they might be doing out there. Then, as her mind spun, remembering Annabelle's angst in the face of Dan's questions earlier, she realised they were standing right at the cliff edge.

She turned her head, wondering if she should panic, wanting to ask someone, but The Old Chapel garden was empty. Indecision stopped her only for a moment, then she began to run towards the cliff, adrenalin turning her legs to wings.

As she approached them, she slowed. She realised they were just inside a wire fence. She forced herself to calm her breathing.

Sylvia was making gestures with her hands, saying something she couldn't hear. Annabelle dropped her arms to her sides and turned her head. Her shirt was plastered to her chest and her hat had blown off, leaving her curls matted and ruined. Mascara was running down her cheeks. She spotted Willa.

'Hello, Willa. We were just having a word with the weather gods. I really can't believe they've let us down so badly. Constance said she'd pray for sun.'

'Oh, I see.' Willa felt an acute sense of embarrassment, as if she'd interrupted something private.

Sylvia turned to Annabelle. 'Willa is a grown woman, Annabelle. You don't need to protect her.'

Annabelle sighed and looked back at the ocean. The silence seemed to stretch on into infinity. Eventually she said, 'You know loss, Willa. You know how it eats you up. When I lost you, I blamed him. Then I blamed Sylvia. But I suppose they would have made me give you up anyway. So in the end, who do I blame?'

'Who was he?' The words formed in Willa's mouth without a thought.

'Andrew Broadhurst,' said Annabelle calmly. 'I did the wrong thing, you see. I made him look at me. Sexually. It felt wonderful, in the beginning.' She had begun to shiver violently. She stared blankly ahead.

'Annabelle, we need to go inside. It's wet. You're freezing,' said Sylvia.

'It was raining that night too,' said Annabelle.

Willa and Sylvia exchanged nervous glances.

'It was handy,' she said, sighing. She turned towards the cliffs. 'It covered the tracks.'

CHAPTER TWENTY-NINE

Annabelle

1977

Lillian tried to turn Andrew's body over, but Annabelle could see it was too heavy. A defeated cry came from her mouth, and she slumped to the ground and turned his head sideways instead. Mud was caked across his nose and chin. She touched her hand to the blood on his temple, then put her fingers to his neck. She looked back up at Annabelle, who was standing staring, frozen to the spot.

'Help me turn him over.'

Annabelle felt the words float over her head.

'Annabelle!'

She squatted down beside Lillian.

'Help me, quick.'

It took a supreme effort for them to lift and turn the body. Lying on his back, Andrew's lips were parted and his eyes were closed. Mud and dirty water were smeared across his whole face.

Lillian undid his jacket and pushed up his shirt. She put her ear to his chest. Then she put it to his mouth.

'He's not breathing.'

Annabelle could hear the beginnings of panic in her voice. It jolted through her. She stood and picked up the ashtray. Some deep-seated need for self-preservation was telling her that perhaps she needed to hide it, or do something with it, but she wasn't sure what.

'A phone…' she whispered. Her voice sounded shaky, unfamiliar. 'Dan said there was a phone… over there.' She nodded towards Merrivale, and Lillian followed her gaze, then dropped her head back to Andrew.

Lillian stood up. 'Yes.' She took a step around Andrew's body, then turned back to Annabelle. 'Are you all right?'

'I'm sorry, Lil.' Annabelle wanted to sob, but she wouldn't. She would be strong. She'd done this and now she must face up to it.

'No. *I'm* sorry. Go inside.'

Annabelle took a few hesitant steps as Lillian sprinted across the garden towards the big house. Suddenly the rain began again. In an instant, it was pelting, furious, as if the gods knew what she had done. A bolt of lightning flashed across the sky, making an eerie spectacle of Andrew's lifeless form. Thunder crashed, and Annabelle jumped, then the lights of The Old Chapel died.

She looked up. Across the road, the porch light of the big house had gone out too. Everything was black. Still holding the long stem of the ashtray, she felt her way through the garden to the edge of the house. A sliver of moonlight began peeping through the clouds, guiding her way.

In the foyer of The Old Chapel she stopped and wiped her muddy bare feet. They felt like blocks of ice. The cold was right through her. The flames of the fire flickered an eerie glow through the dark little house, and she stopped to let her eyes adjust. She began to walk tentatively, one hand out in front of her into the shadows, the other clenching the stem of the ashtray. The light from the fire was stronger as she reached the sink, and she found the dishcloth and began to wipe the mud and blood off the ashtray.

An idea came to her, and she set the ashtray down and felt around under the sink. Yes, the same place as in her own house. Her hand grasped the large box-like form of a torch and her finger pressed at the pliable button on the top. The beam of light brought a small sigh of relief. In the torchlight, she rinsed the cloth then took the ashtray back to the living room and picked up the little removable tray and replaced it. She noticed she was dripping water. She made her way to the bathroom and found a towel. She took off Lillian's jacket and hung it over the bath before drying herself off. She ignored the urge to inspect the ripped top in the mirror. She could feel herself shaking, hammering with the cold.

Holding the torch awkwardly, she climbed the steep stairs to Lillian's room. She ducked across to the bed and pulled off the top, then snatched up one of Lillian's jumpers and threw it on over her head. She tiptoed back down the stairs, fearful that she might wake Len.

Picking up the cloth again, she crossed to the scattered ash and knelt to wipe it up, rubbing some into the rug as she did so. She rinsed out the cloth once more and tiptoed back to the doorway. She wondered how long an ambulance or the police would take, wondered if she would go to jail. What would Sylvia say? What about her father? They'd both be so angry.

Everything hurt, but she tried not to think about it. She wondered why Dan hadn't come back yet. It must be midnight. She turned off the torch and stood at the door and closed her eyes, but behind her lids she saw Andrew and his sneering smile. When she opened them again, she could see two figures coming across the road in the weak moonlight, announced by the beam of another torch.

The woman with the torch darted ahead and passed the door of The Old Chapel, barely glancing at Annabelle. The downpour began to ease, and Annabelle followed the woman and Lillian around the corner. The woman knelt down next to Andrew, shining the torch onto his face. She was small and neat, and Annabelle knew this was Constance Broadhurst. She drove a big silver Mercedes Benz and everyone in town knew her elegant form. Constance put two fingers to Andrew's neck, as Lillian had done, then picked up his arm and did the same to his wrist. Then she put her head on his chest, and finally she rested the back of her hand against his mouth. After a moment, she shook her head and stood up, and Annabelle knew she was in trouble. Her stomach curdled with fear.

Constance turned to her. 'Are you all right?'

'Yes,' said Annabelle.

'What did he do to you?'

This was not the question she had been expecting. Could she really tell this lady what her husband had done? It was too unbelievable. Too disgusting.

Before she could answer, Constance stepped forward and laid the back of her hand on Annabelle's cheek.

'Oh, my dear. I'm so sorry. I'm sorry for what he's done.' She dropped her hand to take Annabelle's. It was warm and kind.

Annabelle felt a well of misery rising up. It began leaking and leaching out of her eyes, her mouth, her body. She started to shudder and sob, and Constance drew her into her arms and let her cry.

'We can't just leave him like this.' Lillian's voice was panicked. 'We've got to try and get help. I'll drive to Dan's and see if his phone's working.'

'There's no hurry, Lillian. He's dead. Nothing's going to help him now.'

'We still need to try! She didn't mean to do it. They'll understand.'

Constance was still holding onto Annabelle. She looked at Lillian. 'Will her lawyers be able to successfully argue self-defence?'

'Constance! We've got to get the authorities. We can work it out later. She's only fifteen – she'll be treated leniently.'

'What does that mean? Prison time?'

'I don't know. Juvenile crime, all that stuff, it's not an area I know.'

'I won't let her go to prison. He was evil.' Constance let go of Annabelle and looked back at Andrew. 'But nobody would have believed me.'

Lillian stared, panic and fear playing out equally on her face. The silence stretched until she said, 'I believe you, Constance.'

'Then listen. The Lord will protect us. You mustn't fear. But it's up to us to find the path he has in mind. What about self-defence? Could you argue that?'

Lillian's hand dropped to her stomach, and Annabelle saw that Constance's eyes had followed it. Lillian's next words were measured. 'He was walking away from her. She stopped him. Self-defence wouldn't work. The danger to her life had to be immediate.'

'He taught you well,' said Constance, flicking her head at Andrew. Then she looked off into the darkness. 'He's not worth a trial. He's not worth the risk. Annabelle, go inside.'

Annabelle turned and followed the beam of Constance's torch. She walked past the gravestone and towards The Old Chapel door. She was used to being told what to do, and something about Constance felt certain and calming.

She stopped as she rounded the corner of the house, listening.

'Back your car up, Lillian. We'll take him down near the path in front of the lighthouse. There's good access there to the cliffs.'

'What?'

'I'll say he was going to find the dog. It's gone missing anyway. Hates the thunder. He was going to look for it.'

'What are you saying?'

'Andrew has powerful friends. Judges. Lawyers. Politicians. They won't stand for a story like yours.'

'It's not a story! It's the truth!'

'I know. Go and get your car keys.'

'Maybe we should get Dan, Constance. He'll know the legalities better than me.'

'He likes Andrew. Loves him. Do you think he'll believe you?'

'Yes!'

'Then don't involve him in all this. Who's to say he won't be pulled down with it?'

'Please, Constance. This is madness.'

'The Bible tells us it's right. Is a child less worthy than an engaged woman?'

'What?'

'Deuteronomy Chapter 22: "But if in the field the man finds the girl who is engaged, and the man forces her and lies with her, then only the man who lies with her shall die… You shall do nothing to the girl; there is no sin in the girl worthy of death."'

'They won't *kill* her, Constance!'

'They won't call her innocent either. And there's no sin in her. Get your car keys. Please.'

The rain was gentle now, and Annabelle could hear every word of their strained conversation. She was shivering as if it was the middle of winter.

'I've lived with his violence for more than twenty years. He was savage and cruel in every possible way. Each year he got worse. Every time he took a new lover. Every time he lost a case. Or gambled the money away. There was no end to it.' Constance's voice dropped to a whisper. 'Please, Lillian. For the sake of your child. Do you want it to know that its father was Lucifer incarnate? All the details will need to come out if we are to save the girl through the courts. His child won't live it down.'

'Constance…'

'The son should not suffer for the sin of the father, Lillian.' Constance sounded like she was preaching, but her next words spewed out in a guttural command. 'Haven't we all suffered enough?'

Annabelle peeped around the corner of the house. Lillian was staring at Andrew's body. She looked up slowly.

'It's just… I didn't know. I didn't know what he was capable of. I thought he was just moody. Difficult. I thought…' She raised both hands to the bruised skin of her neck. Betrayal, sick and terrible, was written across her face. 'I thought he really loved me.'

CHAPTER THIRTY

Willa

'We need to go inside,' said Sylvia. She took Annabelle by the arm and turned her away from the cliff.

Annabelle broke from her daze. 'I'm sorry, Willa. You deserved better.'

Willa took her other arm and they walked across the grass in silence. The rain was light now, but Willa shivered as the water soaked through her coat, ran down her neck, sank into her socks. They neared the entry to The Old Chapel and Willa guided Annabelle towards it. There were too many people at Merrivale and they didn't need to see her like this.

'No,' said Annabelle. 'It's cold in there.'

'I lit the fire,' said Willa, wondering if she could ask Indigo and Constance to leave now that the rain had stopped falling so hard. 'And it's private. Let's just dry off a little inside, and then we can go back over to your house when you're feeling a bit better.'

Annabelle closed her eyes for so long that Willa wondered what to do. She exchanged a worried look with Sylvia.

Eventually Annabelle opened her eyes. 'All right.'

Inside, Constance was alone on the couch. Her face dropped when she saw Annabelle. 'My dear, you're unwell.' She looked at Willa and Sylvia. 'You'll all catch your death in those wet clothes.'

'I'll get a towel,' said Willa. In the bathroom, she found two small hand towels. She returned to the couch, where Annabelle was sitting, mute and staring straight ahead. She handed a towel to Constance, who began dabbing at Annabelle's arms.

She went upstairs and pulled off her wet coat, shivering. Perhaps it was the shock, the knowledge. She was a child created from violence and born into despair. Her hands shook as she picked up a brown woollen blanket to put around Annabelle's shoulders.

The rain began again, and within seconds it was pelting down, pummelling the tin roof of The Old Chapel in an awful cacophony. Downstairs, Sylvia was stoking the fire as the kettle boiled, the sound of it barely audible above the din of the rain.

Willa sat down on the couch next to Annabelle. 'Would you like to talk about it?' she asked gently.

Annabelle was staring blankly at the wall.

'You don't have to, of course.' Willa put her hand on Annabelle's knee. 'You really don't have to. I just thought I'd ask.'

'I never came in here after that night. Not until you invited me in. How silly,' said Annabelle. She let out a deep sigh. 'Now I see that it's just a house.' Her voice was bleak and hollow.

Willa squeezed her knee.

'Just a silly house,' continued Annabelle. 'But it's funny, isn't it, how you associate a place with a feeling?'

'You don't need to talk about it,' said Constance.

'Willa should hear,' said Annabelle. 'She's my baby, you know.'

'I know,' said Constance.

'I told you there was an accident here, Willa,' said Annabelle, turning to her. 'He died here. Andrew.'

'What happened?' asked Willa.

Constance lifted her walking stick and tapped it sharply on the floor. They all looked at her. She sat ramrod straight on the couch.

'I didn't—' said Annabelle, but Constance tapped the stick again, hard.

'Andrew attacked her,' said Constance. She stood slowly and walked to the window.

A strange feeling came over Willa. There was something magnetic in the set of Constance's shoulders. The tilt of her chin.

'He impregnated her. He was a terrible, violent man. He was the Devil,' Constance said, turning to Sylvia. 'I found him in the act, and after, when Annabelle was gone, I struck him. Hard. I killed him.' Her voice was as clear as a mountain stream. She eyed each of them calmly, as if challenging them to react.

Willa pushed her hands between her thighs, but dared not look away.

'There was nothing I could do about it. Obviously I didn't want to go to jail, though, so… I forced Lillian to dispose of his body with me. Over the cliffs.'

The noise of the rain continued above them.

Willa looked up at Sylvia's face. It was haunted, sickened. She was moving her eyes between Constance and Annabelle, who were locked in a stare.

Annabelle shook her head and whispered, 'No.'

Constance laughed, the sound almost lost in the clatter of the rain. There was iron in the look she gave Annabelle. 'Yes. That is what happened. As God is my witness.'

'No,' said Annabelle again, crumbling into herself. 'Please, no. That noise! On the roof. Stop it!' She put her hands to her ears and began to sob. Sylvia crossed to the couch, putting her arm around her sister.

Constance said, 'Annabelle knew nothing about it until later. She was in shock with what he'd done to her.' She paused, then sighed and looked around. Her eyes narrowed as she took in Lillian's artwork, Annabelle's distraught face, the fire. She walked slowly towards the fire, bending to retrieve a piece of wood from the copper bucket. 'It seems to me that we've carried this burden for too long, Annabelle. It's time for this place to be gone.'

She leaned her walking stick against the bucket and carefully opened the door of the stove, then prodded at a burning log with the wood until it fell onto the hearth, glowing and smoking. 'A fire,' she muttered. 'Yes, a fire will cleanse the past.'

'What?' said Willa.

'What are you doing?' snapped Sylvia.

Annabelle's wailing intensified.

Sylvia rubbed her hand up and down Annabelle's back. 'Shh, Anna. It's all right.'

Constance turned back to them. 'It's only fitting, don't you think, that we end this purgatory Annabelle has lived? Waking each day to see this house of Satan's sins? This is no house of God.' She prodded at the log and it rolled along the floorboards.

Sylvia called over Annabelle's shoulder. 'Constance! Stop! Are you mad?'

Yes, Willa thought, with sudden clarity, the woman is mad. But she's right. Annabelle needs The Old Chapel to be gone.

Just as Sylvia propelled herself off the couch, Constance flicked the burning timber across the floor towards the sheer synthetic curtain, which melted instantly, then caught alight in a great whoosh. Barely stopping to look at the flames, she used her walking stick to poke at the woven wicker basket holding kindling and the packet of fire-starters. It tipped over.

Willa was trapped in a trance. She felt time slowing around her. As if through treacle she heard Sylvia crying out, 'No! The paintings!'

'Look at all the faces,' hissed Constance. 'The paintings were her prison. His eyes are in all of them.'

Willa thought: I must move. Do something! But before she could, the fire-starters exploded into a bright vortex of beautiful flames.

'There,' said Constance. There was a fierce, deranged look in her eyes as she stepped back and looked towards Annabelle. 'Daniel should never have left you alone here that night, dear. But you won't be haunted any more.'

Suddenly the flames caught the tasselled edges of the woven raffia mat on the floor and burst sideways and upwards simultaneously. The fire was a metre away from them.

The cloud in Willa's mind cleared and she screamed, pushing herself into action. 'Get out!' She lurched towards the wall of heat, grabbing Constance and forcing her across the room towards the door. She barely registered the cool mist of the rain as she left the old lady on the step outside and turned back.

Sylvia was pulling at Annabelle, who was standing staring at the flames.

'Come on, Annabelle!' screamed Sylvia.

The curtain rod crashed to the floor, igniting the box of Lillian's papers below. It exploded into flames.

'No!' cried Annabelle, as Sylvia dragged at her.

Willa took a step forward, but the air was scorching her face, throwing out a searing, pungent chemical wall of air. She could see the anguish and terror on Annabelle's face as the raffia mat blazed around her. Flames caught the skirt of the fabric armchair beside her.

'Get out!' she screamed again.

The boxes of files and books lining the walls of The Old Chapel were perfect fuel, and one by one they caught fire as The Old Chapel started to burn in earnest.

As the flames seethed around her, Annabelle's face cleared. She put her hands to her head. 'No! It wasn't like that.'

The armchair suddenly ignited, and Sylvia stumbled backwards. Flames began liquefying and multiplying on the mat around Annabelle.

Sylvia was forced further back. 'Anna!' she screamed.

There was a loud crack, and a panel from the ceiling above curled and dislodged, falling onto the couch. With a huge swoosh, the couch ignited.

Annabelle was behind it, shaking her head. 'No,' she mouthed. But Willa couldn't hear the word.

CHAPTER THIRTY-ONE

Annabelle

1977

The noise of the door opening startled her, and Annabelle jumped up from the couch.

Dan was peering into the gloom with a torch. 'Sorry. I must have fallen asleep before the blackout. Thank heavens you still have the fire going.'

'Dan.'

'You all right, little A? The blackout didn't frighten you?'

Annabelle took a deep breath. She wondered if he would notice her wet hair and damp clothes, but between the torch and the dim flicker of the firelight, she hoped he wouldn't.

'A bit.'

'It's really late. I'm surprised Lil's not home yet. Did you check in on Len?'

'Oh no. I forgot. I can do it now.' Annabelle felt a shot of panic. What if Len was dead too?

'That's okay.' Dan moved across the room with the torch and opened Len's door. After a few seconds, he came out. 'Sleeping peacefully.'

'Oh.' Annabelle sank back down onto the couch.

'Annabelle, you okay?' Dan came across and sat down next to her.

'I… Something happened.' She had a terrible, immediate need to tell Dan. To get it off her chest. To ask him what she should do.

'What? Was it Len?'

'No.' She wondered how she could tell him. It was so shameful, the thing with Andrew, and what she'd done. All of it.

'Lillian came back.'

'Where is she? Her car isn't there,' said Dan, frowning.

'She's with Constance. They've… they've gone—'

Car headlights flashed through the small window of The Old Chapel. Annabelle paused. Dan got up and walked to the window. Then he went to the door and opened it, shining the torch into the blackness as the car lights went out.

'Dan,' said Lillian, slipping past him and putting her wet coat on the hook. She looked nervously through the dim light to Annabelle, then back at Dan, before stepping into the living room.

Constance followed her in, and Dan looked confused.

'What's happened? Annabelle said something happened.'

Constance made her way across the room to Annabelle. 'Yes, something has happened,' she said slowly. 'Andrew hasn't come back. He was out looking for the dog in the storm. My phone line's down, or I would have called you.'

'We've been searching for him,' said Lillian.

'Why didn't you come and get me?' asked Dan. 'What time did he go out?'

'Maybe two or three hours ago,' said Constance. 'I fell asleep and woke up half an hour ago. I saw Lillian pulling in, so I just grabbed her and we went along the cliff paths, but we can't find him.'

'Bloody hell, Constance. You should have picked me up! Three hours ago… in this weather? Something must have happened to him.'

The cold of the darkened room seeped further into Annabelle.

'Yes, I think it must,' said Constance.

Dan looked at them curiously. 'We need to get the search-and-rescue guys. The police. You said the phone line was down?'

'When I checked,' said Constance.

'Right. Lil, go and check the phone at my house and ring the police if you can. If not, drive into town and raise the alarm. I'll go out with a torch. Connie, you stay here. I don't want you and Annabelle out in this weather.'

'Nonsense. I'll come,' said Constance. 'You can't go out there alone. Just let me get a better jacket.'

'Will you be all right here, little A?' Dan asked.

Annabelle nodded. She didn't want to be here by herself, but she didn't have much choice.

After they'd left, she sat on the couch, in the dark, shivering. Eventually she went up to Lillian's room and got under the bed covers, but the sheets were freezing and her skirt was wet. Her head throbbed painfully and she didn't dare to think about the dampness in her underwear. The coldness seeped through her until eventually she got out of bed and dragged the blanket back downstairs, huddling into it next to the fire, trying to stop shaking. In the flickering light of the flames, she imagined she was holding onto her mother. She could almost feel the gentle touch of her mother's hand. Then she realised that she had let her mother down tonight, and the lump of sadness that lodged in her belly was as heavy as concrete.

The door opened, startling her. Dan stood with the torch, pointing it towards her.

'Did you... find him?' she asked. She tried to keep the trembling from her voice.

'The police said they're going to search a bit more, but they'll have to stop soon and start again at first light. I need to get you home Annabelle, or Sylvia will worry.' Dan looked edgy, panicky.

'Okay.' Annabelle stood and put the blanket over the back of the couch. She followed Dan outside.

In the car, he was silent until they pulled out onto the highway.

'I'm sorry I left you. You were probably scared in that storm on your own.'

'A bit.'

'You okay?'

Annabelle began to cry. It was pitch dark, so she knew he wouldn't see her tears. She tried desperately to hold her breath, but as he pulled off the highway into their long, pebbled drive, a sob burst out.

'Annabelle?'

'Sorry,' she said. But she couldn't stop the tears.

'They'll find him. You'll see,' said Dan.

Annabelle didn't say anything.

Dan stopped the car outside the house and turned off the engine.

'Andrew's a really great guy,' he said. 'You could probably tell, even though you don't know him very well. It's understandable, to be upset.'

'Mmm,' murmured Annabelle.

'They'll find him, don't worry.' Dan leaned over and gave her a warm hug. Then he leaned in and wiped the tears away from her face with his thumbs. 'I'm so sorry you were there for that. Please don't cry now.' His face was close in the dark.

'Okay,' said Annabelle. Dan's voice sounded so kind that tears kept leaking from her eyes. Her chest was tight and rigid and she could feel herself shaking.

'Maybe I should wake Sylvia. You might need to talk to her,' said Dan pensively.

'No,' said Annabelle. 'Please don't.' She thought how angry Sylvia would be about the ripped top, and about Andrew, if she knew what Annabelle had done. Another huge sob escaped.

Dan reached over and pulled her into a long hug.

'Please, Annabelle, you need to wake Sylvia up. I have to go. To keep looking for Andrew.' He let her go and squeezed her hand.

'No. I'm fine,' said Annabelle, pulling the lever on the door. In one swift movement she was out of the car.

Dan got out his side and spoke across the top of the car. 'Anna, go and wake her. She needs to know what's happened and that you're not feeling okay. You need to talk to her.'

'All right,' said Annabelle. She walked down the pathway towards the kitchen door and listened to Dan's car engine behind her. The headlights came on, and she cringed as her shadow jumped into life. She rubbed away the wetness on her face and took a deep breath. There was no way she was waking Sylvia. If Sylvia found out what she had done, she would never speak to her again.

CHAPTER THIRTY-TWO

Sylvia

Sylvia ducked around the burning couch and lurched into the searing heat. Her lungs were on fire. 'Come *on*, Anna!' She wrenched at Annabelle's arm. When Annabelle didn't react, she moved behind her and heaved, pushing with all her strength.

From nowhere, Willa appeared. She grabbed Annabelle's other arm and together they propelled her out of The Old Chapel, just as there was a crashing sound, and a million tiny embers whooshed past them like fireflies, burning into Sylvia's throat.

Sylvia glanced back as Willa pulled Annabelle down the steps. A ceiling beam had fallen and the fire was crackling and mutating, consuming the boxes. Sylvia stumbled forward and collapsed onto the wet grass.

Indigo was running across the garden. 'Mum!' She had her phone in her hand. 'I've called the fire brigade. What happened?' She pulled Sylvia to her feet.

Sylvia tried to take some deep breaths, but began coughing. When she opened her eyes, there was a flash of movement in front of her. Constance was on the steps of The Old Chapel, moving faster than Sylvia had thought possible. Before she could open her mouth, the old woman had disappeared through the door of the burning house.

'Shit,' said Sylvia. Without hesitating, she ran in after her.

A blanket of chemical smoke was spreading across the ceiling of The Old Chapel like spilled black milk, and Constance was staring up as if it were an apparition. A ravaging wall of golden-orange flame obscured the back half of the building. Smoke was curling down the walls to meet the fire, thickening and blackening as they watched.

'Let me atone!' wailed Constance. She began coughing.

Sylvia pulled her back into the vestibule. The curtains on the nearest window were a tower of writhing liquid orange. All around the room, fire was morphing into huge, shimmering, brilliant walls of flame, pushing an avalanche of heat towards them. Sylvia leaned back in horror, trying to pull at Constance.

Constance jerked away, her eyes shining. '"I will be to her a wall of fire, declared the Lord. I will be the glory in her midst."' She held out her stick to keep Sylvia back as she stepped further into the living room.

'Come back!' screamed Sylvia, but the words were muted, thickened by the smoke in the air.

'You must tell the truth, Sylvia. About the will. Annabelle will be all right if you do.'

Behind her, Sylvia felt a jerk. Indigo was pulling at her shirt. *Indi shouldn't be in here. Too dangerous.* Sylvia tried to lean forward to grasp at Constance, but heat slammed her face, her body, her lungs. There was a great whoosh, and fire seemed to engulf the whole space. Sylvia ducked, but from the corner of her eye, she saw Constance leap forward – as if she were a young woman – straight into the flames. Another explosion roared through the house. The main beam holding up the roof collapsed in a violent crash, sparks and ash and flame spewing across the room. Sylvia stumbled backwards, and Indigo dragged her out through the door and down the steps.

Outside, the rain was harder now, and it swallowed them in a cold, fierce blanket. Sylvia turned her face up to it. The raindrops merged with the sooty tears falling down her face.

A crowd of people were standing in the laneway, pointing, screeching, exclaiming. 'Constance,' breathed Sylvia.

'We can't save her, Mum! We need to get further back. The fire brigade will come.'

'Where's Annabelle?'

'Over there,' said Indigo. She pointed to the group huddled next to the woodshed.

Annabelle was hunched over, keening. Willa was holding onto her, murmuring something. Sylvia stumbled towards them. The sound of breaking glass splintered the air. Flames and black smoke began pluming out through the little window at the top of the house.

In the distance, the wail of a fire engine grew louder.

'Constance,' sobbed Annabelle, looking desperately at Sylvia.

'I'm sorry, Anna. I couldn't get to her.' Sylvia put her hand on Annabelle's shoulder. 'Come away.'

Flames were licking at the timber exterior now. Within minutes, The Old Chapel was engulfed in a crackling blanket that sounded like an angry waterfall.

Willa and Sylvia both held onto Annabelle. 'Come away,' said Sylvia again, walking her backwards. 'We're all too close.' She looked up the roadway as the huge red truck turned the corner, siren and lights blazing.

Annabelle turned to Willa. 'Please, don't let the headstone burn.' She pointed to the blackened stone covered in clumps of newly cut grass. 'Little Maisy kept all my secrets.'

Across the flower garden, a crowd had surged onto the lane, and as the fire engine approached, people stepped back to let it park.

Sylvia ran across the garden and pushed through the crowd. A fireman clad in bright yellow jumped down from the truck and she gestured urgently. 'There's an old lady trapped in there.'

Dan's voice boomed across the chatter. 'Over here for the hoses,' he called, and a second fireman followed him towards the water supply.

Sylvia felt her legs wobble. She ran back across the grass to where Annabelle and Willa were standing. Dan was suddenly beside them.

'What the fuck happened?'

'I don't know. But Constance is in there,' said Sylvia.

'Shit,' said Dan.

Annabelle was panting and crying. Wailing.

'Pull yourself together!' Dan spat the words at her.

Sylvia saw red. The noise of the crowd and the firemen, the flames and the wind was beating into her head in a violent cacophony as she finally understood all her terrible mistakes. She moved in front of Dan, spitting at him with unleashed anger and hate, 'Don't speak to her like that!' Then she turned her back on him and put her hands gently on Annabelle's shoulders. 'Breathe with me, Anna. Breathe as I count.'

Dan turned and strode across the garden towards the fire truck.

Passing him, coming towards them, was the huge, hulking figure of Tippy Heokstrom. He was wearing a pullover that was two sizes too small, and his face was creased with worry. 'You crying, Annabelle?' he said.

Annabelle put her hand to her mouth, then nodded, as her breath slowly normalised.

'Yes, Tippy. My... my friend is in there.' She nodded at The Old Chapel.

'It's a bad house. You was dancing and twirling in there in the kitchen. The night Mister Andrew came and I was hiding in the yard.'

Annabelle nodded.

'He hurt you real bad.' His face wrinkled into a well of sadness. 'Sorry Annabelle.'

Annabelle lifted her hand to Tippy's arm. 'It's all right, Tippy. It wasn't your fault.'

'It's good I helped Lillian throw him in the sea,' said Tippy. 'He was too heavy for her.'

Sylvia's hand fluttered to her mouth.

'I didn't tell,' said Tippy. 'Lillian said I couldn't ever tell.'

Annabelle gave his arm a small squeeze and closed her eyes. 'I always knew it was my fault,' she whispered to Sylvia. 'But I didn't realise. I didn't understand how things worked back then… I didn't mean for it to happen.'

Sylvia drew her little sister towards her, enfolding her, smothering her with conscience-stricken love.

'I never meant for him to come near me, Syl,' said Annabelle bleakly into Sylvia's shoulder, 'and I don't know if I'll ever get away from him.'

CHAPTER THIRTY-THREE

Willa

The Merrivale gardens were empty. Outside, across the lane, an ambulance was parked next to two police cars as dusk settled. One of the fire engines was still there too, and firemen had been poking around in the remains of the blackened building all afternoon.

Sylvia had insisted that Annabelle go to bed a couple of hours ago, and she and Willa had cleaned up the remnants of the ruined fete once they had convinced the last of the committee members to leave. Now they sat on the couch, sipping tea.

'I'm sorry. About your house,' said Sylvia, wincing as she thumbed the bandage on her arm where the fire had singed her.

Willa shrugged.

'And about finding out about your father. What happened to Annabelle – it's… there are no words.'

Willa nodded. She felt hollow.

'Lillian sent me a photograph,' said Sylvia. 'Of you, when you were born. She took it when she went to collect Annabelle in Launceston, at the place your parents were renting.'

A tide of emotion flooded through Willa. A rush of thoughts so enormous that she could barely hold onto any of them. She couldn't speak.

'You were the tiniest little thing. Just so sweet,' continued Sylvia.

'Lillian had one too, in her box of photo albums,' she said eventually.

They both seemed to sink further into the couch, sharing a moment of silent sorrow at the loss of all the photographs. The sound of Dan's Range Rover pulling in near the kitchen door broke the moment. His car door slammed. Willa could barely believe he'd driven off after the fire was brought under control, leaving Annabelle to cope with the aftermath of such a terrible event. What a selfish man he was.

He walked in and ignored them. He opened the fridge and took out a beer, then leaned back on the kitchen bench. 'I thought you were leaving town,' he said, looking at Sylvia.

'Not just yet,' said Sylvia.

'Well I don't know why either of you is still here. You're not wanted.'

'We're here for Annabelle,' said Sylvia. There was ice in her voice.

Willa's stomach clenched in the silence that followed.

'I think it's you who needs to leave, Dan,' said Sylvia. 'You don't love Annabelle. You don't care about anyone but yourself. You should do us all a favour and pack your stuff.'

Dan gave a short, barking laugh. 'What?'

'Anyway, this is Willa's house now,' said Sylvia. She looked around the beautiful living room. Teacups and plates were piled high in plastic crates against the walls, washed and ready to return to the hire company.

'What the hell are you on about?' said Dan. He was angry now. He stood up straighter, his voice disbelieving, but there was a flash of uncertainty in his eyes.

'The will,' said Sylvia.

'What about it? I'm the named beneficiary. Now that Constance is gone, I have a clear title.' He narrowed his eyes at her.

'No, Dan.'

Willa felt a wall of tension between them expand as Sylvia held his glare.

'The other will. The original. Willa is Andrew's daughter.'

Dan scoffed. 'What?'

'It was Andrew who got Annabelle pregnant,' said Sylvia.

'Don't be stupid.'

'It's true.' Annabelle stood at the door, her face wiped clean of make-up. She was wearing her pyjamas.

Dan stared at her, uncomprehending.

Annabelle sighed. 'You need to leave, Dan.'

'Have you all lost the fucking *plot*?' said Dan, looking from Annabelle to Sylvia.

'Please don't speak like that,' said Annabelle. 'For forty years I've gone along with you. I've loved you. Supported you. But now you need to listen.' She looked at him steadily. 'Andrew was violent. He was violent to Constance, to Lillian, to me. He was a violent, sadistic man.'

'He wasn't,' said Dan. His face was tight with disbelief.

'You were young, Dan. I don't blame you for not spotting it. But what he did to me was more than any woman – any child – should have to bear. I did bear it, though. I survived. I always thought that if I told you, you might not believe me.' She looked across at Willa. 'But now I realise I don't need you to believe me.'

Dan turned away, half staring at the floor. Then he turned back. 'You're not taking my house.'

Sylvia said, 'It's Willa's house, Dan. She is in line to inherit. She's Andrew's next of kin. The real will would have recognised her as the beneficiary.'

'Don't be crazy. You go down that road, Sylvia, and you'll rob Annabelle too. Leave things as they are. She'll get half of Merrivale in the wash-up.'

Sylvia shrugged.

Dan spluttered. 'If you want to contest the will, you'd have to admit to committing fraud! To swapping the documents. You signed the damned thing.'

She shrugged again.

Dan exploded. 'Fuck it, Syl! Don't be so stupid! I was saving his arse. You know I was!'

'Dan,' said Sylvia, calmly. 'Don't.'

'I'll fight this. I'm not going to let you ruin my reputation. And what for? You don't even know her!' He gestured at Willa with a flick of his hand.

'She's your cousin, Dan. Your blood, and mine.'

Dan said nothing. Willa's dislike of him twisted in her stomach.

Sylvia sighed. 'Don't be stupid. It doesn't all have to come out. You can just sign the paperwork to transfer Merrivale to Willa and get it all done quietly. It's in your interest to avoid a public scandal. I've read Lillian's diaries. I know what really happened with the trust monies. And not just the once. It happened when that resort investment failed a while back too, didn't it? You borrowed money to prop things up.'

Dan's face cracked.

'Lillian only stayed silent to protect Annabelle from a scandal. So don't be an idiot. Just organise the transfer.' She looked across at Annabelle, who gave a small nod. 'We don't want you here,' said Sylvia.

Dan turned his back, both hands resting on the kitchen bench, as if it was holding him up. Then he turned.

'The diaries are gone,' he said. 'Burned to ash, I'm guessing.'

Sylvia stood. 'Then it's my word against yours, I suppose. I'm happy to take my chances.'

'Who are they going to believe in court, Syl? A respected solicitor with an unblemished forty-year career? Or a drop-out hippy?'

The angry exchange was making Willa's head throb. What were they talking about? Wills? Fraud? 'I don't want Merrivale,' she said quietly. 'I have a house. And a family. This house is a part of who Annabelle is.' She looked out the window, past the fire engine and the charred skeleton of The Old Chapel to the ocean. 'It belongs to Annabelle.'

'No. It doesn't,' said Sylvia. 'In reality, it belongs to you.'

After a pause, Willa spoke again. 'When the house I grew up in was sold after my parents died, it was awful. When we lost Esme, well, of course, that put it into perspective, but when I think about all the losses I've been through in the last few years – both my parents and my daughter – that home, it mattered. When it was sold, it made me feel as though I'd lost my roots. I think I've been looking for somewhere to put them back down. And when I found The Old Chapel, I thought, maybe *this* is my place, because something about being here felt right.' She paused, pulled her gaze away from the window. 'But maybe it was meeting all of you – a sense of people being in a place they belonged to – that satisfied something in me.' She sighed. 'Sylvia, I can't take their house.'

'Dan was going to sell it anyway,' said Sylvia. 'Selling Merrivale in conjunction with The Old Chapel would have made it worth much more. That's why he wanted The Old Chapel.'

'What?' said Annabelle, turning to Dan. 'You were planning to sell Merrivale?'

Dan ignored her. He reached into a cupboard and took out a bottle of whisky.

'Surely you weren't?' said Annabelle tremulously.

'For Christ's sake,' muttered Dan as he poured the whisky.

'Dan? We worked so hard. The gardens, the new business... This was our dream...'

'It was your dream, not mine. The weddings were the only way I could think to keep the whole bloody thing going. It costs me a fortune, the upkeep of this place. I'm sick of spending all weekend mowing lawns and listening to you whingeing about why I haven't trimmed the hedges or mulched the orchard. I'm sixty-six, Annabelle. I'm bloody tired.'

There was so much anger in his voice. Willa felt herself withdrawing into a corner of the couch.

'Well, it's not yours to sell,' said Sylvia. 'In the original will, Andrew's heirs got everything.'

'Oh,' said Annabelle, blinking rapidly. 'Yes.' After a minute, she turned towards Willa. 'Yes, that's how it should be.'

'Well it's a moot point,' said Dan. 'No diaries. No evidence. No proof.'

'I have the diaries,' said Willa quietly. 'I took them to my rental house yesterday.'

All three heads swivelled to look at her.

'And I found the extra box of them. The missing ones.'

Sylvia shot Willa a disbelieving look, but a smile formed on her lips. Then she turned to Dan, triumph showing in the tilt of her chin.

'You'll get nothing if we don't fight for this place, Annabelle!' roared Dan. 'Half of bloody nothing! The other assets are a pittance. I can't retire if I don't have this place to sell. Don't you see?' Dan's face was puce. He slammed the whisky glass down on the bench and Willa jumped.

Annabelle didn't flinch, though. She cocked her head to one side and seemed to consider the idea.

After a moment, she walked to the couch and sat down carefully next to Willa. Then she smiled brightly. 'Yes,' she said. 'I do see.'

CHAPTER THIRTY-FOUR

Annabelle

Twelve months later

Annabelle stared at the email from Ian Enderby. There seemed to be endless rounds of paperwork to sign these days. She found it tiresome, all this work she now needed to be on top of.

She thought back to the moment, just a fortnight after the terrible fire that had killed Constance, when she had finally returned Ian's incessant phone calls.

'I need to talk to you about Constance's estate,' he'd said.

She had sighed, picturing the face of dear, serious Constance. She missed their weekly cups of tea. She missed Constance. She'd been a solid presence in Annabelle's life for more than forty years. She supposed the church would inherit the bulk of her fortune. And some would go to Dan, as surviving family. There was a niece on Constance's side in Melbourne, too. No doubt any remaining relatives would soon come out of the woodwork now that there was an estate to distribute. It was such a vast fortune, so Dan had once told her.

Constance owned a treasured Royal Worcester tea set that Annabelle had often admired. She had hoped that would come to her, so she could think of Constance when she sat down to drink a cup of tea. She raised her hand to the cross around her neck and fingered it; a habit she'd had for most of her life. Constance had gifted her the silver cross when she turned sixteen, and she had worn it ever since, even though she wasn't really sure if she still believed in God. Still, it was sensible to keep your options open.

In the few days since the fire, her grief for Constance seemed to be interspersed with panic about how she'd manage now that she'd thrown Dan out. Emotionally, physically and financially she was a wreck. Still, she had insisted that Willa take ownership of Merrivale as was her birthright, even though it meant Annabelle was now practically destitute and soon to be homeless. Her and Dan's assets, when they removed Merrivale from the equation, were apparently quite limited. Dan had squandered most of their investments and superannuation in a failed property development a few years ago, it turned out. Well, he didn't use the word *squandered*, exactly. 'I was ripped off by a mate' might have been the phrase. She remembered he'd been stressed when a friend's hotel chain went bust years ago, but she knew now that he hadn't told her the full story at the time. Perhaps, she admitted to herself, because she wouldn't have been interested. Still, making Dan sign Merrivale over to Willa was strangely satisfying. It made her happy, despite her panicky moments wondering how she could possibly find a job at her age, with so few skills.

But then she had returned Ian's calls. In Constance's will, he told her, she had been been named as the primary beneficiary. Constance had changed her will almost forty years earlier to recognise her.

Dragging herself from the memory of those first days after the fire, Annabelle pondered the latest email from Ian. It turned out that being rich required a substantial amount of work. There was no relaxing, as one might have expected after inheriting a ridiculously large fortune. Oh no. There were endless meetings with financial advisors, and legal papers to sign with Ian and her new Melbourne lawyers, then constant updates by email about stocks and shares. Then there were property advisors and portfolios, and board papers from companies she owned or had large sharehold-ings in. Charities Constance had been aligned with now needed a new patron, and there were plenty of tax implications to consider; pages and pages and *pages* of really rather tedious paperwork. In the beginning everything was unfathomably difficult. But now she seemed to be getting the hang of it. Indigo had been helping her lately. The girl was incredibly bright.

Annabelle responded to Ian's email, telling him she would be in on Monday to sign the latest round of documents. She pushed the button to turn on the kettle and looked out the window. On the site where The Old Chapel had stood, weeds and thistles had sprung up during the summer. Pete had sprayed them and cut them back a while ago, but there was something about the ash-enriched dirt that drew them back. She let her eyes land briefly on Maisy's gravestone before they settled on the magnificent blue of the endless ocean. Out there, across the nothingness, there was something else waiting for her. She could feel it.

She turned at the sound of the door opening.

Indigo was holding up a magazine. 'I know you like me to chuck anything out that's not worth posting on, but the guests in Bay Cottage left this.'

Annabelle took the magazine and scanned the cover. *British Plants & Gardens.*

'Thought it was up your alley,' said Indigo.

The photograph on the front was of a delightful garden in front of a stone cottage. The trees were strung with colourful bunting and a table was set for high tea with the prettiest china.

'Lovely,' said Annabelle, smiling. 'I might even pop my feet up and read it today. Cuppa?'

'No. Gotta head back into town to the studio. If I don't get these final pieces made, there won't be an exhibition to open next week.'

'How's your mother?' asked Annabelle. 'Is she coming back for the exhibition?'

Indigo hesitated. 'She's fine. And no. I asked her, but she can't get away.'

Annabelle let out a little sigh. 'Never mind.' She missed Sylvia. It had been lovely spending time with her before she left. The Northern Territory was so far away.

Indigo backed out the door, waving goodbye. 'See ya Friday.'

'Bye, Indi. And… just so you know, the real-estate agent said Merrivale will be up on their website by Friday, so I've cancelled the cottage bookings from the start of June.'

'Okay.' Indigo nodded.

Annabelle considered how kind Willa had been, insisting she stay on at Merrivale until her treatment was finished, and she felt ready to decide her future. Well, now she was ready. More than ready. She and Willa had come up with some very exciting plans.

'I'd love you to help me with packing up the house when you've got time to fit in some more hours, Indi. I'd pay you, of course.'

'Sure. I'd love to help. And you definitely won't be paying me.' Indigo waved again as she closed the door.

Annabelle put the magazine on the table and thought of Indigo's renewed passion for weaving. The girl was so talented. Annabelle had been utterly entranced at the state pole-dancing championships a few months ago. She couldn't believe how Indigo had managed to go upside down on that pole and zoom around it like a lusty, semi-naked acrobat. She couldn't believe she had enjoyed watching it. The agility! The core strength! It was captivating. It made her dizzy and proud in equal measure. Sylvia didn't know what she was missing, being such a prude about it.

She looked back down at the magazine. She didn't have time to read it really. There was quite a lot to be done with getting the house ready for sale. Dan had cleaned out the shed before he left, but Annabelle still had to deal with sorting the contents of the house and dividing them up. She looked around at the vast array of knick-knacks, furniture, paintings and lovely antiques.

Her new rental house wouldn't take even a fraction of it. Perhaps Indigo would like to choose a few pieces to squeeze into Sylvia's house down at the beach, which she was now living in. After that, she might help Annabelle to arrange a garage sale or organise the charity van to come and pick things up. What a shame she and Dan didn't have any children to give things to.

Annabelle thought of Willa then, and Hamish, and wondered if it would be appropriate to find them a memento amongst all these *things*. She clicked into her email and reread the one that had arrived from Willa a few days earlier.

To: Annabelleb176@gmail.com
From:Wfairbanks@lightscameraaction.co.uk
So lovely to hear your news…

Hello, Annabelle,

So glad to hear your latest round of tests came back all clear. You must be feeling great. The new therapist sounds lovely, too. I know how beneficial mine has been, and even though it doesn't change the past, sometimes my guy really gives me something to grab onto when everything feels dark. I've finally convinced Hugo (after three years!) that he should also be seeing someone, and the other day he gave me a hug and thanked me for insisting. I think the weight of holding us all together was becoming too much, so I am really thankful that he agreed to go.

We all miss Sisters Cove. Hamish still talks about the surfing. He seems to have grown a few more centimetres and I may have to take out a second mortgage to afford the grocery bill if he doesn't stop soon! It's hard to believe he's turning eighteen in eight weeks. He's adamant he doesn't want a party (huge sigh of relief, actually), so I'm thinking we will just take a few friends to the Cherwell Boathouse for dinner. You know I like an event to plan! It's a favourite special-treat restaurant for us for dinner. I was there just last week for a birthday tea for a friend, and we had a marvellous time watching tourists punting down the river. The kids used to go to school right next door, so it will be lovely to take Hamish back to the place where he and Esme spent so many happy years as children. I find it peaceful to think of her there, watching the gentle flow of the river. Of course I still have awful, dark days, but I'm managing them. I know they'll always be lurking.

Let me know how Indigo's exhibition goes. I emailed her some photos of my weaving efforts from the new class I've been doing, but they were pretty pathetic really. Even so, I loved doing them. I've met some lovely people in the class.

Do let me know about anything I can do to make the sale of Merrivale easier for you. The solicitor is keeping me posted, but I mean practical things.

Better run. My new job with the film company is quite busy. Only three days per week, but it always spills over to four because there are so many events on at the moment. I need to do some work tonight for a meeting I have tomorrow, so bye for now.

Keep well and keep in touch.

Love, Willa

Annabelle sighed, then clicked out of her email. She pulled up the Google search engine and typed in *Cherwell Boathouse, Oxford*. A delightful picture of a multi-gabled dark Edwardian building popped up, set on the banks of a river with punts moored right out the front. She clicked into the other related images – winding waterways, spectacular drooping willow trees in bright green, then others in all the shades of autumnal brilliance framing a passing houseboat. What a beautiful place to live. She smiled to herself, imagining the gardens of the nearby Cotswolds she'd always longed to visit. She'd begun following all sorts of lovely gardens on Instagram, and there were a few from around that area. And some lovely guest houses and hotels.

The photographs lifted her spirits. She'd tried plenty of times to get Dan to visit the UK with her over the years, so she could do a garden tour. But he'd refused, preferring overseas trips with his mates to visit golf courses. But she'd always longed to visit England.

She ran her finger across the magazine and wondered if she might send something to Hamish for his special birthday. Would that be presumptuous? She knew she wasn't really supposed to think of him as her grandson, but sometimes her heart clenched at the thought of his lovely face. Perhaps just a small gift. Nothing too personal. What did teenage boys like? A penknife perhaps? Tickets to something? A nice book? She must ask Indigo. She would know. Then she could order it on the internet. She was getting quite good at online shopping these days. Online everything really. Being unwell for so many months during her treatment had forced her into it.

She closed down the computer and looked across at the magazine. Maybe she did have time to flick through a few pages. She got tired quite easily these days, since the chemotherapy, so perhaps she would sit down for a bit. She picked up her cup of tea and popped two mint slice biscuits onto the saucer.

'Come on, Banjo,' she said. The dog raised one sleepy eyelid from his place on the rug next to the kitchen table. Eventually he struggled to his feet and followed her out onto the veranda. As she passed the rose bush that brushed through the balustrade, she snapped off the droopy head of a Fair Bianca rose that had seen better days. She tossed it in amongst the mulch and wondered if she should go inside and get her secateurs. There were quite a few flowers that needed dead-heading.

No, you won't. You will sit and read and enjoy the beauty of this day and be kind to yourself.

The voice was strong and clear in her mind. She smiled. Perhaps it was the voice of the mindfulness meditation therapist that the Cancer Council had recommended. Tilly. A pretty girl with a sweet, lilting Irish accent. Annabelle had gone to her class every week for nearly three months and it really had helped. Minute by minute. Day by day. That was how she lived now.

She caught sight of another batch of soft-drooping rose heads on the lower branches of the bush and had an insatiable urge to clip them. *Sit down and read that magazine, woman!* She stood still and pondered the voice. Tilly didn't usually sound quite so forthright. As she sat down on the lounger and opened the magazine, she realised with complete clarity that the voice in her head was Sylvia's. She took a sip of her tea and then reached her hand down to ruffle Banjo's ears. Bossy woman; how dare she interfere? Still – she put her feet up on the ottoman and opened the magazine – it really was quite a splendid idea.

CHAPTER THIRTY-FIVE

Sylvia

A few weeks later

'Inhale, up. Square your hips to the front. Exhale. Elbows behind your back, inhale, lift, exhale, forward.' Sylvia leaned down and put her forehead on her knee. From the corner of her eye, the white-orange streak of the horizon was pushing up a bulb of gold through the darkness.

She kept speaking in gentle, rhythmic phrases. 'Right hand up, left fingertips on the ground. Exhale, bend your front leg, step back, go into Vinyasa, exhale, Chaturanga, inhale, Downward Dog.' As she took the class through the final moves, she was warmed by the golden beam of the rising sun spreading across the native grasses, lighting up the enormous shadow of Uluru behind her.

'Coming into Savasana. Final relaxation. Hands are by your sides, palms facing upwards. Allow yourself to relax into this present moment. Enjoy the start of the day and the feel of the new sun on your face.' A fly settled at the entrance to Sylvia's nostril and began exploring. She huffed an out-breath and it jumped onto the bridge of her nose. Now that the sun was up, they would multiply into tiny, winged storm clouds all across the vast expanse of the red-dirt countryside. They would descend into ears and eyes and mouths, driving all those unsuspecting visitors who didn't wear fly nets over their hats to the edge of madness.

'Namaste,' said Sylvia as she raised her hands into prayer position.

'Namaste,' said the group of women back to her.

She let the sadness settle on her chest as she sat still, pondering the vast sky. Eventually the class members stood and stretched, and took in the extraordinary view. Some got out their phones to take photographs as the shadows and colours of the sunrise changed and merged, lighting up the extraordinary beauty of the central Australian desert.

After another ten minutes, the guests piled onto the minibus and headed back along the dirt road to the resort. Some murmured at the prospect of the gourmet breakfast that awaited them, others chatted about the walking tour around Uluru they would be taken on later.

'That was amazing! Thank you so much, Sylvia.' Alana, a woman from the eastern suburbs of Sydney was gushing again. There had been a brokenness about her when she arrived for the five-day yoga retreat, but Sylvia thought that in just a few short days she had taken some baby steps towards self-actualisation.

'It never gets old,' said Sylvia. 'It's worth the start in the dark.' She smiled, and Alana launched into a story about how she was used to the dark anyway, because her husband had always made her get into bed with the light off unless she kept her weight under fifty kilograms. If the scales went over, he'd call her a fat slag and refuse to look at her.

'That's awful,' said Sylvia. 'What a good decision it was to leave him.'

'Oh no, I haven't left him!' said Alana. 'I've just decided to go on lots more retreats this year. He might complain when I'm slow at keeping up the Botox, but he sold his tech company for forty-eight million last year!'

Maybe the baby steps weren't towards self-actualising, pondered Sylvia. Maybe it was more like self-preservation. She felt a little pang of sorrow. The poor woman had sold her soul, yet in some deluded part of her mind she felt she'd gotten a reasonable deal.

Stop judging, Sylvia.

Holding their yoga mats and phones the women hopped off the bus. Sylvia waved to Alana and walked towards the staff tents. The 'tents' were actually hotel rooms with circular white canvas roofs and floor-to-ceiling glassed-in views of the huge red rock formation of Uluru. The staff tents were less luxurious than those of the guests, and only had a view of the desert. Still, Sylvia found hers restful and beautiful, though she wished she hadn't committed to a twelve-month contract. She had needed some space, some time to decide if she should settle down in Tasmania. But now she missed it. It really was home.

She knew she needed time away so she could begin to forgive herself for what she had done to Annabelle, too. When The Old Chapel had burned down, and Sylvia had learned the story of what had happened to her sister, she could hardly function for weeks. She couldn't bear it. Poor darling Annabelle. She wanted to go back and gouge out the eyes of her younger, sillier self. The story was one she could never have imagined, particularly the part where Constance had killed Andrew, although no one had discussed that again. It seemed disrespectful to the old lady's memory.

When Annabelle had started her cancer treatment, Sylvia had taken her to every appointment. But still, her relationship with her sister felt tenuous. Annabelle had accepted her many apologies, but she had been exhausted and sick, and Sylvia wondered if the forgiveness she had bestowed was more to do with pleasing her. Although, there had been a shift in Annabelle's tendency to want to please everyone. Sylvia had felt it.

When a friend had got in touch about this contract in the Northern Territory, Indigo had promised to keep a close eye on

Annabelle. And it seemed that despite the aftermath of the fire, Constance's death and the ongoing cancer treatment, Annabelle had been doing remarkably well. She had so many friends who had wanted to support her.

Dan had moved out the day after the fire, and Sylvia assumed their divorce would be finalised soon. She had been pondering what had happened between herself and Dan. Why did a notion of your perfect first love stay stuck in your head? How had she allowed it to overrule her loyalty to her sister? Teenage love was so different. A moment in time when everything felt extreme – the love, the passion, the disappointment. Somehow, over the decades, Dan had moved in to Sylvia's psyche as the perfect lodger. With the passing of the years, the anger over their fraud and over the fling she imagined between Dan and Annabelle had dimmed. She had cocooned her teenage love from the hurts. She had remembered only the good. No one had ever compared to him. But in the end, he was just a man. A selfish, flawed man. And she had threatened her relationship with Annabelle by falling for him again. The shame felt endless.

There was a quick knock and then the sound of the sliding door into her tent. It was Jenny, the dining room manager. She looked frazzled. 'The new Danish waitress is sick. Any chance you can give us a hand on the breakfast shift, Sylvia?'

Sylvia smiled. 'Sure. I'll just get changed. Be there in five.'

Six minutes later, she walked into the dining tent and headed for the kitchen.

'These are for the couple on table ten,' said Jenny, pointing to two plates under the warmer holding artfully arranged omelettes sprinkled with chives and surrounded by mushrooms. Sylvia picked them up and took them across the room to an American couple, who thanked her profusely in delightful Southern accents. She picked up their empty juice jug and scanned the room for plates to collect.

When she returned, Jenny gestured to two more plates. 'For the lady in the corner, on table three.'

'Both of them?' asked Sylvia.

'She must be hungry,' said Jenny. 'She's certainly talkative. Wanted to know all about the place, the food, the staff. Couldn't get away from her.'

Sylvia picked up the plates and headed towards the back of the tent. The woman was facing away from her, towards the view. There was something familiar about her short greying curls.

'Here you are,' said Sylvia, placing the plates on the table.

'Oh, goody!' The woman grinned and clapped her hands.

'Annabelle?'

'Surprise!' said Annabelle.

Sylvia was dumbstruck. Then she laughed. 'What are you *doing* here?'

'I've come to see you, silly! I'm on the first leg of a little trip I have planned.'

From behind her, Sylvia heard Jenny. 'Well go on then, sit down with your sister.' Jenny smiled. 'Thought we'd surprise you. Frida just popped to the bathroom. She's not really sick.'

Sylvia laughed.

'Order up!' called the chef, and Jenny hurried away.

Annabelle pushed a plate across to Sylvia. 'I ordered you the chia breakfast pudding.' She began cutting into her own bacon and eggs. 'It sounds dreadful, but the lady said it was your favourite.'

'Thanks,' laughed Sylvia, shaking her head. 'This is such a shock. I can't believe you're here.'

'Well, I've never been to Uluru. And I thought to myself, what an opportunity! A personal tour guide on site!'

Sylvia smiled. 'How long are you staying?'

'Eight nights here. Then I head off on the next part of my trip.'

'But this place is extortionate! I mean, are you sure you can afford that many nights?'

'Oh. So Indigo kept her promise not to tell then,' said Annabelle, looking sheepish.

'What promise?'

'Constance left me her estate.'

'What?'

'There was a tithe for the church, of course. And three charities got a few hundred thousand each. But most of it came to me. I couldn't come to terms with it when I found out. You know, with starting treatment and all of the rest. So I didn't tell you. I only told Indigo a couple of months ago because I was completely swamped with the paperwork and needed her help.'

'That's…' Sylvia's spoonful of porridge was suspended half-way between her bowl and her mouth.

'Yes. Amazing, isn't it. She left nothing for poor Dan, which I thought was a little bit harsh, to be honest. But she made a specific provision that he wasn't to have any of it. I'm not sure why she was so set against him.'

Sylvia's eyes widened.

'Not that Dan took it lying down, of course. We had a long marriage, so he says he's entitled to half of any of my income, and you know… blah-di-blah-blah. Says he's going to fight me in the courts.' Annabelle forked some egg into her mouth.

'What will you do?'

'Well, Ian Enderby says Constance's wording in the will about him not taking anything was pretty watertight. But still, apparently we can't be certain. It could cost hundreds of thousands if Dan decides to drag it through all the appeal courts.'

'That would be awful,' said Sylvia.

'I know. So to make him go away, I offered him a huge old house that Constance owned in Prelanah, out the back of Burnie. Near that old quarry. God knows why she had it. The land's not worth much.'

'Well, at least he'll have a roof over his head,' said Sylvia.

'Hmm.' Annabelle sniffed. 'Sort of. Except it's full of asbestos. I got a building report done before I gave it to him.'

'Good Lord,' laughed Sylvia.

Annabelle smiled. 'I'll give him some money eventually. I feel a bit bad for him actually, but I thought I'd make him sweat for a while.'

'Who are you and what have you done with my sister?' asked Sylvia.

'I'm a new woman,' said Annabelle. 'Willa and I have gone into business together. We're building a row of cottages on The Old Chapel block, up the other end, near the eastern cliff face, where it's protected from the winds. Out of sight of Merrivale. One for Willa's family, one for me, and we can rent out the other two to holidaymakers. They'll just be small ones. Willa will only be back now and again, and I don't need much room.'

'Wow, that's fabulous,' said Sylvia. 'What about Merrivale? What's happening there?'

'She's selling it,' said Annabelle. 'And I decided not to buy it. It's too much work for me on my own. I suppose I could afford a team of gardeners now, but really, why lumber myself with all that extra administration? And there's no pleasure in a garden if you don't do it yourself. The Old Chapel gardens will be much more manageable, and quite lovely. Lillian had a pretty good eye, you know. And it's got a better view!'

Sylvia felt a surge of love for her sister. And admiration. Her spirit was so strong, despite all that had happened.

Across the restaurant, the door opened. Alana from the yoga class came in with her girlfriends, make-up applied, hair styled, glamorous walking clothes hugging her beautiful figure. Sylvia thought of love in all its forms. Toxic love, romantic love, sisterly love, motherly love. She thought of Indigo and her foolish pole-dancing job and was suddenly sad that she hadn't been there for the state championships to support her daughter, and that she would miss her weaving exhibition.

'I'm taking a ten-kilometre walking tour around the base of the rock before dusk. Want to come with me?' asked Sylvia.

'Absolutely,' said Annabelle. 'I'm starting a health kick. I've bought some fabulous new shoes.' She stuck her leg out from under the table to reveal bright-green leather walking shoes with pink laces. 'Aren't they just heaven?'

CHAPTER THIRTY-SIX

Willa

One month later

Willa leaned down and clasped the weed in her gloved fingers, ready to tug it out. She hesitated. Perhaps it wasn't a weed. Perhaps it was the beginnings of a flower. The foliage looked a little like the zinnias in the garden of The Old Chapel. She chewed on her lip and wondered what to do. Perhaps she should take a photo of it. Annabelle would know. She could email it. Then she shook the silly thought away and plucked out the weed and tossed it in the heap. She stood and stretched out. She had been weeding for ages and her back was stiff.

Her mind rattled through the rest of her day. Should she go for her walk now, and loosen up her limbs? Perhaps she should check the fridge to see if she needed anything else for the Moroccan lamb dish she wanted to make for dinner. Then there were the groceries to buy, although they didn't need much. Tomorrow night they would be eating out.

It would be a night of celebration tinged with sadness, as big events always were these days. Hamish was turning eighteen and she had booked a table for thirteen. She, Hugo and Hamish, plus their best friends, Elisa and Leo Peterson, with their twin boys, Harry and Jack – who were the same age as Hamish – and their younger sister, Giselle. Then there was Hamish's best mate, Tom Laraday, and his hilarious mother, Mia, a good friend of Willa's since the boys had met in their first year of school. Hamish's godparents, Catherine and Paul Bellamy, would be coming from London for it too. Their children were grown up now, so these days it was just the two of them. The final guest was Hugo's father, Errol, the loveliest man Willa knew, apart from Hugo himself, of course. Hugo's mother had passed away twenty years earlier, and his sister and her family lived in Scotland and were hard to pin down. But although light on family, it was still a lovely group of people.

She sat back and closed her eyes as the sun came out from behind a cloud and threw a warm beam across her back. *Thank you. Thank you for this day.* At Dr Lee's encouragement, she was writing a gratitude diary, and each day she was encouraged to answer three questions: What are you grateful for? Why? What act of kindness have you performed today? It made her much more conscious of the many small positives in her daily life. Sometimes when she got to the end of the day she realised she didn't have anything to report about an act of kindness. So she would make a cup of tea for Hamish, who was hard at work studying for exams, and take it in and fuss around with the mess in his bedroom until he got sick of her. Although, according to him, her fussing didn't qualify as a kindness.

On other days she'd take some flowers or groceries to old Cecil across the road, whose wife had passed away with pneumonia last year. They had both been very kind to the family when Esme died. Whenever she popped across, Cecil would cut some silver beet or pull up some potatoes from his little raised veggie garden for her, and give her tips on mulching or fertilising and she'd end up returning home with full hands and a happy heart.

She pulled off her gloves. 'C'mon, Kettles. C'mon, boy,' she called.

The dog looked up from the butterfly bushes at the back of the garden. He was snapping at insects, but as she called him a second time, he turned his shaggy old frame and followed her towards the house.

At the back door, Willa kicked off her boots and brushed the dirt from her jeans. She peered through the door at the wall clock and was surprised to find it was nearly midday. Friday was her favourite day. She didn't work, and often she would walk into the city centre and meet Hugo for lunch. Today they had no fixed plans, but perhaps she would ring him.

She filled the kettle and placed it on the hob, and the dog settled on his mat. As Willa turned to head for the shower, the doorbell rang. She cursed and crossed quickly to the sink to wash off the dirt that had wormed its way through the hole in her glove, then hurried through to the front door and pulled it open.

'Surprise, surprise!'

Willa took a moment to react. In front of her, a round, colour-fully dressed woman with short curly hair and enormous sunglasses had her arms spread wide. Next to her on the ground was a purple suitcase and a floral pull-along cabin bag. After a moment, the woman pulled off her sunglasses.

'Annabelle,' spluttered Willa.

A fleeting look of uncertainty passed across Annabelle's face, but her bright-pink lips quickly spread back into a grin.

'Hello, Willa! I thought I'd just pop in to surprise Hamish with his birthday present. It's in my bag,' she said, beaming.

'Oh! Well that's wonderful,' said Willa, regaining her compo-sure. She stepped forward and Annabelle drew her into a warm hug. Her perfume smelled comfortingly floral and familiar, and Willa was overcome with a sudden hot welling of tears in her eyes. She stepped back. 'Come in! Do come in.'

'Thank you, lovely girl,' said Annabelle. She picked up the cabin bag and hesitated as she looked at the suitcase.

Willa hesitated too. 'Are you... Give me the case. I'll make up the spare room,' she added, as the thought came to her.

'Oh no!' Annabelle let out a peal of laughter. 'I'm not here to stay with you. Goodness, I wouldn't dream of imposing.' She thrust the handle of the cabin bag at Willa and began fiddling with the extension handle on the case before following Willa into the hall and dragging the case into a nook next to Hugo's treasured antique timber hat stand. 'No, goodness me. I can't check into my hotel until three p.m., though, so I thought, well, why not strike while the iron is hot? I'll go and see Willa!'

Willa motioned her through to the kitchen. 'That's lovely. I'm so pleased you did,' she said, smiling. 'And what a surprise! I'm sorry you've caught me in my dirty gardening gear.'

'Fiddlesticks,' said Annabelle. 'And how wonderful that you're gardening. I was so pleased when you told me you'd taken it up.'

Willa smiled. 'I love your new short hair.'

'Do you really?' asked Annabelle.

Willa nodded.

'I'm getting used to it still. One of my friends who lost hers with the chemo a few years back calls it "cancer chic", so I'm doing my best to get on board and go with that.'

Seeing the fleeting worry in Annabelle's eyes, Willa wanted to reach out and put her arms around her. Instead she said, 'Sorry. I didn't think.'

'Nonsense! It's a bit curlier than it used to be, but I'm embracing the easy-care aspect.' Annabelle grinned, and the awkwardness between them evaporated.

The kettle began to whistle, and Willa lifted it from the hob.

'Oh, what a beautiful Aga!' said Annabelle.

Willa smiled and looked down at the old stove. She supposed it was rather beautiful, although the price of the oil to keep it running made her cringe with terror every time she looked at the bills.

'I just adore these houses,' said Annabelle. 'The architecture was so gorgeous everywhere I looked when I was in the cab. And the cab itself! Black, with the funny door! But so much roomier and nicer than the ones at home.'

'I suppose we take them for granted,' said Willa. 'I'm glad you found us, though.'

'The driver knew your street right away. He was lovely. Took me on a tour around some amazing buildings. Pointed out places for me to visit. Apparently there's an excellent chocolate shop, and also a cheese shop in a place called Covered Market, which sounds right up my alley!'

Willa couldn't help grinning. She'd forgotten how entertaining it was to be swept up into the whirlwind of Annabelle.

'Righto,' she said. 'Well, just let me have a shower and we can go there now. No time like the present, is there? I'll give you a little tour of the city while I'm at it, then we might be able to meet Hugo for something to eat.'

'What fun! Thank you, Willa,' said Annabelle, and she clapped her hands together then leaned down to pat Kettles. 'Off you go then, you go and shower. I'll make myself a cup of tea.'

Willa retreated into her bedroom and hurriedly undressed. In the shower, she had a brilliant idea. Surely Annabelle would agree to come to Hamish's dinner tomorrow night. She would entertain everyone with her delighted chatter.

Washed and dressed for lunch, she hurried back into the kitchen, but it was empty. She turned towards the living room. Annabelle was standing, looking at a framed photo of Willa with her mother and father, taken on the day of her graduation from Sydney University.

Annabelle looked up. 'Your parents,' she said, with a hint of sadness.

'Yes,' said Willa.

'They were lovely to me.'

'To me too. They were wonderful.'

'I'm so glad,' said Annabelle earnestly. 'I did often wonder, you know. All the time, actually. I used to say to myself, "Annabelle, no doubt your little girl is having the best childhood ever, because Arthur and Janice were so kind."' She smiled. 'And they *so* wanted a baby. They'd been trying for such a long time before you came along, but it just didn't happen for them. I lived with them for five months, until you were born.' She looked out the window for a moment, then turned back to Willa. 'They were so kind to me, but I was horrid to them at the end. I was rude and upset and angry. Lillian did her best to calm me down, but I didn't really want to let you go, you see. I called you Bee-Bee, and the only thing I wanted was to keep you.' She looked back at the photograph. 'But I couldn't.'

'You did the best you could,' said Willa, crossing the room. She picked up the photograph and looked at it. 'And you picked the best family for me. They were very loving. I had a wonderful childhood. A wonderful life with them.' She put her hand on Annabelle's arm. There was nothing else she could think to say. She knew now. She understood the loss, and they both knew what it meant, and that was enough.

Annabelle gave her a small, grateful smile, then moved to the window, where she gave a quick shake of her head. 'I'm so excited,' she said. 'A local to show me around Oxford. The city of dreaming spires!'

'Well I probably don't really qualify as a local yet. We've only been here for fifteen years. Still, I know my way around.'

'Excellent. Where shall we start?'

'It depends. How long are you staying? There's lots to see.'

'I've booked into a darling boutique hotel near Broad Street for a week. Found it on Instagram! It's ridiculously expensive, but then I thought, if Constance left me all this money, she probably wouldn't mind me travelling in style.'

'How wonderful,' said Willa. 'You deserve every penny.'

'Actually, I gave a bit to Dan recently, because, well, she was his relative, not mine. I felt a bit bad that she'd written him out of the will. Anyway, my treat this week. Let's have a very fancy high tea somewhere later on.'

'Gosh, all right,' said Willa.

'Next week I have tickets to the Chelsea Flower Show, so I'm heading back to London. I bought a spare, just in case you were able to get a day off, but it doesn't matter if you can't, of course. I wouldn't want to impose. I can give it to someone else.'

Annabelle was smiling so hopefully that Willa heard herself say, 'I'd love to join you.' Then she realised that she meant it. She'd never been to the Chelsea Flower Show, and every gardener amongst her friends said it was an event not to be missed.

There was the sound of the mud-room door opening and closing. Annabelle turned around as Hamish slung his bag down and came into the living room.

He stopped for a moment, staring, then he grinned. 'Hi, Annabelle.' He strode across the room and gave her a hug, then kissed Willa on the cheek. 'Hi, Mum.'

Willa found it amusing how unsurprised he seemed to be that Annabelle was standing in their living room.

'Oh Hamish!' said Annabelle, flushing pink. 'You're so tall!'

'Thanks,' he said. He went into the kitchen and dug his hand into the glass biscuit jar, plucking out three chocolate creams.

'I've got some free periods because of exams, so I thought I'd come home and bribe Mum to cook something good for lunch.'

'Oh Hame,' said Willa. 'Sorry, but we're about to go out.'

'Can Hamish come too?' asked Annabelle. 'I'd love to feed him up!' Her eyes shone with anticipation.

Willa shrugged agreeably.

'Oh good! Now, Hamish,' said Annabelle, 'where's the best place for lunch around here for a growing boy? Somewhere that also does excellent dessert.'

Hamish sidled up to her and put his arm around her, then looked across at Willa and winked. 'How long are you staying, Nana Anna? Because I can think of at least four or five.'

Willa felt the tears well in her eyes, and she looked down to blink them away. She realised the room had gone silent, and when she looked up again, Annabelle was retrieving a handkerchief from her pants pocket. She blew her nose vigorously.

'Just a week, darling boy,' she said quickly. 'This time's just a flying visit. But I can come back again another time if you like, and we can try them all.'

'Awesome,' said Hamish, cramming a chocolate cream into his mouth. 'Let's go and eat. I'm starving.'

A LETTER FROM SARAH

My sincere thanks to you for reading *The Daughter's Promise*. I loved writing it while spending time around the windy cliffs and the stunning beach that inspired its Tasmanian setting. If you'd like to be one of the first to hear about my next book, you can sign up at the following link. Your email address will never be shared and you can unsubscribe at any time.

www.bookouture.com/sarah-clutton

If you enjoyed *The Daughter's Promise*, I'd be so grateful if you could write a short public review so that other readers can have the benefit of your recommendation and insights. It really helps people to discover my books.

I love hearing from readers. So please, do get in touch via my Facebook page, through Twitter or on Goodreads.

Thanks, and happy reading!
Sarah Clutton

@sarahmclutton

sarahcluttonauthor

www.sarahclutton.com.au

ACKNOWLEDGEMENTS

I always said that if I wrote a book set near the ocean, it would be based around my favourite little beachside hamlet in north-west Tasmania. Sisters Cove is a fictional town, but for those of you who live on the north-west coast, you might recognise the beach and the windy capes that inspired this novel.

For me, this book is about finding the feeling of home. For those who have moved around a bit in life, sometimes it's the search for that feeling that forges our path. I have dedicated it to my mother and my big sister because a long time ago, the farmland around the real Sisters Cove was a place the three of us called home. It is a special place for us, filled with memories of enormous family gatherings, with my beautiful grandmother Judy Sadler always in the middle, seeking out stories. To those three extraordinary women, thank you for always looking after me and encouraging me to write.

To my extended Tasmanian family, who constantly welcome us back with open arms, thank you for inspiring this book. To my stepfather, Greg Clutton, who adopted our place and our huge family, you taught me that a home can be made wherever you go, as long as there is love.

To Jan Sadler, Ruth Stendrup and Missy Bennett, my first readers, who have lived large parts of their lives on the north-west coast of Tasmania, thank you for your wonderful input and suggestions. And Ruthie – thank you for inspiring the Merrivale gardens.

To Sally and Duncan Sadler, your beach house with the glorious views is where my character of Willa stayed when she visited Sisters Cove, and it is where I managed to hammer out a large part of the story, inspired by the sound of the waves. Thank you for letting me use it.

To my mother, Helen Clutton, and my sisters Kate Clutton and Sam Jenkins, thank you for your initial chapter-by-chapter encouragement, input and ideas.

To Ann Brooks, Sarah Jones, Lisa Cornes, Judith Jenkins and Meg Jenkins, you are superstars. Your willingness to slog through the finer detail helped to shape and shine the final story. Fiona Leahy, thank you for running your legal-eagle eye over the almost final version. I take full responsibility for any erroneous applications of estate law. (It may well have been my worst subject at law school, although my friend Susan might quite reasonably tell you that was tax law.)

To my brilliant mate Dr Stephen Barnett, thank you for your medical input, although sadly, much of it was chopped when my lovely editor and I decided to send Dan's character in a different direction. (It saved Dan quite a lot of medical intervention, so at least the hospital system was a winner there.)

To my editor, Emily Gowers, you are endlessly positive and a pleasure to work with. You also have brilliant story sense. You improved everything about this book and I dedicate the climax (and this well-deserved exclamation mark) to you! To the rest of the incredible Bookouture team, I feel very lucky to have found you. What an inspiring and energetic group of professionals you are to work with.

A particular thanks to my lovely husband, Justin Lewis, who under strict time requirements gave me detailed feedback on early drafts and also said quite nice things about my writing, even though I had already offered to cook dinner and take the rubbish out. You could only have been raised in a fabulous and kind family, and I owe a huge debt of gratitude to your parents, John and Judith Lewis. This book is also about the love between parents and children, and about family, and I am so grateful to be part of yours.

Finally, because my writing life revolves around them, I need to mention my children, Henry, Grace and Georgina. Thank you for putting up with my distracted head, and for pretty much raising yourselves. Full marks for the amazing job you are doing. I am very lucky.

Lightning Source UK Ltd.
Milton Keynes UK
UKHW011445270520
363925UK00011B/3470

9 781838 880323